RYANN FLETCHER

Sewing Deceit

First edition

ISBN: 978-1-7399953-0-0

This book was professionally typeset on Reedsy.
Find out more at reedsy.com

Be the radical outlaw you wish to see in the world.

Contents

Chapter 1

Bailey lifted a box of expensive rum, the bottles clinking gently despite the careful packaging.

"And don't forget, it's your turn to scrub out the loading bay," the captain of the ship shouted after her.

"Yeah, yeah, Marshall, I know," she replied, shifting the weight of the heavy crate in her arms. "Don't worry, the work always gets done."

"Make sure you tell Bertie that if she's late back again, we're leaving without her. I don't care what her gods-damned navigating credentials are."

"Mhmm," she agreed, stepping off the ramp, rolling her eyes. The captain was a good man, as far as she could tell, but she missed the freedom that Hjarta had given her. Making a living as a rum runner was fine, most of the time, but between the heartache of losing her family, friends, and the woman she loved and the constant fatigue, she was merely drifting through consciousness. Detached. Apart.

The uneven cobblestone streets of Bradach wound their way from the port to the Purple Pig tavern, where her delivery was scheduled. Three heavy-as-hell crates full of top shelf illegal liquor sloshed in her hands. She'd make the delivery and head straight back to the ship. The Pig wasn't somewhere she wanted to linger for too long.

The rough wood and the ragged nails of the crates bit into her hands. It wasn't the weight so much, she was used to carrying heavy loads, but the old, splinter-ridden boxes that made this part of the job almost unbearable. It was worse in some of the more rural settlements, where the roads were

1

unpaved, mounds of dirt tripping her up. Or that one place where she'd had to carry the delivery for miles because the roads were so bad that no cart could carry the shipment. In Bradach, it was a shorter, more manageable walk, even if her hands were already throbbing in pain.

Bailey dragged herself up the slight incline to the tavern, a little pleased with herself that it was easier now than it had been when she'd first taken this job. It paid not to skip leg day, literally. The faster she delivered shipments, the more likely it was that she'd get a second of rest before the next one. The Pig was the only tavern they delivered to in Bradach, after that embarrassing altercation with the Bronze Bell at the other end of the city. She'd never seen Captain Marshall so angry before or since.

Slipping through the open back door, she stacked the crates on the floor near a mound of potatoes. "I just need a signature," she called, craning her neck.

"Bailey!"

She jumped. "Larkin, you scared the hell out of me. Why do you always have to sneak around like that?"

Larkin shrugged. "Old habits."

"I just need a signature for your shipment, and I'll get outta your hair."

"Why don't you stay a minute? Have a drink, catch up—"

Bailey waved her off. "Can't. Got more deliveries to make," she lied.

"You and I both know that's bullshit after what happened at the Bell. What, do I smell, or something? You don't like Evie's food here? What is it?"

"No, no, nothing like that. Just... busy."

"Busy. Sure."

"The job keeps me occupied, that's all I can say."

"How long has it been, now?" Larkin asked, signing the invoice with a tiny, scrawled signature that was illegible. Old habits, indeed. "Six months?"

"Seven."

"No complaints?"

Bailey shrugged. "No more than any other job, I guess. Rum running pays the bills."

"Any word about your people?"

"No." The word burned like bile in her mouth, the shame of not being the hero they'd all needed that day. "No word."

"I'm sure Eves will hear some intel soon, she's cracked a new code, you know. With the help of—" she stopped short.

"Yeah. I heard."

Larkin cleared her throat, squinting up at the ceiling. "Right, right, of course you did. I'm just being a grapefruit."

"Mm." Bailey held out the clipboard. "You have to sign here, too."

"Come on, you should stay, just for a minute. Catch up. I'll fix you one of my new specialties, it blends some very interesting botanicals that really brings out the woodiness of the whiskey, and—"

"I can't, I'm sorry."

"They're not here, you know. Not even in port, and only left last week. It's not like she's going to swan in here and rub it in your face."

Bailey sighed, the clipboard dropping to her side. "She wouldn't do that, anyway. It's not in her nature to be cruel."

"Yikes. Still got it bad, huh?"

"Like not even a day has passed."

Larkin grimaced. "Shit. I'm sorry. Listen, if you'd rather just go, I'll just sign that copy and let you be on your way. Hell knows I wouldn't stick around here if I were you. Probably would have tossed the crates through the back door and forged the signature. Would have run all the way back to the ship. When I thought I lost Evie to that - *woman*... well. It wasn't a fun time."

"Captain says anyone caught forging invoices spends the next month on dish duty. I have terrible handwriting and hate dishes, so..." She looked at the scrawled signature. "Although, I reckon I'd have gotten away with yours."

"Oh, piss off," Larkin said with a laugh. "Now, are you staying for a drink, or not?"

The afternoon light glowed at the door, the shadows growing longer with every passing minute. She didn't have plans that night, not really. Eating cold leftovers by herself in the ship's crappy old kitchen didn't really count as plans. "Yeah, alright then. Let's have this new drink you've concocted." Bailey set the clipboard on the counter and sauntered through the backroom door into the main room of the tavern, a beautiful establishment with gilded accents on the walls, thick velvet upholstery, and the delicate dance of lantern light at each little table.

"Did you hear we started having live music on the weekends, now?"

"No, that's..." Bailey felt her fingers itch for the strings of a fiddle. How long had it even been since she had stomped and shredded some notes with her friends? "That's really great."

"It's nice to give something back to the community, you know? With all the refugees coming in from all over the Near Systems, the pool of talent has grown exponentially. Besides, it keeps the regulars happy, and it's better than the alternative."

"What's the alternative?"

Larkin wrinkled her nose. "Comedy."

"What, you don't like to laugh?" Bailey punched her lightly in the arm.

"A bunch of drunks telling old jokes is hardly worth laughing at. Here, take a seat, I'll fix you up that new cocktail."

"Seems like you're really settling into this mixology thing."

"Yeah, well, when you spend most of your life knowing the delicate ins and outs of hiding poison, it's not a far jump to finding yourself in the kitchen with your old mortar and pestle, grinding up some new herbs and spices for some seriously good drinks."

Bailey eyed the glass in Larkin's hand suspiciously. "Old mortar and pestle? As in, the one you used for poisons?"

"Oh, please, I washed it, *obviously*."

"Maybe I should pass on that drink, actually—"

Larkin burst out laughing. "Hey, *relax*. It's one Eves bought me special when we got this place. My old one is in a trunk somewhere." She winked. "Probably." She ground some leafy stems into the marble bowl and turned to crack the wax seal on a new bottle. "See? Breaking out the good stuff for you."

"Why? I'm just your courier."

"Let's just say I want to make sure that my connection to the top shelf stuff stays intact." Larkin shook the green pulp with a healthy shot of amber liquid and strained it. "Anyway, I like you. You're much nicer to talk to than the last asshole who had your job."

"I think he got fired."

"Not surprising, given that attitude. I almost socked him in the jaw one day. Here," Larkin said, pushing the drink across the bar, "try this."

Bailey sipped at the drink, savoring the simple yet satisfying flavors. Mint cooled her tongue, while the smoky liquor warmed her throat. "It's good. What's it called?"

"Dunno. Doesn't have a name yet."

"When's this one going on the menu?"

Larkin wiped down the bar. "As soon as it has a name, I guess."

"Where's Evie?" The short, bookish barkeep was always a welcome sight to Bailey, especially as she was usually offering her food.

"Out. Down at the research tent, I expect."

Bailey tensed and sipped at the drink. "Oh?"

"I told you, she's not in Bradach. Her lab partner is, though, I think he's starting to take on more down there. Something about weather pattern predictions, I don't know. After they figured out how all that was happening, and disabled those satellites, it sounds like they're trying to figure out how to turn it back on the Coalition." Larkin shrugged. "I dunno. I'm an assassin and a bartender, not a scientist."

"I bet those damn scientists couldn't mix a drink this good, though."

"You're gods-damned right, they couldn't," Larkin said proudly. "You're not bothered by the lab partner, are you? If you are, I can make sure—"

Bailey waved her away. "No, no. Roger's fine. Glad to hear he's healing up."

"He seems to be happier on the ground than in the sky. The Cricket can be a bit of a maze inside."

"Yeah." Bailey's heart ached at the memory. She'd never set foot on that ship again. It would be too painful. "It can." She drained her glass and slid it across the polished, freshly lacquered wood. "Thanks for the drink."

5

"If you want to stay for dinner, I can see what Evie is making—"

"Nah. Thanks, though. I've gotta scrub the loading bay before bed tonight. Some lemon sold us a crate of unsealed gin. The pressure change in the bay made them leak everywhere."

"What a waste."

"Marshall was raging for days."

Larkin rinsed the glass under a tap and dried it. "I would be too. Good gin is hard to come by, everyone across every backwater settlement thinks their undistilled bathtub swill is worth selling." She set the glass back on the shelf. "It isn't."

"You can say that again," Bailey said with a snort. "Gods, there have been some seriously gross taste tests over the past few months."

"So, where to next?"

"Dunno. Could be anywhere. Marshall tries not to let things get too routine, no circular shipment patterns. Coalition is getting too smart, too many patrols all over the place."

"Sometimes I forget how frantic it gets out there. I'm getting soft now, all snuggled up with a cushy job here."

Bailey nodded. "It's worse than before, too. No rest for the weary."

"Don't be a stranger, okay? You're always welcome here."

"We'll see. There's only so much torture a woman can bear, you know?"

Larkin looked at her with pity. "You'll meet someone else."

"Not like her, I won't."

"You will." The bartender flipped her long, shiny braid over her shoulder and tucked the bar rag into a belt loop. "Now go on, get out of here. Don't you have work to do? I swear, you rum runners are all the same, kicking back when you have swill to deliver."

Bailey snorted. "Be nice, or yours might just accidentally get dumped into a storm drain."

* * *

Bailey wiped her brow and shoved the disgusting, slimy, gin-soaked mop back into the bucket. Gods-damned, half-assed bathtub distillers and their shoddy bottling, creating more work on the Starling's Storm. It was getting late now, the mirrors above the city that directed the distant rays of sunlight now turned inward, plunging Bradach into night. As much as she enjoyed seeing Larkin and Evie, she preferred being as far away as she could get. The danger of running into one Henrietta Weaver there was far too high, and Bailey's heart couldn't take much more of that particularly acute heartbreak.

She loved easily, and loved often, but she'd gotten so hung up on Henry that she could barely focus on anything else - until that janitor swooped in and swept Henry off her feet. Though, technically, she'd done the sweeping before Bailey ever met Henry back in Hjarta. No matter. Her heart was broken nonetheless.

"Oi, Stockton, are you done with that yet?"

"Just finishing. I swear, Marshall, if you ever do business with them again, I'm going to swap out your personal stash for this mop water."

The captain leaned against the frame of the airlock. "No danger of that. One and done, that's what I always say. In this economy, there's no room for second chances."

"Good. From what I can tell, it wouldn't have been very good gin anyway."

"Listen, Bailey..." he trailed off, his face scrunched and sheepish.

"What?"

"I have a job needs doing. Big payout, and I mean *big*. Enough to buy half a settlement."

"What's the catch?"

He sighed. "I can't do it. Nor can anyone else on this ship."

The handle of the mop slowly slid down against the wall of the loading bay, the worn wood screeching gently against the unfinished sheet metal. "Sounds like one hell of a catch."

"It's on Gamma-3."

Bailey burst out laughing. "Good one, Marsh. Hilarious, in fact. Go on, why don't you pull my other leg while you're at it?"

"Come on, I'm serious."

"And so am I! What kind of foolish nonsense is this? You seriously want to risk a delivery to the most Coalition-controlled planet in all the Near Systems? What, shall we just land the ship on the steps to the Capitol Building?" She laughed and shook her head. "It sounds like a one-way trip into prison."

"That kind of money would be life changing." The captain squeezed his eyes shut and puffed out his cheeks before continuing, "It could help you get your people back."

Bailey sucked in a breath. "Don't play with me like that."

"I'm not. That's the kind of money we're talking about. Piles upon piles of credits."

"And how, if no one on this ship can go there without ending up arrested, would you propose to execute this harebrained scheme?"

He shuffled his boots, resting his hand at the back of his bald, shiny head. "None of us... except you. You're basically invisible, if we get you a solid enough identification chip. You don't have a record on Gamma-3, you were born off-world, and—"

"I know where I was born, thank you." Her soul ached for home, but home was gone, now. Destroyed. Gutted by the Coalition, razed, the fields she plowed salted. It wasn't home, not anymore.

"We could get you pretty close. We'll get a transport chartered, and—"

"How much swill are we talking about here? That much money and I'm thinking whole cargo ships full of booze."

Marshall winced. "Twenty crates."

"*Twenty*?!"

"The last of the private reserve stock. The fifty-year-old whiskey."

Bailey gave a low whistle. No wonder it was big money. "Gods."

"It would set us all up for years."

"But you need me."

"We can't do it without you, Stockton. You're the linchpin. The cornerstone of the plan, the—"

"Alright, I got it." She leaned against the wall and picked at the frayed buttonhole at her wrist, the grey threads poking out in every direction. "How long do I have to think about it?"

The captain looked at the floor, guilt written all over his face.

"How *long*, Marshall?" she demanded.

"Tomorrow morning."

"Have you completely lost whatever was left of your marbles? What kind of half-cocked plan is this? How long have you known? Have you just been skulking around, waiting to ask me?"

He held up his hands in surrender. "I only just got the wire today. The plan is solid, Bertie already put out some feelers for some contacts on the ground, and it looks good."

"Does her husband know about this?"

"She said she'd tell him as soon as the money came in."

"And if it doesn't, you're out a navigator and a courier."

"You don't have to do it. You could say no, right now, and that's the last you'd ever hear of it. No one on this scrap heap of a ship knows better than me how dangerous shit has gotten, and there are days I wonder what we're even doing risking our tails delivering top shelf liquor."

Bailey tugged at her long braid, glistening crimson in the fading light. "We'd have to discuss share split. If I'm the one putting my whole ass on the line..."

"Of course."

"And I need more details before I make a decision. Who are Bertie's contacts? Where exactly is this being delivered on Gamma-3? What happens if it all goes horribly wrong?"

"Let's just say you weren't totally off-base when you mentioned the Capitol Building."

"The Capital—Marshall, come on. That's suicide."

"Not if we do it right. And it's not the Capitol Building, per se, it's just in the Capital. Some back-alley speakeasy popular with the governors and regional managers when they're in town to lobby the senate for funding and troops."

"Oh good, so, no pressure then," Bailey snarked. "Only a ninety percent chance of arrest and execution."

"Money talks."

"Yeah, don't I know it," she sighed. Lack of money was one of the reasons why information on her people was still so scarce. Private investigators were expensive, even more so if it involved the Coalition. "So, some speakeasy in the Capital, then what?"

"We get you a disguise."

"What, like, a fake mustache and some thick glasses?"

"No, like a Coalition employee uniform."

"Where are we going to get one of those, I wonder? Are you hiding one under your pillow?"

"There's a tailor in town here, she's the best of the best. She'll get you suited and booted as a Coalition Sergeant, and we'll go from there."

Bailey shook her head violently. "You want me to impersonate a military officer? No. Hell no, in fact. Absolutely the fuck not."

"It's the best way to make sure no one questions you directing a porter with a steamcar to the speakeasy."

"Yeah, and a guaranteed vacation in Gamma-3's finest high security prison if I fuck it up."

"You won't fuck it up."

"Can't I go as a janitor, or something?"

"No. Janitors on Gamma-3 are almost exclusively prisoners working for free labor."

"What about a porter then, or a driver, or..."

"It has to be this, Bailey. It's an airtight plan. Get in, get out, collect the credits, we all get to move on." He stroked his beard. "Maybe give up this shit forever."

"How do we know this isn't some big trap?"

"We have contacts who have vetted the request."

"And we have to cut them in on the profits too, I imagine."

"They've already been paid. Bertie thought it was for the best, it keeps things cleaner if all the informants are kept in the dark."

Bailey nudged the bucket towards the drain in the corner. "I miss my people, Marshall. And Yannick especially, despite his stubborn horseshit.

They could be anywhere."

"I know."

"It's possible they're in a prison somewhere, and even if I found them, I wouldn't be able to get them out."

He nodded. "It's possible, yes."

"But what if they're not? What if they've been moved on to a settlement, like some were in Skelm? What if I could have the opportunity to get them out, rebuild what we lost? Not back home, not... not anymore, but somewhere else, maybe. There's gotta be a rock somewhere out there up for grabs." After months of nightmares, of waking up in a cold sweat, months of heartbreak, and loneliness, and pain, the faint glimmer of hope was almost too much to bear.

"If we pull this off, if you do this for me - for us, then I swear, the gods as witnesses, I will scour every gods forsaken hole in the Near Systems to get your people back. I'll need a hobby after I give up rum running, anyway."

Bailey picked at the split ends of her thick braid, contemplating if it was worth the risk. It was the best chance she had at righting her wrongs. She sighed and stuck her hand out. "We have a deal."

Chapter 2

Mae resisted the urge to *accidentally* stab a pin into her client's thigh. She didn't get paid enough to deal with this jerk's attitude, and she earned more than most people did. "How's that for length?" she asked through gritted teeth.

"No, no, it's all wrong," the man said, sighing heavily. "I was assured you could accomplish this very simple task, yet it doesn't seem as though you are capable."

"If you could just be a little more specific, maybe—"

"All due respect, Ms. Machenet, but the specifics are *your* job, not mine."

"Yes, Mr. Clements, but I am unfortunately not a mind reader. I assure you, I can sew just about anything you can dream up, but I can't even begin to guess at what's inside your mind." She stood, straightening her full skirts. "Now, let's begin again, shall we? You're looking for a formal occasion, that much has been established, but it seems as though you're throwing out every suggestion I make."

"I told you, I want to dazzle. These people I am working for, they appreciate a well-dressed individual. I mean to impress."

"There aren't many ways to dazzle in plain black, and you've outright refused any injection of color or pattern—" she shook her head, interrupting herself. "Hmm. That won't do at all." Holding the straight pins in her mouth now, she moved around him on his pedestal, appraising his masculine figure with a trained eye. She tucked here, and lifted there, manipulating the rich fabric into flat pleats across the waistcoat, and gathering the excess at the seam. She reached for another pin, poked into the cushion at her wrist.

"There, now, I think we have a start."

"Can I turn towards the mirror?"

"No. Be patient, I won't be long. It wouldn't do the suit justice to peek before the vision is realized." She stood back and scanned his form, chewing the inside of her lip. "Stay there, I need something from my storeroom. And *don't* look at the mirror."

"But—"

She ignored him, sweeping out of the room, the crisp taffeta of her dress whispering across the beautifully hand-woven rug she'd bought from a market just before the shop opened years back. The back of the shop was empty this time of day, with her right-hand woman not due in until lunch. Mae didn't mind the early mornings. Normally, they were quiet and serene, with routine dress fittings and calm, methodical work at the sewing machine.

Her hands brushed past thick velvet and lustrous satin, landing on a particularly beautiful crisp brocade she'd just bought in the last week. It was perfect for Mr. Clements, pain that he was, and it would suit him excellently, so long as he let her do her job and stopped trying to interfere. Some monied men thought they knew everything about everything, when in reality their sphere of knowledge and influence was less than that of a child's.

"Okay," she said brightly, reentering the front room with a beaming smile. "Let's try this on for size, shall we?" She draped a section of the fabric over his left shoulder, pinning and adjusting once again. Yes, it would do very nicely. If he didn't choose this, he was a fool. "Right then, you can have a look. Mind the pins, now, don't move around too much. I'd hate for you to get pricked."

"Oh, Ms. Machenet," he breathed, admiring himself in the full-length mirror. "I don't think I've ever looked better."

"I don't think you have, either. So, are we settled, then?"

He tilted his chin up, twisting his shoulders so that the half cape swished at his waist. "I never would have thought to ask for a cape, but it's perfect." He laughed and shook his head. "You said you aren't a mind reader, but I think that maybe you are."

"If you're settled on this, I can have it ready for you to collect..." she rounded the small counter in the corner and perched a set of glasses on her nose as she examined the date book. "The end of next week."

"But that's no good! I'm leaving Bradach in a few days!"

"We offer a rush service, but I'm afraid it will cost you. My assistant will have to work overtime to complete it, and I have to compensate her fairly."

He frowned. "Fine, fine." He turned back to the mirror and smiled at his reflection. "It will be worth the cost."

"It will, I can assure you of that, sir. If you would please transfer a fifty percent deposit, we will get started on your bespoke suit right away. Assuming prompt payment, it will be ready the day after tomorrow."

"Perfect," he said, beginning to remove the pinned cape.

"Oh, careful," Mae said, rushing over. "You'll end up with a pin precisely where you don't want one." The bells that hung on the shop door tinkled lightly, and the latch snapped open and then shut again. "I'll be with you in just a moment," she said, pushing each pin back into the cushion on her wrist, noting down measurements in a black, fabric-bound book. "Mr. Clements, you are free to go. I look forward to seeing you in the afternoon, the day after tomorrow. Any earlier and your suit won't have been pressed."

"Understood." He tipped his silk top hat and smiled. "And Ms. Machenet, apologies for my rudeness. My friends were right when they said you work miracles."

"I am pleased we were able to reach an accord."

As he left, she bent to pull a stray pin from the rug. He absolutely had looked in the mirror while she was out of the room. The man was a child. She tucked the glasses that were still on her nose up onto her head and snapped the notebook shut. "I'm sorry, one more moment," she said, without looking at the new customer. "I have to make a note of a special rush order."

"It's alright," the customer replied, in a voice that sounded like a perfectly aged red wine. Throaty and smooth, and left you craving another sip.

Mae looked up with interest, and her breath caught in her throat. It was the most effortlessly gorgeous woman she'd ever seen, leaned against the far wall, her hands clasped behind her back. She was taller than Mae, and broad in the shoulders, her biceps clearly visible even beneath the jumpsuit she was wearing. A smattering of freckles danced across her cheeks and nose, and a long braid sparkled like fire in the city's mirrored light. Mae cleared her throat. "What can I help you with?"

The woman flashed her a smile for just a moment before casting her glance down at the woven rug. "Marsh - er, Captain Marshall sent me, said you knew why I'd be here?"

"Oh, it's you. Yes, of course. Let me get my tools." It was one of the weirdest, cagiest requests she'd ever gotten. A Coalition officer's uniform, with no reason why it was needed. It wasn't her job to know why, only to take jobs, complete them, and provide the citizens of and visitors to Bradach with impeccable clothing. "Before we begin, I need to tell you that there will be a wait if there are significant alterations to be made."

"We, uh, leave tomorrow morning."

Mae blinked. "Of course." She sighed, tucking a tape measure into the pocket of her dress. "Your captain didn't inform me that it would be such a delicate deadline."

"Marshall isn't really one for planning ahead."

"And no one else on your crew thought to send us a wire ahead?" Mae asked.

"I didn't know until late last night."

"Perhaps he should invest in a date book."

The woman laughed. "He'd lose it in five minutes."

"Are you quite sure that there is no room for debate on the departure time?"

"It's my understanding that this is possibly the most time-sensitive thing our crew has ever done."

Mae gestured for her to step up onto the small platform. "All I can do is offer my level best with such a tight schedule. I'm sure you heard as you arrived, we already have an important rush job that needs to be completed."

"Well, if even half of what I've heard about this place is true, I'm sure it will be perfect."

Mae was no stranger to praise, she'd worked hard to build a reputable business, but coming from this muscled mystery woman it made her blush. "Thank you. We do try."

"I'm not supposed to tell you why we need this."

"I assumed as such. There's no legal reason you'd need an officer's uniform, not from me."

"I'm Bailey. Stockton."

"You know my name, it's on the door. You seem nervous, Bailey Stockton."

"I am, in fact, the most nervous I have ever been in my whole entire life."

"Hold still, I have to get your measurements. A time scale like this, there's no room for error. I'll be up all night as it is."

"Sorry."

Mae glanced up at her before noting down a measurement. "I might have something we can work with. Might shave a little time off, in any case. I'll have a look." There was a similarly sized suit somewhere in the back, one the client had never returned for. It had been over a year now. Safe to say it had been abandoned. She glanced back over her shoulder at the woman and smiled, feeling her face grow too eager and too open. Pushing past the velvet curtain that hid the back room, Mae pinched herself on the arm. *Get a hold of yourself*, she thought. *She's just a client.*

"Should I follow you?" Bailey called, stepping towards the curtain.

"No, just stay there. I'll only be a minute!" The suit was buttoned inside a garment bag at the back of the pickup rack. It was pure white, just as she remembered, with turquoise accents. It wouldn't be too terrible to rip out the existing ones and replace them with the signature yellow and purple of the Coalition. "I hope you don't need any medals or anything, I don't have that kind of thing here. With more time, I could get it, but—"

"Just the suit, he said. If all goes well we should be in and out before anyone knows the difference, anyhow."

"Here, try this on," Mae said, pushing the suit into Bailey's arms. "It should be okay, but might need some tightening up in the leg. Officers never look sloppy."

16

"Have you met one before?"

Mae grimaced. "My fair share." And if she never met another, it would be too soon. Even looking at the similarly cut suit in Bailey's arms made her stomach churn threateningly. "Enough to know how to make a near-perfect replica." She gestured at the curtained changing room in the corner. "Try it on, and we'll have a look."

"Aye," Bailey said with a dimpled smirk. She disappeared behind the curtain, the sounds of clothes dropping to the floor. "So how did Marshall know you'd be able to do this job, and at short notice?"

"I can do almost anything, so long as it can be accomplished with a needle and thread." Mae looked around for her glasses. Where the hell had she left them? "And I've done a job or two for him before, though nothing this specific, or with this kind of time crunch." Had she set them down on the desk? No, the desk was empty. "I hope he knows this kind of last-minute nonsense will cost him."

"I'm sure he'll spare no expense."

"It does make me wonder what you're getting up to, with that kind of payout."

"Um..." Bailey trailed off.

"Don't worry, I know you can't tell me. It's just my inquisitive nature, I can't help it." Were her glasses in the back room? She thrust aside the curtain and squinted across the racks of fabric. No, not there, either. "How are you getting on with that suit?"

"It's a decent fit, I don't think it needs altering, to be honest."

"What? Impossible." Mae swished back into the main room and looked at the lumpy suit, hanging awkwardly off Bailey's hips and bulging at the shoulders. Without thinking, she laughed.

"Why are you laughing?"

Mae clamped her jaw shut, swallowing the remnants of a chuckle. "Oh. Er—it does need alterations, actually. Rather significant ones."

"Does it? Seems fine to me."

"Yes, it does. You'd stick out like a sore thumb next to a real officer."

Bailey frowned at herself in the mirror. "I'll never understand fashion."

"It's not fashion, it's... never mind. Here, I need to pin some adjustments." She pulled pins from her wrist and circled Bailey like a shark, turning the ill-fitting suit into something any Coalition officer would be proud to wear. It was a skill that returned almost too easily. "I need your inseam measurement," she said, whipping the tape from her pocket. "The intended recipient was a good deal taller than you."

"I'm hardly short."

"No, but she was very tall."

"Do you ever get bored?"

Mae looked up at her. "No?"

"Never?"

"Would I have opened a shop and put my name on the sign if I didn't enjoy what I do?"

"I suppose not, but the thought of... sewing... fills me with the kind of dread most people get when they're caught smuggling illegal booze."

"That's why people like me have a job. I enjoy this, you enjoy... whatever it is you do. I'm sure I would be no good at hopping from ship to ship, putting my life in danger so that some rich fool can have a wild evening."

Bailey shifted her weight from foot to foot. "You don't drink?"

"Stop moving, please. I do occasionally indulge in a glass of a good red wine, but you can keep the hard stuff. Had a bad experience once, and that was enough for me. I don't enjoy feeling like my brain is too large for my skull."

"I don't think anyone *enjoys* that—"

"I'm going to measure your inseam, now," Mae interrupted, with more sharpness in her tone than she had intended. She softened, and continued, "I hope you can stay and wait for me to finish this. I don't like dragging myself down to the docks first thing in the morning. Always takes me far too long to find the right ship. And I can never see clearly enough in the dark to deliver it after closing."

"I'll stay. Don't have anywhere else to be, anyway."

Mae squinted at her notebook. Without her glasses, the numbers blurred and danced across the page. "Hmm," she mumbled to herself.

"They're on your head."

"I'm sorry?"

"Your glasses. They're on your head." Bailey gestured towards her own head, pausing to tuck a stray strawberry lock back into her braid.

"Oh. Right. Thank you." Mae's cheeks burned, despite having no real reason to feel embarrassed. She noted down the inseam and stepped back to assess the suit. "Still not quite right. That shoulder seam is a bit strained. It will need letting out, if there's any allowance for it."

"I've always been very broad in the shoulder."

"Yes, I can see that." Mae wrote herself a note about the fit in her natural, florid script. Her affinity for purchasing surplus stationery had been a lifelong habit. "Okay, let me help you out of the jacket, at least. I trust you can slip out of the trousers carefully, to keep the pins in place."

"How long do you think it will take? The alterations, I mean. No rush. I mean, we're leaving in the morning, so there's *some* rush, but—"

"A few hours, most likely. My assistant will be in at noon. She can handle any other walk-in clients we may have. You're very lucky, you know, most days we wouldn't have the space for a job like this."

"My aunt always did say I was lucky."

"Long may it continue."

Bailey shrugged out of the jacket, laying it carefully over Mae's outstretched arm. "I'll just be a minute, then."

"I might be able to convince my assistant to deliver it this evening—"

"I said I'll stay. It's alright. The ship is old and dusty, and I don't like Bradach much. Might as well stay here. Better than anywhere else."

"They serve a nice lunch at the Purple Pig, you know."

"Yup. I know. I'll stay."

Mae examined the pins in the jacket, calculating how long it would take her to finish the job, and how much Captain Marshall was going to owe her for dumping this kind of job on her at the last minute. He should know better, really, after all these years. You can't rush these things, not if you want a good job done. "Well, take a seat," she said with a sigh, "this shouldn't take too long."

Chapter 3

Bailey lay awake in her bunk, staring at the suit hidden inside the plain grey garment bag with the monogrammed M in the top right corner. Marshall was thrilled they wouldn't have to delay their plan. Mae finished the suit in plenty of time, the stitching impeccable and perfectly matched. Even the official uniforms weren't this accurate. The suit gave her a strange feeling, like she was buttoned into someone else's skin. It was more than a costume.

She'd turned off the lights hours before, hoping to find some much-needed rest. They'd been flying for weeks, doing two, sometimes three deliveries a day. Being the only courier in the crew, she was tired. Her muscles ached. It wasn't so much the weight of the crates, but the awkward size. The ale shipments were the worst of them all - all those glass bottles clinking angrily inside with every step or slight jostle. There was no sneaking around with those.

It would only take a day or so to get to the goods pickup location, a backwater trading beacon in the middle of nowhere that even the Coalition had no interest in. There wasn't much commerce there, not for a base so far out of the way of any major flight paths, but the owners of that place made a tidy sum dealing in swill. People would travel anywhere to get hold of something other than the watered-down cat piss most speakeasies served.

Kicking the blanket off, she sat up in bed and rubbed her eyes. Clearly, sleep wasn't going to come. Not tonight. She stumbled into the bathroom and lit the kinetic lamp, twisting the handle until the tiny bulb cast a dim, yellow glow over the tub and the sink. The mirror revealed dark circles under her eyes, and a messy, unkempt braid. "Gods, I look terrible," Bailey said aloud to her reflection. It was no wonder Henry hadn't wanted her. No. Shouldn't think about that, not now. She'd spent too much time thinking about that already.

Her heart ached. She'd lost so much, and yet, guilt still settled deep in her bones. Guilt that she hadn't been taken, too, that she hadn't found them all and rescued them, that she was just too broke and too cowardly to be the woman her friends and family needed her to be. Her mothers would have been ashamed, if they'd been alive to witness how she hid that day, watching everyone they'd ever loved get shoved onto a Coalition transport. Watching her do nothing about it. Watching her rely on tips that other people uncovered. It was shameful.

"Enough," she whispered, trying to believe her own words. The cold water splashed on her face washed away the grit of Bradach and the thoughts of all those she'd let down. There was no time for wallowing. If she pulled off this job, if everything went to plan, then she could find them all, every one of them, and work on getting them out of whatever hellhole the Coalition had dumped them into. She had to focus now. How long now, before they reached Gamma-3?

Bailey tugged on her boots and laced them tightly, just the way she liked them. Nothing gave her blisters faster than ill-fitting shoes. She snatched her gloves and cap from the hook behind the door, pulling them on. The ship was drafty and often cold in the common areas. It was a cargo ship, with a wide, cavernous loading bay and tiny, cramped quarters. She didn't mind the size of her room, after all, she didn't spend much time in there, but the icy gusts that rushed through the corridors let the damp cold settle beneath her skin. An almost permanent chill.

The door swung closed, but the wood had swelled with the wet air, and caught on the lock. Bailey delivered a swift, targeted kick, and the latch engaged. It would be hell getting it open again later. The ship thrummed beneath her boots, a quiet, lifelike breathing that hung somewhere between comfort and worry. It was quiet, for the most part. Everyone could hear Marshall snoring from across the whole ship when he slept, a monstrous growl so loud, they wondered how he actually got any sleep at all. Even now, in the middle of the night, his telltale labored breathing echoed through the halls. He said it was because he used to work in one of the Coalition factories when he was younger.

Jogging up the ramp to the mess hall, Bailey jerked back in surprise when she found it occupied, nearly sending her tumbling back down. "Bertie," she wheezed, her hand over her pounding heart, "you scared me!"

"All I'm doing is sitting, that's hardly a crime," the woman said, her boots up on the table.

"I didn't think anyone would be up this late."

"You thought wrong."

"Obviously."

Bertie nodded her head towards the kitchen. "Some leftovers in there, if you're angling for some food."

"Yeah, maybe. Thanks."

"What's on your mind?"

"The usual." Bailey poked at the remaining nut loaf and sighed. "Is there anything else?"

"Not until we get to the beacon. Should be able to get some fresh stuff there, though I don't know what passes for fresh all the way out here."

"We've been there dozens of times. What do you mean you don't know?"

Bertie scowled. "As you know, I rarely leave the ship except on shore leave. I'm a navigator, not a courier. I'm also not the cook, though everyone seems to think so."

"I guess I don't pay much attention when we're parked at the beacons, except to load or unload crates."

"I'm surprised you agreed to this wild plan, to be honest."

"Why?"

"Most people would say it's a fool's errand. A good way to get caught."

The knot of nervousness in Bailey's stomach tightened. "Marshall said the plan was ironclad."

"It is, and of course it is, it's *my* plan," Bertie said, balancing the chair on the two back legs. "But plans don't always go the way we intend."

"If we pull this off, though, it could right a lot of wrongs."

"Honey, if you pull this off, I'm retiring the second those credits hit my account. I'll take my husband and we'll get a nice little place back on Gamma-3."

"Why there?"

"I miss the air. I miss being able to plant things and know that they'll grow without intervention. As a child, I spent hours looking up at the starry night sky, dreaming that I'd be up there someday. Well, now I'm an old woman, and after decades out here, I'm tired of the stars. I'm ready for some rest."

"Don't you worry about being on a Coalition planet?"

Bertie shrugged. "We've all gotta live somewhere. Not many places left that aren't, these days, and I'm not crazy about Bradach. It feels too small, too contained. Too secretive, maybe. I miss driving my steamcar down the wide open road in the middle of nowhere, across land no one ever wanted to build on. I miss my kids." She poked at her nut loaf slice. "I miss eating stuff that doesn't look like regurgitated compost."

"Marshall should get a staff cook."

"Marshall is too gods-damned cheap."

Bailey laughed. "Yeah, he is that."

"If you promise not to tell anyone—"

"I promise."

"There's a can of beans in the bottom cabinet."

"Beans?" Bailey had been hoping for something more exciting than legumes.

"If you push those beans to the side, you'll find my secret stash."

"Oh!" And there it was, a small tin marked with a skull and crossbones. "DO NOT EAT," it read, "PROPERTY OF BERTIE. CONSUME ON PAIN OF DEATH."

"Bring it here."

Bailey slid the tin across the table, where it rested against the toe of Bertie's boot until she lifted it off the table. "Got this back on Delta-4. High quality stuff."

"It's nice of you to share it."

"I mean it, don't tell anyone. If it goes missing, I'll know that you either ate it yourself or squealed to Marshall." Bertie removed the lid and set it aside. "And then I'll never share with you again. Ever."

"Understood."

"Here, try this." An individually wrapped square slid across the table and dropped into Bailey's lap. "I'm told it's some of the best chocolate in the Near Systems. From a small place in the restaurant district."

Bailey tore at the wax paper eagerly, her mouth watering greedily. She popped the square into her mouth and struggled to bite back the grimace that spread across her face. "Oh. It's... interesting."

"Gods, this is terrible, isn't it?" Bertie said, laughing. "I've never had anything so bitter."

"Does anyone actually like this?" Bailey asked, swallowing hard. The unpleasant taste lingered in her mouth, coating her throat. "It doesn't taste like any candy I've ever had."

"Either I was swindled, or rich people like disgusting food."

"I might have to eat some nut loaf to cleanse my palette."

Bertie pushed her plate across the table. "Here, eat mine. I've lost my appetite now, anyway."

"How long until we reach the beacon?"

"Tomorrow, mid-afternoon, most likely. Assuming no checkpoints we'll have to swerve around."

"Then how long to Gamma-3?"

"Eh. About a week, give or take."

Bailey poked at the nut loaf, chasing a seed across her plate with her fork. "I thought it might be sooner."

"Nah. Not with all the new flight path restrictions and monitoring. Nope, it ain't like it used to be, can't be taking short cuts anymore, not unless you want to draw attention to yourself. Dangerous, in these times, a recipe for disaster."

"I just want to get it over with now."

"Won't be long. Just imagine, two weeks from now we'll be feasting on something other than this crap, celebrating an easy win. It will be bliss."

* * *

When the Starling's Storm pulled into the port, Bailey's chest squeezed a little tighter. After Marshall paid for the crates, there would be no going back. Failing the mission would put them all into deep debt. She took as deep a breath as she could, given the grip of panic around her lungs, and tightened the laces on her boots, tucking the excess under the tongue.

"You ready to grab some crates?" Marshall asked, poking his head through the airlock into the loading bay.

"Ready as I'll ever be."

"Last chance to back out. You sure you want to do this?"

She squeezed her eyes shut, picturing all the people she'd let down. "Yes. Could be my only shot at getting what I need."

"Need some help?"

"No. I'll use the wagon for most of it."

"Is there anything I can do? Feels wrong to let you do all the work and be the one on the front lines when we get to Gamma-3."

Bailey laughed. "As a matter of fact, you can get us some better food. That nut loaf tastes like garbage."

"I thought you liked nut loaves!"

"Yeah, good ones, not whatever the hell that thing is."

He held his hands up in surrender. "Alright, alright, I hear you. Gods, between you and Bertie I barely get a moment's rest."

"Can it, Marshall. You know we put up with a hell of a lot more here than many would."

"Yeah, and *some* captains command respect," he grumbled, but smiled at the end. "So, what do you want, then? Won't be much here other than fuel and booze, but I'll do my best."

"What, you mean I can't ask for lightly braised eggplants and a flaky mushroom pie?"

Marshall raised an eyebrow, bemused. "You'll be damned lucky to get a decent loaf of bread."

"Get a few, then. And don't skimp on the toppings this time. When we're on the other side of this, you won't even care about the money."

"I'll *always* care about the money, Bailey."

"Move your meat, old man," she said with a laugh. "Let a courier do her damned job." She lifted the large wagon out of its storage space and wheeled it to the loading bay ramp, waiting for the doors to lock into the open position. "Twenty crates should take two trips. Given the size of this beacon, it shouldn't take too long."

"Excellent. Bertie already has our path plotted out, we can head off as soon as the crates are secured."

The huge overhead doors clicked into place, and she descended the ramp, heading off to the pickup location on the other side of the beacon. Backwater or no, they weren't going to keep the illegal shit in plain view. "Don't forget to get something that resembles a vegetable," she called over her shoulder. "No one would believe a Coalition officer with rickets."

Chapter 4

"Abigail, do you mind delivering this to Mr. Clements? The man grates on my nerves."

"If he grates on yours, I'll probably hate him, too."

"Yeah, but my name is on the door."

"Alright, fine. But you owe me."

Mae pushed her glasses up onto her head and smirked. "How about I sign your paycheck and we call it even?"

"When does he need it by?"

"I told him tomorrow, but I'd rather just get him out of my hair. I have a feeling if we let him into the shop tomorrow for a final fitting, he's going to have second thoughts, and this suit is perfect as it is. No, it's better to exceed his expectations with a personalized drop off and be done with it."

"I still have that hem for Mrs. Spratt to finish."

"Don't worry, I'll finish that for you. Is she picking up later today?"

Abigail nodded, her bouncy brunette curls shining in the mid-afternoon light. "She has a party next week, but it's off-world, so needs it today. I think her transport leaves in the morning."

"No problem. I assume it's the garish orange taffeta number hanging in the back?"

"That's the one."

"Sometimes, Abs, I feel like our efforts are wasted on ugly clothes."

"Don't tell Mrs. Spratt that," Abigail said with a snort. "She thinks it's the most beautiful thing she's ever seen."

"It's really a pity that tailors like that piss pot across town mark up cheap fabrics so much. I guarantee if she'd just come to us first, she'd have a beautiful sunset of a frock in a textile that doesn't scrape across your skin like sandpaper." Mae shuddered. "He really does a disservice to the profession."

"I'm surprised he hasn't been run out of town yet."

"He's cheaper than us, that's why he stays in business. People think they can scrimp on handmade, custom garments. That old fool uses the cheapest fabrics he can find, and can't even manage to sew a straight steam. You know it's going to be torture for me to finish that hem and not rip out every seam to redo it, right?"

"Do *not* do that, we have enough work without you creating more."

"I have pride in my work!"

"Yes, but she only paid us to hem it, not dismantle it and rebuild it. Besides, you'd just end up disgusted with that fabric, hunt through the back room for something comparable, which I can guarantee you we don't have because I just reorganized everything last week, you'd ignore me and spend all night trying to remake it." Abigail took the dress from the hanger and gently laid it across her arm. "I don't think I can even trust you here with this. I'll take it with me."

"Excuse you, I—"

"Tell me I'm wrong, then."

Mae narrowed her eyes. "I can do the hem."

"I know you can do the hem. What I *don't* know is whether you will resist the siren song of remaking it to prove some kind of point against your competition. He doesn't even care, you know."

"Of course he doesn't, he's a hack."

"Then why do you bother?"

"Pride! And besides, it's good customer service."

"I might agree with you, if Mrs. Spratt had paid for a custom ball gown, but Mae, she paid for a gods-damned hem."

"Fine! Have it your way!" Mae snatched the dress from Abigail's arms. "Go deliver the suit to Mr. Clements. I'll do the hem, and—"

"Promise me you won't take it apart."

"And I promise I probably won't take it apart."

Abigail laughed. "I will take every single seam ripper in this place, I swear."

"It's fine, it's fine," Mae said, waving her off. "Could you stop by the port on your way back? I got a wire that someone sent something, it should be waiting at package claim."

"Ooh, a present! What is it?"

"No presents, I'm afraid. Likely just a shipment of fabric."

"Still exciting. Anything I'd like?"

"What *don't* you like? If I let you, you'd spend your entire pay packet on fabrics we buy in. And don't think I don't know how much you already have stashed in that trunk at your apartment."

"How *dare* you," Abigail said with a mock gasp, a smile crinkling at her eyes. "Okay, I'm off. I mean it, don't take that ugly dress apart. We have enough work to do."

"Get us dinner on the way back too, will you? My treat. The Pig's special, if they haven't run out of it by the time you get there."

"I'm certainly not one to turn down free food, am I?" Abigail checked the pockets of her long, dark blue dress and closed the door as she left, making the tiny chimes tinkle amicably.

Mae frowned at the orange dress. It was true, she did want to take it apart. Gods, had he even bothered to cut the base layer on the bias? This dress probably hung off Mrs. Spratt like dirty laundry left out in the rain for weeks, stiff and uncomfortable and entirely inappropriate for a gala. Her fingers itched to take it apart, reassemble it, make it better, make it something to be proud of. She reached for her seam ripper on the table, but it was missing.

Abigail. Of course. She smirked at her apprentice's cheek. Abigail would have her own shop one day, and if she decided to stay in Bradach, she'd be some real competition. Not like the fraud across town. He had no pride in his work, no creative streak, nothing more than cheap fabric and flashy prices.

Her fingers brushed against the layers of orange taffeta, and she cringed. Pulling out her pocket watch, she frowned at the time. Abigail was right, there really wasn't time to remake the dress. *Unless...* she thought, pawing through an open drawer looking for a seam ripper. There might be time, if she pulled an all-nighter.

"Where the hell is it?" she growled, her fingers closing around a slip of paper.

"I took this one, too," it read.

Mae barked out a laugh. "Alright, alright," she said to the dress. "Let's just get you hemmed, then."

She threaded the machine and set to work on the dress, grimacing with every stitch. Poor quality fabric. It would wind up in a trash heap or an incinerator the week after the gala. A hem wouldn't fix what was wrong with this dress. She hesitated, her hand floating over the dress. The temptation to pick at the seams with scissors was almost overwhelming. She didn't like waste, and there was enough cheap clothing being tossed away to clothe generations of people.

The machine snagged at the material, looping the stitches. After hemming just half of the full skirt, Mae considered gently feeding the dress into an incinerator herself. The urge to tear at the dress with her stubby fingernails intensified. Why hadn't Mrs. Spratt just come to her first? She'd have a beautiful dress made to order for only slightly more than the tailor charged. Though, perhaps her experience with the tailor is what had led her to Mae's door. If that was the case, then surely the best thing to do would be remaking the dress.

Abigail was right, they didn't have any orange satin or taffeta. They didn't have much orange at all, in fact, other than some brocade she'd used as a wedding vest the previous year. She racked her brain, hoping she'd ordered some with the shipment that had just come in.

The invoices piled on the front desk were stacked neatly, alphabetized by name, sorted into ingoing and outgoing. Mae had to admit it, Abigail was amazing at keeping the place organized. Owning a shop was one thing, the upkeep was another entirely. She rifled through the papers, locating the order form.

"AHA!" she shouted to the empty shop, the afternoon rays allowing the dust in the air to sparkle like fire on the water. "I did order some orange."

She'd just remake it when Abigail got back. That was the only thing she could manage. What was she supposed to do, let Mrs. Spratt pick up a lazily made dress? She'd repurpose the existing fabric, so it wouldn't go to waste. A cape, maybe, or a matching cropped jacket. She eyed the dress, chewing on her lip. Yes, a cropped jacket would be best, it would keep Mrs. Spratt warm, and it would allow the dress to be worn no matter the season.

Mae smiled smugly to herself. It was a fabulous plan. Who cared if Abigail was right? She was always right, anyway.

The door flew open, and Abigail tumbled inside with a mess of takeout boxes. "The Pig gave us desserts, too," she said, out of breath.

"That was nice of them."

"Larkin said she needs to talk to you about a new waistcoat, maybe next week."

"I'll make a note of it. Does she think she can bribe me for the best appointment times?"

"Can't she?"

"Depends on the dessert."

Abigail swished past the back room curtain, setting the food on a table near the back door. "Evie says hot fudge brownies."

"Then, yes, she can absolutely bribe me."

"She said it's important."

"It always is, with Larkin."

"What's wrong, did the machine break? How come this dress is still sitting here?"

Mae busied herself unpacking the food, unwilling to look her assistant in the face. "I thought I'd make some alternative adjustments," she mumbled.

"I see you didn't get far, given I took all the seam rippers." Abigail tipped a pile of them out onto the sewing table, clattering softly. "I bet you went looking for fabric too, didn't you?"

"I ordered some with that shipment you were picking up." Mae glanced around, her brow furrowed. "Where is that shipment? It should have been sizable. Too heavy to carry back? I'll call for a porter—"

"They said that shipment was delayed, they don't expect it until next week, now. Too many blockades cropping up. So you'll have to just hem the dress, then, not remake it. Although maybe it's better if I do it, I'm not so sure you can manage handing over that dress to Mrs. Spratt tomorrow."

"Gods be damned," Mae cursed. "I really thought I'd be able to pull this out of my hat."

"The only thing we'll be pulling out of our hats is the hem she paid for," Abigail scolded gently. "There was this for you, though. Must be what you got the note about." She tossed a small brown box across the room, and Mae snatched it out of the air, her mouth full of crispy fried tofu.

The return address made bile leap into her throat. No. Not now. Not after all this time.

"What is it?" Abigail asked, eating straight from the takeout container.

"It's nothing."

"Ooh, a secret admirer?"

"No. It's nothing." Mae pushed away her food, too sick to eat.

"Mae, what's wrong?"

"I told you, nothing to worry about. I might head upstairs early, I'm not feeling well all of a sudden."

"You don't want your brownie?"

Mae shook her head. "You have it, take it home if you want to. Are you alright to lock up tonight?"

"Of course. Are you sure you're alright?"

"I said, I'm fine!" Mae snapped, and stomped up the back stairs to her apartment, the box clutched in her white-knuckled fist.

* * *

Mae stood in her kitchen, staring across at the box sitting on the sturdy green table. Why now? Surely the answer laid inside of the box, beneath the thin wrapping of brown paper, tied with twine. And yet, she knew that the answer was likely more dangerous than the mystery.

Her stomach roiled angrily. She'd barely eaten two bites before she'd seen it, and the acids had already eaten through her meager dinner and now pelted at the lining with vigor. It was closing time now, and the sound of the shop's metal gate echoed up the narrow staircase that led to her door. She was all alone. Abigail would be headed home, wondering why her boss was losing her marbles.

The apartment was quiet, the only sound coming from the ornate clock on the wall that ticked away the seconds, an ever-present reminder of the marching of time. Someone on the street below sneezed, leaving Mae to delve further into her own solitude. The box remained on the table, looking perfectly innocent, but she knew better.

She shouldn't have been surprised, not really. It was inevitable that she would be summoned back eventually, pulled down into the swirling vortex she'd worked so hard to escape. She'd barely done it the first time. Would she even be able to this time? Now, after time had dulled the memories into a blunt blade? Still deadly, though not as quick.

"Fuck," she whispered, edging closer to the box. Maybe she could just toss it into one of the bins destined for the incinerator. Pretend she'd never gotten it, and hope another identical box didn't appear next week, or the week after that. They'd paid a great deal of money to send it with a private courier. They wouldn't be ignored. She knew this, and yet, the temptation to hurl it out the window into the street made her fingers twitch with anticipation.

It could be nothing.

The box could be empty, an attempt to leave her unsettled, draw her out of hiding, or maybe it had been sent years ago, lost in the cargo hold of some courier ship. Maybe it was a false alarm. Perhaps someone was just trying to rile her up. She could think of a few who might do a thing like that, as payback for slights, real or imagined.

She stepped closer, reaching out her hand for it. The paper was smooth and crinkled under her touch. The twine had been triple knotted, and it easily fell away when she snipped at it with the tiny scissors she'd pulled from her pocket. Mae tore gently at the paper, the sound so loud and abrasive that she may as well have been standing next to one of the ships on the port. Grating. All-encompassing. Unavoidable.

Her breathing had lapsed into a pant. Short, shallow, inefficient and inadequate. The room tilted around her, vision swimming. No.

The wrought-iron chair scraped across the floor as she pulled it out, the silk of her skirts crackling against the legs of the table when she sat down. She tore at the paper again, and this time, it fell to the floor, revealing a pine wood box etched with her initials. The clasp in the middle was bronze and matched the shining hinges. Whatever inside wasn't going to be good. She still hoped it was old, moot, irrelevant. A gift sent fifteen years ago, maybe.

Unlikely.

She picked at the clasp, prying it open. Wherever it had been stored, the humidity had swollen the wood. Inside, there was a note, folded crisply into quarters. The florid, elaborate handwriting couldn't be mistaken for anyone else's. Her blood ran cold, and pounded in her ears. Hands shaking, she unfolded it.

"Dearest," it read, the first letter of the word much larger and more ornate than the rest, "it is time for you to come home. Your father needs you. Don't make us send someone looking for you like last time, or you won't like the results. You've been booked passage from your nearest beacon. We trust you can find your way there post haste. Love, Mother."

Chapter 5

"You ready, Officer?" Marshall asked, trying to smile wide enough to cover his worry. Bailey had been around long enough to know that face, and it didn't make her feel any better about what they were about to do.

"As ready as I'll ever be, I guess."

"Alright. We've booked you on the next transport out of this beacon to Gamma-3. It's headed straight to the Capital, so you won't have to worry about extra stops."

Bailey tugged at the uncomfortable uniform. "And the shipment?"

"Already on board. It's apparently a free service for officers to have their belongings couriered from ship to ship."

"Fancy."

"We told them you're headed to a gala in the Capital to celebrate the new colony near the Outer Rim. You know, to explain the very obvious clinking in the crates. Officially, it's sparkling grape juice." He cleared his throat nervously. "It will be fine. You're in, you're out, big payday, we're all thrilled."

"I hope you know you're going to need to spot me some credits to pay for a porter when I get to the dock."

Marshall shook his head. "No, the speakeasy will be collecting the goods and you."

"If they're collecting it, why the hell do I have to be there at all?"

"The tax clerks on the dock won't question an officer. It also means they'll be less likely to be stopped while it's being transported to the speakeasy."

"Unless I'm found out and they throw me into prison."

"Yes, well. Let's hope it doesn't come to that."

"Come to think of it, I really should be getting a larger share of this payday. What did you do to make it happen?"

"Took out the largest and most terrifying loan from some even larger and more terrifying crooks. If this doesn't go well, I have a very strong inkling they might break my legs."

Bailey stared at him. "Gods, Marshall, why the hell would you go and do a thing like that?"

"Because when we pull it off, it will all have been worth it." He sighed, shoving his hands into his pockets. "But, I take your point. We'll work some kinda bonus out when you get back, alright?"

"Don't let me rot in a work camp if they catch me."

"Darling, if they catch you, we're all going to end up in a gods-damned work camp." He tried for a smile again, but it warped across his face, leaving him looking like he was beginning to regret this whole wild plan. "But don't worry. You'll be grand! It's going to go smoothly, and you'll be stripping off that hideous uniform before you know it."

"Yeah, I hope so. I feel like I'm being strangled. Who designed these ugly things, anyway?"

"I always thought they looked sharp."

"No." Bailey wrinkled her nose. "Don't even give them that, Marsh. They're hideous and itchy and I've never felt more like I wanted to crawl out of my own skin."

He laid a hand on her arm. "Not long. In, out, done. You'll be great."

"I feel like an impostor."

"You *are* an impostor." He handed her a small satchel. "But a damn good one. Here, some emergency funds. Just in case."

"I thought they only use credits on Gamma-3."

"They do, but I don't think you'll find a back alley merchant that won't accept gold, if it comes to that."

"What about a chip?"

"That one's on me," Bertie said, jogging down off the ramp. "You'll need this at the docks, they scan everyone. You're Officer Jones. It's a legit tag, but she's off-world, so as long as you don't stick around, you'll be long gone before they figure anything out."

"What if this Officer Jones comes back while I'm there?"

"She won't. She's stationed in that new colony, and it takes weeks to get back to Gamma-3 from there. Take off your jacket a minute." Bertie pressed a small, snub-nosed gun to Bailey's bare arm.

"Ouch!"

"The pain will fade in a minute. Trust me, this is better than the old way of doing things, when we had to implant them surgically, and then remove them."

A tiny drop of blood bloomed on Bailey's skin, but just like Bertie said, the pain faded as quickly as it came. "Am I good?"

"You're good." Bertie threw her arms around her. "Please be safe. Be smart. Don't get into any trouble."

"I promise."

Marshall shifted his weight from foot to foot before holding out his hand. "See you soon, Stockton."

"Don't be ridiculous," Bailey said, hugging him. "I'm going off to battle, I deserve a hug."

"I didn't want to presume," he replied, his voice muffled against Bailey's uniform. He was short enough that his face only came up to Bailey's shoulder. "Like Bertie said, stay safe. We'll be waiting for you right here."

"You're parking? Isn't that dangerous? If I get caught—"

"You won't get caught, and we aren't going to leave you on your own when you're finished. We'll wait right here. It's a promise."

Was he wiping a tear from his eye? It was hard to tell under the harsh lighting of the transport beacon. "Well, here I go," she said, slinging a small canvas sack over her shoulder. A real officer would have standard Military Police issued extras in their pack, everything bleached white with the signature yellow and purple accents embroidered over the top of the thick wool fabric. Bailey had tossed in a handful of stuff from her quarters, including a few pairs of underwear, half a dozen mismatched socks, her journal, a hairbrush, and three protein ration bars she had no intention of eating unless it was life or death. Those things tasted like they'd already been digested once. She should know, she'd been around enough livestock to know.

"The next transport back up here is the day after you land. There's one in, and one out, every day. Don't be lollygagging down there, just get the job done and get the hell out of there."

"Yeah, yeah, I heard you the first time." She gave a mock salute. "See you soon, soldiers."

As she walked away, her heart grew heavier. She'd grown close to the crew in the seven months since she'd left the Cricket. They were a little rough around the edges, but who wasn't nowadays? She had baggage, too. Everyone did.

The ticket grew sweaty, gripped in her hands. In and out, that's what Marshall said, and that's what she intended to do. There was no point in dwelling on what might happen. It was much better to think positive. She sighed. Thinking positive had never done much for her before. Why would it now?

"Now boarding in terminal four, express transport shuttle to Gamma-3, The Capital," the overhead speaker barked.

Bailey's hands shook as she approached the iron gate, guarded by an MPO, a military police officer. She held out the ticket, half expecting the man to immediately see straight through her ruse and throw her directly into the nearest prison.

"Thank you for your service, ma'am," he said, standing at attention.

"Oh, er—at ease," she said, forgetting that her fake persona outranked MPOs. "Thank you. You too."

His brow knitted in confusion. "But, ma'am, it's obvious I've never seen active duty, not like you. You're one of the most decorated officers I've ever met."

"Yes! Well!" Her mouth went dry as she searched for an answer that would satisfy him. "Maintaining peace at our transport hubs is of the utmost galactic importance. Without hardworking men like you, we'd be overrun."

"That's very kind of you!" he chirped, brightening. "Fuck the rebels, am

I right?" He playfully elbowed her in the arm, grinning. "We'll string them all up, one by one!"

Bailey blinked. "Sure."

"Have a good flight!"

She edged past him, taking her stamped ticket back and folding it neatly into her breast pocket. That seamstress had done a good job. An excellent one, if she had so easily fooled another MPO. Her seat was at the front of the transport, away from civilians. Lucky for her, there wasn't another military staff member on board, at least, not yet. She relaxed into the plush seat, shoving her bag beneath. *In and out*, she thought, pulling her cap down over her eyes for a nap. *Easy as pie.*

* * *

"Attention, passengers," the loudspeaker barked. "We will be passing through the Gamma-3 atmosphere shortly. Please be sure to fasten your seatbelt and brace your hands against your knees. We will be landing at the Capital port in approximately ten minutes."

Bailey opened a bleary eye, her mouth tasting like hot sand. Had she really slept the entire flight? Maybe she'd been more tired than she thought. The seatbelt was clasped around her hips, just as she'd left it, and just as the announcement had promised, the ship began to shudder and shake. Her heart pounded in her chest - it always did when setting down somewhere new, and she'd never been to Gamma-3 before. It was where people had begun, but unlike most, she'd been born and raised off-world.

Without windows, she had no idea what time it was as they exited the troposphere, allowing the shuttle to return to its smooth flight. There were never windows on these things, not anymore. Too many people couldn't handle seeing flames lick up the side of the ship, no matter how normal and expected it was. People were never even meant to fly, and now traveling to distant planets, moons, and beacons was an everyday occurrence. Hell, the bored looks on her fellow passengers' faces said it plainly enough.

"Please remember to take all of your personal belongings with you as you leave the vessel. Capital Air cannot be held responsible for any unattended luggage or effects. If you think you may have lost personal effects, please check with our lost items office on level three of the port, in suite thirty-four."

Bailey reached under her seat, half expecting her bag to be missing after that pre-recorded speech, but it was there, all the same. Who'd want to steal some socks and underwear, anyway? And from an officer? It would be one hell of a gutsy move if they did.

Though she was tempted to look inside her bag, made paranoid by the lengthy warning, she resisted the urge and hung it over her shoulder. Preparing to wait her turn to exit the shuttle, she found that people ushered her ahead, bowing their heads with murmured words of thanks. It was weird. Maligned her whole life by the Coalition, now respected by strangers because she wore a uniform. It wasn't hard to see the attraction of joining the force in the first place.

Sunlight nearly blinded her as she stepped off the transport onto the dock. Gods, she'd never seen sunlight so staunchly bright before, and it threatened to burn her retinas. She shielded her eyes, squinting across the dock for a sign of the speakeasy porter that was due to meet her. Maybe they'd be waiting until the cargo was unloaded. That would take a few minutes, at least.

She leaned against one of the wooden posts that lined the dock, trying to stay out of the way as the other passengers streamed past her on their way to wherever they were going. Ten minutes passed, and then twenty. The huge clock in the center of the city towered over every other building, casting a menacing shadow. Bailey's stomach growled impatiently for breakfast, and she winced through a hunger pang. How the hell long did it take to unload a few crates, anyway? If it was her doing the unloading, it would have been done already.

There was still no sign of the porter, and no sign of the crates, either. What if she'd been found out? Panic danced from one neuron to the next in preparation for an all-out sprint, or a scrap to save her own skin. It was too bad the uniform was so tight it would hinder her killer right hook. Her knuckles tingled in anticipation, waiting for the moment someone would point her out as the fraud she was.

"General Fineglass!" someone shouted. "General Fineglass, I can't apologize enough for our tardiness, I—"

Bailey jerked at the weight of someone's hand on her arm, yanking back her elbow to throw that punch.

"General!" a short, bearded man said, leaping back to avoid the potential collision with his nose. "It's just me, I'm sorry I'm late, I'm here to take your things for you."

"Are you from—"

"Yes, yes, I'm from the welcoming committee. We're thrilled to welcome you home to the Capital. If you'll just follow me, I'll escort you to your lodgings."

"I think you have me mixed up with someone else."

The man threw back his head and laughed. "Oh, good one, General! You know, they told me you were a joker, but I didn't think you'd be this funny!"

Bailey stared, that slow ballet of panic rapidly accelerating into a wild tango of fight or flight. "I have some things, er—" Should she mention the crates? He didn't seem like he was from the speakeasy. Bertie said they'd approach her with the code phrase: 'Tarantula Juice.'

"Yes, don't worry, they'll have everything delivered to your accommodation for you. Oh yes, I know you're accustomed to doing things for yourself, but at least for the next few days, allow us to do all the heavy lifting. Literally!" He laughed at his own joke, taking his glasses off to clean them with a silk handkerchief. "What a pair we are, aren't we, General? A pair of comedians!"

What in the gods-damned hell, Bailey thought, still staring at the man. What was she supposed to do now? Where was the porter? Where were the damned crates of whiskey? "I might like to see my belongings unloaded," she said finally, standing up straight. "You know these shuttle workers, never careful enough with valuables." She grimaced. Valuables like twenty crates of illegal whiskey.

"Oh, I can assure you they will take the utmost care in transporting your belongings," he said, glancing at the huge clock. "I don't mean to rush you, ma'am, but the rest of the committee is anxious for you to be safe at the hotel. I just can't believe I'm talking to the fabled General Fineglass, pioneer of the Outer Systems!"

Fuck.

"If you'll just follow me, I'll show you to your car. They've reserved a new model, top of the line for your use while you're with us here in the Capital!" He smiled broadly, gesturing towards the busy street beyond the port. "I do understand why you'd want to wait here, but as I've said I can assure you, we will take the utmost care."

She was stuck now. Refusing would be a dead giveaway. It's not as though there were loads of other decorated officers in uniform on that transport. In fact, she was the only one. None of this made a damn bit of sense. She'd follow him, wait until he left her in her room, and hot foot it back down here to the port and hope to hell the crates were still there. "Excellent. Thank you, Mr...?"

"You can call me Davey."

"Mr. Davey. Lead on—"

"It's just Davey, ma'am."

"Right. Davey. I do appreciate your patience with me. I have been gone a long time." Knowing fuck-all about the real General Fineglass was going to make it harder to lie, and she wasn't a good liar to begin with. Her mother always said she had a very honest face.

"Right this way, ma'am." He led her to a shiny, sleek, ebony black steamcar with tinted windows. He opened the door to reveal a soft, buttery interior, with a driver in the front seat wearing a cap that matched the steamcar's paint job.

Every cell in her body was screaming at her to not get into the car. "I could just walk, it might be good exercise, if you'd just direct me—"

"Another hilarious joke, ma'am!" Davey said, slapping his knee. "Who'd want to spend hours walking across the city after a journey that had taken almost a month?"

Gritting her teeth, she slid across the smooth fabric of the seats. Davey followed, and closed the door once he was buckled in.

"Where are we going?" she asked, hoping it wasn't a question that would give her away. Where the hell was the real General Fineglass, anyway?

"To the Rockford Arms, the finest lodgings here in the Capital. As liaison from the welcoming committee, we wanted you to know that we spared no expense to cushion your reentry into society. It can't be easy after spending so long in such desolate places."

"I appreciate the sentiment."

"The drive shouldn't be long, ma'am. Not with the new high speed tunnel that's just been finished! It's for high-ranking military and envoys only—well, with the exception of certain paying customers. We have to pay for the maintenance somehow, don't we?"

"Mm," Bailey agreed. Once she ditched this fool, it would take her ages to get back to the port. She watched the shuttle disappear from the rear-view mirror and slumped back in her seat.

Chapter 6

The knot in Mae's stomach only grew harder with every gated doorway she passed. She'd never wanted to come back here, to relive all the reasons why she left in the first place. Yet there she was, carrying her suitcase past houses so huge, you could fit three families in them. She'd grown used to Bradach, to conservation and attention to stopping the Coalition's crawl of control across the Near Systems and the galaxy. In another life, she would turn around and head straight back to the port and board the first shuttle out of there - or maybe she wouldn't have come at all.

Direct flights were expensive, but she wasn't the one footing the bill. One ticket on an express transport had at least saved her a few days of transit time, but in truth, she could have used the extra time to process, to wonder why they'd summoned her back after so many years. What could they possibly need from her? They had everything they could want right there on Gamma-3.

"Hey lady, move out of the way!" a courier shouted from her steambike, pulling a small trailer of luggage.

"Sorry!"

The courier stopped, a quizzical expression on her face. "You new around here or something? This street is for steambikes only. The pedestrian crossing is overhead."

Mae shielded her eyes against the harsh rays of the sun, squinting into the glare from the glass above. When had they installed that? "Not new, exactly. Just been a while since I've been here."

"Don't let the MPOs catch you. There are fines for jaywalking, you know."

She nodded. "Thanks." No one had to tell her about the dangers of MPOs. Larkin at the Purple Pig back home had been thrown into prison for nonpayment of a jaywalking fine after an MPO conned her out of her last credits. She slipped down a narrow alley and climbed the stairs to the overhead walkway. The elevator was functional, but she had a deep fear of the hollow shafts they traveled through. She imagined what it would be like to fall down one of those shafts, and shuddered.

Her steps were slow and shallow. She was in no rush to get to her destination. No doubt it would be a barrage of questions and insults, an interrogation matched only by the Inspectors that the Coalition employed to extract information from rebels and pirates. People like her.

Commuters stalked past her, knocking into her shoulders and her suitcase as they went. Rudeness certainly hadn't gone out of fashion here in the years she'd been gone. The city was just as mean and disconnected as it had always been. The cacophony of hundreds of heeled shoes on the thick glass echoed against the red brick of the high-rise buildings so loud, she could barely hear herself think. If she took her time, then she could drag out the march to the house for at least another twenty minutes.

Shops along the glass walkway boasted the best the city had to offer: coffee, sweets, bakeries, and newsstands selling the latest Coalition propaganda. Mae stopped to purchase a newspaper, waving the black market chip she'd bought years ago in Bradach but never used. She'd never needed to before now.

The newsprint felt like a bomb in her hands, so incendiary and righteous. After so much time living in Bradach, the only truly hidden pirate colony in the Near Systems, it was a shock to see what passed for truth outside its borders. Blatant lies splashed across the front page, presented as fact instead of fiction. Scaremongering. Fairy tales told to all the good little Coalition citizens to get them to behave, to stay in line, shut up, do their work, don't ask questions. The weight of it laid itself across Mae's shoulders, and she began to stoop under it.

She'd only just arrived, but already she was desperate to leave. If there was any viable way to avoid walking through that door, she would. Unfortunately, there wasn't. They'd found her, again, and she couldn't risk the lives of her friends, especially Abigail, or even more so, the secrecy of Bradach. The letter had threats written between the lines: "Do as we say, or we'll burn it all down." It was how they'd always operated. She could only imagine what fresh hells awaited her past the lacquered green door that was now only steps away.

Her fist was raised in the air, poised to knock, when the door opened in front of her. "Maevestra. It's about time you showed up."

"I came as soon as I received your letter."

"Which I'm sure you left in the port for several days before bothering to retrieve it."

"No, actually, I—"

Her mother sighed, her slight frame with a rigid posture, the same way it had always been. "You might as well come inside, I suppose."

Stepping over the threshold was like stepping into a time machine, and just like that, Mae felt like she was a child again, with no autonomy or control over her own life, the glittering plaything of her parents to live vicariously through, instead of the confident, business-owning adult she'd worked so hard to become. "Why did you send for me?"

"I told you, your father needs you."

"You said as much, yes, but I'm wondering about the specifics. After all, I have a shop to look after, and—"

"Oh, please, Maevestra, how could you be so callous? After everything we sacrificed for you, everything we've done! It's bad enough that you continually ran away, putting us through the shame of having to drag you back, but to abandon us in your father's hour of need? You've always been such a selfish, ungrateful child."

"I'm here, aren't I?"

"Unwillingly."

"With greetings like this, is it any wonder?" Mae set her suitcase down and latched the lock behind her. "Let's not do this right now, Mother. Tell me why you've summoned me back here."

"We'll talk after dinner. Go to your room and freshen up, you're all

46

wrinkled from travel, and I'm sure you'll want to put something nice on for supper."

"Fine." There was no sense in arguing, not with her mother. She'd get home quicker if she did what they wanted. It was easier not to fight them. "What time is dinner?"

Her mother laughed, an empty, hollow sound. "The same time it's always been!"

"Right. I'll see you at dinner, then." She pushed past her mother to the wrought-iron spiral staircase in the corner of the room that led to her room on the top floor of the house. At least it was furthest away from the parlour, even if it didn't have a lock on the door. Their house, their rules, they'd always said.

The heels of her boots clattered against each stair as she climbed, her suitcase bumping against the claustrophobic railing with every step. The iron was cold under her fingers, and without realizing, she moved her hand away right where there was a snag on the underside. Even after years away, this place had never really left her. Maybe it never would.

A long, pained creak whined from the brass hinges when she swung open the door to her room, the golden oak wood dull in the afternoon light that streamed through the far window. Dust hung in the air, thick and undisturbed. Mae sneezed, the force of it rattling her brain and leaving her dizzy. She thrust open the window, and didn't even mind the crisp, early spring breeze that whistled through. The cold was better than breathing in the years of stagnation that gathered in every corner, and in a fine haze over the formerly gleaming trophies stacked atop the white shelves. Nothing had changed. Everything was as she'd left it, waiting for her to come back. Waiting to pull her back in.

Mae sighed, tears gathering in her eyes. She never wanted to be back here. Defeated, she unpacked her suitcase, hanging her spare dress in the closet, and setting her underthings inside an empty drawer.

* * *

"Maevestra," her mother called from the base of the stairs. "Are you coming down for supper, or are you going to sulk in your room like a child?"

"I'm coming," Mae replied, smoothing her skirts and tucking a long black lock of hair back into the elaborate braid she'd pinned to the top of her head. "Just give me a moment." It was strange, hearing her full name. She didn't so much dislike the sound of it, as had a very clear connection to being scolded.

"You've had all afternoon! Though I suppose I shouldn't be surprised that you've lost all sense of punctuality in that heathen place. I'd be surprised if they can even manage to keep from eating each other when there's not enough food to go around."

Mae grimaced. It was going to be a long week, or however long they expected her to be there. She closed the door behind her and descended the stairs, the taffeta of her skirts sighing heavily against every step. "Where's Father?"

"In the dining room, clearly. Some of us manage to be on time for meals."

"What are we having?"

"Don't be so rude! Have you forgotten *all* your manners in that place?"

"I can't wait to get out of here," Mae mumbled under her breath.

"What was that?"

"Nothing, Mother."

The house was different than the last time she'd seen it. Her mother loved nothing more than to remodel rooms one at a time, in an endless race to show up the neighbors, to impress people who didn't care at all once they left. An infinite, expensive quest. The wallpaper was blue when she'd left, and now it was a crisp white, with all the furnishings to match. The dining room chairs were upholstered with a thick white brocade on the seats and backs. Mae frowned.

"Stop with the sour face, dear, it's not becoming," her mother said, ushering her into the large, airy room. The table held three vases of flowers, all brimming with pure white roses to match the interior. As always, everything was perfect, unfit for mere humans to enjoy.

"Father," Mae said, extending her hand.

"Maevestra, it's been so long," he said, wrapping her in an awkward hug. "I thought you'd never come home."

"Well, here I am." Mae stepped back from his grip and sat in the chair she'd always sat in. "What did you need from me?"

Her mother huffed quietly. "Don't be rude, we will eat supper first like the civilized family that we are, and then we will discuss business matters after the plates have been cleared, in the study."

Impatience bubbled in Mae's stomach, her fists clenched under the thick white linens. Why wouldn't they just tell her what they wanted? "Of course."

"Your mother says your trip took longer than expected. I hope your shuttle didn't run into any pirates."

Mae stifled a laugh. The theoretical competition to have dinner with hardened pirates or her family was not a close one. "No, we didn't run into pirates."

"Why are you so delayed, then? We sent that letter weeks ago."

"I left for the transport beacon the morning after I received it."

Her father sighed heavily. "You see, Gladys, I told you that we shouldn't trust those courier services. I've always said, if you want something done right, you have to do it yourself."

"Yes, Gerard, and if you wish to do it yourself next time, I shan't stand in your way. I suppose I'll just handle the business while you're gone fetching our wayward daughter, just like I always do." She waved in a servant with a shining silver cart. "Genevieve would never do this to us, make us wait weeks upon weeks, and then appear with wrinkled clothes and a sullen face."

"I notice that I'm the one sitting here, not Genevieve."

"She's far too busy with her new job, dear. She can't take time away, she's too important."

"You realize that I have a job, too? I have clients and a business, and employees—"

"Yes, we know all about your little business, Maevestra," her mother interrupted. "Now, let's eat, shall we? I hear the cook has prepared something extra special for our prodigal daughter."

The servant, a man with skin so pale it was almost translucent, removed the lid of the cart with a flourish. "Tonight's feast is flame grilled sea bass on a bed of wilted greens, with a side of garlic and lemon sauteed potatoes." He set a plate in front of each of them, so graceful it was almost a dance. "Enjoy."

"Fish?" Mae asked, when he had exited the room. "I thought seafood was banned now, due to all the overfishing."

"Oh, don't be silly! There's always somewhere to get what you want, despite all the disgusting Coalition restrictions."

Her father sliced into the fish, steam rising from his plate and swirling into the air like a translucent ribbon. "It's a damn shame what they've done to the fishing industry here. But when you consider the alternative to this government, it's an easy choice at the ballot box every ten years."

Mae frowned at her plate, poking at the fish with her fork. "And what's the alternative, then?"

"Chaos! You've seen the news, haven't you? Or don't they have papers wherever it is you're living now?"

"We have papers, yes." She was thanking her past self for setting up that fake post address and having it forwarded to her on Bradach. The last thing she needed was for them to find out about the city, they'd probably skip all the way to the MPO branch to report it, and her. "They just aren't as... biased."

"Biased!" her father barked with a guffaw. "What do you mean, biased?"

"I bought a paper when I landed here. It's quite bombastic. Propaganda, I'd say."

"How do you have propaganda against *pirates*? They're thieves, for the gods' sakes! Hardly a defensible profession!"

"Yes, well, they're not the only thing to worry about off-world, let's just say that."

"And what else is there to worry about? It's not as though we're the ones doing the looting—"

"I think Maevestra should eat her food," her mother interrupted, a smile on her lips but daggers in her eyes. "And Gerard, you know better than to talk politics at the table. It's unseemly."

He harrumphed quietly and piled potatoes on his silver fork. "Yes, darling, I suppose you're right."

Mae didn't like the idea of eating the fish, but she took a bite, anyway. It wasn't as good as anything she'd had at the Purple Pig. "It's good."

"Just good? Our poor chef chased around for days trying to put together this meal for you." Her mother speared a potato before cutting it into four equally tiny pieces. "It seems you've lost whatever decorum you once had while you've been away on Delta-4."

"You didn't know when I'd even be here! You admitted yourselves you expected me days ago."

"Eat your dinner, Maevestra," her mother hissed.

"I think the fish is sublime," her father said, wiping his mouth after the last bite. "Truly a culinary accomplishment. I'll have to give my compliments to the chef." He stood, tugging at his tailored jacket. "I'll do that right now."

"I thought we were going to talk after dinner," Mae protested.

"You aren't even finished eating, dear," her mother said.

Mae shoved the rest of the fish into her mouth and pushed the plate away. "There," she said, her mouth full, "I'm finished."

"Gods!"

"I want to know why I'm here, Mother."

"Well, I simply can't talk to you when you're like this. So willful! The rudeness! I won't have it, not at my dinner table. You're excused. We'll talk in the morning, when you've calmed down."

"Tell me right now why you summoned me, or I'm leaving on the first shuttle out of the port tomorrow."

Her father paused at the door, his palm resting against the smooth lacquered wood. "There's no need for your theatrics. It's obvious you're too upset to discuss anything of substance right now. Your mother and I just want what's best for you, Lamb. We will tell you everything tomorrow morning, at breakfast."

"Tell me now."

"At. Breakfast." He shut the door behind him, not quite a slam, but enough to show his seething anger. He'd be locked in his study until the wee hours. It had always been like that, and likely would never change. A man of few words and a short fuse.

"See what you've done, Maevestra? I begged you to calm down, but you refused, and now you've upset him."

"I don't think it's asking too much to want to know why I'm here."

"You act like coming to see your parents is some kind of detestable chore! As if we're just some rubbish stuck to the bottom of your boot. Your father just wanted one meal together before we embark on this business proposition, and you've ruined it."

"Business proposition?"

Her mother turned away, patting the coif of hair at the nape of her neck. "No, now I've said too much. That's all you'll get from me until tomorrow morning."

Chapter 7

Bailey stepped into her room, the uncomfortable uniform chafing at her arms and behind her knees. How the hell did MPOs wear this crap? "Thank you, Davey."

"My absolute and entire pleasure, General. I trust you'd like some time to get comfortable, clean up?"

"Yes, that would be most appreciated."

"I would gently remind you, ma'am, that the welcoming breakfast in the morning will be very well attended. I hear they'll be serving quail's eggs!"

She'd be long gone by the time that happened. "That sounds delightful."

"Can I fetch anything else for you? A drink? I can order room service—"

"That will be all, Davey, thank you." She turned to close the door, and spotted something odd in the corner, a small black box with an ominous, flashing red light. "Wait. What is that?"

He pouted apologetically. "Ah, yes, of course you won't have known, you've been gone so long. The Coalition is taking steps to stamp out corruption in the higher ranks, and so they have ordered for the installation of closed-circuit camera surveillance."

Bailey's eyes grew wide in horror. *"Cameras?"*

"Yes, ma'am, but I assure you, it's for your own safety as well. There has been a rash of abductions of late, high-ranking officials being swept up in rebel raids. The surveillance is for your protection, to be sure we can have MPOs on hand immediately if something happens."

"This is ridiculous. What about privacy?"

"I'm sure you'd agree that the safety and security of the Near Systems demands some sacrifice?"

"Yes, of course," she grumbled. "And am I free to come and go as I please?"

Davey laughed. "General, you outrank almost everyone in this hotel. I doubt anyone would stop you. However, due to these abductions, I've been advised to caution you that security services are on high alert, and that it is inadvisable to travel by yourself. If there's anywhere you'd like to go, I'm sure we can arrange a driver for you."

"Fuck," Bailey said plainly.

"I'm sorry?"

"Apologies, Davey. I'm sure my language has become rather coarse while I've been away. I'm just so damned disappointed that our society has resorted to the abduction of the brave souls who defend us."

"Indeed, ma'am." He held out her canvas bag. "Is there anything else?"

She sighed. "No, that will be all."

"I'll see you bright and early, General."

"Yes, I suppose you will."

As the door latched close, Bailey bent double with a low, frustrated moan. Of course they'd have their employees penned up like animals. At least the goats back home had some semblance of independence, in that no one sat around watching them all day, just waiting for an excuse to jump over the fence and haul them back to the barn for questioning. She sat on the large bed, staring up at the camera, internalizing the rhythm of the blinking red light and wondering who was looking back at her.

Davey hadn't mentioned if there was audio on these things. He also hadn't mentioned how exactly to get hold of a driver, not that she really wanted to risk someone realizing what she was up to. The port was miles away, and that was if she could even get out of the building without being caught.

The small window on the far end of the room was secured with bars that were bolted into the wall. She was on the ground floor, at least, but without tools there was no way she was getting through that - plus, the sight of a highly decorated general making an escape attempt through the bars was sure to raise suspicions.

"Fuck," she said again, this time under her breath.

She moved to the other side of the room and positioned herself under the camera, hunting for a wire to detach, or some way to train it on a different part of the room. No dice. The wiring was all hidden behind the wood paneling of the wall.

Alright, fine. If she couldn't sneak out, then she'd just waltz right out the front door. She draped the strap of her canvas bag over her shoulders again and yanked the door open. To her relief and surprise, there was no armed guard waiting in the hall. Like a prison with the cell door standing open. Was it just a temptation? Was Davey part of some kind of elaborate trap to ensnare her?

Stepping back through the hotel lobby, the soft leather of her boots didn't snap against the marble the way the other MPOs' did. If she didn't give herself away by saying something foolish, then her damned shoes would.

"Excuse me, General?" the concierge said as she passed. "Can I get something for you?"

"No thank you, just going for a walk," Bailey replied, blazing ahead towards the revolving doors at the front of the building.

"We can arrange—"

"No thank you!"

With that, she was back out in the fresh air, or as fresh as the air in the Capital would get with all the traffic from the port. Even so, Gamma-3 was a damn sight better than many of the settlements she'd been to, and there was something intoxicating about breathing air that hadn't been cycled through a terraforming machine a few hundred thousand times. How could anyone grow up in a place so huge, open, and free, and ever want to leave? She just couldn't even begin to wrap her mind around that.

Squinting into the last of the fading sunlight, Bailey held a hand to shade her eyes. Where the hell had they come from? Where was the port? She had to get back there as soon as possible, even if it meant running the whole way.

The Capital's skyline was a deep tear in the fabric of the orange sunset, the high-rise buildings blocking the streaks of purple that shot across the sky. The port was near the city, she'd seen that big ugly clock when they disembarked. To the clock, then, with the huge hour and minute hands ticking the day towards its close, despite the fact its chimes were inaudible at this distance. She bent, tightening her laces, and headed off on a manicured path that pointed towards the city's center.

She was trying her best to look casual, like a powerful general who had been away for a while, not a born and raised rebel who'd never set foot on Gamma-3 before that day. The ease with which flowers sprang from the earth was astounding. In Hjarta, they had to be so precisely careful, nurturing each seedling through the imported dirt, praying to all the long-dead gods that you wouldn't wind up starving if the conditions ruined your crops. Here, unwanted, scraggly plants broke through wherever they could, before being cut down. Odd that nutritious plants were shunned for aesthetic ones, garish purple and yellow bulbs that lined the pavement she walked on.

If Gamma-3 was different, if it hadn't fallen to the Coalition so long ago, if it had never birthed it into existence in the first place, it would be exactly the kind of place Bailey would want to build a life. To have the freedom of air that would always replenish, to have independence from terraformers, and engines, and the thick clouds of steam that blocked out whatever faint rays of sun they could steal, was an existence she couldn't have fathomed before she stepped off that transport. But, now that she had, it was the only thing she could imagine wanting.

Her steps scraped softly against the black tar of the path, the fabric of the ugly uniform threatening to chafe between her thighs. Ahead, the stark grey concrete of a wall rose out of the ground, shunting the path off to the left.

"Damn," she whispered to no one. "Blocked."

The wall stretched out in either direction, as far as the eye could see. If she couldn't go around it, well, then, she'd have to climb over it, instead. Chewing her lip, Bailey eyed up a tree near the wall, one with thin, fragile branches that stretched over the narrow wall, dropping pink petals over the other side. With a quick glance around, she leaped into the tree, scaling its trunk, scampering up the limbs that creaked under her weight. Decorative trees weren't meant for climbing, nor were they particularly suited to subterfuge.

Straddling the wall, Bailey's stomach dropped when she peered over the other side. No trees, no soft grass or ugly flowers to shimmy down or drop into, just a ten-foot drop onto cold, unforgiving brick. She squeezed her eyes shut and released her grip on the wall, landing hard, her knees sore from absorbing the impact. At least she hadn't broken anything. Small mercies.

There was no path there, no guidance from maps or signs, and now her view was blocked by a labyrinth of buildings just tall enough to obscure the distant skyline. If there had been a car, she'd have stolen it, but the streets were bare. Identical little houses were lined up against the roads, their yellow and purple flower gardens fenced off by white posts. The monotony of one neighborhood after the next disrupted her natural sense of direction, every home swimming in her vision as the last one had.

In Hjarta, no two homes ever looked alike, being defined by their occupants instead of the builders. Some chose to live in airy tents with plush rugs laid over each other, some chose to live in small huts made of recycled building materials. Rarely did people live in houses, and if they did, they certainly didn't look like these did.

The neighborhood dissolved into a wide road, choked with steamcars. It was people from the city, driving home for the day. Each one emerged from a vast tunnel that disappeared below ground. Bailey hesitated, unwilling to trap herself underground but also unsure of how to get into the city quickest. The sun was almost down now, the street lamps beginning to flicker on, one by one, as darkness laid heavy over the Capital.

"Fuck it," she said, marching into the tunnel. The walkway was narrow, with room only for one person, and so Bailey shuffled along, the steam nearly choking her as it lingered, thick and inescapable, within the tunnel. She must have walked for miles, the friction between her thighs wearing an inconvenient and painful hole in her Coalition uniform. People in their cars must have been wondering what the hell a general was doing down there, but if they were, no one mentioned it.

By the time she emerged into the city, the inside of her thighs was a mess of raw meat, her skin worn raw from hours of walking. Tears stung her eyes as she approached the port, thankful this would all be over soon. She'd buy her ticket back the second the last crate was safe inside that speakeasy, and her first purchases with her ill-gotten credit hoard would be gel packs for her thighs and a night's stay in an inn with a deep bathtub.

She was almost feeling the soft caress of oat-infused warm water when someone angrily yanked her behind a palette of crates.

"Where the hell have you been? We've been waiting for hours!" The angry person shouting at her had a tangle of tight blond curls and eyes that flashed with rage. "Your people said you were reliable!"

"Relax! I'm here now. They got me mixed up with some real general and dragged me across the whole damn city."

"Why didn't you just tell them to fuck off? You outrank them, that's the whole point of this transfer!"

"It wasn't like that, it was—you know what, it doesn't matter. Let's go collect the crates."

The woman rolled her eyes, jabbing a finger into Bailey's ribs. "You are a sorry excuse for a courier, you limp, rotted carrot. The shuttle is gone, it's been gone for hours."

Fear gripped Bailey's stomach again, an unwelcome addition to the fiery pain in her thighs. "So where are the crates?"

"Taken to Central Claim, obviously. We'll have to get up there and drag all those crates out of hock."

"Let's get a steamcar, I can't walk anymore. It took me hours just to get here from that gods-damned hotel."

"What, and risk getting caught? Hell, no. I don't think so. We're going to have to hike up there."

Her thighs throbbed, and she briefly considered stripping off the uniform entirely and burning it in effigy. "Where is Central Claim?"

"Back where you came from."

Bailey moaned. "Are you sure they aren't just lying around here some-where? What if—"

"Listen, whatever your name is, my boss paid a veritable fortune to secure

58

this shipment. If you bail out now—"

"This never would have happened if you had been on time. I was waiting for ages, and then some guy with a clipboard all but shoved me into a steamcar and drove me to some fancy ass hotel for Coalition ass kissers."

"We were... unavoidably delayed."

"Fine. Pair that with my unavoidable detention in an up-jumped prison cell, and we've got a hell of a problem."

The woman crouched lower behind the crates. "Okay, alright, fine. We can still work this out. We thought something like this might happen if we weren't careful."

"Kind of you to, you know, fucking warn me, then."

"Our communications with your captain have been limited. Much of the wires in or out of the Capital are monitored. We couldn't risk it."

"I guess I'll just remember that for next time, shall I?"

"Enough complaining. We need to get our booze out of Central Claim. We need to get up there and show ID, and then we're golden."

"ID?"

"Yeah, ID. You must have one."

Bailey pulled at her now frizzy, ratted braid. "I really, really hope you mean the chip they gave me."

"What?! Of course that's not what I mean! Are you serious right now?"

"I guess they didn't think I'd need one, if I was collecting them here at the port."

"We told them to prepare for any and all contingencies." The woman clawed at the side of her face. "What are you people, amateurs? It's like you've never been to Gamma-3 before!"

It probably wasn't the right moment to tell her that, no, in fact, Bailey hadn't ever been to Gamma-3 before, and her crew hadn't been there since they were children. "I'm sure we can figure this out, let's not panic, okay?"

"Where are you going to get an ID from?"

"They already think I'm some joker named General Fineglass, maybe I could just ask for a replacement?"

"As absolutely childish as that solution sounds, it might be our best option of getting out of this without either of us ending up in prison."

"So what now?"

"You need to get back to your room and pretend you just wanted a casual walk that inexplicably lasted for what, four hours?"

"Five."

"Gods. I'd be surprised if they weren't already combing the city looking for you." Headlights from a steamcar illuminated the port, and the sound of a door slamming echoed across the empty bay. "You'll need to know where to find us if you manage to not land yourself in the clink. We're on Gardener Street, use the back entrance next to the old library."

Bailey poked her head out from their hiding place and sucked in a breath. "It's him. The guy who picked me up earlier." She turned to the woman. "Should I hide?" she hissed.

"Not if you want a ride back home," the woman said, shoving her out from behind the crates.

"What the hell do you think you're—"

"General Fineglass! Oh, ma'am, we're so glad to find you, we've been worried sick! The receptionist said you didn't ask for a driver, no one could find you within the hotel's property, we've all been running ragged, we thought you'd been abducted!"

"Er, no, I—"

"Why are you back here at the port? Surely there are nicer walks much closer to the hotel, and much more secure, to boot!"

"I, uh..." she trailed off, racking her brain for an answer. "I thought I dropped something."

"No problem, of course! We'll take you up to Administration tomorrow and get a new one ordered."

"That would be helpful, thank you." Maybe this ID plan wasn't too bad, after all. "The walk was refreshing, exhilarating, in fact, after spending so much time away."

"I'm sure." He opened the door, just like he had earlier that day, and gestured for her to get into the steamcar. "Shall we head back? If you like, we can order supper to your room."

Bailey sighed. "Supper sounds wonderful."

Chapter 8

Mae drummed the tips of her fingers against the crisp white linen fabric of the dining room tablecloth. She hadn't slept—too angry, or at least frustrated by the lack of information as to why she was even here. She shouldn't have come. She should have just ignored the letter, and hoped they wouldn't go poking around at her fake address, which was really just a locked mailbox in a huge warehouse. Paying extra for the post forwarding helped keep Bradach, and her real life, a secret.

The morning sun streamed through the tall windows, wispy drapes tied back with matching sashes that fell to the floor, weighted by thick tassels. Breakfast should have been at least an hour ago, if her parents were still keeping the same kind of schedule they had before she left home. Yet, the kitchen was quiet, except for trapped air creaking in the pipes. She huffed angrily, tired of being kept waiting. Dark circles ringed her eyes, reflected back at her in the crystal panes of glass.

Her stomach rumbled in protest, despite the previous night's fish not agreeing with her. Though, she may have had a better chance had she not horked the entire thing down in one bite. "This is ridiculous," she grumbled. "I'm not a child." She stood up from the table and marched into the kitchen, expecting to find the cook waiting on orders, but instead found it empty, not a scrap of prepared food in sight. The ice box was empty, the cupboard shelves stocked with grains but not much else. What in the hell was going on?

"Mother?" she shouted, striding back to the steps that led to their room. "Mother, I've had enough of this. Either tell me why I'm here, or I'm leaving for the port right this instant." There was no answer, not even a cursory tut or sigh. "Father?" Still nothing. The house was empty.

"Fine, I guess I'll find my own breakfast," she announced, apparently to no one. Taking her coat from the rack near the front door, she shrugged it on and unlocked the deadbolt. It wasn't her fault they hadn't given her a key. After all, the locks had been changed years ago, right after she left, or so they'd said. Even so, she'd thrown her key off the bow of a ship a long time ago. It was probably at the bottom of the ocean somewhere. She slammed the door behind her, guilt nestling between her shoulder blades.

"Maevestra!"

She turned, face to face with her mother. Freedom had been so close, and now, so far. "Mother."

"Were you going to leave our home *unlocked?*"

"I didn't know where you were!"

"It's Tuesday. We were at breakfast, as usual! And then you never bothered to show up, despite that horrid display last night!"

Mae blinked. "How the hell was I supposed to know you went out for breakfast?"

"Such language! If you bothered to pay attention, dear, you'd know these things. As it happens, I came back to fetch you, to see why you abandoned us at our meal. Your father had assumed you decided to sleep in, instead."

"No, I've been sitting at the dining table for at least an hour, wondering where you both were."

"If you'd have been up earlier, then you could have walked there with us. But I suppose you're used to a rather lackadaisical way of living, now."

A hot flush of rage began to creep up Mae's neck. "I work very hard, thank you."

"Yes, however, we have differing ideas of what hard work entails. Your sister Genevieve—"

"Gen isn't here, and you still haven't bothered to tell me why *I* am."

"Honestly, Maevestra, you made such a fuss last night about this, and then you couldn't even be bothered to join us for breakfast. You're the same as you've always been, willful and headstrong, completely unmanageable."

"If you won't tell me, then direct me to wherever you were having breakfast, and I'll ask Father, instead."

"As I said, I came to fetch you. Perhaps we can all eat together as a family without any little dramas? Do you still like pancakes?"

"Of course I like pancakes. Who doesn't like pancakes?"

"Stop being hostile. This place has lovely pancakes, topped with freshly picked strawberries, and cream newly churned. Now, will you join us, or are you going to insist upon rummaging through the cupboards in the kitchen?"

Mae sighed. "Yes, I'll come." She stepped aside for her mother to lock the door, and followed her down the few steps to the brick-paved street. "How come the kitchen is so bare, anyway?"

"It's Chef's shopping day. I'm sure he's at the market right now, stocking up for this week's meals. I would have asked what you wanted, but you slept in too late."

"I was up at dawn."

"You know what they say, dear, about birds and worms. Sleeping in is for lazy rebels and filthy pirates."

"Sure," Mae responded with a snort.

"Don't be rude. I've about had my fill of rudeness from you, and we've barely gotten started."

"Gotten started with what?"

"Stop prying, you'll know soon enough."

"I don't understand why everything has to be so secretive."

Her mother gave a fake, irritating laugh. "It's not about being secretive, it's about being savvy, and about having some sense of decorum."

"Right. How far is this place?"

"Around the corner. Your father will be waiting there for us, we've already eaten, but you can order something. It's so late, though, it may as well be lunch."

"Mother, it's hours from midday. This is when normal people eat breakfast."

"If you say so."

The little cafe was charming, but it was no Purple Pig. The tables and

64

chairs all matched, for one thing, which had an overwhelming sense of manufactured appeal. The black, wrought-iron furniture stood in stark contrast to the whitewashed floor and the crystal vases stuffed full with pristine daisies. No wonder her mother liked this place. It looked as though she'd designed it herself.

"Good of you to finally show up," her father said, with a smile that didn't reach his eyes. "Apparently, they are still serving breakfast."

"I imagine most places serve breakfast in the morning," Mae quipped, returning the forced smirk.

"Can I get you something?" the server asked, her severe bun piled high on top of her head. "I can tell you the specials, if you'd like."

"Thank you," Mae replied, "but I know what I'd like. A stack of pancakes with the fresh strawberries if you have any left, and two eggs, scrambled, with a side of potato hash if you've got it."

"Sure thing, won't be long."

"Are you planning on feeding half the Coalition army?" her mother muttered under her breath.

"You said I should order something if I was hungry, and I am."

"I didn't realize you'd order half the menu. Men like a woman who watches her figure."

"I've told you before, I have no interest in men."

"Women also like other women who don't eat their weight in pancakes."

Mae gripped the side of the table with so much force, she thought she might dent it. "Mother," she said through gritted teeth, "if you don't lay off, I will leave, and not care what was so important that you dragged me halfway across the Near Systems for."

"Delta-4 is hardly halfway, dear."

"Mother."

"I only say these things because I love you, Maevestra. I just want you to be happy!"

"I am very happy," Mae uttered through gritted teeth, her knuckles white with pressure. "Thrilled, in fact."

"A mother just wants the best for her children, isn't that right, Gerard?"

"Yes, dear," he agreed, his face buried deep in that morning's newspaper.

"In any case, that's why your father and I called you here to see us."

Mae released her grip on the table, but only slightly. "Because you think I'm not happy?"

"Because we think you could be much happier here with us."

Not if the last sixteen hours are any indication, Mae thought, but kept her mouth clamped shut.

"You see, love, your father and I are getting on in years. We won't be around forever, you know. We have the business to think of, and where it will go when we're gone."

"You want me to take over the family business of blackmailing politicians?"

"Shh! Don't be ridiculous, dear. And keep your voice down. You know that we have a long and established history of working within the financial district here in the Capital, and, well, we'd like to see you take it on for yourself, settle down, raise a family."

Mae raised an eyebrow. "What about your golden child, Genevieve?"

"Oh, your sister is successful enough on her own. She doesn't need our charity. She's much too busy building her own legacy to rely on ours."

"No."

"What?"

Mae bristled. "I said, no. It's a complete sentence. No."

"And why not?"

The server swooped in with plates stacked high, setting them on the small table. "Did you need anything to drink, ma'am?"

"Coffee. Black." She sighed. "Please," she added.

"Of course, I'll be right back."

"Thank you so much," Mae said politely. As soon as the server was out of sight, she continued, "Because I have my own business, and my own life, far from here, and I like it. I have no interest in taking over whatever it is you do here." She cut a large chunk of pancake and stabbed into it with the fork, layering it with a slice of strawberry. She shoved it into her mouth, relishing the taste. At least coming here wasn't a total waste. Fruit off-world rarely tasted this good.

"Maevestra, this could be very lucrative for you. It could change your life!"

"No."

"Think of the possibilities, dear. Think of the influence you would have! Gods, you've always been so stubborn with your strange political ideas, and now you actually have the opportunity to make a difference, to enact the changes you want to see here on Gamma-3! Why would you ever turn away from that kind of impact?"

Mae swallowed her food before loading up another forkful. "Because this place is toxic. It ruins people. Chews them up and spits them back out again, and that's if they don't mysteriously vanish for having the wrong kind of opinion. Look at you, Mother, even now you're nervously looking around, afraid someone will overhear. No. It's not for me. Thank you, but no."

"What are we supposed to do, then?"

"I don't know. I don't care, really. Why can't you just retire, like all the other rich snobs around here?" Mae sliced another sliver off the stack of pancakes. "It's very strange to me that you would offer me the family business, when all morning you've been making snide comments about my work ethic."

"I'm sorry. I shouldn't have said those things. It's just... you've been gone so long. I feel like I don't really know you anymore."

"And you want to hand your business over to someone you don't know?"

"You're staying here, Maevestra, and that's final," her father said, still reading the paper, or at least pretending to. "The business needs a leader, and unfortunately, you're our only option now that your sister has raised her station above ours."

Mae choked back a laugh. "Absolutely not."

"It's not a request."

"And I'm not a child, nor am I a prisoner or—" she lowered her voice now, "or one of the many I'm sure you're blackmailing."

"We only deal in information, we don't question where that information came from."

"Please, you deal in blood. And I'm not interested. Thank you for breakfast, but I'm going back home on the first shuttle." Mae stood, snatching the last strawberry from the plate and popping it into her mouth. "Good luck with the business."

Her mother grabbed her by the wrist before she could walk away. "Please. Don't make us do this."

"Don't make you do what?"

"You should sit back down," her father said, folding the newspaper in half, "unless you want your precious Bradach to be compromised."

Mae's breath caught in her throat. Her worst fear, realized. Thousands of lives, reduced down to one angry man's vendetta against his daughter. "Excuse me?" she whispered, sliding back into the chair.

"I'll bet you thought you were so clever, didn't you? Setting up a fake residence on Delta-4, paying an extortionate fee for courier forwarding. I'll admit, I didn't think you were capable. You proved me wrong, and for that, I am proud of you."

"For hiding?"

"For covering your tracks. It's smart. It's what I would have done. But—" he flagged down the server, waving his hand casually, "I would have made damn sure that the courier I was paying knew better than to be followed."

"You still couldn't know the coordinates. All transports in and out of Bradach are piloted, and only those pilots and their navigators know where it is."

"I know enough. Based on how long it took you to get here, we can make very educated guesses. Wouldn't it be a shame if that information just slipped into the wrong hands? Oh, sure, the Coalition has known about a secret settlement for years, never able to quite pin it down. But with a little extra information—"

"What do you want, exactly?"

"I told you. We want you to take over the family business."

"Is there anything I can get for you, sir?" the server interrupted.

"We're finished, just the bill, please."

"Of course," she said, floating back into the kitchen.

Mae shifted uncomfortably in her seat. "How do I know you're not lying?"

"When have you ever known me to lie?"

It was true, he was a man of his word, even when his word was stitched together from dozens of illicit backroom meetings. He was the person who knew everything about everyone, and used it to stockpile his bank account. "So you're just going to blackmail me to run your business for you, is that it? Keep the money flowing in while you two have a luxurious retirement?" Her hands shook.

"Blackmail is such a... a *strong* word, don't you think?" her mother interjected.

"What the hell else would you call it?"

"Persuasion," her father answered. "We tried going about this the right way, inviting you here to see us, inviting you to breakfast—"

"Where you knew I wouldn't make a scene."

"Well now, we couldn't risk you shouting the house down, now could we? Despite our thick walls, your voice does carry, my dear. I'm sure you will find that of advantage in certain situations."

Mae's heart pounded in her ears. This was like a nightmare she couldn't wake up from. The worst-case scenario. She'd spent so long trying to get away from this place, and now she was tied to it indefinitely, so long as she wanted to keep everyone back in Bradach safe. Her friends at the Purple Pig. The refugees. The research station. Abigail, who would be running the shop by herself now. At least she'd left it in good hands. "Why have you done this to me?"

"You're our daughter. The business is your birthright."

She shook her head. "But I don't want it."

"Sometimes, for the good of humanity, it doesn't matter what you want. What matters is working to nudge things in the right direction."

"Give it to Genevieve."

"Your sister has other gifts."

"What you think is the right direction is in direct opposition to what I think."

Her father furrowed his brow. "Open your eyes, Maevestra. Stop being naïve. I can't keep protecting you from the scum you call your friends."

"You're the scum," she hissed, as the server set down the bill. She stood, waiting. Mae's father opened up his newspaper again, and her mother averted her gaze. Mae held out her arm, and the server scanned it with a chip before departing with a chirpy "Thank you!" and moving to the next table.

"You're broke," Mae said. "That's why you brought me here."

He set his fork down. "Yes. And I have a job for you, you'll have to start immediately."

Chapter 9

"General Fineglass?" Someone pounded on the door.

Who the hell is that? Bailey wondered dreamily, and pulled the covers in tighter.

"General Fineglass! Are you alright in there? We have your welcome breakfast in ten minutes!"

Her eyes flew open. *Shit.* "Uh, yes, I'm fine! Running a little behind schedule, I'll be right out."

"Ma'am, I took the liberty of having your uniform cleaned and pressed, I'll just hang it here on the doorknob. I, uh... also had it repaired."

"Thank you, Davey," she said, throwing off the blankets, deeply resenting the gust of frosty air that swirled around her ankles. At least the hole in her uniform had been sewn up. She couldn't bear another day of chafing, and the insides of her thighs were still red raw and swollen from the day before. What a gods-forsaken mess. Marshall and Bertie would probably assume she was caught, or dead, when she didn't show up on the transport that would be leaving the docks that morning.

Opening the door just a crack, she pulled the uniform inside and examined it. The hole had been patched, and now it was all but invisible. She slid into the pants and tucked in her shirt, shrugging the jacket around her shoulders. Her boot laces tightened, she strode out into the hall. "I'm ready."

"Uh, ma'am," Davey said, looking down at the shining marble floor, "if you need any... personal items, I'm sure the front desk would be more than happy to provide."

"Anyone who thinks I don't look presentable can shut their damned mouths," she said with a laugh, before remembering who she was supposed to be. "I mean, after so long away, it's turning out to be a difficult transition."

"Of course, understandable. I just meant that you may want to... brush your hair. Before we go."

"Oh." Bailey leaned back into the room, her reflection proving Davey's point. Her vibrant, sunset-colored hair was a tangled rat's nest. She looked like an orphan someone just dragged in off the street. "Yes, of course. My apologies, Davey, the time difference has me a little out of whack."

"I thought that all official expeditions ran on Capital time?"

Gods, she was never going to make it out of this alive. "Oh, yes, but the civilian transports don't." She hoped she wasn't totally full of shit, but she probably was. Who was she to be impersonating a general on a planet she'd never even been to? If she didn't end up dead or imprisoned, it would be some kind of untold miracle.

"Ma'am, I hate to rush you, but—"

"Yes, yes, okay," she replied, digging through her canvas bag for her hairbrush. It was made from pine wood and bristles, with a carving of a deer on the handle. It had been a gift from her mothers.

"Beautiful trinket, if I may say so," Davey said, clearly trying to make up for his indiscretion of telling her to brush her hair. "Ornate, even. Wherever did you get it from?"

"It was a gift." She should work on giving shorter answers if she had a shot in hell of keeping all the lies straight. She dragged the brush through her tangled hair, wincing every time it found a tangle. When this was all over, she'd give some serious consideration to shaving her head bald. Braiding her hair quickly, she tied it off. "Let's head to this breakfast, then."

"Excellent. Apologies if I was too familiar, ma'am, I only mean to ease your transition back to Gamma-3. Given your shining record and history of being one of the most capable and decorated officers in the Capital, I'm positive you won't need me for long."

"I may need you longer than you think," she admitted. "The transition has been difficult."

72

"Don't be too hard on yourself, General. You've not even been back a full day!"

"Tell me more about this breakfast, then."

Davey gave her a worried look. "Surely the itinerary was sent to you weeks ago?"

"I'm afraid I never received it."

He flipped through his clipboard, his hands flying over the pages. "We received your confirmation, I'm sure of it. Yes, here it is," he said, showing her the page and a stranger's signature. "Oh no, oh gods, do we have a leak? Is there a mole? Has someone been intercepting—"

"Davey. Relax. I'm sure I just forgot." She tried to create a mental picture of the signature, in case that came up. There was an ornamental loop on every L. *General Fineglass.* It couldn't hurt, anyway, even though she was probably moments away from getting caught.

His shoulders returned to their normal position. "Ah, well. Yes. Of course. In that case, would it be appropriate to refresh your memory?"

"Yes, please, if you would."

"This morning is your welcome breakfast. You'll be meeting with the ambassadors of a few different colonies, as well as several civilians involved in the expansion project. It will be a sparse offering, I'm afraid, as the main bulk of the budget has been reallocated to the gala."

Bailey swallowed hard. "Gala?" When Davey started to look concerned again, she continued, "The gala, yes. Who will be there?"

"A few hundred people. Nothing too big."

She nearly choked on her own saliva. Someone was bound to realize she wasn't General Fineglass eventually, and that danger increased with every extra person she met. She had to get the hell off this rock as soon as she could. "Davey, I don't suppose you have a copy of my notes?" Assuming there were any notes, anyway. She could use all the help she could get.

"I do, in fact," he said, pulling a leaf of paper from the stack. It was sparse. A few scribbles here and there about the expansion project, and not much else. Most of the notes were about what the general expected upon landing, and the lodgings she preferred.

"Thank you," Bailey said, and knew that she hadn't quite muted the disappointment in her voice. "Davey, I was hoping we could sort out a replacement identification today. I feel very strange without it."

"Your chip should get you whatever you need, General—"

"I know it's an imposition, but I just want it with me, just in case."

"Begging your pardon, ma'am, but in case of what? We have fantastic security here at the hotel, we'll cater for your every need until you head back out to manage the rest of the project."

"You said it wouldn't be a problem."

Davey gestured for her to follow him down the left fork off the atrium, their voices echoing freely now in the larger space, the room being built out of a glass dome that let the sun warm the air. Bailey appreciated it after her chilly wake-up. "It's not a problem, ma'am, I just wasn't sure that you needed to waste your time on such a trivial matter."

"Perhaps you could get it for me?" she asked hopefully. The less contact she had with officials, the better.

He barked out a laugh, shaking his head. "They never told me you'd be this funny. The notes you sent never captured your sense of humor."

That was a no, then. "I've never enjoyed written jokes," she replied.

"Your breakfast is in the main hall," he said, opening the door. It was a large conference room, lit from the skylight above, and populated by a dozen people. "I'll be waiting here when you're finished to take you to your next meeting."

"My next—"

Before she could finish, a huge, hulking man in a finely tailored suit rushed up to her, snatching at her hand to shake it. "General!" he boomed. "What an honor to finally meet you. Glory to the Coalition!"

"Yes, glory," she echoed, pumping his hand just as hard.

"My name is Marcus Winter, I'm the envoy from Eelry. We're big fans of your work there, big fans."

Bailey's breath caught in her throat. She'd delivered a cask of ale there just a month ago. "I trust the windmills are nearing completion?"

"Yes, yes they are! How did you know about our windmills?"

"Oh, you know, I find it's responsible to keep a keen eye on projects across the Near Systems. It helps to... coalesce."

"We are honored that you keep a keen eye on us, and I for one feel much safer knowing that you do. Now please, please, don't let me keep you from breakfast."

He shifted away from the door, and Bailey's eyes grew wide. Davey had said it would be a meager spread, but there was anything you could ever want in the morning, from bowls of fresh fruit, to scrambled eggs, to piles of pancakes stacked next to dishes of butter and tiny carafes of syrup. Her stomach growled noisily. "Excuse me," she said, having to focus on not sprinting towards the tables of food, suddenly overcome with the desire to stuff herself full to bursting. Her room service dinner the night before had been underwhelming, consisting of a small salad and a side of soggy tofu.

"General!" someone else said, approaching, and Bailey resisted the urge to growl at them for getting between her and her breakfast.

"If you'll excuse me, I just—" she stopped dead in her tracks. It was the tailor from Bradach, dressed in a blue dress, spectacles perched on top of her neatly coiffed hair. Relieved as she was to see a familiar face, she wondered what in all the gods' names was going on. "*Mae?*"

"General Fineglass," the seamstress replied forcefully, her eyes wide. "What are you doing here?"

"I'm at my welcome breakfast, obviously," Bailey replied, keenly aware of all the eyes on them. "What are *you* doing here?"

"Ah, you two know each other! Excellent!" Marcus said, his plate teeming with food. "Are you friends from way back, or...?"

"Something like that," Mae replied tersely.

"Yes, something like that," Bailey echoed, still eyeing the food. If she was going to get dragged off to prison, she might as well have a decent meal before she went. "I was just going to get some breakfast, if you don't mind, Ms—"

"Machenet," Mae interrupted. "And yes, of course. It is, after all, your welcome breakfast, to celebrate your four and a half years away on an expedition in the outer rim, working to build the new habitation beacon that will allow the Coalition to expand our glorious empire."

Marcus laughed. "I think she knows where she has been!"

Bailey nodded, grateful that Mae seemed to be feeding her information. Whatever the reason she was here, she was helping Bailey save her own skin. "Yes, it's good to be back after so long away. I look forward to meeting with envoys such as yourselves while I am here, to learn and exchange information before I head back out again. It is, after all, a rare opportunity."

"You have to tell us what we're all dying to know!" Marcus said enthusiastically, his eyes wide with excitement. "Don't keep us waiting!"

"And what might that be?" Bailey said, fear taking hold again. She might not even survive the breakfast, much less get the whiskey out of storage.

"Ha!" He guffawed, throwing his head back with laughter. "I've never met a high-ranking official with such a sense of humor! Come, now, do tell us."

The incredible weight of his gaze landed on Bailey, thick and impervious. They had caught the attention of the other attendees, too. "I will tell you, just as soon as I use the washroom," she announced. "Could you please direct me?"

"Of course, ma'am, it's right through there," he replied, disappointed.

"Thank you, I'll be right back, I promise!" She sped across the hall, aiming for the sweet freedom of the bathroom. She'd escape through the window, or something, strongarm someone into releasing the whiskey, and get off the planet without somehow getting caught. The longer she stayed, the more dangerous things got. Throwing open the washroom door, she gasped for air, unaware she'd stopped breathing. She tumbled inside and pulled the door closed, irritated there was no lock. The extreme hypocrisy that she should be under close surveillance while the High Council enjoyed unprecedented levels of privacy did not escape her.

The window was small and high up, too small for Bailey to fit through. Fuck. Gods be damned! They'd never let her walk through the front door without an escort again, not after going missing the night before. She was trapped, a hunted animal backed into a corner. Panic bloomed, the long, snaking tendrils crawling up her spine.

"What the hell do you think you're doing?" Mae asked, flinging open the door. "You're going to get yourself killed, you know." She closed the door and wedged it shut with the back of a chair.

"I was only supposed to be doing a shipment, they got me confused with some actual damn general and now I'm stuck here."

"Just leave! You outrank all of them, make your delivery and go!"

Bailey sighed heavily. "The crates are in Central Claim."

"Whatever's in there, it's not worth it. This place is dangerous, like a pit of scorpions looking for someone to sting. Go home."

"You don't understand, the money we could make from this—"

"Isn't worth it. Trust me. If I had known why Captain Marshall asked me to make you this uniform, I never would have agreed. He should know better than to put his crew in danger like this."

"I mean, it's a damned good copy, though. No one has even looked at it twice."

Mae glanced at the door. "Yes, well, it should be, given that... you know what, never mind. Here, I'll help you through that window."

"I'll never fit through that window."

"Yes, you can, I'll shove you."

"General?" someone called from the hall. "General, are you alright?"

"Er—"

"We heard voices, and with all the new protections—"

Bailey coughed loudly. "I'm fine! Just a tickle in my throat."

"We heard voices."

Mae grabbed her by the wrist. "Tell them to go away, and that's an order," she mouthed, pointing at the badges on the uniform.

"I, er—I'm fine. Go back to the hall, I'll be there shortly."

"But General—"

"That's an order," Bailey finished, hoping she sounded like an authoritarian.

Their reluctant steps echoed back up the hall floor until they faded.

"That was close," Mae said, releasing Bailey's wrist. "Too close."

"You'd think with a rank like this you'd get a little more privacy."

"Not with the abductions lately. Higher-ups are getting nervous about losing information to rebels." Mae frowned at her. "Stand up straighter. You're supposed to be a general, for all the gods' sakes." She pressed her palms against Bailey's collarbone. "And square your shoulders."

Bailey sucked in a breath at Mae's touch, and coughed to try and play it off. "I don't think they suspect."

"They will, and soon. You need to get out of here as soon as you can."

"So what are you doing here? What about your shop in Bradach?"

"Don't even say that name here, you understand? Don't even think about it. They'd piss themselves with happiness if they found it." Mae rubbed her temples. "And it's a long story, not one I want to recount in a bathroom hiding with a stranger that shouldn't even be here."

Bailey grabbed Mae's shoulders in desperation. "Please, I need your help. I can't do this on my own, and if I fail..." She didn't even want to consider what failure would look like. Destitution for Marshall. Prison for the rest of the crew. Her own people, still scattered across the Near Systems, homeless and desperate. "Please, I'm begging you."

"Why should I risk my own life so that you can make some credits shilling booze?"

"Because it's more than that. The credits we get from this job... it could help me find people that are lost. Work camps, most likely, though some may be in prison by now."

Mae sighed. "What is it you need, exactly?"

"I don't know! It's not like I went into this expecting to become a spy!"

"Shh! You need to learn how to keep your voice down." Mae removed the chair from the door. "Come back to the hall in five minutes. They won't wait much longer."

"But what about—"

"I'll do what I can, but trust me, this facade isn't going to be easy to maintain. Your best bet is to get the hell out of here as soon as you can." She opened the door, her skirts swishing against the floor. "And when you get back, tell Abigail the shop is hers. Tell her to take care of it."

"Wait!" Bailey hissed, but she was already walking back up the corridor.

At least she might have an ally, even if Mae was clearly uninterested in helping her to get the crates and complete her job before heading home. And giving away her shop? Something was up.

Five minutes later, she waltzed back into the hall like nothing had happened, though now Mae was noticeably avoiding eye contact. Bailey loaded up her plate, letting the envoys do most of the talking. "General Fineglass!" Marcus said, butting in again, and Bailey was really beginning to resent him. "Will you tell us now?"

"I have to admit, Mr. Winter, I don't know what answer you are angling for. Given the breadth of this project, I can only guess what it is you're hoping to hear."

He bellowed a laugh again, this time spraying a fine mist of orange juice across the crisply marbled floor. "Why, we're hoping to hear when contracts will be available, of course! We all have expertise to offer with the expansion project. For example, in Eelry we have several contracts to strip mine the nearby asteroids for rhodium. We'd be thrilled to be the main suppliers as we move forward into the outer rim."

Bailey raised an eyebrow. "I'm not sure we're quite there yet, Mr. Winter."

"Oh." His face fell, and his shoulders slumped. "They said we'd be able to start pitching for contracts. If I'd known, we'd have focused our efforts elsewhere, maybe in Skelm for the rebuilding of some of their buildings."

"I'm merely suggesting that a modicum of patience would prove prudent." What the hell was she even talking about? It was like a word salad, whatever was coming out of her mouth. Still, at least it seemed to appease the envoys. "I say the same to the rest of you," she said, raising her voice to echo across the room. "Contracts will be chosen on merit only, and will be decided in due course. I look forward to hearing from each of you in turn." Before anyone could ask her anything else, she shoved a huge bite of pancake into her mouth. It was rude to talk with your mouth full.

Chapter 10

"So what did you learn today at the breakfast?" her father asked, leaning greedily over the desk in his study.

"The general seems as though she will be harder to appease than other high ranking management. She made a statement that all contracts will be chosen on merit."

He laughed. "That's what they all say, before the bribes start to roll in."

"I think she's serious."

"Maevestra, you have much to learn about how people work here in the Capital. The highest bidder will win, and failing that, whoever has the most dangerous gossip."

"We'll see."

"Is that all?"

Mae chewed the inside of her cheek. She sure as hell wasn't about to tell him about Bailey Stockton. "There's an envoy from Eelry who has access to much of the rhodium in that sector. I think that unless there are any other early front-runners, it will likely be awarded to him."

"Hmm." Her father flipped through worn pages of an old, leather-bound notebook. "Marcus Winter?"

"Yes, that's him. He has proximity to both the launch beacon and Skelm, and everyone knows how much they've reinvested in their manufacturing infrastructure."

"It's a fool's errand, unless they've found a way to stop those storms."

"Mm." She wasn't going to tell him anything more than she had to. If she was being forced to live here, then she wouldn't make it easy for them.

"You're sure there was nothing else of note?"

She smoothed her skirts. "It was a boring and uneventful breakfast. Truth be told, I'm surprised that you sent me to such a lackluster event. Have you squandered your influence as well as your savings?"

"We can't just be sending you into top level briefings off the bat, it would raise too many eyebrows. You need to work your way up. You'll see in a few months how they'll all start crawling to you, begging you to give them the information to swing a contract, or which representatives plan to flout guidelines."

"I don't even want to be here at all, much less wait months for anything interesting to happen."

"You would see your mother and father starve?"

Mae rankled. "I would have seen them stop gambling intrigue years ago and be satisfied to live out their days in peace, without interfering in the business of dangerous criminals."

"Funny for you to say that, given your chosen abode."

"It's not my fault you gave some bad advice that landed you in this mess, and yet, you've dragged me back here, threatened to blackmail me with the lives of my friends, and you seem surprised that I'm in no rush to repair the father-daughter bond that never existed to begin with. I've given you all I learned today, I don't know what else you expect."

"I expect a little less hostility."

"Don't count on it."

"Mae..." he trailed off, pulling open a desk drawer and retrieving a bottle of whiskey. "I know you're not happy to be here. Trust me, we never wanted to do this."

"Then agree to leave Bradach alone, and let me go." She'd never believe him, though. Bradach wouldn't be safe as long as he was alive.

"If it wasn't this desperate, we never would have had to rely on you." He poured himself a glass, then gestured to her. "Care to join me?"

"I don't care for whiskey."

"Suit yourself." He put the stopper back into the bottle, the rubber squeaking gently. "I've long looked forward to the day you'd take over for me, you know."

"I'm surprised that you would cede control, to be quite honest. You've always been too proud for your own good."

"You know that I am a careful man. This one time, someone got the drop on me. They out-maneuvered me. I was bested." He took a long sip of whiskey, his eyes squeezed shut. "A parent never wants to rely on their child. It's a failure on my part as your father."

"What happened?"

He waved her away. "It's not important. I know better, now, and so will you. Together, we'll climb higher than our family ever has before, using the information you'll glean. You'll see. You never know, you might grow to love this line of work."

"I sincerely doubt that."

"You sit there, trying to convince me that this little shop of yours is enough." He shook his head. "I don't buy it. Not from you, Maevestra."

"I wish I could accurately describe to you just how desperately I'd rather be there than here right now."

"Sewing buttons on waistcoats? Taking in seams, hemming trousers? You've always been a lively child, someone with fierce intelligence and curiosity. Fabric doesn't change, it's predictable, unchanging. I always thought you'd be clamoring to take my place at the head of the family."

"Genevieve is far more suited to galas and boardrooms than I am."

"I don't agree. Your sister has other gifts. You are quicker on your feet. Observant. Even as a toddler you were always listening, learning. I was heartbroken when you left."

Mae drummed her fingers against the smooth sphere at the end of the arm of the chair. "Odd, then, that you never reached out before you needed me to drag the family name out of the mud."

"Despite what I say sometimes, you did a good job covering your tracks. I tried a few times to find where you really lived. It didn't take long to discover that the fake Delta-4 address was a warehouse, but from there? It was almost impossible to track you down." He set the empty glass back on the desk. "I've been actively searching for you for over a year."

"Is that how long you've been in trouble?"

"I saw the writing on the wall, in some respects."

"Why not just leave, then? Sell this house, move somewhere quiet? Why did you have to drag me all the way out here to save you?"

"We have a lot of enemies, daughter, and there is no escaping the fact that losing our access and influence leaves us vulnerable."

She rolled her eyes. "Leaves *you* vulnerable, you mean."

"No, I mean us. You're a part of this too now, like it or not. If we can't protect ourselves, we'll all end up with targets on our backs."

"Who exactly did you piss off to such a degree that all this is necessary? Shouldn't you - we - be protected by all the people you sucked up to over the years? What, are you telling me that all those asses you kissed were for nothing?"

"Language, Maevestra. The tides have changed. The sands shifted. Things aren't the way they used to be. It's sharper, now. Every dignitary and envoy you'll meet will have their claws out. Now that credit distribution is based on contracts, not populace, their desperation makes them greedy."

"I'm not sure I agree with you."

"It doesn't matter if you agree with me or not. These are the facts. This is why we're in this predicament. And so, I will ask you again, what else you may have heard this morning at the general's breakfast. What is she like? I've heard from others who worked with her prior to the Outer Rim expansion project that she was rather cold and unforgiving."

"She seems like any other general," Mae said, focusing on keeping her face even and undetectable. The only thing worse than the Coalition discovering Bailey's subterfuge, would be her father uncovering it. "And I've told you, Marcus Winter is vying for one of the contracts. Beyond that, people were keeping their cards very close to their chests."

"Next time you'll have to do more digging. Everyone from here to Theta-8 knows Winter will be trying to snatch every contract he can. With his proximity to the ore-rich asteroids and how many people he's been importing from the work camps, he'll have to keep them all fed if he doesn't want to find himself out of a job."

"It would be helpful if I knew what kind of information you were after. If I really knew where to look."

He traced his finger tip around the rim of the empty whiskey glass. "Oh, you know. Affairs. Back-alley dealings. Anything we can use."

"If you'd tell me who we're after, then I can be more focused."

"He's untouchable, and you don't need to know who he is. Better to find smaller pieces of information we can use to assemble a ring of protection, to begin building assets up again. We've not held a dinner here at the house in over a year, because we don't want people to see the truth. It would make us—"

"Vulnerable," Mae finished. "Yes, I got that much." She stood and leaned against the back of the high backed, impeccably upholstered chair. "I'll do what I can. But I'm warning you, I still don't think I'm the right daughter for the job." Afternoon sunlight streamed through the stained glass window, casting dancing rivulets of color across the stark desk. "And just to be clear—we're done, as family. I'll fulfill my duties, so as to keep Bradach safe. But beyond that, I don't care about you at all."

* * *

Mae gently eased the front door open and moved to slip through it, undetected.

"Where are you going?"

Damn.

"Out," she answered her mother. "Nowhere special."

"Where is *out?*"

"Just—out!"

"If you leave—"

"Yes, I know. If I leave, Father will hand over the information and thousands of people will die. I got it."

"Maevestra, it's not that simple—"

"I just need to go for a walk, alright? I'll be back later." She slipped through the door and closed it behind her, walking towards the end of the block with a fast, punishing pace. She wanted to be long gone before her mother had the time to put her shoes on and come after her. If she even would.

The Capital was largely how she remembered it. A sprawling city packed with high-rise buildings, stuffed with people all scrabbling against each other to be top of the heap, to curry enough favor to move up the ranks, or blackmail their way into prominence. Why anyone would choose that life was beyond her imagining. Yet, here she was, in the exact position she'd never wanted to be in, because her parents decided they couldn't fend for themselves. She'd rather cart them back to Bradach and have their wire access revoked. Tempting though it was, trying to traffic people on or off Gamma-3 was near impossible after all those new regulations. Too many citizens running off to become rebels and taking their families with them.

Who would say no to the siren song of land to work, a roof over their heads, and to be left alone? Rebel ranks were swelling, and with them, pirates. Abigail would have a hell of a time keeping up with the shop on her own. She'd have to hire someone in. Mae's heart ached at the thought of never seeing her little shop again, never walking the cobblestone streets up the hill to the Purple Pig for lunch. Her parents would never let her go, and she wouldn't risk it.

She walked for at least an hour, finding herself standing outside a bookshop, closed at this time of day, peering in through the window. There was nothing worth reading in the display, stuffed full with Coalition propaganda stories about the glorious empire, of the value of hard work and efficiency. A long time ago, before Mae had left, this place had a back room with all the banned books, stories about bravery and loyalty, but if the sign over the door was any indication, the shop had changed hands. One by one, dissidents were rooted out. A bookshop owner. A labor activist. A rum runner.

Her thoughts turned to Bailey, and she cringed. What a mess that was. Why was she even here? She'd get herself killed, or worse, if she wasn't careful, and by what Mae had seen that morning, she was being anything but. Rum runners were frequently reckless, and that's why so many ended up in work camps. They delivered the goods everyone wanted, and were punished by the same people who kept bottles of the stuff in their drawers.

The night was cloudy, the stars invisible. Bradach had carefully controlled weather patterns, designed to keep the city balanced and the inhabitants happy. As the first fat droplets splashed against her skin, she realized it had been years since she'd been caught in the rain. Despite the inconvenience, she had to admit to herself that she enjoyed the spontaneity that unpredictable weather offered. And thus, that's how she found herself ducking into a little cafe on the other side of the Capital, drenched.

"Evening", the man behind the counter said. "Can I get you anything?"

The limited credits on her grey market chip wouldn't last forever, especially now that she'd have to take care of her parents, too. "No, thank you. Would it be alright if I just waited out the rain in here?"

"You'll be waiting a while. Last storm we got lasted all night long—" he checked his pocket watch before continuing, "and we close in an hour."

"That's alright. I'll be on my way in just a minute, as soon as I wipe down my spectacles." She rubbed at the lenses with a handkerchief, but it was so saturated that all it accomplished was to smear water across the glass.

"Here." He came out from behind the counter and handed her a fresh cloth. "That ought to do the trick, though I'm not sure how much good it will do once you're back out there in it."

"Thank you."

"Are you sure I can't get you anything?"

"Thank you, but I should probably be getting home."

"You look familiar."

The words knotted her stomach as she searched his face. Had she done a fitting for him once? "Oh?" she squeaked out.

"Yeah." He let the word hang there in the air, a dangerous omen. She couldn't have anyone here knowing where she'd been, one wrong word to the wrong person, and she'd be as good as dead, along with everyone else who lived in Bradach. That information wouldn't stay hidden once an inspector started poking around.

"I'm so sorry, I'm terrible with faces," she said, cleaning her glasses.

"And these certainly don't help."

His face fell. "I thought for sure you'd recognize me, Mae. My wife still talks about you."

"Your wife?" she echoed.

"Don't worry, we won't say anything."

"About what?" she asked innocently.

"You know," he said quietly. "The thing."

"What thing?"

He flipped the open sign over and turned out the lights. Panic seeded at the nape of Mae's neck. She was wishing she'd stayed out in the rain. He was right, it didn't look like it was letting up. "I should go," she said, laying the cloth on one of the tables. "My mother will be wondering where I've gone to."

"Mae, relax. Why are you acting like I'm about to murder you?" He flipped the lock on the door. "I just wanted to catch up, and I'm sure Amy will as well!"

Amy. Who the hell was Amy? She could only remember—"OH," she said, heaving a sigh of relief. "Amy! Of course! Gods, I haven't seen you two since school!" Amy and Aran. Of course.

"I heard you took off right after school. Someone said you joined up with the rebels," he said, an eyebrow raised.

Mae snorted. "Some people like to tell stories." Dangerous information, and surprising her parents hadn't gotten wind of that. Or perhaps they had. "Who said that?"

"I don't remember. People say a lot of things."

"So how have you two been?"

Aran grinned, waving his arms around the cafe. "Well, we got this place a few years back. Our pride and joy, you know."

"It's cute."

"I did all the decorating. We both know Amy can't be trusted with that."

"Did her eyebrows ever grow back?"

"Eventually. The scorch marks from those fireworks are still on that building, though."

"I'm amazed we never got caught," Mae said with a laugh. "It's a good thing you never told anyone."

"These days we'd get thrown into a work camp for a prank like that." He sobered, looking around again as though he expected to see someone hiding in a dark corner, ready to report them for a teenage offense from years back. "Seems harsh."

Mae shrugged. "I guess." He was fishing for information. She'd seen her father do it hundreds of times.

"Would you like a drink? Whiskey? Gin?"

"No, thank you." Her immediate instinct was to get the hell out of there, but she wanted to know why he was needling her for information. "I will take a pastry, though, if you have any spare."

"Of course!" He jumped over the counter and disappeared into the back room, returning with one glass of whiskey, one pastry, and a stack of towels. "Here, let's move to a different table. I brought you these, they might help."

"Thank you," she said, taking the towels. They were blissfully warm, a welcome change from the cold, damp feel of her sodden skirts. "So strange to run into you like this."

"Well, I suppose it was bound to happen, really. This is the only place for blocks. You still live with your folks up the road?"

"I was traveling for a while, but yes, I'm back. For now, anyway."

"Why the sudden return?"

She shrugged, biting into the pastry. "Ran out of credits."

"Tale as old as time. We had to save for years to get this place."

"Where is Amy?"

"She has the night off. Probably spending it with her parents, if I had to guess." He sipped his whiskey. "She'll be so disappointed that she missed you."

"It's a shame."

"So, traveling! Where have you been laying your head all these years?"

He was still scraping for information. Mae shrugged again, nonchalant. "Oh, you know. Around Gamma-3 a piece. Delta-4 for a while." She was cautious to say anything that could be challenged or verified. Who was he working for?

"No rebel settlements, then?" he asked with a laugh. He was bad at extracting information.

"Of course not, what do you take me for?"

"I'm just teasing, Mae. Everyone knows that your family would be the last ones to commit treason."

Mae snorted. "What a strange thing to say."

"I just mean, you've always been very connected."

"My parents are. I'm just a nobody."

"A nobody that came back to the Capital after more than a decade away. It's unusual. People will want to know where you've been."

"And I just told you."

He smirked. "Relax, I'm just teasing. To old times," he said, holding up his glass.

"To old times," Mae repeated, tapping his glass with the last bite of her pastry before shoving it into her mouth. "May the powers that be never discover our youthful indiscretions."

"Or any other indiscretions," he added.

"I'm afraid you'll find me rather boring after all these years, Aran."

"Oh, I don't know about that. What do you do?"

Aside from being a question that she hated, especially in the Capital, a way for people to measure your importance with cruel efficiency, it was one that could lead to more probing queries if she was truthful. And so, she lied. "I work in administration, filling temporary vacancies."

"A paper pusher?"

"I told you I was boring." He was new to the investigation game if he thought that someone with access to classified documents was unworthy. So, he wasn't a practiced hand. Then what was he doing interrogating her? Maybe she was just being paranoid. He was a school friend and a bakery owner, not a spy.

"I always thought that Mae Machenet would wind up a top of the line designer. That seemed like where you were headed."

Mae folded the towel she'd wrapped around her shoulders, setting it on the table. "Things change."

Chapter 11

"Davey, I feel like you're inventing excuses. You said yesterday that we would go to get my identification replaced, yet here we are, today, and I am still without it."

"Ma'am, once that planning committee ran long, there just wasn't enough time. Speaking of which, did you want me to log a copy of your notes from that meeting?"

Bailey snatched her notebook back, safely out of his grasp. "No, thank you. I have some revisions to make first." In truth, those pages were filled with inane doodles, not her thoughts on the rapid expansion project. It would have been interesting, had they been talking about rebels or pirates, or even illegal trade routes, but it was dry, bone dry conversation about melting points of stressed ore and blueprints of efficiency housing planned for the Outer Rim.

"We can go right now, if you like."

"Yes, please." With any luck she'd be well on her way back to the beacon as soon as possible. "After, I might like to have dinner. Alone. In the city."

"That's highly inadvisable, ma'am, as I explained—"

She squared her shoulders. "Do I outrank you, or not?"

"Of course, ma'am, but—"

"Then I will be having dinner, alone, in the city, as soon as I get my replacement ID." She laid a benevolent hand on his shoulder. "I know you're just trying to do your job. Let me do mine. Part of it is taking some time outside this hotel to see what the average Gamma-3 resident says or does. After all, the Outer Rim exploration project will need plenty of eager souls if it is to succeed."

"Will you at least let me organize a steamcar for you?"

"Only if the driver won't argue with me like my assistant does."

Davey blushed a deep crimson. "She will take you wherever you want to go. My apologies, General, I forget myself."

"You've been a great help to me, and I appreciate your efforts. Please just trust my intuition. It's kept me alive this long, no?"

"Understood." He began the march towards the front of the building, making notes as he walked. Bailey followed, her hands clasped behind her back the way she'd seen other officers do. "Ma'am, not to intrude, I just wanted to gently remind you that the gala is tomorrow evening."

"Yes, I'm aware." There was no way she was going to that gala. Aside from being an excellent way to get herself arrested, it sounded boring as hell. No, she'd be long gone by then.

"And I'm sure you're also aware that it's a black-tie event?"

"Of course."

"Surely your dress uniform is in your room? You've not asked to have it cleaned and pressed."

"Er—yes, absolutely. It's already been cleaned and pressed."

His brow furrowed in confusion as he looked over his shoulder at her. "When? I've not seen it since you got here, and all you had was that canvas bag—"

"Very late. After you'd gone home."

"Sure, yes. Right. Of course." He opened the door of the awaiting steamcar for her. "Did you want me to accompany you to have your ID reinstated?"

"That's not necessary, Davey."

"Excellent, ma'am. In that case, your driver, Amy, will take you anywhere you wish to go that isn't illegal." He snorted a laugh. "Not that you'd ask that, ma'am."

"You can take the rest of the day off, Davey. Enjoy it."

"But ma'am—"

"See you tomorrow!" Bailey said as she slammed the door, erasing him through the deeply tinted windows. She sighed heavily.

The steamcar's engine rumbled quietly under her, a weirdly comforting sound despite her unfamiliarity with models this sleek and updated. The steamcars she'd seen in settlements were either cobbled together from junkyard parts, or imported castoffs, older models and ones with flaws in the bodywork. "Where to?" the driver asked.

"The Administration building," Bailey answered. "I have to reauthorize a printed identification card."

"Sure thing. We'll be there in a snap." The steamcar pulled away from the hotel, leaving the huge edifice in the rear-view mirror. "Long time away?"

"Yes, at the Outer Rim. Working on the colonization and expansion project."

"That's very impressive. Do you like the work?"

"Sure."

"When do you head back?"

"Uh, soon. Next week, I believe."

Amy's black-gloved hands rested, relaxed, on the steering wheel. "What do you need an ID for, then? Aren't those mostly for protocol?"

"I may be expecting an imported shipment before I leave."

"Oh?"

This driver was starting to get on Bailey's nerves. Why was it any of her business, anyway? "I'd prefer not to talk, if that's okay with you. All these meetings have left me feeling rather overwhelmed."

"I bet. All those people, all that talking..." Amy trailed off. "It can be exhausting, if you aren't used to it." She locked eyes with Bailey in the rear-view mirror. "If you know what I mean."

"It's all part of the job."

"Sure, sure, but that would be quite the transition, coming from the Outer Rim, landing here, immediately having to... acclimate."

"I'm fine, thank you."

"You know, *General*, there are plenty of people who would kill to be in your shoes. All that power, the accolades... "

Bailey's mouth went dry. "I don't wish to carry on this conversation. How long until we reach the destination?"

"About fifteen minutes."

"Excellent. Then I wish to spend those fifteen minutes in silence."

"Aye," the driver answered sullenly.

The sudden interrogation had Bailey at the edge of her seat, fidgeting, and then trying to hide the fact that she was fidgeting. She sat on her hands to keep her fingers from picking at the one frayed thread that had escaped the seam. Drivers shouldn't be this nosy or brazen. She must be a spy, planted because someone suspected Bailey of not being who she said she was. She'd undoubtedly report back to her boss wherever Bailey asked to go - so she'd have to walk to the Central Claim building to get the crates out of hock after she got the identification. Gods, this was a whole mess.

The Capital was invisible from within the car, the windows being too dark to see anything other than blurry outlines of the harsh architecture that shot into the blue, cloudless sky. If there was one thing Bailey loved, it was the vast expanse of sky, wide and huge, that stretched out to every horizon, full of possibility and opportunity. Why had people ever left this place? It was beautiful. It was miraculous and perfect, aside from the hordes of fascists that swarmed the city every day on their way to and from the offices in which they worked.

If things were different, she'd never leave. The blissful freedom of an entire planet devoid of terraformers, or mirrors, or space suits. No poorly maintenanced air filtration units that hummed and clanked irregularly. She could only imagine what it would feel like to sift her hands through wet earth that hadn't been imported at an extortionate cost. What luxury, what beauty there was in the random miracle of a life-giving planet.

"Ma'am? We're here." The car stopped, though the engine continued to run.

"You're not coming inside?"

"Better to keep the steamcar running. Even these quick-firing boilers need a couple minutes to get going."

"Oh, good," Bailey said, relieved. "I mean, good that we'll be able to leave promptly."

"I'll be here."

The building was unremarkable, three stories of red brick peeking through the thick vines of deeply green ivy that crawled across each window and nestled around the doors. The sign read *Administration Building.* Bailey wedged herself though the narrow revolving door, which dumped her into a starkly bland waiting room, the whitewashed walls blinding in the afternoon light. "Good day," she said to the man behind the desk. "My name is General Fineglass. I need a new printed identification card."

"Of course, ma'am. Follow me down the corridor and we'll get your chip scanned."

Bailey's heart pounded in her chest, pushing panic into her veins and capillaries with every beat. "My chip?"

"Yes, it's the quickest way," he said, nodding his head towards the long hall. "I imagine a woman of your stature has no time to waste."

"Uh—" Bailey stuttered, searching desperately for a solution. Her chip was linked to an Officer Jones, not General Fineglass. "My chip may have been damaged, our transport was raided, and they used an electromagnetic pulse." Plausible.

"Damn brigands," he uttered darkly. "They should all be strung up for their crimes against the Coalition. How can anyone push for progress with hoards of pirates all across the Near Systems, disrupting shipments and engaging in petty thievery?"

"Er—agreed."

"In that case, ma'am, we'll have to look up your file. Name?"

"General Fineglass."

He stopped at a large filing cabinet, pulling out the drawer marked with a large, florid F. "I need the first name, too, ma'am."

Fuck, Bailey thought with a panic. No one had ever mentioned a first name. "Excuse me," she said, working to keep her tone even, to hide the fluster building beneath the uniform's stifling collar. "I didn't work hard my entire life to obtain this ranking, just to be undercut when attempting to perform minor errands."

"Of course, ma'am." He pulled a file and edged past her, before sitting back in the reception chair. "We'll just need to check the photo in the file to confirm."

"Wait—" He flipped open the file and began to leaf through the pages. This was it. This was how she got caught. She only hoped that Marshall and Bertie were smart enough to get the hell off that transport beacon before the Coalition tortured the information out of her. "I don't have time for this, I—"

"Did you want to keep your existing photo, or have a new one taken?" he asked in a neutral voice.

"I'm sorry?"

"We always ask. Some people prefer to keep them up to date."

"Do I look... different?" Whatever the hell was going on, it didn't make any sense. He had the file in front of his face, and hadn't called the guards yet. At least, not to her knowledge.

He shrugged. "I don't know. A bit, I guess? The scar on your forehead faded."

"My—" Bailey cut herself off, shaking her head. "Yes, of course. A fantastic doctor on one of the military beacons is pioneering a new treatment." For being a bad liar, she was improving at an exponential rate. The words flew out of her mouth so easily that she nearly startled herself.

"So, a new photo?"

"Yes, thank you."

"Stand to the left." He stood from his chair and dragged the camera on its tripod out in front of the desk. "Look just above the lens. Three, two, one..."

The camera flashed, a temporary blindness that left her disoriented, fumbling for the upholstered seats that lined the wall. "Gods," she grunted, catching the toe of her boot against the leg of a chair.

"I'd have thought a woman of your rank would be used to that by now," the secretary mused. "I'll just be a few moments as I arrange your card for printing. Wait here." He disappeared into the back amid the gentle sound of blades through thick paper.

Was this some kind of elaborate ruse? Was she being watched? Maybe the obvious spy, planted as her driver, wasn't the only thing the Coalition was doing to mess with her. Were they hoping to get more information, or discover who was helping her? None of it made any sense, and she was starting to get incredibly nervous. She shifted her weight from foot to foot, as though preparing to run at the first sign of trouble. She more than half expected a battalion of MPOs to burst through the spotless glass doors at any moment.

"Right then, here you are," the man said casually, handing her an identification card over the top of the glass partition at the desk. "Is there anything else I can do for you?"

"No, that will be all," she said, blinking, the card coming into focus. General Wilhemina Fineglass. "Thank you kindly."

"If I may, General, I think you should have kept the old photo. It's much more intimidating."

"I'll keep that in mind for next time." She pushed through the door, her hands shaking. Whatever was going on, it couldn't be good. She needed to get the hell off this planet, and fast. She piled back into the steamcar with a heavy sigh. "Take me to Central Claim, please."

"I'd be happy to, ma'am, but I received a message for you while you were in there. Davey dropped it by." Amy passed a crisp, folded piece of paper back to her. "He said it was of utmost importance."

"Great." Bailey carefully opened the note to reveal Davey's careful, practiced handwriting. It said to meet him for an urgent meeting. "Damn," she hissed under her breath.

"Ma'am?"

"It's nothing, he told me that I had the rest of the day to myself, but he needs me at the court."

Amy shifted the steamcar into gear, the boiler bubbling quietly beneath the sound of the engine. "I'm sure you're used to that, aren't you?"

"Unfortunately."

"Shall I take you there, then?"

Bailey chewed on the inside of her cheek. If she refused, it might clue them in, if they weren't already. But what if it was a trap? Her stomach clenched as she weighed the equally dangerous options, regretting having agreed to this scheme to begin with. "Yes, that's for the best. Thank you."

* * *

When Bailey climbed out of the steamcar, she sucked in a surprised breath. The court, aptly named the Judicature, was an immense edifice that stretched high into the sky, floors and floors of identical green-tinted glass that disappeared into the clouds. She gave a half wave to Amy and pushed into the building through the huge revolving doors.

"General!" Davey shouted, leaping up out of the plushly upholstered chair he'd been sitting in. "Thank you for coming, I know you're busy, and—"

"Of course. What's the matter?"

"Nothing necessarily—"

"Why am I here?"

Davey clasped his hands in front of him. "The staff here were eager to meet you, ma'am, and to show you around. Your stellar reputation precedes you."

"You called me here urgently for a *tour*?"

"No, no, of course not, that would be inefficient and self-indulgent. The tour is merely secondary. The truth is, General, they're a little short staffed today."

"Did you want me to fill in behind a desk, then?" she asked with a laugh. "Surely there are others better suited to this than me."

He furrowed his brow in confusion. "No, ma'am, that would be a ridiculous request, given your skill and experience. Unfortunately, the Judge is out sick today. Nothing serious, I expect, but now they have an influx of prisoners and no one to sign the paperwork to move them along. I knew that you'd jump at the chance, so..."

"Yeah. I mean, yes. Sure." Her heart pounded in her chest. The last thing she wanted was to be responsible for the lives of prisoners. The weight of it hung heavily around her neck. "I assume this is just a formality, the sentences already handed down?"

"Most of them, yes."

"How many?"

"A dozen, give or take."

Bailey's lungs resisted taking on the breath she desperately needed. "I suppose we should get started, then."

"I can't go with you, ma'am. Closed proceedings."

"Of course."

"It's on the tenth floor, ma'am."

She nodded, her feet carrying her toward the elevator at the end of the corridor which hissed and popped with the weight of its passengers. She hated elevators. It wasn't the small spaces so much as the potential threat of falling to her death, crashing into the basement that cast fear into her heart, but she boarded it anyway, her eyes squeezed shut.

"Ah, you must be General Fineglass," the attendant said. "Tenth floor."

When the iron cage of the elevator opened, Bailey opened one eye and peeked out into the long, domineering hallway lined with thick steel doors. At the end was a small judicial chambers, the heavy, engraved oak door propped open with a stack of books. She sat at the desk tentatively, afraid to touch anything.

"Good afternoon, ma'am!" a chirpy woman with a thick brogue announced. "I'm so sorry to interrupt your day, but I'd be lying if I said I wasn't excited to see you here. Seems that the Judge's bad luck is our good fortune! It's not often we see a general in here, much less one of your stature."

"Mm," Bailey mumbled in a non-committal tone.

"As I'm sure your assistant mentioned, we're extremely low on space here, and we need official authorization to move these prisoners on. If we don't, we'll have people sleeping in the halls by tomorrow morning." She snorted a laugh. "And that would be ridiculous."

"I suppose I'm confused why you couldn't have had this paperwork delivered to the Judge at home."

"Truth be told, ma'am, perhaps we could have."

Bailey stood. "In that case, I shall take my leave, and warn you not to waste my time—" she stopped short. A prisoner was being led down the corridor. A prisoner that looked a great deal like Ned Beckett from the Cricket. "Which prisoner is that?"

"Oh," the woman said, turning, "I'm not sure. Some pirate."

"As I was saying," Bailey said, sitting back down, "this is the last time I will allow this wasteful and inefficient use of my time. I trust the Judge will be back at her bench tomorrow?"

"We would assume so, yes. I'm sorry for bothering you, General, it's just—"

Bailey held up her hand. "It's fine. I'll process these, and then you can show me your facility. I am planning for the Outer Rim habitation project, and we are always looking for innovative ways to structure colonies. I hope that you will be patient with me, as I don't have duties like this where I am stationed."

"Yes! I mean, of course, ma'am!" the woman gushed. "The papers are just here, and we just need your signature on the ones you approve. It's just a formality, really." She handed over a thick yellow folder, stuffed with pages.

"What if... what if I don't approve of one?"

"You're funny, General!" she said with a laugh. "I'll be in the next room if you need me or have any questions." She shuffled out of the room, her navy blue skirts trailing behind her.

Hoping that Ned hadn't been sentenced, Bailey tentatively opened the folder. The first prisoner was a man convicted for a violent assault on a coworker. The description made her stomach turn.

Picturing the signature she'd tried to memorize, she signed. It wasn't a challenge to her moral compass to send him to a work camp. Nor the next man, who had gotten caught trafficking children to colonies for cheap labor, or the woman caught swindling old people out of their life savings. But then, a woman convicted of rum-running surfaced in the folder, and it gave Bailey pause. She had been sentenced to a hard labor camp until her debts were paid, and given how the system worked, that would likely be the rest of her life. She hesitated, holding the fountain pen in her hand above the paper. Could she sign off on a woman being punished for the same thing that filled her own account with credits?

Bailey set the paper aside, shuffling the rest into place. Another assault, someone accused of embezzling from their workplace, a man who stole a steamcar and crashed it into a barrier. Each of them a life, and they were asking her to sign off on signing away their rights and freedoms. And then, Ned. It was him in that cell down the hall. He'd been picked up on suspicion of terrorist activities. The name didn't match, though the enclosed photo did. He'd already been sentenced to a high security prison on the other end of the Near Systems, with a note in his file to interrogate him for more information, the underlying implication being that they'd torture it out of him.

She didn't know what to do. If she signed, she was complicit. If she didn't, she'd be found out, and Marshall and Bertie would end up in the exact same position. The pen dipped into the well of ink and rested there. Her hand shook as she laid it against the smooth wood of the desk, tears gathering in the corners of her eyes. She wasn't cut out for this. She was barely cut out for rum-running. The only reason Marshall had given her the job in the first place was because she could easily heft huge crates of product where the wagons couldn't go.

Now here she was, in way over her head. Impersonating a general. Being asked to condemn people to a painful, short life of hard labor. "Fuck," she whispered under her breath. Even if she got herself out, she'd be leaving Ned here alone to die. And only the gods knew why the hell Mae was on Gamma-3, but at least she wasn't in a prison.

Chapter 12

"I might as well be in a damned prison!" Mae shouted, already sick of the incessant arguments with her domineering parents. "I told you, I met an old friend from school."

"Keep your voice down!" her mother hissed, dragging her into the dining room. "Do you want everyone to know our business?"

"I don't know why you're making such a big deal about this. I'm a grown woman, Mother. I've managed perfectly well on my own for a long time now."

"Not here, you haven't. The papers say there are more pirates and rebels sneaking through the ports every day."

Mae snorted. "I'm not worried about pirates or rebels."

"You should be. I've heard what they can do to people, and it's terrible. Really horrifying. Just last month one of our old friends was found tied up in his basement, robbed of everything he had! Do you want that to happen to your father and I?"

"What would they steal? You're broke."

Her mother's face grew scarlet with rage. "I told Gerard it was a bad idea to bring you back here. You've only ever brought hardship and heartbreak to us."

"And yet, here I am, expected to save your asses from financial ruin."

"Language, Maevestra!"

"I have to ask again why Genevieve isn't here. Surely your golden child wouldn't disobey you the way I have."

"Stop bringing up your sister. We've told you time and again, she is occupied with garnering respect for our family name elsewhere." Her mother sighed, melting into one of the dining chairs. "Why must it always be so difficult with you?"

"All I did was go out for a walk."

"You were gone for hours! For all we knew, you were lying dead in a gutter somewhere on the wrong side of the city."

"I grew up here, remember? I can handle myself."

"You have to be careful, my darling. There are a good many people trying to take us down. One wrong word, and—"

Mae shoved her hands into her dress pockets to hide her clenched fists. "And we'll all go down, I know. *I know*, Mother. If you'd let me finish for once, I'd have told you that I think he was fishing around for information."

"What did he ask?"

"Nothing specific. Seemed to think I was running with a rebel cell. I told him I wasn't, obviously."

"He could be working for the security division."

"I doubt it," Mae replied, shaking her head. "He's too clumsy with his interrogation. He doesn't even know what he's looking for."

"Curious."

"I thought so too. Which is why I swiped a photo of him and his wife from their water closet." She freed it from her pocket and handed it over. "I hadn't seen him or his wife since school. They own a little cafe on the north side now."

"He doesn't look familiar."

"His wife's name is Amy."

"Hmm." Her mother shook her head. "No, I've never seen him. I would know, I have a memory like a steel trap."

"So you've said."

"How could he have known you were coming? Did you alert him, or make some sort of clandestine plans with someone to meet there?"

The thought of Bailey briefly flashed in Mae's mind. "No, I didn't have plans with anyone. I didn't even know I was going to end up there until I got caught in the rain."

"He must have known *something*."

"I think he just remembered that I was always well-connected and hoped for a confession. Aren't they paying people to snitch on their neighbors these days?"

Her mother harrumphed softly. "It's a community safety initiative."

"It's horse shit, is what it is."

"*Language.*"

"Where is my father? I need to discuss tomorrow's agenda."

"Oh, so you're done with me, just like that, are you?"

"Mother—"

"I've always been desperate for a warmer relationship with you, but all you ever do is push me away."

Mae blinked, chewing her lip. "Sorry."

"He's in his study," her mother sighed, standing to straighten the vase in the center of the table, the wilting white flowers now offensively slumped towards the wrinkling linens. "I'm sure he's waiting to hear why you were so late coming home last night."

"I'm sure he heard the shouting, the walls aren't that thick," Mae mumbled under her breath, climbing the stairs to her father's office. He was right where she knew he'd be, sitting behind his desk, his hands steepled together, resting on the lab-grown leather surface.

"Maevestra," he said in a low, warning voice, "you need to remember how things work here. You cannot go wandering off at all hours of the day and night. Though I disagree with your mother about the source of the risks, if you were seen walking the streets at midnight, people might start to assume things."

"Like what, I have a drinking problem?"

"No. That you're a liability." He gestured to the chair. "Relax for a moment."

"What if we used it to our benefit? Make people think that we're more vulnerable than we are, to bring them out of the woodwork?"

"Too dangerous."

She sat in the chair and stared him down across the desk. "I can handle it."

"I don't think you fully appreciate what we're dealing with here. These are not run-of-the-mill brigands and upstarts, they are seasoned predators."

"I can't help you if you're not honest with me. You've sent me to one lackluster welcome breakfast, without much of a clue what I'm even looking for or what my title is while I'm here."

Her father leaned back with an eyebrow arched with a challenge. "I'm told you had words with General Fineglass at that breakfast. A worthy contact, if she can be trusted."

She coughed, to buy herself time to find an answer, making a show of unfolding her handkerchief. "It was unimportant."

"An acquaintanceship to build on, perhaps."

"The general merely asked to borrow my powder in the wash room. I obliged, and we parted ways."

"Seems rather familiar for a general, no?"

Mae shrugged. "She seemed like anyone would after years at the Outer Rim. Distant. Cold. Uninterested in small talk."

"We could use a strong ally like her. Think of the connections and information that would net us! In six months, our finances would be solvent again."

"General Fineglass doesn't seem like the kind of military official who takes bribes or engages in backroom dealings."

"Why didn't you tell me that you had a conversation with the general, Maevestra? What are you hiding?"

Her father had been in his seedy line of work for far too long. He was like a bloodhound for blackmail. "Nothing. I told you, it wasn't useful. I would have mentioned it otherwise."

"Then why all the sneaking around last night?"

"I was hardly sneaking." She sighed, closing her eyes so that she could roll them undetected. "I needed some air."

"The next time you need air, try the gardens." He opened a drawer and pulled out an envelope embossed in gold, and sealed with matching wax. "We have an opportunity. Our star has not fallen so far yet, it seems. There is a gala tomorrow, and we have been invited." Pushing the envelope across the desk, he continued, "That is to say, *you* are invited."

Mae took the letter in her hands, running a fingertip over the raised lettering that spelled out her family name. "Who's my target?"

"The chancellor, Arnold Weaver. Before your mother and I fell from grace, we were friendly. I am in hopes that he will be curious enough about your presence in our stead that he may entertain a conversation. If he does, then perhaps we can start to try to repair that particular relationship. He could have any number of valuable connections or grudges."

"And if he ignores me?"

"Then you should move around, try to position yourself near those who speak a little too loudly, or those who may be drinking from a hip flask, enough to let something useful slip. After all," he said, an eerie grin spreading across his face, "it only takes a whisper."

* * *

Mae was sitting in the front room, hand-sewing beads to the front of the other dress she'd brought, trying not to think too much about the gala. Bailey would be there, unless she'd wised up and gotten the hell out of the Capital already. Even though that was for the best, the slight pang in her chest took her by surprise. She was probably just grasping for anything and anyone who felt familiar. Aran, at the cafe. Bailey, masquerading as a high-powered general.

A sharp knock at the door yanked her from her wonderings. "Just a moment!" she shouted towards the impatient soul on the other side of the green lacquered door, who was continuing to knock aggressively. Mae laid the dress delicately over the back of the chair she'd been sitting in, sliding the needle in and out of the fabric to secure it for when she returned. She unlocked the door and pulled it open, expecting to see a courier or a salesperson. She did not expect to see Bailey.

"Bai—I mean, General Fineglass! What an unexpected honor to find you at the door to my family home, where my parents are living, and are in fact just in the next room!"

"I know you don't know me, not really, but I need your help. I, uh... got your address from the court office files. Your father has been a witness in multiple cases."

"Come in."

The faux general stepped over the threshold, her cap in her hands. "Is there somewhere we can go?"

Mae chewed her lip. "My room is probably safest. Are you alright? You're not on the run, are you?"

"I'm fine."

"Follow me, then." It was a strange sensation, leading Bailey up to her childhood room, hearing her boots on the stairs just behind her own. It was like the first time she'd ever led a girl up to her room, except now everything was much more dangerous. She closed her door behind them, wedging a chair beneath the handle. "What happened?"

"I saw someone. A friend. They've got him in one of the detention cells at the Judicature. They asked me to fill in for the Judge today, wanted me to sign off..."

"What did you do?"

"I just left!" Bailey hissed. "I spilled my ink well over the paperwork and told them I was feeling ill. I didn't know what else to do. I didn't want my name signing off on any of it."

"It *wouldn't* be your name. But I wouldn't mention more of that here. The walls may have ears."

Bailey nodded, pulling anxiously at her braid. "What should I do? I can't just leave him there. He's a friend. He was always so kind to me on the ship, he—I was pretty low for a while, and he never judged me for it, not once."

"You can't pardon him?"

"No, the judgment had already been handed down. Besides, I'd feel guilty leaving the others—"

"Listen to me. You cannot help him, not if you don't want to get caught. You break him out, any hope of getting your swill out of hock is gone. They'll uncover your secret, the whole damnable thing, and no one will see you except through iron bars for the rest of your life."

"Please, Mae."

Something about the quiet desperation in Bailey's voice tugged at Mae's heartstrings. "It's dangerous."

"I don't care. I can't leave a friend to be sent to a high security prison. You and I both know that with the beefed up protocols, there'd be no hope of getting him out. It's now or never."

"It's going to have to be before he's transferred, then."

"We need a plan."

Mae couldn't help but laugh. "How have you already roped me into this? You may be a better negotiator than the real... well, you know."

"Are you going to the gala tomorrow night?"

"Yes. But we can't do anything then, it's in a different building, and—"

"I don't know what to wear."

"Oh. I suppose your dress uniform."

Bailey stared at her. "Are you forgetting...?"

"Gods. I almost did, for a moment." She racked her mind for a solution. "A formal dress would also be acceptable."

"No," Bailey said firmly, wrinkling her nose. "I'd rather go naked."

"Well, *that* would certainly cause a stir."

"I mean it!"

Mae instinctively reached out to smooth the wrinkled fabric at Bailey's wrist. "Leave it with me. I'll figure something out. But just so you're aware, the rush fee on this one is *really* going to cost you."

"Deal," Bailey said with a snort.

"You might have to wear a dress. Beggars can't be choosers when they're asking for black tie formal wear less than twenty-four hours before an event, especially not when I'm several hundred thousand kilometers from my shop."

"Do you need my measurements, or something?"

"No," Mae said thoughtfully. "I remember your measurements." Broad at the shoulder and hip, muscular thighs, well-built biceps. It would be difficult altering anything in this house to fit, but she'd do it. If nothing else, it was an excuse to be near her again. "Go back to the Judicature. Say you ate something for lunch didn't agree with you. Apologize profusely to the staff and promise to make it up to them."

"What about Ned? They said the Judge would only be out for today—"

"I've never once heard of a Judge taking a sick day. If she didn't show up, she's on her deathbed or trying to secure passage out of the city. That paperwork will take until tomorrow afternoon to retype. Your friend has a very brief stay of execution, and if you're—we're extremely lucky, we might be able to figure something out between now and then." Mae took Bailey's hands in her own, and she was almost surprised at the calluses. "Not a word of this to anyone else, okay? Your story is that you felt ill, you left for a while to recover. Got it?"

Bailey rubbed her thumb across the back of Mae's hand before pulling away. "Of course. I can't thank you enough for this, you know."

"If we ever make it back to the Pig, you owe me dinner."

"If we make it back there, I'll buy you dinner every night for a month."

Chapter 13

Bailey paced in her security-monitored room the next morning, staring at her—or rather, General Fineglass' uniform. The gala weighed heavily on her mind, and not because she didn't have anything to wear yet. It would be the most likely venue for getting caught in her very tangled web of lies; the bullshit she'd been feeding Davey would only cover her tracks for so long.

Pulling on the freshly pressed pants (it was a nightly service, apparently), she fastened the buckle at her waist and tucked in her undershirt.

"General?"

"Yes, Davey, I'll be right out."

"There's a delivery for you."

She shrugged on her jacket and buttoned it. "You can come in, I'm just tying my boot laces."

"Okay, I'm just going to sign for you. Is that alright?"

"*Yes*, Davey." She was double knotting her laces when he eased open the door, a garment bag in his hand. "You can take more initiative, you know. I won't get angry if you make a decision without me."

"Noted, ma'am. May I ask what you've had delivered?"

"It's for the gala."

"Ah, you've opted for a dress!" He hung it from the hook next to the door. "May I?" Before she could answer, he flipped open the toggles that held the bag closed, revealing a perfect dress uniform. He frowned. "Ma'am, you already have a dress uniform, you told me as such the other day."

"This is the same uniform," Bailey lied. "I sent it to be cleaned and pressed."

"But they do that here at the hotel! They've cleaned and pressed your everyday uniform every day since you arrived!"

"Yes, and don't think I didn't notice that they're so harsh with my things that the cuffs are beginning to fray. I didn't want my dress uniform to suffer the same fate."

"You could have asked me," he said, wounded.

Bailey stood and clapped a hand on his shoulder. "You've been so busy for me, I didn't want to add to your workload. Thank you for all you do."

"You're welcome, ma'am!" he exclaimed, instantly brightening. "The gala is going to be the highlight of the year, just you wait."

"I'm sure." She motioned to the door, but took one last look at the uniform, crisp black with yellow and purple accents. How the hell had Mae pulled that off, so far from her shop? "Let's get some breakfast, shall we? I'm starved, and I'm sure you have a full day for me."

"Today is Thursday, ma'am."

"Yes, I know."

"You were very clear in the instructions you sent ahead that Thursdays are to be kept free for you to have time to train."

"Thursdays, yes! Of course!" Train for what, exactly? It's not as though the real General Fineglass had time for athletics, spending so much of her time at the Outer Rim.

"So unless there's anything you need from me, I shall depart after breakfast. I do apologize that the gala is tonight, I tried to get them to change the day, but they insisted."

Bailey pulled her cap on. "It's no worry, Davey. The gala is a special event, after all." The possibility of having some free time was almost dizzying with potential, even if she was being aggressively monitored by cameras in her room and around the Capital. An afternoon without her assistant running after her with a clipboard might just be the best thing that had happened since she arrived.

Just before they entered the breakfast room, she paused. "I'm not feeling like a hot breakfast today, actually. I think I will take this roll and get started on training early."

"Are you sure? I heard they're making waffles today."

She wavered, tempted by the sticky sweetness of one of her favorite foods. "I'm sure. I don't get much time to focus on training here, as you know." She pocketed the roll and backed out of the room, determined to do at least one thing right today.

* * *

"General Fineglass, you said?" The angry woman behind the counter was flustered, her hair falling out of its once prim braid. "I'm sorry, we don't have any shipments here under that name."

"Try Officer Jones."

"But you said—"

"She asked me to pick it up for her." Bailey's heart was thudding almost painfully in her chest. The risk of being found out here was immense. The name on the crates wouldn't match her shiny new identification card, and she was coasting on laying thick pressure, backed up by her sparkling white uniform.

"This is highly irregular. We ask that people send us a wire first."

"I know, but she got busy. I'm sure you know how it is."

The woman flipped open a thick file with a heavy, aggravated sigh. "I mean no disrespect, General, it's just that this is a very busy port, and we have protocols for a reason, you see."

Bailey did feel guilty, having worked in service-oriented jobs before. She'd lasted exactly three days as the outgoing shipping clerk in Hjarta before she'd thrown the clipboard into a fire and stalked out. She'd always been better suited to manual labor, anyway. "I understand."

"We'll need to verify with Officer Jones that she's clearing you to pick up these twenty crates."

"That won't be necessary," Bailey said, bile leeching into the back of her throat, the anxiety pooling in her stomach as corrosive acid. It would be a miracle if she made it out of this without an ulcer. "She will be unavailable for the rest of the day."

"But, ma'am—"

"I promised Officer Jones that I would do this for her. She's had a real shit time of it lately—" at that, the woman's eyes grew wide with horror, and so Bailey rephrased, "Officer Jones has had a difficult time lately, I'm sure you've heard."

"I didn't hear, what happened?"

"Her ship was boarded! By *pirates*!" The woman gasped, and Bailey had to bite down hard on her tongue to keep from laughing at how absurd it was. "Poor thing has to attend meeting after meeting, accounting for all the losses, meeting with the High Council to discuss how best to reinforce the trading vessels."

"Oh," the woman breathed, suitably impressed. "I suppose the least we can do will be to make sure her delivery reaches her. Where did you say she was staying?"

"Don't worry about that, I'll take care of everything."

"No, no, I insist, ma'am! Just give me an address and we'll have a courier deliver it later today."

She knew what she had to do, but she hated herself for it. "Listen here, we've spent days trying to find the time to come down here to get her shipment because it was taken from the docks by mistake in the first place. We're both busy, especially with the onslaught of attacks from thieves and rebels alike, not that there's much difference between the two anyhow, and don't even get me started on the scheduled delivery that never took place. So if you don't mind, I'd like to take them myself, as this office is clearly too incompetent to do so." Bailey held out her hand expectantly. "The keys for the storage unit they are in, if you will, *please*. I don't have all day."

The woman leafed through the file frantically, clearly flustered. "I don't have any record of a delivery request—"

"As I said, the incompetence is staggering. It's a marvel you're even allowed to operate in the Capital. The keys, if you will."

"Of course, ma'am," the woman said, pulling a bronze key from a peg behind her. "I am very sorry, please pass our apology to Officer Jones—"

"You'd be luckier if she never found out about this," Bailey hissed, while simultaneously ashamed of her actions. "You don't want to know what she's done in the past when faced with such brazen and unrepentant inefficiency."

"Understood. Thank you, ma'am. The warehouse access is around the back of the building, I assume you have a porter?"

"Of course I have a porter!"

"Ah, yes, of course you do. Good day."

"Indeed."

Bailey stalked out of the office, a mess of emotions, from anxiety, to embarrassment, to absolute victory. The hard part was over. Now they just had to move them to the speakeasy, and they'd be done.

"Did you get it?" the woman from the speakeasy asked, leaned casually against an old, beat up steamtruck.

"Of course I got it. I told you I would."

"I gotta say, we were awful shocked when you rolled up this morning. We thought you'd be long gone by now. Boss was saying how thrilled she was that she was smart enough not to pre-pay the whole amount."

"Tell her she better get ready to pay it now. You're lucky we're not adding hazard pay on top of the agreed price."

The woman snorted. "After what we're already paying you? Get lost, *General.* You were late, besides."

"I wasn't late! You were late, and that's why any of us are in this mess to begin with!"

"What mess? You're the only one I'm seeing in uniform here."

Bailey rolled her eyes, which was probably not something the real General Fineglass would do. "Whatever. Let's just get this shit loaded up."

"I have a bad back."

"Of course you do." She rolled up her sleeves and strode in the side entrance, unlocking storage room A and hefting the crates, four at a time, out to the truck. With every trip she grew warmer and sweatier, eventually having to mop at her brow with the cuff of her uniform. "Alright, that's the last of it."

"Hop in. She'll sign off on payment after they're all in the shop."

"Yeah, alright."

The woman jumped into the truck, the boiler warm and ready. "It's not far. Maybe five minutes."

"I'm Bailey, by the way."

"I know."

"What's yours?"

"Boss says not to share details with rum-runners. Says you never know when one will get caught, and give us up as collateral."

"I already know where your speakeasy is, I'd just tell them that if it came to it."

"Ha! Good luck using it in your interrogation. Half the MPOs in this trash heap of a city know about us. They'd never do anything to jeopardize their favorite watering hole."

"Right."

"As long as we're trading secrets, how the hell in all the gods' names have you managed to pull this off? I thought after the identification card problem that was it."

Ignoring the fact that the woman hadn't told any secrets at all, actually, Bailey leaned her head against the old, water-stained window. "It just worked out in our favor, this time."

"I'd be careful, if I was you. Enough surveillance in this city to fuel ten years of investigations. Hell, I'd leave here and never come back if I'd done what you have. Shit like that makes people remember your face, you know? Better to be invisible. Off the grid. Undetectable."

"Aren't all steamtruck journeys logged and recorded?"

"Yeah, but me driving from an import depot to my place of work, where it's registered to, is hardly going to set off any alarms, now is it?"

Bailey shrugged. "You never know."

"I think you have bigger fish to fry than worrying about my work commute, yeah? Weren't you worried the real General Fineglass was going to show up?"

"Of course I was. But she didn't. Lucky me."

"Luckier than you realize, lady. Not many people could pull off what you've done without getting thrown into the highest security prison they have."

Poor Ned. That was his fate, if Bailey didn't get her shit together and help him. "Yeah."

"We're here. The door is just there. Once you're all unloaded, the boss will sign off on that payment. I'll give you a lift back to the docks, because I'm nice."

Bailey shook her head. "Thanks, but I'm going to stick around for a couple more days."

"What is this, hollow?" the woman asked, tapping at Bailey's head. "You've gotta have mushy watermelons for brains if you stay in the Capital. You're damned lucky you got away with this, and you aren't already working on rotting away in a cell somewhere."

"I saw someone. A friend. They're going to transfer him to a maximum security facility if I don't do something."

The woman gave a low whistle. "Yeah, that's a tough one. I wouldn't want to leave someone I cared about in the hands of these fascist fucks. Still, it's a hell of a risk to take. Would he do the same for you?"

"Yes. In a heartbeat."

"Then let's just say I'm glad I'm not walking in your boots." She climbed out of the steamtruck and lumbered inside, returning with a small wagon. "Here. Use this."

"Thanks." It wasn't long before Bailey had all the crates unloaded, resting safely inside the speakeasy. The owner of the club was perched on top of the bar, her legs crossed at the knees, the crisp white of her trousers almost glowing in the dark room. Her dark hair was pulled back into a fierce bun that tugged at the sides of her round face, and she was sipping at a complicated looking cocktail. "It's done. You have your stuff."

"Aye, so I do," the boss answered, making notes on a small clipboard. "You can go."

"Are you going to transfer the payment?"

"Probably."

Blood ran hot and surged through Bailey's veins, rushing color into her cheeks. "*Probably?* Do you have any idea what I—"

"Relax, love. This is standard procedure."

"That's not what I was told."

"Regardless of what you heard, this is how it is. Thank you for delivering my shipment. Once we verify the age and quality of the booze, we'll pay. Don't you worry."

"And how the hell long is that going to take?"

"It will take as long as it takes."

"Verify it now. I'm not leaving until the invoice is paid in full."

The club owner laughed. "Don't you have somewhere to be? Dressed in all that fancy-pants uniform, I can only imagine what pressing obligations you have. You wouldn't want to be late, now would you?"

"I'll be late if it means Marshall gets paid his due."

"All this talk of payment and credits is making me rethink this whole transaction. If I was a harsher woman, I'd take some of the price off the top for being three days late. What if the party had been scheduled, and the time passed already?"

"It wasn't, and it hasn't," Bailey replied through gritted teeth. "I'm really not in the mood for mind games."

"They aren't games, love, this is just how business is done here on Gamma-3." She leaned back and lit a fat cigar, her ruby lips pressed around it. "If you were as experienced in deliveries as your captain said you were, you would know that."

Maybe this *was* how things were done in the Capital, but she didn't trust this stranger. "Alright, lady, level with me. Your porter was late at the docks for the scheduled pickup, which is why the shipment is three days late, and why I'm standing here dressed like a fancy penguin in this gods-forsaken uniform. If you're threatening to charge a late fee, then I'm afraid I'll be forced to charge the biggest hazard fee you've ever seen. I am not trying to undermine you, or your business, I just want what's owed to us."

"How about *you* level with *me?* How would I know if what's in these crates is genuine without having it authenticated? I'm paying a stack of creamy credits for this swill, so I'll be damned if I'm not going to make sure it's not a fucking swindle, yeah?"

She had a point. For all she knew, she had twenty crates in her speakeasy full of cheap, catpiss rum. "Fine. But I'll be back tomorrow. You have until then to authenticate it, and no longer."

"Gods be damned, the woman *can* see reason," the owner said with an oddly charming smile. "I'm not trying to cheat you, darling. On my honor."

"Do speakeasy owners have much honor?"

"More than most."

Chapter 14

The hall was strewn with soft, twinkling lights, the overhead lamps dimmed, and the night outside dark. No moon hung in the sky. Mae smoothed her skirts, the deep blue of the taffeta fabric glistening in the dim light. She straightened the black fingerless gloves, the lace soft against the inside of her wrist. Her father had practically shoved her out the door into the street with a small purse which included emergency bartering gold, her old identification card, and a recording device. It weighed her down far more than it should have.

"Mae?" someone said behind her. She turned and stifled a gasp.

"Mr. Hawkins, what a surprise!"

"It's so good to see you back in the Capital. I can assure you, your absence was deeply felt."

"That's very kind of you to say."

"So, where have you been hiding all these years? You were building the career of a lifetime, one to surpass even my own, and then - poof - you disappeared into thin air."

"Oh, here and there. I've enjoyed my travels."

He took her hands in his own weathered palms. "I hope you will stay awhile."

"It's my understanding I will be here much longer than I had planned."

"I do hope your family is well?"

Mae grimaced. "Very well, indeed."

"I must say, your frock this evening is a great deal more conservative than I might once have guessed from you."

"I didn't anticipate attending a gala so shortly after returning home. If I'd had more than a day's notice, I might have designed something new."

"Still, it's very fetching. However did you achieve that delicate sparkle at the bodice?"

"Micro-beading. Impossible to do by machine, and the supplies can be difficult to come by."

He smiled proudly. "One day's notice, and you managed this work of art? My apprentice has become the master, and more skilled than I, dare I say."

"And you?" Mae asked, eager to change the topic, the ache in her chest at the loss of her shop in Bradach deep and inescapable. "What have you been up to, all these years?"

"Still teaching, though none of the students are ever as gifted as you were."

"No need to flatter me, Mr. Hawkins."

"It's not flattery if it's truth. You were always my favorite. Even Hector knew it, and despite all those years together, he rarely took an interest in the school's pupils. He always loved you, though."

"Where is Hector tonight?" Mae asked, and as his face fell, she knew she shouldn't have asked. "I'm so sorry. How long ago?"

"Two years, now. He was on a trip to Delta-4 to research a new ore seam, determine its viability. His ship was hijacked by pirates. There were no survivors."

"Gods," Mae breathed. "How awful."

"He was the love of my life. Still, life goes on, doesn't it? At some point, you have to pick yourself up, dust yourself off, and confront those demons head on. He'll always be with me, in my heart. There's a little piece of him in everything I create."

"That's a really beautiful sentiment."

"Ah, well, you know me, a sentimental old fool, same as I've always been." He folded his hands in front of him, and tilted his head, the motion swaying the long tails of his impeccably tailored black coat. "And you? Anyone special?"

"You know me, always working. No time for romantic entanglements."

"Mae!" Bailey shouted from the doorway. "Mae, I've been looking everywhere for you!" She hurried across the waxed dance floor and grabbed her hand to pull her away. "I need to speak to you."

"Uh—" Mae said, taken aback at how handsome Bailey was in the formal occasion dress uniform.

"Who's this?" Mr. Hawkins said, extending his hand. "Oh, General Fineglass, I presume! It's an honor to meet you, ma'am."

"Er—yeah, you too," Bailey said, her voice rushed. "Mae?"

"This is Mr. Hawkins," Mae said, ignoring the urgency in Bailey's voice. One of them had to keep composure, or they'd both end up in prison. "He is one of the finest instructors at the Capital University."

"Ms. Machenet is too kind, I am but a humble teacher."

"A teacher who is responsible for three quarters of the fashion in this city."

He beamed. "I like to think I learn from the young as much as they learn from me."

"*Mae*," Bailey repeated. "I would very much like to speak with you."

Mr. Hawkins had a furrowed brow, examining the fabric of the fake uniform. They were in trouble if he said anything. "Yes, General, right away, apologies," Mae said, shooing Bailey towards the corridor. "Mr. Hawkins, I hope to chat with you later?"

"Of course," he replied, still squinting at the uniform. "Anytime."

In the corridor, Mae spun on Bailey. "Have you lost your senses? What are you thinking, running around screaming my name like that?"

"What was I supposed to do, wait for you to notice me?"

"It's not like you're hard to notice!" Mae shot back, before realizing what she'd said. "You know. You're... tall."

Bailey raised an eyebrow. "And I look good in this uniform?"

"Yes. And you look good in the uniform." She reached up and straightened the lapel. "Now, what the hell are you doing, going around screaming my name? You do realize we're trying not to draw attention to ourselves, right?"

"I have an idea."

"Okay...?"

"To get Ned out," Bailey whispered. "During the gala."

Mae choked on her own saliva. "No. Absolutely not. No. We have a much better chance of going through the proper channels, I'm sure that you could pardon him, or... or..." she trailed off.

"You and I both know that overturning a well-respected judge's decision will draw a hell of a lot more attention than whispering in a corridor."

"Do you have any idea what you're asking me to risk, *General*?"

Tears began to gather in Bailey's eyes. "I know, I just—Ned is a good person, and he doesn't deserve whatever they're about to throw his way. I can't leave him here, Mae! It would tear me up inside, I'd never be able to look any of them in the face again, knowing I could have at least tried and didn't."

Softened, Mae took her hands. "Alright. Tell me the plan."

"We break him out during the gala."

"*That's* your plan?"

"Everyone of note is here, not at the Judicature. Security has been increased here, so it might be thinner on the ground over there."

"I want to help, I just really don't like the sound of *might*."

"If we get there and it's swarmed, we stop. I won't push. I know as well as you do that this is wildly irresponsible, but..."

"How do you plan on getting there?"

Bailey smirked. "I can drive."

"All the journeys are logged into the central server."

"Not if you rip out the navigation." She held up a mangled handful of wires that she'd pulled out of her pocket.

"That's going to flag a repair notice."

"Tomorrow, it will, when the central servers reset."

"And if someone notices that we're gone? You do realize that half the scum-sucking cretins in this room are only here to cozy up to you, General Fineglass?"

"Then I guess we'll have to be quick. We don't have much time to mull this over, as much as I'd like to give it to you."

Mae chewed at her lip. "Fine. Yes. Alright, let's go. But you'd better be working on a hell of an excuse in case we get caught."

"There's a back entrance over here. There's a camera, but I wandered over here earlier and pointed it just slightly off center. Should give us enough wiggle room to get out and back in without too much surveillance."

"What if there's a guard?"

"I'm a general, remember? I can do whatever I like. Then the real general can deal with the fallout once we're long gone."

Mae didn't have the heart to tell Bailey that she'd be staying in the Capital, probably forever. Not the heart, nor the time. "Lead the way, General."

They slipped out the back entrance, and Bailey wedged a brick in the door to keep it ajar until they returned. "The car is parked around the corner."

"Did you steal that, too?"

"Maybe."

She climbed into the passenger seat, being careful to tuck all the layers of her dress inside before slamming the door of the steamcar. She saw now why Bailey had been so frantic in the hall - she'd left the boiler running, to make sure the car would be ready to go. "Don't get us pulled over."

Bailey set a small yellow and purple card in the back window. "We won't get pulled over. I have immunity as a high-ranking official."

"I hate it here."

"It will keep us out of trouble, and that's what we need." She shifted the car into gear, and they set off towards the Judicature. "Shouldn't be a long drive. A few minutes, maybe."

"You're not taking the tunnel, are you?" Mae asked, her panic apparent in her tone.

"How the hell else am I supposed to get there?"

"Bailey, they use all kinds of tracking and facial recognition crap in that tunnel!"

"Shit." She pulled the car over to the side of the road. "What now?"

"Get out."

"What?"

"Get out. I'll drive."

"I didn't know you could drive."

Mae flung open her door. "It's been about ten years, but I imagine it's like riding a bike."

"You haven't driven a steamcar in *ten years?*"

"No! Why would I? Brada—I mean, why would I, when other options are widely available?"

"It's just me, Mae, I know where you live."

"You never know what kind of recording devices are built into these things." Her own device still weighed heavily on her mind. Her father wouldn't be impressed with another event yielding no information. "Come on, get out!"

"Alright, alright," Bailey relented, moving to the passenger side. "Don't get us killed or caught."

"I think we can both agree that I'm not the biggest liability in this steamcar right now."

"Just drive, Machenet. Let's go do this thing."

Mae threw the car into gear and started down the road, taking the winding back roads she'd memorized as a teenager, a lifetime ago. When she left, she never expected she'd come back, at least, not like this. Bailey was unusually quiet, staring out the darkly tinted windows as though she was trying to memorize the entire city. "Are you alright?"

"Just nervous."

"Understandable." She turned the car down an alley so narrow, the side mirrors of the steamcar scraped against the weathered red brick. They both cringed at the sound, and Mae struggled to focus on keeping the car perfectly in line. "I hope this isn't a rental. They'll charge you a fortune for the body work."

"Very funny," Bailey replied through gritted teeth, gripping the edge of her seat.

The car pulled out of the alley, and they both heaved an audible sigh of relief. "Next stop, the Judicature." Mae couldn't help but be smug that she'd pulled off driving through that alley. Maybe growing up in this festering sore of a city hadn't been a total waste, after all. "I hope you have a plan for getting back before anyone notices we're gone. That is, if they haven't already."

"Let's just say I'm winging it."

"Ah yes, famous last words from people who tend to wind up in prison."

"You didn't have to help me, you know."

Mae smirked. "Please. You might have a handle on lifting huge crates and being an incredible impersonator, but I have the handle on polite society."

"I don't think anyone has ever described me as being incredible."

"They should. You are." Mae put the car into park at the edge of the lot, just under a large willow tree. The extra coverage certainly wouldn't hurt. "So what's next?" She climbed out of the car and motioned for Bailey to do the same, and they stood beneath the gently swaying, trailing branches.

"I figure we have two options. The first being we try to sneak in through the back and break him out without anyone noticing."

"That sounds like a plan I can get behind. What's the other choice?"

Bailey turned, an eyebrow playfully raised, despite the seriousness of their situation. "I walk in like I own the place, release him myself, and we walk out."

"And what would your explanation be?"

"Further interrogation?"

"The first method means fewer questions, I vote for that. The back entrance is close by."

"Are you sure you want to come with me? I mean, in that dress?"

"Why, do you have a different dress in the car you'd rather I wore? Is the color not quite your style?" Mae snarked lightly.

"No, you look amazing in the dress—it's just—" Bailey coughed. "I wouldn't want you to mess it up."

"The dress is fine. Did you forget that I made you that suit in record time? Any tears that may or may not happen are easily fixed. Not easy for everyone, maybe, but easy for me."

"I really thought you were going to put me in a dress."

Mae hitched up her skirts and headed for the back entrance. "You made it rather clear that you'd rather be seen dead than in a dress."

"I appreciate it."

"You'd better. Do you have any idea how hard it is to find the right fabric with no notice? Hell, I thought we were rumbled when Mr. Hawkins was inspecting the twill. If anyone is going to notice that your regulation dress uniform is made primarily from my bedroom curtains, it's him."

"You made this from *curtains*?" Bailey said with a laugh, following behind. "Gods."

"I've done more with less. Not for a long time, mind you. Back home I was able to get my hands on exactly what I wanted. Silks, taffeta, thick satins, lightweight cotton, it was all right at my fingertips."

"It sounds like you miss it."

"So much that it hurts."

Bailey approached the back door, rolling up her sleeves. "I hope we all get back there soon. I can't say that my time here has been anything other than stressful. I can't imagine growing up in a place like this."

"You get through it."

"I love the sky, though. Endless. No terraformers. Sometimes, the air feels crisp in the mornings when I first wake up, and it reminds me of home."

Mae caught herself smiling at Bailey, and staring a little. If only circumstances were different, but... no. There was no time for that. They had to break a man out of prison. "So how are we dealing with this door, then?"

Bailey pulled a small pair of pliers from her breast pocket and yanked the pins out of the hinges, before gently lifting the door off and setting it aside. "What door?" she asked mischievously.

"Where the hell did you get tools from?"

Bailey shrugged. "I stole the pliers from a janitorial cart."

"You'd think that they'd reinforce the hinges to prevent something like this," Mae said, stepping over the threshold into the Judicature.

"Most people aren't strong enough to lift the door. It has a solid steel core."

"I bet you'd be a thief's best friend."

"I don't know any thieves, but I do know an assassin."

Mae laughed. "Please, everyone knows Larkin. She loves the Pig. It's just a shame I don't like cocktails, since she's found her calling as a mixologist."

"They're good."

"What floor is this friend of yours on?"

"Ned is on the third floor."

"Stairs are on your left. It's better if we don't take the service elevator, you never know who you might find on those."

Bailey glanced over her shoulder as she started up the steep, steel plated stairs. "What, other than a janitor or a mechanic?"

"Half the dirt my father ever dug up on people took place in a service elevator. Affairs, bodies, you name it."

"Stairs it is, then."

"Easy for you, you're in sensible boots," Mae grumbled, following Bailey up the stairs, her skirts bunched in one hand so she wouldn't trip on them. "The next time we do this, I vote that we don't do it in formal wear."

"I did ask you about the dress," Bailey countered, easily climbing each step, "and what is this next time stuff? I'm not built for treason."

"You seem built enough to me," Mae said, before realizing what she'd said. "For whatever you want to do. Not just treason. Maybe no treason at all. Some light sedition, perhaps."

"Can we please stop talking about treason?"

"We're here, anyway," Mae said, gesturing at the large number three plaque near the service entrance door to the floor. This one wasn't locked, and swung open without hesitation.

Bailey stuck her head out, looking one way, and then the next. "The coast looks clear."

"Let's grab him and get the hell out of here before someone notices that the back door has been ripped off," Mae whispered.

"I didn't rip it off, I just dismantled it."

"Either way, they're going to think that there are far more of us in here, and I'd rather be far away by the time the reinforcements arrive."

"He's on the left side of the corridor. Come on."

Their boots clicked quietly against the polished marble floors, echoing gently down the corridor. "It's quiet."

"I told you it would be," Bailey agreed, approaching the cell door. It was solid, painted beige to match the interior walls, with a small window high up at eye level. "Ned?"

"Look, I already told you knuckleheads, I'm not telling you anything!"

"Ned, it's me. Bailey!"

A man's face appeared at the small window. He looked tired, and had a black eye with a bruise that spread down over his cheekbone. "What the hell are you doing in a general's uniform?"

"It's a long story. We're here to break you out. Stand back." She took out the pliers again and began working on the pins. "I'm going to need a minute," she said, working the pins back and forth. "These have been painted over."

"You'd better hurry, they do rounds every ten minutes," Ned said, his voice a mixture of hope and worry. "How did you know I was here? Captain Violet? Alice?" He paused a moment. "Barnaby?"

"No, I saw you yesterday when they brought you in."

"Why are you posing as a general? What kind of dangerous nonsense has Marshall gotten you mixed up in?"

"Shh! I'll tell you as soon as we get out of here."

"Who's she?" He squinted. "Looks familiar."

Mae gave a half curtsy and a wide smile to try to reassure him, to distract him, and let Bailey work on those hinges. "Mae Machenet. Pleased to meet you."

"The seamstress?" he hissed. "From—well, you know where."

"That's me."

"This just keeps getting weirder. Didn't Captain Violet have a jacket made recently?"

"Last month. Dark blue brocade with mother-of-pearl buttons. Cropped length and sleeves. Double-breasted."

"Does she know you're here? Did she send you?"

Bailey smacked the top pin, and it fell to the floor with a clatter. "Got one."

"No, I'm here on... unrelated business," Mae answered. "But Bailey needed my help, so here I am."

"If you get me out of this, I swear I'll order a suit from you three times a year until I'm dead."

Mae smiled sadly, knowing she wouldn't be at her little shop in Bradach to make them. "You'd really suit a plum colored crushed velvet jacket, I think."

"I've always wanted one of those."

Bailey smacked at the second pin, swearing under her breath. "This shitting pin is stuck."

"So what now?" Ned asked. "They'll be back any minute—"

"Let me give it one more try." She wound back her arm, her face scrunched in concentration, before giving the hinge an almighty crack that bounced off the walls, the ugly, piercing sound akin to a gunshot. "Shit." The pin fell free, and bounced along on the marble, creating its own rippled echoes that melded with the others with an ominous dissonance. "I'm going to guess someone might have heard that."

Boots thudded down the neighboring corridor, at least three pairs. Mae tensed, her instincts wildly cycling from running to staying, and back again. "General Fineglass!" an MPO said, stopping short. "What are you doing here?"

Bailey held the pliers behind her back, stealthily stepping on the pins to hide them from sight. "I have urgent business with this prisoner."

"We don't have any record—"

"Some things are above your pay grade and your clearance level. Move along."

"But—"

"I said, move along! Or would you three rather be ensigns in the morning?"

"We have to log this, General, you know the protocols."

Bailey narrowed her eyes, baring her teeth slightly. "Write whatever you need to in that silly notebook of yours, Officer. But don't come crying to me when your dedication to clipboards and formalities stunts your career. Sometimes, you have to do what needs to be done. Who will stand at the hard line between us and them? You? With your paperwork, and your files?"

"General, I—"

"Are you going to paper cut the rebels into submission? Or will you stand and fight for our glorious empire?"

"But the protocols—"

"Get out of my sight. You disgust me. I'll be having words with your superiors."

"Just to be clear, we will be logging—"

"I said, *get out of my sight*," Bailey spat, staring them down. One by one, they all retreated back up the hallway.

"Gods," Mae whispered under her breath.

"Fucking hell," Ned said from inside the cell. "I haven't seen a dressing down like that since Boss caught Barnaby stealing from the loading bay." His face fell at that, and he rubbed his eyes. "Can we get me out of here, please?"

Bailey lifted the door, propping it against the wall. "I'll have to put the hinges back. Those assholes are going to report this, and we can't have any more questions than we already will." Tears were gathered in her eyes, but she quickly brushed them away. "I didn't enjoy that."

"I know," Mae said, reaching out to squeeze Bailey's arm. She had an overwhelming urge to wrap her in a hug, to comfort her, but there was no time for that now. They had to get back to the gala.

Chapter 15

Bailey was grateful that Mae was driving the steamcar, given that her own hands were still shaking from the encounter with the MPOs. She hated shouting, and confrontation, and wanted to crawl into a hole for several days, not be speeding back to a huge party, riddled with credit-hungry representatives desperate for their next deal. "Thank you for driving," she said.

"My pleasure. It's been nice to get back behind the wheel, actually."

"You're good at it."

Mae leaned away, as though she was trying to hide the blush that crept up her face. "Needs must."

"Ned, what should we do with you? Is there anywhere we should take you, or...?" Bailey was realizing that she hadn't thought this plan through quite as much as she should have.

"They'll be looking for me soon. I suppose you can try to distract them for a few hours, but they'll figure it out, and you need to be long gone before then."

"We should get back to the gala," Mae offered, turning down a side street. "If nothing else, it will delay them figuring out that you removed a prisoner."

"I can hide in the car," Ned said.

Bailey shook her head. "No. It would be a disaster if someone found you in here."

"He can't go anywhere near the gala or your hotel, there're cameras everywhere."

Ned leaned forward, his head jutting out between the two front seats. "If

131

you know where I can get an orange jumpsuit, I have an idea."

"Hiding in plain sight. Always a good plan," Bailey agreed. "I bet we can borrow one from a janitorial cart at the gala venue."

"I'll do it," Mae said, parking the car. "You're too recognizable, Bai."

"Better hurry up, then."

"I'll be right back." She disappeared around the corner, heading for the door they'd propped open.

"You didn't have to do this," Ned whispered. "You could have just left me there."

"I'd never do that," Bailey replied. "You're my friend. You were in trouble. Hell, you're still in trouble if we can't smuggle you out of here."

"I thought I was a goner for sure." A tear dripped down his weathered face, disappearing into his fluffy ginger beard. "I was just sitting in that cell, waiting for death."

"If you start crying, I will too, and I'm told that real generals never do that."

"Why is Mae helping us?"

"I... don't know. I don't even know the real reason she's here."

"Hell of a surprise."

"I'd have been caught at least three times over if she wasn't helping me."

Ned wiped his tear-stained cheeks with the back of his hand. "You know, General, you'd always be welcome back on the Cricket. The boss likes you, always has. Hell, even Kady likes you, and she never likes anyone."

"I can't come back, Ned." That old, familiar pang of heartbreak thrummed in her chest. "Not while she's there."

"She still cares about you."

"That just makes it worse. Harder. Sharper. It's easier when she's not around. That's why I left in the first place."

Mae came around the corner, her face in a panic. She threw the orange jumpsuit through the open door. "We need to get in there," she said, panting.

"What's wrong?" Bailey asked.

"They're all going wild looking for you. They're about to send out a search party."

"Shit. Well, what now?"

"I have an idea. You're not going to like it."

"Try me. If it means we're less likely to end up in prison, I'll do just about anything."

"Follow me," Mae said, grabbing her hand. "Ned, we propped open the back entrance in case you need to get in, but it's probably best if you stay away from the main hall."

"Aye," he agreed, pulling the jumpsuit on over his prison clothes.

Bailey followed Mae up into the building, leaving the door almost invisibly ajar, blocking the latch with the handkerchief from her breast pocket.

"Hey, that's silk, you know," Mae said with a smirk.

"Sorry."

"I'm kidding, Bai. It's part of an old set of curtains. A bitch to seam, though it's apparently rather effective for that." Mae pulled her towards a door and wrenched it open, revealing a small storage cupboard. "In here."

"*What?*"

"Do you trust me?"

Bailey furrowed her brow. "Yes, I guess so."

"Then get in. Come on, this is the only way."

"Okay, okay," Bailey said, relenting, edging herself into the cupboard. "Can you at least tell me what the plan is?"

"We need to make sure they think you never left the building. We need witnesses to that effect, and the bombshell story of a high-ranking general in the cupboard with the daughter of the former intelligence secretary will hopefully shield you."

"But those MPOs at the Judicature, they saw me—"

"Plausible deniability, Bai. You didn't sign in, there's evidence of a break-in with those hinges you so expertly removed. We say there's a lookalike, a doppelganger, pretending to be you in order to wreak havoc."

"That's ridiculous," Bailey said with a laugh. "Who's going to fall for that?"

"Everyone, if we make it convincing enough."

"What do you mean?"

Mae pulled the door to the hinge but didn't latch it. "Someone will notice this door is open. They're about to do a sweep of the building to try to find you." She wedged herself in next to Bailey, the cupboard barely wide enough for both of them, their bodies pressed against each other.

"And... and then what?" Bailey's heart skipped a beat, not sure if it was the threat of getting discovered as a fraud or the proximity of Mae's hips pressed against hers.

"I told you that you wouldn't like it."

"Just tell me!"

Mae stood on her tiptoes, pulling Bailey's face closer. "We have to make them believe it."

"Oh," Bailey breathed, her head swimming. "I think we can probably manage that."

"Someone's coming."

"Yes."

"Here we go," Mae said, and pulled her in for a kiss.

It was light and sweet, like a field of freshly cut hay, before deepening into something more like the feeling she got when slipping into a hot bath, wet and all-encompassing, with a hint of danger if she wasn't careful. Bailey's hands were resting on Mae's hips, and she pulled her closer, tighter, and a strange need rose up within her, something she hadn't felt since that ill-fated kiss with Henry, but this time there was no pulling back, no rejection, and she thought she might drown in it.

She hoped they'd never be discovered, and they could stay there forever, lost in each other's arms. *Get a grip*, she thought to herself. *This is just for show.*

Mae kissed her again, this time resting her hands against Bailey's neck, and it may have been the thrill of getting caught, or the soft pressure of Mae's fingertips against her skin that shot electricity through her, sizzling through her veins like she was on fire. She thought she might be lost forever, when the door was yanked open, flooding the small cupboard with harsh, invasive light from the corridor.

"General Fineglass!" Davey gasped, his hands over his mouth.

Bailey squinted at the light. "What do you want, Davey?"

"Ma'am, everyone has been looking for you! I was worried sick! We thought you may have been abducted from the gala by ruffians or rebels, or—"

"I was not abducted, as you can clearly see."

"Well, no, but this behavior could get you brought before the board of ethics! This woman isn't your spouse!"

"I'll only be brought before the board of ethics if you say anything, Davey."

"But—ma'am—I am duty bound—"

"How dare you threaten us?" Mae shouted, her voice reverberating off the marble floors and gilded ceiling. "What the general does in her private life is of no concern of yours! The audacity that you, a personal assistant, could be scolding one of the most highly decorated officers of our time is astounding! Leave, now, sir! Leave, before I report you to your superiors for impropriety!"

Several MPOs tumbled into the corridor at the sound of Mae's yelling. There was no turning back now. "General!" one of them crowed triumphantly. "We found you!"

"In... a broom closet?" the other said, taking in the scene. "With a woman."

"I'm not just a woman, you fools," Mae spat. "I am Gerard Machenet's daughter. I demand our secret, our incendiary secret, the one that could probably be sold to a tabloid for a fat stack of credits, be kept, or I'll have your heads on a platter."

"Er—aye, Ms. Machenet," the first one said. "General Fineglass, they are waiting for you in the main hall. To make your speech."

Bailey narrowed her eyes at Davey. "What speech?"

"All due respect, ma'am, the speech you're here for. About the importance of expansion past the Outer Rim."

"Of course. That speech."

"General?" the guard prompted.

Bailey squeezed out of the closet, dusting herself off. "Yes, yes, alright, I heard you."

"I'm sorry, ma'am, you just gave everyone such a fright. We were about to mount a full-scale search," Davey explained. "With all the abductions of late, it's what we all think when someone as important as yourself turns up missing."

"I said, alright. Gods forbid anyone have even one single iota of privacy in this damned place."

Mae cleared her throat loudly and poked her hard in the back.

"That is to say, I am embarrassed and aghast at my behavior. I would be ruined if the papers got hold of this story, my reputation ruined. I would appreciate discretion."

"This way, General," Davey said quietly, gesturing for her to follow him into the main hall.

Her footsteps were uneven and unsure, the panic lodging itself deep in her chest, below her ribcage and encasing her lungs. He threw open the doors, and she stepped over the threshold to greet the hundreds of shocked eyes, all staring back at her. Out of the frying pan, and into the blazing inferno of all the hells combined.

"Good evening, everyone," Bailey said, working hard to keep her voice even. "I apologize for causing worry. I had some business to attend to." From the corner of her eye, she saw one of the MPOs who had discovered them whispering to a server in the corner. And so it began. "If you'll all take your seats, I will begin the talk shortly."

She was considering escaping, climbing out a bathroom window, or just sprinting out the front door and throwing herself into the first cargo hold she found. If there was anything she hated more than the gross overreach of the Coalition, it was being unprepared. She was no stranger to public speaking, she would frequently attend community meetings in Hjarta, but making a speech without any background information to a room full of people desperate to climb over someone's corpse to rise to the top? It was the most terrified she'd ever been.

"General Fineglass, the podium is next to your seat on the top table."

Of course. Of course she was to be seated at the most visible table in the entire hall. The hope of escape evaporated, and the panic of making a speech settled in her chest. "Thank you, Davey."

"We can't begin to serve until after your speech, so..."

"So I need to get a move on. Yes, fine, I hear you." She swallowed back a sigh and climbed up onto the platform, keenly aware of the dull thud echoing around the silent room. The podium stood before her, imposing, threatening. Like it was laughing at her from the core of its lacquered oak center. She laid her hands on the smooth wood before adjusting the microphone that jutted out from underneath the hollow structure. "Hello. As many of you already know, my name is General Fineglass."

She cleared her throat, trying to swallow back the bile that threatened to make her retch. It was a good thing she hadn't eaten anything yet. "I am here to tell you about the importance of expansion past the Outer Rim." Her mind raced, and she frantically fought to remember anything from the boring meetings she'd been forced into over the past few days. "Some of you are here to convince me that your settlement, or your private company, would be best to take on operations there." A few gasps littered the crowd. *Okay, maybe a different direction, then.* "What I am here to explain is the fierce barrenness of the Outer Rim. It is not like you imagine."

Bailey had no idea what the Outer Rim was like, but she continued on anyway. "It is cold, and there is little light that far from the sun. It will take hard graft to make things work there, but having spent a good deal of time near the Rim, I know that it is worth the risks for the rewards of expanding our glorious empire further across the universe." The words burned in her mouth and threatened to choke her with the insincerity. "There could be rhodium out past the Rim in huge quantities. Early expeditions have been very fascinating."

This might be total garbage, but as they all sat in rapt attention, she felt compelled to keep talking. "It will take years before the expedition site at the Outer Rim is habitable for civilians, but we will need support from the private sector to complete the renovations to the station, primarily gravity generators, followed by expanded living quarters. We officers know that civilians are accustomed to far more privacy and comfort than we get in the military." Titters skipped through the hall, some officers hiding laughter behind polite palms. "So... er, that's my speech."

She ran the risk of incriminating herself if she kept trying to bullshit her way through this. She had to keep it together long enough to get them all off the damn planet alive. "The end." She took in the confused faces in the audience. "That is, unless, anyone has questions?" A hand shot up, and Bailey nodded at her. "You, in the front."

"Good evening General Fineglass, and a delight to finally meet you. I am from Sector Fifteen. Overseer Allemande."

Bailey's mouth went dry at the name. She'd heard plenty of stories about this woman, and all of them were terrifying. "Yes, Overseer, please continue."

"My sector is home to Skelm, jewel of the Coalition." Someone in the back snorted a laugh, but when her steely gaze landed on the offender, they swallowed it back with a cough. "We produce a great deal of products for the Coalition with our hyper-efficient factories, and we are already set up to take on challenging workloads. What would you say to someone like me, who already knows that their proposal will far outstrip all the competition? After all, you must know at your elevated rank that it makes more sense to keep production within the Coalition, rather than outsource it to private entities."

"Piss off, Amaranth," Marcus Winter spat loudly from the other side of the room. "Submit your application like the rest of us. There's no need for these theatrics."

"That's Overseer Allemande to you, *sir*."

"Whatever. You know, some of us from other sectors are getting real tired of Skelm sucking up all the most rewarding contracts."

Allemande raised an eyebrow. "Then perhaps other sectors should focus more on improving their efficiency, instead of publicly complaining."

"I'm just saying what everyone else is thinking. You accuse me of publicly complaining, but clearly you have no problem with attempting to influence the general's opinion before she's even seen the applications. It's uncouth, Amaranth."

"A show of hands, then, who thinks I am being unseemly?" Allemande asked, casting her steely gaze across the rest of the audience, twisted in her chair. No one moved a muscle. "Seems you're not speaking for the majority, then, Marcus. General Fineglass, please continue. I can't apologize enough for this unbelievably rude interruption. It turns out, not all envoys are properly trained."

"I—er, thank you," Bailey said, tripping over her words. Her mouth was dry, her throat parched from the fear. "I would say, Overseer Allemande, that I cannot comment publicly on how contracts are chosen. There are many... factors... which go into these decisions, not just my own personal opinion."

"Your *educated* opinion," Allemande emphasized, smiling politely. "Not a soul here can debate your efficacy or efficiency with the Outer Rim expansion."

"That is very kind of you to say." Bailey swallowed hard, her mind racing with all the threads of lies she had to keep track of if she was going to keep everyone out of prison and far from the clutches of Coalition blowhards like Allemande. "If there are no more questions, then I think we should allow everyone to dig in!"

A few exchanged concerned glances, but no one spoke, so she backed away from the podium, turning back to her seat. She could smell the first course, and it made her stomach rumble noisily. The scent was so deep and rich, she could almost taste it. Her mouth began to water in anticipation as she pulled out her chair to sit down.

"Er, General?"

"What is it, Davey?" Bailey asked with a sigh.

"Could I have a word with you in the corridor?"

"Can't it wait?"

"We'd best not, I'm afraid."

"Right." Glancing over her shoulder at the trays of food beginning to flood the hall, she followed her assistant - well, General Fineglass' assistant, anyway - down off the elevated platform into the hall. "Can we make this quick?"

"General... are you not at all concerned about what transpired... earlier?"

"What's done is done. Worrying about it is... inefficient." She couldn't wait until she was done with this farce and would be able to stop talking like some kind of brainwashed boot licker. "Is there anything else?"

"Your speech was abbreviated. I'm afraid that some of the envoys and overseers who traveled a long way might be disappointed that it wasn't more informative."

"I'm not running for election, Davey."

He ran his hands through his wavy black hair. "No, ma'am, of course not—"

"Spit it out. What's going on?"

"I overheard some talk earlier, that they might ask you to cut your visit short."

Bailey tried to resist the urge to scream with excitement. "Why?"

"The organizers here had hoped you would... favor some of the attendees, and you haven't shown any indication of what contracts you might be leaning toward."

"They'll just have to wait for my decision. But if they want me to go, then—"

"General, news of your... I am reticent to say, but your... indiscretion... from earlier, is already making the rounds tonight. I heard Marcus Winter grumbling that he wants to file a formal inquiry into you, to bring before the ethics board."

"For kissing someone in a broom closet?"

"For kissing someone who isn't *your husband* in the broom closet, ma'am."

Bailey snorted a laugh. "Surely, my private life is my own."

He furrowed his brow. "General, you know as well as I do that the Coalition military has strictly enforced rules on family life." He squinted at her, like he could see right through her. "Ma'am—"

"Bai—er, General Fineglass!" Mae gasped, hurrying around the corner. "I need to speak with you urgently."

"Haven't you caused enough trouble tonight?" Davey asked, acid in his tone. "We're having a conversation."

"Hey, don't talk to her like that!"

"I don't think you're grasping the gravity of the situation, General," he said.

Mae tugged at her arm. "It's important, it's about—"

"Davey, can't this wait until later?" Bailey begged.

He looked from her, to Mae, and back again, a horrible realization washing across his aghast face. "You're not really the general, are you?"

The three of them stared at each other for what felt like seven years, the panic mounting in Bailey's gut, adrenaline pumping into her veins, leaching into her muscles. Their tenuous plan was crumbling out from beneath them. They had to tell Ned. They had to get out of there before Davey said something to one of the higher ups, or reported her to the local guard station. They'd all get thrown into prison and rot in a work camp somewhere, and it would be all her fault.

"General! It's so nice to meet you!"

Bailey turned, and came face to face with a pretty young girl who was about seventeen, dressed in a sharp yet modest deep aubergine dress, cinched in at the waist. She was the picture-perfect epitome of a fancy finishing school graduate. "Hello, and you are...?"

"Emeline Allemande."

Of course, of all the people to show up, it would be Henry's girlfriend's sister. The one who had been effectively kidnapped and, apparently, adopted by the overseer. "It's nice to meet you as well," Bailey managed to choke out after a moment. Did she know who she was? Was she trying to ask for help? "Was there something you needed?"

"The overseer is such a great admirer of yours, General. I know she hopes to work with you more in the future." Emeline gave a winning smile and held out her hand. Bailey shook it. "You know, if you had any questions about her proposal, or about operations in Skelm, I'd be more than happy to answer them."

"Oh, er—no. I'm familiar with Skelm and its factories."

"I just know that some people think that Overseer Allemande is too forthright in her ambitions, but she really just wants what's best for the Coalition. She's loyal, and hardworking, and—"

"Are you alright?" Bailey blurted out.

"Pardon me?"

"I just mean—"

"Ms. Allemande, the general is a very busy woman. I'm sure you understand," Davey interrupted. "Run along back to your mother now, and be sure to remind her that trying to influence this decision could result in her demotion."

Emeline curtsied and smiled at him like she wanted to tear him limb from limb. "I shall. May I remind you, sir, that she has rather a lot of influence even beyond her sector."

"Noted. Good night, Ms. Allemande."

"General Fineglass, if you decide you need some more information, you know where to find me."

Bailey blinked. Was that a hint to rescue her? "And where's that again?"

"We have a home nearby. Two streets away, house number twenty-four. The overseer keeps late hours, in case you want information straight from the source - but I'd recommend making an appointment at your earliest convenience. She's a very busy woman, given her meteoric rise." Emeline swished away, back into the gala with a beaming smile for anyone who looked.

"Mae," Bailey said. "Do you know who that is?"

"Yes."

"I'm sorry. Did you misunderstand me?" Davey asked. "I asked—"

Bailey lifted him off his feet and threw him over her shoulder. "Make any noise, and this won't go well for you."

"Hang on—" Mae hissed, rushing after her. "You can't just—"

"He knows, Mae."

"Well, he sure as hell does now!"

"Put me down, or I'll scream the place down!" Davey cried, wriggling in her grasp.

She wrenched open the same closet door and set him down inside, preparing to slam the door shut and lock it. "No one will hear you from in here, not until—"

"Wait," Mae said, pulling her hands away from the door frame. "Davey, is it?" He nodded petulantly. "Davey, I imagine you feel the impulse to try to escape us right now, and report this to the first guard you see. Is that correct?"

"Yes."

"Let me present an alternative scenario to you, then - you say nothing, and we all go about our business as usual."

"And why the hell would I do that?"

"For one thing, admitting to your superiors that you mistook an impostor for a general and brought her into classified meetings is probably likely to get you fired."

He scowled. "The real general could show up any minute. You're fools for not running."

Mae shrugged. "Perhaps. But I also know that we're not the only impostors here, are we?"

"I'm no impostor."

"Please. I could sense it from a mile off that you're hiding something. You overcompensate, Davey. So tell me, who are you working for? Is it Intelligence? No, it can't be, even a rookie wouldn't make a mistake like this."

"I'm not with Intelligence," he grumbled. "In my defense, she does have a remarkable likeness to the real general. Though I suppose that's why she was chosen for this job in the first place, no?"

Bailey opened her mouth to protest the accusation, or to ask more about the real general, but Mae laid a land on her arm and squeezed lightly, as if to say, *let me handle this.*

"I'm sure you realize you're not really in a position to be asking questions, here. Out with it. Who's your boss?"

"I'm not telling you a damn thing, not until I know your allegiance."

"Allegiance," Mae repeated, an eyebrow raised. "You're with The Scattered."

He shrugged. "I assume you'll turn me in now, to save your own necks."

"Not necessarily. Maybe we can work out a compromise. I suppose you've infiltrated the Coalition in order to gain intel, yes? And you assumed that would come from General Fineglass?"

"Something like that."

"You might still be able to get information, given the opportunity. Far be it from us to stand in your way - our objectives aren't in opposition."

"Why trust me?"

Mae tucked a stray black hair back into her elaborate updo, secured with a jeweled silver comb. "I try not to waste opportunities. I need information, as much as I can get. I'd be willing to throw some credits your way for nuggets of gossip you overhear. I know The Scattered doesn't pay well."

"We work for a better society, not to get rich."

"Be that as it may, you still have to eat, and judging by that suit you're wearing, you have good taste. Those fabrics aren't cheap. Someone's been paying you, because that pure wool isn't affordable on an assistant's salary. I'm merely offering to pay for services rendered. Tips for tips, if you will."

He fidgeted with his pocket watch before tucking it back into his waistcoat. "Fine. But I want to know who you're working for," he said, glaring at Bailey.

"This was all some weird accident. I'm just a rum-runner."

"Horseshit."

"It's true."

"What the hell are you still doing here, then?"

Bailey tugged at her long, auburn braid. "I wanted to help some friends."

"Unbelievable," he said, shaking his head. "I agree to these terms. You don't say anything, and I won't either. I can't believe I've wasted this entire week spying on a spy."

"I'm not a spy."

"Whatever. You're hardly a reliable source of information on the Outer Rim." He buried his face in his hands. "Do you have any idea how long I trained for this? How many hoops I had to jump through in order to get this assignment? How many months have been wasted on this?" He ruffled his hair. "Gods, do you have any idea how much damage this has done? How much planning you've ruined?"

"It's not her fault you snatched her off the docks, now is it?" Mae interjected. "Adapt. Find someone else to haunt."

"We were trying to get intel on whatever they're doing out there at the Outer Rim. Whatever it is, it can't be good."

"Given Overseer Allemande's insistence over that proposal, I'd say she's a better mark than Bailey."

He looked up at Bailey. "That's your real name?"

"Yeah. Keep it under your hat, will you? We still have to figure out how to get the hell out of here."

"I have an idea for that, actually," Mae said proudly. "I think if we play our cards right, it's a sure win."

"What about Emeline?"

"What about her?"

Bailey frowned. "We can't just leave her here. What if she needs help? She was basically abducted by the overseer after starting union efforts in Skelm."

"You'll never get her off Gamma-3," Davey said. "People who get close to Allemande, well... they don't fare well."

"So I've heard, but she's just a kid."

He smoothed back his hair. "It's your funeral."

"Yeah," Bailey admitted, "I'm afraid you might be right about that."

Chapter 16

The temptation of Bailey's kiss still lingering on her lips, Mae strode back into the main hall, smiling at everyone who would risk eye contact with her. No doubt gossip of her cupboard dalliance was already spreading like wildfire, traded in dark corners between envoys and officers alike. It was all part of the plan to cover up the obvious scandal with Ned going missing, and as long as Davey kept his mouth shut, it would work. She'd seen her father do it dozens of times. The media fell for it every time - secret trysts and infidelity were much sexier headlines than potential government corruption.

Still, even with her plan, she still had to get Bailey and Ned off Gamma-3 as soon as they safely could. There was a shuttle leaving in two day's time, and the owner owed Mae a favor she'd waited a decade to cash in. She still didn't know how she was going to break it to Bailey that she wouldn't be going with, not with her own mess to figure out. Her parents were still a major and frustrating threat, not just to her own well-being, but the whole of Bradach. They were bastards, really, but irritatingly effective bastards, much to her immense fatigue.

"Mr Hawkins!" she called out, approaching her table. "I'm so glad that they seated us together."

"I'd ask where you disappeared to, but it seems like the whole hall is talking about it."

She waved him off. "Jealous gossip."

"You know, they say most lies have a grain of truth."

"Between you and me, sir, this story has several."

"You could do worse than a general. Good salary, employment security, and hell, you'd be free to pursue whatever you wanted here in the Capital while she's off exploring the Outer Rim."

"I believe it's the husband that's the real problem."

He snorted, taking a drink from his glass. "Yes, I imagine the papers will have plenty to say about that. You may want to steel yourself for the inevitable confrontation with him, however."

"He's off-world." She arranged her skirts around the chair and sat down, tucking into the bowl of soup, now mostly cold. "Thank goodness."

"Yes, I'm sure that's a complication you didn't need."

"Complication?"

"Mm. I'd assumed your father brought you back to join the family business. Am I mistaken?"

Her father's reputation wasn't unknown, but most people didn't dare say it publicly. Not when anyone could be targeted with blackmail. "I'm here to visit with my parents, and maybe, open up a shop."

"You could do more than have a shop. You were one of the foremost designers a decade ago, Mae. Your career was on an exponential trajectory before you disappeared."

"There's nothing wrong with having a shop."

"No, but we both know your penchant for perfection, not to mention your artistic eye. You could have been designing for the High Council by now."

She resisted the urge to wrinkle her nose. "Things change."

"What changed for you?"

Couldn't handle the shame of clothing monsters, she thought, but said, "Wanderlust."

"Is Delta-4 really all that exciting?"

"It's new, at least. Sometimes you just need a change of scenery."

"Ms. Machenet?" That girl from before, Emeline, sat down next to her, swapping the name tag on the table with her own. "It's such a nice coincidence we're seated together, isn't it?"

"Er—yes?"

"From what I hear, you have the general's ear. Even her trust, maybe?"

Mae slurped at her soup, enjoying the look of horror that crossed the faces of the others at the table, temporarily distracting them from their own conversations. "What's this about, Emeline?"

"As I said before, the overseer's proposal—"

"I can't influence the general's decision on those matters."

"Oh, come now, I would never ask something like that, I'm just offering to clarify anything that might put it at risk."

"Maybe we should discuss it later."

Emeline leaned back in her chair and gave a slight smirk. "I'm sure there's something we can work out. The overseer is enthusiastic about motivating others to compromise."

"You were adopted, right? Why don't you call her your mother?"

"That's inappropriate." The girl was visibly irritated at the question, smoothing imaginary wrinkles from the taffeta of her skirt. "It would be unprofessional to refer to her in familial terms in public, not that it's any of your business."

"Come on, Mae, she's just a child. A bit young to be pushed, no?" Mr. Hawkins said kindly. He always had been an incredible advocate for his students, and his affinity for mentorship hadn't left him.

"I'm nearly eighteen," Emeline answered. "Hardly a child."

"Perhaps not, then. Still, rather young to be put on the prowl for business dealings. You're the same age as Mae was when she completed her first informational transaction."

Mae cleared her throat loudly. "I don't think that's relevant."

"If you change your mind, you know where you can find me." Emeline stood, swishing away from the table, taking her name tag with her.

"What's your angle here, Mae?" Mr. Hawkins asked, taking a bite of salad. "Why are you interested in that girl's adoption?"

"It's complicated."

"Your food is going to get cold."

"I'm not very hungry."

He laughed. "That's a change from the Mae I knew." He wiped his mouth with the thick cloth napkin before setting it back in his lap. "I don't mean to pry."

"Yes, you do."

"Maybe so, but it's only because I'm an old man without much excitement in his life. I live alone, now, my students are far and few between, and the ones I do have, none even come close to measuring up to you. Spoiled brats whose parents paid the studio to let them in, despite the fact that most of them can't even thread a needle."

An idea was dawning in her mind. "Let me come teach."

"I'm sure you have better things to do than—"

"Please, Mr. Hawkins. I miss being at the machine so much. If I'm... if I'm going to be stuck in the Capital a while, it might be nice to have an outlet."

"We'd be honored to have you, of course. Next week we start on alterations, if—"

"I'll be there." She'd need a distraction after Bailey and Ned were gone, and hanging around a bunch of snotty, upperclass teenagers was a good way to grab some intel, maybe even enough to lift her family out of the trough they'd fallen into. Children had far less tact and discretion than their guarded, world-weary parents.

Mae stole a glance at the top table where Bailey was seated, looking very fine in that last minute dress uniform she'd whipped up. There was a never-ending stream of envoys and private investors wandering past her seat, dropping proposals, notes, even gifts, in the hopes she'd reward them with the contracts. Gamma-3 was nothing but a damned snake pit.

"They are being particularly brazen," he said, following Mae's gaze. "It must be a lucrative contract."

"I wouldn't know."

"Wouldn't you?"

"I'm sorry, Mr. Hawkins, but I have to go. No doubt I'll already have reporters at my door, my parents will be livid." She stood, gathering her skirts in her hand. "It's been lovely to see you again, and I'll come up to the school to try to teach the hopeless cases something."

"Good night, Mae."

She nodded, heading to the door. Before she could leave, Davey grabbed her arm and pulled her into the corridor. "Ouch!" she hissed, yanking her elbow back from his grasp. "What the hell?"

"I thought you said you didn't know anything about The Scattered."

"I don't!"

"Then what are you doing talking to Hawkins?"

Mae snorted. "He was my teacher a long time ago. There's no way he's part of your cult."

"We're not a cult."

"Tell that to your acolytes who plan the destruction of whole cities to prove a point to the High Council."

"Those are special circumstances. Answer my question, what are you doing with Hawkins?"

"I told you, just catching up. He asked me to do some teaching at his studio. How do *you* know him?"

Davey sighed heavily. "I don't, not really—but his husband asked me to keep an eye out for him while I'm here."

"His—no. Mr. Hawkins said that Hector died two years ago."

"He did not."

"Does Mr. Hawkins know that?"

"He may suspect, it's hard to tell, but no, he doesn't know. Hector doesn't even think he knew throughout their marriage about his involvement with us."

"Gods." Mae rubbed at her eyes, aware she was probably smearing kohl all over her cheeks. "I can assure you, I didn't know."

"I find it a challenge to believe you."

"Believe what you want, then. Nothing I say is likely to sway your opinion, anyway." She pushed past him, heading for one of the exits.

"Do you have any idea how much hot water I'm going to be in? Your little stunt with the general is going to blow this whole thing out of the water. They're going to figure out she's not Fineglass. She's not brilliant at acting, either."

"Good enough to fool you."

Davey rankled. "You know, I don't buy that cock-and-bull story that she's a rum-runner. Who are you two really working for? Is this an Intelligence mission, to test protocol?"

"If it was, you'd be in prison already."

"Unless you need more time to test barriers, and arresting me would end the experiment too early."

"We're not from Intelligence." She pushed the door open, stepping out into the night air. "Stop following me. Don't you have a general to look after?"

"I need to know who you're working for!"

"Keep your damned voice down!" she hissed. "Do you want us all to get caught, you moldy potato?"

"Get away from her!" Ned boomed, shovel menacingly in hand. "Where's Bailey?"

"Gods, can you men please *shut the hell up*? Sound carries here." She grabbed the shovel, yanking it away from Ned. "We have a new plan, but you have to come with me."

"Who the fuck is this?" Davey asked. "Some big, hulking..." Ned stepped into the light, pooling from the corridor lights inside the building and spilling out the glass door. "...handsome bodyguard?" Davey finished. "Hi, I'm Davey."

"Mae, who's this?"

"A pain in the ass." When Ned raised an eyebrow, she sighed. "He's Scattered."

"Oh. I didn't realize you folks were down here on Gamma-3."

"Officially, we're not."

"This is a gods-damned mess," Mae huffed. "You people have secrets even within a secret organization? What next?"

"You should be thanking your lucky stars that I wasn't a real assistant, desperate for clout. You'd already be in a cell."

Ned stroked his thick red beard. "As a recent occupant, I can't recommend them. I've stayed in much nicer prisons."

"You *broke* him *out*?" Davey demanded. "They're going to be on your asses any second." He started to back away, casting furtive glances behind him. "You are the worst organized outfit I've ever seen. Whoever you're working for, they should be ashamed of your clumsy, hack-eyed—"

"We're pirates," Ned interrupted. "Well, not Mae, not really."

"Excuse me? I'm as pirate as you," she shot back.

"Apologies. Most don't like that label."

"I told you, Davey, we're here to help a friend, that's all."

"You should have enlisted help from an organization, instead of coming down here and stomping through carefully laid plans. It's highly irresponsible, and—"

Mae put her hand up to silence him. "I'm going to be frank with you. We don't give one solitary shit about your carefully laid plans. Just go about your business, and leave us out of it."

"You involved me the second she decided to pose as a general."

"You're the one who grabbed her off the docks!"

"It's not my fault she looks like her!"

Mae barked out a laugh. "Please, they can't look that much alike. You're both damned lucky this isn't Fineglass' normal base of operations, no one knows her here, not personally."

"May I humbly suggest having this conversation elsewhere?" Ned interjected. "Could be recording devices around."

Davey shook his head. "Not here. They remove all recording devices for officially sponsored events, as a mutual agreement to cover all their asses."

"That's not right, actually," Mae said. "There are still some around, probably planted by Intelligence. Ned is right, we need to get out of here."

"I thought you said you're not with Intelligence?"

"Where's Bailey?" Ned asked.

"I have other methods of gaining information," Mae said to Davey. "And she has to stay here, at least for now. It would rouse too much suspicion otherwise."

"Feels a little like we're leaving her to the wolves."

"It would be a nice vacation from what we're really dealing with here—wolves are more civilized. I have a plan. Get in the car."

Chapter 17

Bailey sat in her chair, already exhausted from the evening's activities. It already felt like days ago that they'd sprung Ned from his cell, and her stomach agreed, growling ferociously. Her first course was tepid at best, grown cold from the time spent in the corridor. She shoveled it into her mouth anyway, a welcome abatement from the constant questions and speeches, followed by the endless parade of envoys and representatives trying to casually bribe her into choosing them for the expansion project. If she had her way, she'd slink back to the hotel with pockets full of food pilfered from the trays near the kitchen doors.

Her eyes flicked over the other attendees, trying to memorize their faces and names. Unless Mae had a top secret ship that could get in and out of Gamma-3 undetected, she was going to be here a little while longer. She could only imagine how panicked Marshall and Bertie were, probably pacing the length of the transport beacon over and over, aggravating Bertie's bad knee and Marshall's frayed nerves. If only there was a way to get word, but there wasn't, not unless she wanted to raise even more suspicion than she already had.

What she couldn't figure out was whether Emeline was asking for their help. She'd been gone for seven months. Plenty could have happened in that amount of time - she might be a desperate kid trying to get away, but there was also the possibility that she had absorbed all the inevitable brainwashing from whatever boarding school she'd been dropped into. It didn't matter that it was Henry's lover's sister, the responsibility for the girl still weighed heavily on Bailey's shoulders.

"General?"

When Bailey turned, she had to resist the urge to roll her eyes at yet another desperate envoy. But it was Overseer Allemande, so Bailey nearly choked on her cold soup. "Overseer."

"My daughter Emeline says you had a friendly chat in the corridor."

"We did, yes."

"What we can't discern is whether you can fill us in on any other information."

"Ah." Bailey sucked her teeth. "As I told her, my decision will be made within the next few days."

"I know you must be busy, with all these proposals to go through. Perhaps I could save you some time?" When Bailey didn't answer, Allemande sat in the chair next to her, pushing the plate of food out of Bailey's reach. "You see, most of these aren't even worth the paper they are printed on." She pulled one out and frowned at it. "See here? They don't have the kind of capacity to handle the demands of the Outer Rim project."

"That will all be determined, I assure you."

"I had hoped to have an answer before I head back to my sector tomorrow. It would be so wonderful to return to my people with good news."

"I apologize, Overseer, this is a matter that requires close attention and some time to determine the outcome." Of all the things she didn't want to be doing on Gamma-3, handing Allemande more power was at the very top of the list. "As I've said several times now, my decision will be made when it's made."

Allemande narrowed her eyes. "General Fineglass, I have to ask - is there anything you've always wanted to accomplish, but never had the opportunity to? A woman of your lofty achievements, I'm sure you have at least a dozen."

"Er—"

"No one understands the frustration of bureaucracy more than I do, and I am merely offering my assistance in helping you realize those dreams. I could influence grant proposal hearings, or put you in contact with department heads, or—"

"Aren't you the one who got bamboozled by those pirates last year?"

"Excuse me?"

"That is you, isn't it. I just wonder if it's the best use of project funds to hand them over to someone so easily taken in by a dirty group of scallywags, no?"

Allemande's mouth opened and closed soundlessly for a moment. "How did you hear about that? It's classified, I—"

"I have access to a good deal of classified files, especially when they could potentially impact a decision of this magnitude."

"General, I—"

Bailey pulled the plate of food back towards herself and sliced a cold roasted potato in half. "Let me be crystal clear with you, Overseer. All of the things you mentioned, I can already achieve under my own steam. I outrank you, militarily, politically, and socially. Your clumsy attempts to influence this decision are embarrassing, even more so when you consider that you roped your own daughter into it as well."

"Of course, ma'am," Allemande said through gritted teeth, her eyes flashing dangerously. "My deepest apologies. I look forward to hearing your decision." The overseer hesitated, her gaze flickering over Bailey's face. "Until we meet again, then."

As she turned to walk away, Bailey stifled a sigh of relief. Mae's plan had better be good, or they'd never outrun Allemande. Every moment spent with her was another opportunity to be found out. Their risk levels increased every time she showed her face, and if Emeline was indeed working for her, then that would only double their odds that some piece of inconsistent information would make its way back to her. The sooner Allemande was on a transport off Gamma-3, the better.

Bailey shoved another frigid, half congealed potato into her mouth. It was better than the crap Marshall served on the ship, but only barely—though had she gotten to it while it was hot, it was probably markedly better. She'd never liked eating hot food cold or at room temperature. Roasted potatoes should be eaten piping hot, gods be damned.

"Ma'am?"

She bit her tongue to keep from lashing out at whoever was interrupting her again. How the hell did the real General Fineglass put up with this shit day in and day out? "Yes?"

"The rest of the guests are wondering when you will kick off the dancing portion of the gala."

"Dancing?" Panic began to crawl up her spine, sending shivers down her skin. She hated dancing. It was always far better to be the one playing the music than the one dancing. Having everyone stare at you, while you tried to move your body in graceful ways it could not fathom, was her idea of a nightmare.

"Yes, the string quartet is all ready for you."

"Who am I supposed to dance with?"

The woman blushed, looking down at the floor. "Many assumed you'd dance with the woman you were seen with earlier this evening. Begging your pardon, ma'am."

"She left the gala."

"Oh."

"Can I nominate another couple to begin the dance?"

"That would be highly irregular."

Bailey pulled at the fine hairs poking out of the tail of her braid. "Fine. Tell them I'll be ready shortly."

"Excellent, and I'll just take that plate for you," the woman said, whisking away the mostly full plate of food. Despite having resented it mere moments prior, Bailey was sad to see it go, her stomach still rumbling to be fed. Although, panicky bile was beginning to mingle with her hunger, and the unpleasant burning in her chest made her want to heave what little she'd eaten into the nearest bucket.

"Davey!" she hissed, scanning the crowd. "Gods be damned, where are you?" She left her seat, scrambling through empty corridors to no avail. "Fuck," she whispered to herself, leaning against the wall. She could never live like this, no matter what the salary was. Expectations, obligations, surveillance. It was all too much for her.

Her assistant was nowhere to be found. She'd have to ask a stranger to dance, and the truth of her inability to do these formal routines would be laid bare for all to see. People would get suspicious. They might look into her more closely and start to ask questions she wouldn't be able to answer. Ned would be apprehended along with her and probably wind up dead, all because she never bothered to learn how to do a silly dance.

Breaths came fast and shallow now, the horror of the situation settling at the base of her skull, radiating out into every cell. She wasn't built for espionage. All she'd wanted to do was deliver a shipment of overpriced, over-aged booze and go home with her pockets full of credits, plenty to hire some investigators to find her people. That dream felt very silly, and very far away in that moment.

"Looking for me?" Mae asked, closing the door quietly behind her.

Bailey gasped with delight and scooped her up, relieved. "Please, you have to help me."

"The dance?"

"Yeah, how did you know?"

"It's customary."

"Where are Davey and...?"

Mae squeezed her hand reassuringly. "Safe, don't worry."

"So, this dance—"

"I'll lead. It's not too hard, and halfway through other couples will start to join the floor. We just have to hold it together until then, okay?"

There was something about the way that Mae said *we* that instantly put Bailey at ease. She'd be doomed if Mae wasn't in her corner. "Yeah, I can handle that."

"Come on, Bai, let's go put on a show."

"Why are you doing this for me?"

"Because I like you, you damned pineapple." Mae took her by the hand, gently pulling her back toward the main hall. "And I have business of my own that needs attending to, and this just means I get to dance with someone that doesn't repulse me."

"Happy to hear I don't repulse you."

Mae chewed on her lip for a moment before replying. "No. Rather the

157

opposite, actually."

Before Bailey could say anything else, a blush cascaded over her face, the heat burning the tips of her ears. Mae eased open the frosted glass door, the carved brass embellishments of the handle glinting in the dim light of the hall, now given solely from tall lanterns that hung from the ceiling. If it wasn't so terrifying, Bailey might have been almost enchanted by the way the beams sparkled on the shining dance floor. The string quartet was getting ready to play, the warm notes from their strings reverberating across the room as they tuned.

Her fingers itched to snatch the violin from the musician and start playing a barn-burner of a dance. These stuck up busybodies would never know what had hit them. Mae took Bailey's hands and gently led her to the edge of the dance floor.

"Ready?" she asked.

Bailey nodded. "I'm sorry in advance if I step on your toes."

"Don't worry, these dancing shoes have iron toes."

"Really?"

"No, not really, I was just trying to make you feel a little less nervous." Mae stiffened her posture and the angle of her arms, raising her chin delicately to maintain eye contact with Bailey. "Right foot first."

The strings played the introduction. *Shit*, Bailey thought, *this is much faster than I thought it would be.* Her right foot forward, they stuttered into rhythm, despite being far too aware of her feet. She'd never thought so much about her feet in her entire life.

"Turn to the right, right foot first," Mae uttered, her frame and dazzling, performative smile utterly unshakable. How did she do that? "And turn."

They swirled around the dance floor, and with Mae in her arms, Bailey was only half as aware that everyone was staring.

"Get ready for another turn, to the left this time."

"How are you so good at this?"

"Finishing school. Turn."

"That is not a thing where I am from."

Mae smirked. "Focus, please."

"I don't know, I think maybe I'm a natural."

"I'm going to do a twirl, put your arm out for me."

Bailey did as she was told, and watched in awe as the shining blue silk swirled around Mae's ankles, swishing gently against the floor. She really was very pretty, in addition to being whip smart. Something stirred in her chest when Mae took her hand again, but Bailey shoved it down. *No,* she thought, *not again. And definitely not now.*

"Right turn in three steps. We're almost there, General." Mae squeezed her hand. "And turn."

"Didn't you say people would start to enter?"

"We might be creating an absolute scandal at this very moment, General. Enjoy it, you can't buy this kind of infamy."

"Do we want to be infamous?"

"Turn. Trust me, this will work."

"The overseer is staring daggers at us like she wants to strike us dead."

Mae squeezed her hand again, indicating another turn. "She probably does. No doubt her dance card is perpetually empty."

"She tried to bribe me earlier." The strings swelled even louder, and Bailey was grateful for the opportunity to talk to Mae. "Said she could sign off on projects."

"Be careful of her, she's... dangerous."

"I know."

"Final twirl to close us out, ready?"

"Ready." Bailey held out her arm, and Mae took her hand and pulled her in close for the final steps as the music swayed into the final cadence. "Expertly done, Ms. Machenet."

"Damn well better be, with what my parents spent on that education. Now hush, they can hear. Release me and then bow."

"A pleasure dancing with you, my lady," Bailey said, sweeping into a deep bow. Mae replied with a delicate curtsy, and they backed off the dance floor just as the first notes from the next dance began to sound. A few couples stepped hesitantly onto the waxed wood and began to dance.

"General Fineglass, can I please get a photo of you two for the paper?"

"What? No—"

The flashbulb went off, filling her vision with exploding stars, and she fumbled around for something to hold on to until they cleared.

"Thank you, ma'am!" he said, scuttling away, melting back into the throng of people.

"That will be the front page tomorrow," Mae said, leading her to the dessert table at the far end of the room. "It's good," she whispered, "all part of the plan."

"If you scheme half as well as you dance, then we're all set. I'm not thrilled about having my mug splashed across the Capital newspaper, though."

"I think you mean, the general's mug," Mae whispered behind her hand. "And I wouldn't worry about that. You look great."

"The suit helps."

"Of course it does. I made it. Here, have some cake, you must be starving." She handed Bailey a small plate, almost entirely eclipsed by the enormous slice of cake atop it. "It's pretty good, so long as it's fresh. It will be drier than dirt tomorrow."

"Cake! Hell yes," Bailey said, cutting off a chunk with her fork.

"May I have this dance, General?" Emeline asked, taking the plate away and setting it on the table.

"There are plenty of other people to dance with." Bailey reached for the plate, but the girl pulled her away.

"I feel like perhaps our conversation wasn't entirely clear earlier."

"It was as clear as it needed to be. Now, if you'll excuse me—"

Emeline gripped her with a fierce, unpredictable strength. "You wouldn't want the cameras to catch you pushing away an innocent girl, would you, General? I suspect they'll be watching you closely, now."

"Is that a clumsy attempt at blackmail?"

"I'm merely asking for a dance, ma'am." The girl flashed a smile.

Mae gave Bailey a cautious wave, chewing the inside of her cheek. It was no secret how dangerous Allemande could be, and now that she had this girl under her wing, she had even more tools of manipulation close at hand.

"Fine," Bailey sighed, holding her an arm's length away. "One dance."

The music's pace slowed, but she didn't know whether she should be grateful or miserable. "What is it that you want, other than unilateral confirmation that your mother's proposal will be chosen?"

"General!" Emeline gasped. "I would never suggest such a thing. I merely offered clarification."

"Do you need help?" Bailey asked it plainly, hoping it would spark some kind of reaction.

"Help with what?"

"With anything."

"What do you mean by anything?"

"I'm just curious why you're so desperate to continually start a conversation, only to pretend that you aren't actually asking what you're angling for."

Emeline looked away, flustered. "I'm sure you understand my situation."

"No, why don't you fill me in?" Bailey waited, barely even moving.

"Skelm is a proud city, and an efficient one. A contract like the one on offer could stabilize the region for decades. I grew up there, General."

"I see."

"So for me, it's not about aggrandizing the overseer's legacy, or political sport. It's about securing safety and a financial net for a place that holds a place deep in my heart."

Bailey felt herself soften. "I can understand that. We all miss home, sometimes."

"I bet you're glad to be home, if only for a little while."

"What? Oh. Yes. Home."

"What's it like near the Outer Rim?"

"Cold, mostly. Dark. The work is hard, and brutal, with no room for mistakes."

Emeline twirled by herself, never releasing her grip on Bailey's hand. "It sounds terribly exciting."

"It is, if you enjoy that sort of thing." The Outer Rim sounded like a hellscape, really. "Do you want to be an explorer?"

"No."

"No?"

"I would rather spend my time advocating for settlements, in truth. Besides, I doubt there are many galas there."

"You're right about that." Bailey willed the musicians to wind down the song, so she could be released from this prison of propriety. "Do you like galas?"

"Of course, who doesn't?"

Me, Bailey thought. Being an esteemed and honored guest was, frankly, garbage. "Not many galas in Skelm, I should think."

"No. Not now, anyway - but if they had a decade-long contract—"

"I told you, I can't give you any assurances."

Emeline huffed and jerked her hand away. "You know, General, I was led to believe that you would have a sympathetic ear."

Interesting. So the real general might be known for taking bribes. Bailey put her hands down at her sides, resisting the urge to make eye contact with Mae across the room. "Who said I wasn't sympathetic?"

"Oh."

"I realize that you are young, Miss Allemande, but there is a certain level of... decorum that I must present. You understand."

"Yes, yes, of course, I'm sorry ma'am, I—so does this mean that you'll be giving the contract to Skelm?"

"It means that I have heard you, and an appropriate decision will be announced in the coming days."

Emeline held her hands out again to dance. "I do apologize for my outburst, General. I assure you that it is quite out of character."

"We all do outlandish things to accomplish goals close to our hearts."

"You're stepping on my toes, General."

"Sorry."

"I would have thought a woman of your rank would be a fantastic dancer, given all the mandatory military balls you've attended over the years."

"There isn't much dancing at the Outer Rim."

"Still..." Emeline trailed off, and suspicion clouded her face. It was time to cut this short.

"I'm very sorry, Miss Allemande. Suddenly I am very tired. I think I need to sit down."

"Thank you for the dance, ma'am."

As the girl backed away, something like dread dropped like a rock into Bailey's stomach. There was no way she could leave Gamma-3 without taking her back to her family. If Emeline was her little sister, she'd never forgive someone if they had the opportunity to rescue her, and chose not to. She'd spend the rest of her life haunting them, and continue in the hereafter. Georgie Payne already hated her, and made that clear once Henry told her that Bailey confessed her love while she was stuck in Skelm. Stuck there protecting her little sister, who was now twirling around the dance floor with a young officer, probably not even out of school yet.

"What's wrong?" Mae asked, handing the plate of cake back to her.

"Nothing. Or... something, but it probably makes me the biggest fool that's ever lived."

"What happened with the Allemande girl?"

"I think we have to save her."

Chapter 18

Mae was waiting on the front steps for the morning newspaper, and snatched it eagerly the moment it landed. Her own face was staring back at her from the front page, just as she'd hoped. A slow, sly smile spread across her face. Maybe she wasn't too bad at this, after all.

"Where's the paper?" her father asked, standing behind her in the hall. "I heard the delivery kid's steambike bell."

She hadn't, however, quite figured out how to play this to her parents. "I have it here. You want the political section?" She began to leaf through the pages, separating out the sections as she kicked the door closed behind her. "I assume Mother will want to read the economic—"

"Maevestra, you know I always read the paper from front to back with my breakfast."

"That was before you dragged me back here to do your dirty work. You'll have to learn to share."

"Give me the paper."

"No!" she said with a laugh, holding it to her chest. "You can have it when I am finished."

"Why does everything have to be such a battle with you? Every day, a new thing to argue about. It's as though you were raised by beasts, or some impostor has moved into my home, eating my food, while my real daughter dines on delicacies somewhere."

"I wouldn't be standing here arguing with you about the damn newspaper if you hadn't dropped a pile of blackmail in my lap."

"Keep your voice down, please."

"What, are you worried someone might hear?" she shouted.

Her father narrowed his eyes and lunged forward to snatch the paper. "It's as though you don't have a single ounce of self-preservation."

"I do, actually, that's why I left." She thrust the pages at him, sending them all flying, but making sure to keep hold of the damning evidence on the front page. If they saw her with who they thought was General Fineglass, they'd press her to use that to their advantage. And, well, Bailey wasn't the general, and had no access to the kind of information they wanted. No, she had to do this her way.

She stalked into the kitchen and carved herself a messy, uneven chunk of day-old bread. Slathering it with butter and raspberry jam, she made no effort to not let every dish and utensil clatter noisily.

"Why must you agitate him like that?" her mother asked, her face set into a disapproving frown. "I know you're not happy to be back here, but he only called on you out of desperation. He is a proud man, Maevestra, you should allow him some grace."

Mae snorted. "Why? It's not my fault he got into bed with the wrong people and lost everything. Neither is it yours, I might add, Mother."

"Your father and I are a team, til death do us part. I know that you don't understand that, but—"

"Don't patronize me."

"It's true! You're not married, you don't have anyone, it's no surprise you can't fathom that kind of lifelong bond."

"You don't know anything about me."

Her mother wiped crumbs from the counter top with a smug smile. "What, are you hiding a spouse inside your suitcase? You might want to let her out, I hear that's no good for your posture."

"If I was married, I sure in all the gods' names wouldn't tell *you*."

"You're a demon of a child."

Mae slammed the plate against the table. "I'm here to save you! I'm doing *you* a favor! Yet it's as though I've come crawling home after years away, desperate for assistance despite the mountain of bullshit you make me listen to. Here's a clue - I was fine before I came back here. I don't need this, or you, and I'm only here because if I leave, Father will allow an entire city of people to be ruined." She sighed angrily. "Probably killed."

"Where is the front page?" her father asked from the doorway.

"How the hell should I know?"

"Because you were the one to snatch it from the steps, and then throw it into the air."

"I don't know where your page is."

"Fine, then give me a few credits, and I'll go buy one."

A scream welled up in Mae's throat. "Why do you care so much about the front page, anyway? You always said it was always manufactured outrage, or a public relations story, or—"

"Yes, and that is precisely why I want to see it. Our family may be down and out—"

"Don't lump me into that."

"—But I might be able to tell from the style who it is who's got the puppet strings these days." He sighed, rubbing his temples. "Please, Mae, does everything have to be such a fight? I know you don't want to be here. I wouldn't have summoned you unless it was important. Besides, it's high time you took your place in the family business."

"If you weren't holding a threat over my head, I'd have been on the first transport back home," she said, cutting another slice of stale bread. "You've discovered something I care about - the safety of that city. And you'll use it to manipulate me, every time, because you know it will work and you'll get your way."

"You never used to be like this."

"I was naïve."

"I would argue that you're more so now than before. You see everything as black and white, when the reality is so many shades of—"

"Don't you dare lecture me," Mae spat. "You sit up there in your office, doing your best to control the narrative, to cover for one person to send another to prison, all to enrich your accounts, to buy stability with blood money. Yes, I left. I did so when I was ashamed to look at myself in the mirror."

"You had such a bright career ahead of you. You could have been draping yourself in the finest silks, instead of tearing down your bed curtains and sewing appliques to tired old frocks," her mother said in an eerily placid tone. That was never good. "But you made your choices, and so did we, and now here we all are, having to make the best of it."

The chime of the front doorbell rang, clattering in Mae's ears. "You didn't say you were expecting guests."

"We aren't."

Wordlessly, her father returned to the front door, his footsteps silent against the hand-woven rugs. While he was gone, Mae ate her breakfast contemptuously, swallowing every bite with a murderous rage. How dare they force her into helping them, only to belittle her at every turn? It wasn't enough to destroy her career, her shop, her future, they had to be sure to break down her spirit day by day, too. There was a day, shortly after she'd left, when she wondered if she would ever regret severing those ties. That was the *real* wide-eyed nonsense, not her refusal to engage in bureaucratic horseshit.

Her mother glared at Mae over the top of her teacup, no doubt plotting something else hideous to say. "What?" Mae demanded, eager for a fight, some way to release the pent-up rage that had accumulated since she arrived.

"Nothing." Her mother sipped at her tea delicately. "I'm just wondering what you're hiding."

"Always so suspicious, Mother."

"Never without cause."

"If you would spend as much energy on digging up information about the rich jerks you lunch with as you do watching me for any sign of impropriety, you two wouldn't be in this mess."

"I would, if I hadn't been uninvited the moment we lost our standing."

Mae examined the crumbs on her empty plate. "Oh."

The Capital had always been a snake pit, and apparently now more than ever. People always looking for another back to stab, someone else to drown so they could climb another rung of the socialite ladder. It was a never-ending, exhausting existence, in Mae's opinion. Even well-established people like her parents could easily fall prey to the broken system.

Her father hovered in the doorway, a crisply addressed note in his hand. "Maevestra, I don't know what you did, but I've been invited to dinner with an overseer. It's incredible access. How did you achieve this?"

"If it's Amaranth Allemande, you're not going."

Her father threw his head back and laughed. "Don't be ridiculous."

"She's dangerous."

"So are we."

"We are children's toys compared to that monster. Trust me when I say, we don't want this alliance."

"Beggars can't be choosers, my dear."

Mae sliced another piece of bread, this one ragged and uneven from her agitated sawing. "She will turn on you the moment it's convenient for her."

"That's true of anyone."

"Don't eat *all* the bread, Maevestra," her mother said with disdain.

"I'll buy you another loaf," Mae replied through gritted teeth. She had to get out of the house before she said or did something she'd regret. "Father, I am asking you, please, do not agree to this meeting."

"I already did, it's tonight at eight." He set a telegram down on the counter, sliding it across. "You're invited, too."

"I'm not going."

"Surely if you think she's so dangerous, it makes sense to have a show of force. A united familial team, father and daughter, and not just a lonely old man who's passed his expiration date."

Her mother bristled, setting down her teacup on the saucer with an angry rattle. "Am *I* not invited?"

"You aren't mentioned, Gladys, but I'm sure you wouldn't be turned away at the door if you wish to come along."

"I'm just as much a part of this as Maevestra, Gerard. You forget that I'm the one who forged the connections with the Exchequer."

"Tell that to Overseer Allemande, then, not me."

"This is so... so... uncouth."

At least they were distracted from the front page for a few moments, not that it mattered. That invitation was a direct result of it, and would no doubt be the topic of conversation at that dinner. Gods, how she hated the Capital. Her plan was working, but at what cost? Still, at least the paper had no mention of a prisoner going missing, and no connection to General Fineglass, real or impersonated. The time they'd bought with the scandal would hopefully be enough to get Bailey and Ned back home.

"We're going, Maevestra, and that's final."

They were going to find out sooner or later. "You may change your mind once you know why." She tossed the crumpled ball of newspaper at him.

"I knew you had it," he said, rolling his eyes. He unfurled the front page, a frown forming, and then deepening. "This is shameful."

Her mother snatched it from him and gasped. "A married, monogamous woman, Maevestra? In public? What are you thinking?"

"I was thinking that you were demanding access, and that seemed like a good way to get it. The general may be suggestible."

"Carrying on affairs in rooms with cameras is foolish. And at a gala? Have you lost what little sense you had?"

It was almost humorous that he couldn't see that she was employing one of his favorite tricks, all because he thought she was too foolish to manage it. "Why did you bother bringing me here, if I'm so useless, then?"

"Please, stop. I'm tired of the constant arguing," Mae's mother said, covering her face with her hands. "Mae, this is a terrible setback. We may never recover from this, now. You've created even more work for yourself, young lady."

The doorbell sounded again, and Mae cocked an eyebrow. "A setback, eh? Sounds like another telegram delivery to me."

Her father returned again, this time handing her an ivory envelope. "It's for you. Sent priority."

Sliding her finger underneath the seam, she opened it. The letter was from Mr. Fineglass, sending his sympathies. He separated from the real General Fineglass over a year earlier, and was wishing her luck in maintaining a relationship with "a callous and monstrous woman." Interesting, and wholly unexpected.

"Who's it from, dear?" her mother asked expectantly. "Is it another invitation?"

"It's from the general's husband. He's threatening to press ethics charges if I don't stop seeing her."

"You must have expected that, really, I—"

Mae smirked. "I'm going to keep seeing her."

"Don't you think we have enough problems to deal with, without this little schoolgirl crush causing headlines?" her father hissed, reaching for the envelope.

She snatched back the envelope and folded it into her pocket. "If you want access, then this is how we do it. I don't care about the machinations of some man, off-world, consumed by petty jealousy and vindictiveness. I care about getting the job done."

"You're going to drag this entire family into scandal!"

"Would you rather be rich and scandalous, or flat broke and pious?" When neither of them answered, she smiled broadly. "That's what I thought. Mother, press your favorite dress. We're going to dinner tonight, and it's important we make a good impression, isn't it, Father?"

"I—"

"I'm going out. I'll make my own way there, and I'll send a steamcar for you at half past seven." She pushed past her parents, leaving her crumbs on the counter. With her coat folded over her arm, she stepped out into the street, savoring the warm sun on her face. She needed to see Bailey.

Chapter 19

"So what's on the agenda today, *General* Fineglass?"

"You'd better do better than that at pretending, Davey, or we'll both be staring at the inside of a cell," Bailey hissed.

"I don't think you're fully appreciating just how much you've screwed me over. Weeks of planning, down the drain!"

Bailey poked at her breakfast of toast and half an orange. "Can we please not get into this again? Where did you go last night, anyway?"

"I'll tell you later." He drained his mug and set it on the tray. "You have that meeting later."

"What meeting?"

"With the ethics adviser. Did you forget that your face is splashed across the front page today?"

"Of course I didn't forget, how could I? Seems like every person I pass in the hall is whispering behind their hands."

Davey snorted. "Trust me, they are."

"I feel like we're in too deep."

"*We*? No. *You're* in too deep. You're lucky you're still sitting here eating cold toast, and not on your way to a prison hearing." He sighed and sat back. "Listen, I said I'd help, but you need to help me accomplish what I came for, too."

"I already gave you the detailed list of all the bribes and proposals."

"Please, I could have gotten that by just being your assistant. I need real information. I need you to find out who's heading the insurgency taskforce, who's hunting down members of The—of my organization. I also need you to get me access to weapons development information."

"Even if I was... you know, I still wouldn't be able to get that for you. She—I don't have access to those divisions."

"Then get access. You're a general, you can strongarm someone into doing your bidding."

"Not without getting caught."

Davey shrugged. "Then don't get caught. I don't care how you get it, but if you want me to stay quiet, then you need to give a little back."

"I didn't ask to get roped into this! I was only here to—well, you know—and I'm only here because you made a mistake!"

"It's not my fault the file I was given had inaccurate information. Hell, if that dock attendant hadn't called up to the hotel the second you arrived, I'd still be waiting around for the real general to show up. Which should be any day now, if you haven't forgotten."

"I know. I know!" Bailey pulled at her braid. "I can't leave until we get Emeline and Ned safe, too."

"You sure that girl even wants saving? She seemed very keen to do her mother's bidding at the gala last night."

"I'm sure that even if she doesn't want to be saved, she should be."

"You're getting yourself into one hell of a mess."

Bailey sighed. "Probably."

"Have you always had such an irritating savior complex?"

Thinking of all the people she'd watched be loaded onto a transport, she blinked back the encroaching tears. "No."

"No wonder you're so bad at it."

"Can you just lay off? I'm doing my damned best, no matter how shit that is."

Davey smirked. "Touchy."

"I have to get to that delivery before this ethics committee meeting."

"I thought you already delivered."

"I did, but I have to go back to finalize things."

"How do you expect me to keep covering for your absences, *General*?"

"My face is all over the newspaper today, just tell anyone who asks that

I'm talking to my husband, or something."

"A crisis counselor!"

"Whatever, I don't care. We need to keep an eye on the docks, in case she shows up early, given the news. I'm almost surprised I wasn't dragged out of bed and thrown into prison in the middle of the night."

"This plan of your girlfriend's is definitely risky."

"She's... not my girlfriend."

"Perhaps not, but you sure made it look convincing on that dance floor last night."

Bailey pushed away the remains of her breakfast, hungry for something more substantial than bread and fruit. She'd gotten up too late to enjoy the full breakfast spread the hotel usually had on. "Hmm. I have to go. Cover for me."

"You'd better bring me back some good intel."

"Yeah." She slid her chair away from the table, the iron legs scraping against the polished marble floor. "Maybe I'll get you the information to bring this whole thing down, eh?"

"That would be great, actually." He checked his pocket watch and made a note on the pad of paper he pulled from inside his jacket. "Hey, do you happen to know where Ned usually stays? Like, where he lives?"

"Yes."

"Can you tell me?"

"Will it count as part of the intel you're so hungry for?"

Davey rolled his eyes. "Just go. Don't be late for that meeting or they'll have patrols all over the city hunting you down."

"I won't be late." She left the hotel, missing the softness of the dress uniform. Bedroom curtains or not, it was more comfortable than this one, especially with the patch job between the thighs that continued to rub. The soreness of the inflamed skin was a constant reminder it had only been a few days since she got here, despite feeling like it had been weeks. Climbing into the car, she slammed the door shut. "Morning, Amy."

"Good morning ma'am, and might I say, you are looking fresh as a daisy today."

"You're a terrible liar."

"I try. Where to?"

"I have a... meeting in the city center. You can drop me anywhere."

The driver turned around in her seat, the blond ringlets peeking out from beneath her cap. "Are you sure? This is a diplomatic vehicle, we don't have to abide by the road law. I can park anywhere."

"I'm sure. A little walking might do me good."

"Perhaps it's too forward of me to say, but I think that the ethics laws here are far too strict."

"It is too forward."

"Apologies, General. And will you need transport back to the hotel?"

"Yes. I shouldn't be long in the city, so I'll just meet you back where you drop me an hour or so after."

Amy tipped her cap and shifted the steamcar into gear. "Gives me a moment or two to grab some lunch from my husband at our shop."

"Could... could you bring me a sandwich?"

"They not feeding you properly in there? I'm surprised, usually the spreads are legendary."

"It's been surprisingly challenging to eat a full meal since I arrived. And a sandwich sounds amazing, if it's not too much trouble."

"Of course, ma'am, it's no trouble at all."

"I'll pay for it."

"There's no need for that."

The deep black of the tunnel loomed ahead. "Don't be ridiculous," Bailey said, leaning her head against the tinted window. "Just tell me what I owe you when we get back this afternoon."

* * *

"Are you ready to sign off on this yet?"

The speakeasy owner's gold earrings dripped down her neck, glinting in the dim light of the saloon. "I hear you got yourself into one hell of a pickle."

"You could say that."

"It's no wonder you're so desperate to get out of here. What other job are you pulling? I was under the impression that we'd be your only clients on this trip, and seeing the front page today, it's suddenly very clear why you were so late in delivering our crates."

"I'm not pulling anything. And you have them now, and have had ample time to check them all, so I'd rather you just transferred the rest of the credits to Marshall so I can get on with it."

"Yeah, we checked them. Everything seems on the up and up."

"Okay, so what's the hold up?"

The owner rolled up the sleeves of her crisp white shirt, which bulged over her ample breasts. "Marshall never said we'd be expected to be a halfway house for waifs and strays."

"What the hell are you talking about?"

"That friend of yours, the one in the newspaper, dropping off some hulking huge man in the middle of the night."

"Ned's here?" She knew that Mae had stashed him somewhere safe, but had no idea it was here—though it made sense. Nowhere was safer than a speakeasy's cellar these days. "Ned!" she shouted. "Hey, it's me!"

He burst through the swinging doors, a stack of crates in one hand, a cane in the other, fashioned from a curtain rod. "Bailey, as I live and breathe!"

"You put him to *work*?"

The owner smirked. "No one stays at The Dark Owl tavern for free, darling."

"It's alright, I'd rather have something to do other than sit around and worry. And it's a hell of a lot better than sitting around and waiting to be sent to some toxic waste work camp. I'd be dead without you, Stocky," Ned said.

"Told you not to call me that, old man," she replied, a grin spreading across her face. Knowing Ned was safe and sound was a hell of a balm after the last twenty-four hours, and made all the chaos worth it.

He set the crates down and leaned against his cane. "Fuckers took my good cane. At least Marina here was good enough to make me one."

"You're just lucky some of that crap down there was sturdy enough," Marina replied, tugging at one of her gold earrings. "And you're a hell of a cook in the kitchen. You stick around here much longer, and I'm liable to offer you a job as one of our chefs."

"Thank you for taking him in," Bailey said, extending her hand. "Really."

"I'm not going to let him get picked up by the swine who run this town. Plus, if I pushed him out into the street, I doubt Marshall would send you back here with more shipments."

"Does that mean you're going to sign off on those crates?"

Marina hopped down off the bar. "Already did. Credits transferred this morning. Pleasure doing business." She shook Bailey's hand firmly, the bangles on her wrist rattling pleasantly. "How long will my guest be staying?"

"Hopefully not long. We've got a shuttle booked in a couple of days, then we'll be out of your hair."

"You're brave souls, to stick around here after all that ruckus. I'd be halfway to... well, you know, by now."

"Might be nice to see you there sometime," Ned added.

"Maybe," Marina said with a shrug. "Hard to get away from this place for too long. It's a good thing I love it so much - but I wouldn't mind stealing some of those cocktails I hear about so much from the travelers in and out of there."

Bailey laughed. "I'm sure Larkin would be thrilled to hear that."

"Yeah, don't tell her," Ned grumbled, "or she'll be on the first transport out here, despite all those warrants for her arrest." He turned to Bailey and clapped a hand on her shoulder. "You're putting yourself in the line of fire for me, and I won't ever forget that."

"You'd better not, this is pretty intense. Much more so than my average delivery, yeah?"

"Boss is gonna want you back on the ship after this. You'll have a hard time telling her no."

"Ned..."

176

"I know, I know. I'm just saying." He released his grip on her shoulder and melted back into one of the iron stools at the bar. "The offer will always be open."

"Let's focus on getting out of here first, alright?" The clock on the wall chimed at the hour, a deep, resonating sound that was both reassuring and hurrying. "Gods, I have to get back, my driver—"

"Hey, Marina, I'm just dropping by to—Bailey! I didn't know you'd be here." Mae slammed the door shut behind her and threw her arms around Bailey's neck. "I'm so sorry about the papers, it's all part of the plan, I just—"

"I trust you."

"You do?"

Bailey hugged her tightly, the memory of the previous night's kiss still fresh in her mind. "Of course I do. I sure as hell don't know how things work around here, and given there's not a peep about Ned's jailbreak, I think it went pretty well."

"Those MPOs are going to be raked over the coals. Their bosses will likely think they were blind drunk when they say it was you who broke him out. Still, we should be careful, unless they start thinking there's two of you running around the Capital."

"Not yet, anyway." Bailey released her. "What did you need here?"

"Nothing, really. Just wanted to make sure Ned was settling in alright." He waved her away. "I'm fine, they're fine here."

"As long as he keeps cooking us breakfast, we'll let him stay," Marina added with a laugh that was deeply booming and contagious. "Your secrets are safe with us. Just don't be bringing any more refugees here without letting us know first, yeah? The cellar isn't that big."

"I have to go," Bailey said again, despite a tingling desire to stay near Mae. She felt safer around someone who knew the ropes of Gamma-3. "I have an ethics meeting, or something."

"Gods, already?" Mae asked. "They sure as hell didn't waste any time. Listen, the husband sent me a wire, he's not going to step in. Seems they separated over a year ago. Some friend of his sent a message about the papers."

"Small mercies, I guess."

"Play it cool at the meeting. Don't accept blame for anything. No comment is going to be your best friend in there. Don't give them anything to go on. Any inquiry this early on is purely a formality to satisfy the press. They shouldn't press too hard, none of them want to be on the receiving end if their indiscretions wind up in the gossip columns."

"Anything else?"

"Yeah, don't get caught."

"Excellent advice."

Mae smirked. "The best, in fact. Now get going before they send out the dogs looking for you."

"There are dogs?"

"It's just an expression."

Bailey frowned. "Oh. Alright... keep in touch, I guess. You know where to find me. What's the plan now?"

"I have a dinner with the Allemandes tonight."

"No!" Ned shouted. "That's way too risky, Mae."

"Don't worry, I'll have my parents with me. She can't lock us all up at once."

"You'd be surprised."

"I've got things under control for now. Now Bailey, go! Get moving!"

Bailey hugged Mae around the waist, lifting her gently off the ground with the force of the embrace. "I can't thank you enough, Mae. We never would have gotten this far without you."

"Anything for my favorite customer." Mae squeezed her arms around Bailey's shoulders. "Ned's right, you need to get going!"

Chapter 20

Mae stepped into the hall of her old conservatory, and was almost surprised that it still smelled the same. The faint scent of mothballs, heavily suppressed by the thick cinnamon potpourri that Mr. Hawkins had always preferred. It was strange to be back, considering she never thought she'd see the inside of the building ever again. She pulled the roped tassel that sounded a shrill bell and waited, her hands deep in her pockets.

"Ms. Machenet!" Mr. Hawkins shouted, hurrying down the stairs as fast as an old man could go. "I wasn't expecting you until next week."

"I need a favor, I'm afraid."

"Anything."

"I have a dinner this evening, and I didn't bring anything appropriate. Perhaps one of your students has made something suitable?"

He wrinkled his nose. "Not this bunch. I'd never dream of dressing you in one of their monstrosities. No, I should ask a favor from you in return - make something, start to finish, and let them observe."

"That's too kind of you. I don't have long, unfortunately—"

"When was a time constraint ever a problem for you?"

"I just don't want to get in the way."

"I'm telling you, dear, you won't! Come, now, let me show you what we have in the storeroom. Do you have your heart set on anything?"

"Red satin, if you have it."

He turned, his eyebrows arched in surprise. "Red was never your signature color."

"No, but I'm trying to make a statement."

"I suppose I shouldn't be surprised, after last night. That was quite a show you were putting on for the press."

"Mm."

"Care to tell me what you're up to?"

She stopped at the doorway to the storeroom, words bubbling up inside her. It was wrong that she should know his husband was still alive, with him still mourning the loss. Yet, telling him could endanger not just Davey, but all of The Scattered. She bit her tongue, swallowing it back down. "I have a dinner with Overseer Allemande."

"Oh?"

"I have a feeling she's going to try to leverage the scandal against me. If I wear it proudly, she'll be on the back foot."

"You always were one of my smartest, cleverest pupils. Here, take your pick of anything in here. I'll round the students up, and you can use my machine in the classroom next door."

"I'll be right in."

The racks of fabric had the same effect on her as they always had. Bolts of kinetic energy, waiting to be unleashed into their sartorial destiny. Taffetas, silks, linens, in every color, in bold patterns and gentle textures. Left to her own devices, she could easily spend weeks in there, sewing a new wardrobe. There was power in dress, there always had been. Her hands landed on a crimson silk, and then a matching taffeta, and then scarlet binding. The image was coming together in her mind, an ostentatious, brazen dress with asymmetrical straps and a full skirt. Crinoline fell into her arms like fire from the gods so many eons ago.

The classroom was packed full with bored-looking students, many of them children of generals or high-ranking officials. None of them would ever know hardship. She set the bolts of fabric on the table, and wordlessly began. She wouldn't use a pattern, not for this. She'd sew by instinct and wow them all. It was a challenge, one she hadn't undertaken in years, but the shears in her hands felt like home.

"Class, I have a special treat for you today. Ms. Machenet is here to show you what real design looks like. See what she's chosen here, a selection of textiles that work well together to achieve certain shapes. She will sew from start to finish in just a few hours."

"I don't believe that," one of the students said, a young woman with deep red hair sitting at the back of the room. "No one can sew that fast."

"Then prepare to be amazed," Mr. Hawkins said. "She is by far the most skilled designer and seamstress I have ever had the privilege to teach or observe. You all might learn something, if you're not careful."

Mae spread out the first fabric, eyeballing the measurements. She would never do that if she was sewing for a client - too much room for error - but she knew her own measurements, and besides, she'd made something like this before, years ago, for a fancy dinner at the Pig. Tansy had pulled out all the stops for that one. "Who can tell me the proper procedure for seam allowances?" she asked, keeping her eyes on the fabric as she cut.

When there was no answer, she tutted quietly. "Really? No one?" She raised her eyebrows. "I know Mr. Hawkins taught you that already." She sliced through fabric, setting each piece aside once it had been cut from the bolt. She sat at the machine, placed her foot on the pedal, and began to assemble the most ostentatious dress she'd ever made for herself. It would be rivaled only by something she'd made for a customer soon after she'd opened her shop in Bradach, a bright orange suit with purple trim. While not to her personal taste, she had impressed herself with the result.

It restored a sense of normality to be sitting at a good machine. The one in her parents' attic was adequate, but only barely. It needed to be serviced, and it was always a bastard with thicker textiles. She'd nearly thrown it out the window when sewing the dress uniform for Bailey.

The machine's soft rhythm calmed her, and it was as though she wasn't sitting in front of dozing students and her former teacher, but alone in the back of her shop. With every snip of thread, she came closer to completing the dress. She was pressed for time, so she'd avoid the long line of buttons up the back that she might typically choose, and opted instead to use the straps to secure the bodice.

None of the students spoke above a whisper, but Mae paid them no mind anyway, instead preparing the crinoline for the underskirt. The sweet crunch of the fabric would swish delicately and fill out the silks nicely. She didn't know precisely what time it was, but the golden glow of the setting sun outside the windows told her she didn't have long left to complete her masterpiece.

She began to assemble the larger pieces, and when complete, she draped and buttoned it around the dress form that most matched her body shape from the dozens stacked in the corner. "I'm finished," she announced, folding her hands in front of her.

"Marvelous!" Mr. Hawkins shouted proudly, examining her work. "Such perfection in every stitch, the evenness and precision is enviable even for me." He turned back to the students, some of whom still looked like they'd rather be anywhere else, but a few leaning forward in their seats now. "Does anyone have questions for our guest?"

The student in the back raised her hand. "Is it true you designed the Coalition uniforms?"

She has expected the question, yet, it still knocked the wind from her lungs. She steadied herself on the desk and cleared her throat. "Yes."

"They're so much nicer than the old ones. My father has photos from years ago, that lumpy grey cut was pretty gross."

Mae could only bring herself to nod affirmatively, such was the guilt that clenched in her gut. Some would say that uniforms were just clothing, unimportant, but she knew the truth. Allowing MPOs, and by extension, the Coalition, to look approachable, chic, and fashionable, had only made it more attractive. Easier to vote for. Relatable. The fabric people chose to wear was an expression of themselves, of their beliefs, sometimes, and her efforts had allowed the Coalition to recruit probably thousands of new soldiers with the crisp, tailored lines.

"Thank you for the opportunity," Mae said politely to Mr. Hawkins, sweeping the fabric scraps into her hands. "It's been a delight."

"The pleasure is all mine, I assure you," he replied, taking the scraps from her. "Any time you wish to come back, the door is open for you. I'm sure these students learned... something. Hopefully." He gave her a sad smile, and the guilt grew roots into her bones. This school was all he had left now.

What would he do if he knew that his husband was alive and well?

Mae chewed the inside of her cheek. "Yes, hopefully." She began to take the dress from the dress form, handling the luxurious fabric with care. One snag and she'd be cursing herself for days. "I'm afraid I do have to go, sir. I have a dinner to get to."

"Yes, of course, silly me! I do hope that you will return?"

She nodded. "When I am able, yes. There's a certain sense of calm, being back here."

"I know precisely what you mean, my dear. The dress really is beautiful."

"It will do. If I'd had more time, I would have—"

"Put in the buttons, yes, I thought you might. It is your signature with evening wear, after all."

"Maybe next time."

He reached out and squeezed her hand. "Yes, perhaps next time. You can change in the dressing room, it's in the same place it always has been. Don't be a stranger, Mae."

* * *

Mae stepped out of the steamcar in front of the Allemandes' house fashionably late, with an emphasis on the fashion. Her newly sewn red dress caught the last rays of the late spring light and almost glowed. "Thank you," she told the driver, and held her arm to the grey rectangular console on the mirror to pay for her fare, plus a twenty percent tip for their discretion.

"Hey listen," the driver said through the open window. "If you need more drives, you can reach me directly via telegram at this number. You can book rides early. Discretion guaranteed."

"I'll remember that," she replied, taking the card. Silence was something that you could rarely pay for in the Capital, not when information was more than worth its weight in credits. The driver might be full of it, but it might be a better option than rolling the dice with a randomly assigned steamcar.

As the car sped off, she approached the intimidatingly painted yellow and purple door, embossed with the Coalition insignia. It was a bit much, really, tantamount to screaming through a megaphone how much the inhabitants supported the corrupt government. She shouldn't have been surprised, given who those occupants were.

"Ms. Machenet, you've finally arrived," Emeline said, opening the door before she could knock.

"Were you watching for me through the window?"

"It can't be helped when you're delaying everyone's supper."

"My apologies, the lateness couldn't be helped. I was at a prior engagement."

The girl raised an eyebrow. "Interesting dress."

"Thank you." Mae stepped over the threshold into a blandly decorated room, all grey and white with yellow and purple accents to match the door and the fascism it stood for. Without waiting for an invitation, she swished her way into the dining room, the silk of her skirts sighing prettily against the plush rug underfoot. "Good evening, everyone," she said pleasantly. "Thank you so much for asking us to supper. What an honor it is to dine with the famed Overseer Allemande and her very charming daughter."

When she sat in her chair, dropping the cloth napkin into her lap, Mae caught her mother's disapproving glare, her jaw wired tense with disdain.

"Maevestra," her mother said in a terrifyingly even tone, "wherever did you get that dress? I don't recognize it as one from your closet."

"No, you wouldn't. I just whipped it up this afternoon."

"What a compelling shade you've chosen."

"Thank you."

Emeline joined them at the table, her modest green dress a fetching color against her pale features. "You sewed that in one afternoon?"

The overseer cocked an eyebrow. "Oh, yes, Ms. Machenet is renowned for her skill in design and seamstressing. In fact, she created the military uniforms. What was that now, over ten years since?"

"Around that, yes." Mae knew she couldn't escape her shameful legacy here, but it was still a sharp reminder of her sins.

"Fascinating, then, that she seems to have abandoned her career in favor of wreaking havoc," Emeline said pointedly.

"Oh, I wouldn't call it that," Mae said, reaching for a hot bread roll.

"Not many of us would be caught dead on the front page, publicly engaged in what some would describe as rather an embarrassing indiscretion."

"I'm not embarrassed."

Overseer Allemande flicked her gaze across the strappy red gown and cocked an eyebrow. "Clearly."

"We are honored to be here," Mae's father interjected. "I've long wanted to meet the renowned Overseer Allemande, a woman with what some would call a meteoric rise through the ranks. Why, it wasn't so long ago that you were a highly respected inspector."

"And you, Mr. Machenet, architect of so many careers. It's said you had a hand in placing a third of the High Council positions."

"In a manner of speaking, yes."

"That's an impressive resume. Yet, your name has been absent from so many discussions of late. Why might that be?"

Mae's father bristled. "We can't always control how things unfold, despite our best efforts. Unfortunately."

"Personally, I think it's nearly a crime how you've been tossed aside, sir, after decades of loyal service to the Coalition, making sure the best people have access to the jobs where they can affect the most change in our noble and ever-expanding empire."

"You flatter me, ma'am."

Mae resisted the urge to roll her eyes. She'd need some boots to wade through all this horseshit. "Overseer, I can't be the only one wondering why you did invite us here today," she said sweetly. "We've had no business in the past, and as you said, I'm dealing with a scandal of my own at the moment."

"It was my idea," Emeline chimed in, taking a bowl of spiced rice from the quiet servant dressed head to toe in black. "It's foolish to waste opportunities to build bridges, wouldn't you agree?"

"Sure."

"Especially when we know that you are trying to hide the release of a prisoner."

Mae choked on the sip of water she was taking. "Excuse me?"

"A Francoise Frederickson from the Judicature. Oh, it didn't make the papers, but he's gone, all right."

Ned must have given them a fake name. Thank the gods for that, at least. "What makes you think I had anything to do with that?"

"No self-respecting member of a family with a former standing like yours would ever be so careless as to do what you did last night," Allemande said, her plate conspicuously empty.

"We will not stand for this kind of insinuation," Mae's father said firmly, and started to stand from his seat.

"Sit down, Gerard," Allemande continued coolly. "I am merely trying to unearth the truth of the matter."

"You have no jurisdiction here!"

"And do you see MPOs lined up at the door to take you away? No. We are here to discuss solutions in a civil and dignified manner."

He sat back down, but not before loading his plate with a second helping. "Alright then," he relented.

"I'm not trying to make wild accusations. We all know how inquiries make life... difficult. It's always been my personal and professional belief that jobs are better done without the inefficiency of oversight."

"And how many inquiries have you been the subject of?" Mae asked, harsher now that the evening's tone had shifted into a far more dangerous position.

Overseer Allemande folded her hands primly next to her clean, untouched plate. "I do believe you'll find that there is no public record of any examination of my ethics or behavior."

"There wouldn't be if you were exonerated."

"Precisely. And that's all you need to know about that."

Mae's father sipped water from his glass. "I'm no fool, ma'am, I can see what it is you're asking of us —but as I'm sure you're aware, we've lost our access in many sectors. I don't have the kind of influence I once did."

"Yes, I know all about how the Exchequer tossed you away like last week's refuse once you were no longer as useful to him. He is a disloyal man, and I have it on good authority that he's been pilfering from Coalition budgets to fill his personal coffers for years."

"No!" Mae's mother blurted out . "He would never!"

The overseer leaned forward in her chair, almost imperceptibly. "Why do you defend a man who was so keen to cut ties with you? With all due respect. Mrs. Machenet, I should think your family would be grappling for any kind of influence right now. New alliances for a new age."

"With the Outer Rim expansion project, we are set to enter an era of prosperity and pride in the Coalition," Emeline said, each word emphasized for maximum effect. She was an excellent public speaker for someone so young. "There is room for new legacies, for those who do not delay in their decisions. We will need families to band together and support the right proposals, the ones which will feed credits back into the Coalition for reinvestment, in the meantime earning a comfortable existence for themselves."

Mae stifled a performative yawn. "So what this is all about, is that you want me to put pressure on the general to approve your proposal?"

Allemande's face contorted as though she smelled something rancid. "That is rather a crass way of putting things. But yes."

"What makes you think I have that kind of influence?"

"A picture says a thousand words, Ms. Machenet, and yours on the front page says a thousand more. I'm not suggesting you have unilateral control, but a woman of your..." she trailed off, casting a displeased eye over Mae's crimson dress, "...talents, I'm sure knows how to seed an idea."

"And if I don't, you'll set up some kind of investigation into this random prisoner's escape, I assume." Mae shoveled a huge bite of rice into her mouth, a forkful her mother would have described as 'unladylike,' along with two chunks of roasted red peppers. "You are assuming a great deal about a jailbreak, Overseer," she said, her mouth full, garnering a cold glare from her mother.

"I don't *make* assumptions."

The cold, clinical statement sent a chill through Mae's bones, even if it was mostly bluff and bluster. It was unlikely that Allemande knew the whole truth, but based on her confidence, she was taking the eyewitness account from the MPOs more seriously than their commanding officers. She knew something was amiss. "Be that as it may, I cannot make guarantees. The general is her own woman, with her own mind, and not easily swayed." No way in any god's hell was she going to agree to hand over more power to one of the most sadistic shits she'd ever met. *Unless.* "Although, I can promise to do my level best, so long as we all lay our cards on the table."

"What kind of *cards* are you referring to?"

"I don't think we need to ask the overseer to—" her father interjected.

Mae put her hand up to quiet him. "I want to know why this project is drawing such insistence from you. After all, as your daughter said, with this expansion project, there will be many opportunities for communities to grow and climb the ladder. Why this contract? Why now?"

"Skelm is poised on the precipice of greatness," Emeline explained. "With an influx of funding into their infrastructure to shore up existing factories, and retrofitting equipment to improve efficiency, it would reduce emissions there by a significant amount."

"So it's a humanitarian effort."

"In part," the overseer continued. "Skelm could be the jewel of Sector Fifteen, if only the correct proposals were chosen. It could be the finest settlement for industry, given a boost of investment."

Mae's father pushed his plate away, now empty. His brows were knitted together in thought, no doubt dreaming up every possible way this partnership would personally benefit him. His ambition had always been his best and worst quality. "You were governor of Skelm, were you not, Overseer?"

"I was, yes. And while I was living there, I saw all the potential of that city. An eager workforce, existing machinery, a well-organized dock that could easily be doubled or tripled in size. It's always been my mantra to never waste opportunity, which unfortunately is what previous governors to me did."

"And what of the current governor?" he asked. "Have they carried on your legacy of efficiency?"

"She is... adequate. She is not as abysmal as my predecessor, but nor does she have the confidence and ability to advocate for her city to be awarded a contract such as this. She asked me personally to intervene, and I graciously accepted."

"I'm sure your magnanimous behavior has nothing to do with the fact that Skelm, being in your sector, would be a fine feather in your cap?" Mae asked acerbically. "It doesn't take a genius to see that the city growing in importance would no doubt enhance your own personal position within the Coalition."

"I advocate for my sector because it's my job as overseer. I can understand why someone with your background would struggle to understand doing something without first thinking of your own personal gain, but as you know, my beloved daughter was raised in Skelm. She has a deep love of where she came from." Allemande sighed gently. "Sometimes it makes me want to weep, thinking about the conditions she was raised in. Mr. Machenet, Mrs. Machenet, I'm sure you can understand, as parents, the importance of a child's education and stability."

Emeline's expression remained unmoved. Did she miss her family at all? Or was she just a very good actor? Without knowing her, it was difficult to tell, but Bailey was hell bent on getting the girl off Gamma-3 and back to her real mother. That might prove to be more of a challenge than she'd anticipated.

Allemande continued, "The poor thing was raised half her life in a drafty tenement after her father left them to fend for themselves. Her family then shared one room between all of them, sometimes not even having enough food to keep them fed. She had no one advocating for her, no one to lift her out of a bad situation and give her the education she was so desperately craving."

"Would this influx of investment get rid of the tenements?" Mae asked. "Seems to me that's where a great deal of problems originate there."

"Not entirely, but it would allow established workers to move up, have small residences of their own, if they meet certain stipulations and agree to the work credit scheme," Emeline answered. "While not a perfect solution—"

"I disagree, dear daughter, I think it's the best idea anyone's had about the housing in Skelm in years. After all, we will need the tenement building space for new arrivals who will be making a life in Skelm once we have an increased need for workers to run the expanded mills."

"What would this workforce look like to you, Overseer?" Mae's father asked. "Poaching workers from other cities?"

"No, nothing like that. The majority of workers in Skelm right now were rescued from a broken down rebel settlement. They'd all have died, if not for our intervention. The others from that settlement ended up in a work camp near Delta-4, I'm sorry to say. Those who ended up in Skelm have rehabilitated themselves remarkably." Allemande waved her hand, and the servant swooped in to clear the plates. "Some might linger too long on the idea of class, Mr. Machenet, but I find that ideology inefficient. There are many diamonds in the rough, just waiting for the education or opportunity to help build us an even more glorious existence."

Mae's father frowned. He was a man who thrived on the idea of class distinctions. "How do you determine the diamonds from the coal, ma'am? Begging your pardon, but my experience has shown that class is an incredibly efficient indicator of potential and achievement."

"They make themselves known, like my intelligent daughter here. There will always be far more rabble than forward-minded thinkers, to be sure. Our proposal will have children who exhibit a keen desire to learn, or express special talent in certain areas, to be removed from tenements and other unsuitable housing, and placed with loving families eager to support them on their journey."

"That's cultural genocide," Mae spat, her emotions getting the better of her.

"The Coalition is the only culture that matters, and the only one worth preserving," Allemande said simply. "The regressive attitudes of these rebels slow progress, and in my opinion, that is tantamount to treason. Better that we try to save what children we can from the beasts, rather than condemn them to a life of servitude to an outdated code of ideals that no longer serves the human race."

Mae flinched at the twisted, calculated answer. The moral superiority hung above the table like a fog, threatening and cold. A plan began to unfold in Mae's mind, and she allowed a smile to spread across her cheeks. "I see your point, ma'am. How silly of me to suggest otherwise."

"This could be a very valuable partnership, Mr. Machenet. With your skills, and your family's access, we could achieve great and important things. If you agree to put my plans first, above any other clients you may take on in the future, then I can foresee a comfortable future for you and your wife. And Maevestra too, should she decide to stay on Gamma-3, and not spend another ten years gallivanting around the Near Systems."

Mae bristled, but her father stood and extended his hand. "Overseer, I think we have an accord."

Chapter 21

"Yes, that's right, Ms. Dodson," Bailey said to the reporter. "The new proposal for the Outer Rim project will go to Skelm, in Sector Fifteen."

"Can you give our readers any insight as to why you chose that settlement above some of the others, which are already larger and more efficient?"

"Erm—" she stole a furtive glance at her palms, where Mae had written the answers to the questions she'd be asked. "Proximity was a major factor in this decision. While other locations were... um... better fitted out with regards to machinery, we will save years in getting materials to the new station over time."

"And what would you say to those, like Marcus Winter, who have accused you of taking bribes?"

Shit. That wasn't written on her hand. "I, er... uh... actually—"

"In fact, we have an eyewitness account that there was nearly an altercation between Winter and Overseer Allemande at the gala the other night." The reporter smiled, and Bailey took it as a threat. "Among other accounts, as well."

Bailey cleared her throat. "As I was saying, it's important to take into account that Marcus Winter is angry that his proposal was ultimately unsuccessful, and is lashing out in an attempt to salvage his reputation before he returns home." Damn, that sounded almost decent. "As for other accounts, off the record, they were unrelated to the proposal consideration. I'm sure you can understand why I am hesitant to remark on my personal life right now."

"Yes, General, that is understood. Now, for my final question, some are wondering whether this signifies a new shrewd political alliance between yourself and the overseer. What would you say to such speculations?"

"I would say that they are reading too far into what is no more than a routine decision, made to help advance the Outer Rim project."

"Great! Thank you so much for your time today, ma'am, and may I just say what a huge fan I am of your work."

"Oh. Thank you?"

"I hope someday to be the first member of the Coalition press corps at the Outer Rim." She slid the notebook into her leather briefcase and smoothed her skirts. "Perhaps you could lean on that decision?"

"I, uh—sure. Maybe. Good luck."

"A recommendation from someone like you could go a very long way in boosting one's chances to ascend up the career ladder, you know. You have incredible influence, General Fineglass."

Gods, was everyone here corrupt? "I'll think about it." Bailey paused, her hand poised on the back of the chair she'd been sitting in. "I guess it depends what your article says." When in the Capital, do as they do. Her own moral compass had no place in a city like this.

"I can assure you it will be nothing but glowing praise. You should be grateful, you know. I bet some presses would be itching to rake you over the coals for... well. You know." She gave her a razor sharp, brilliant smile. False reassurances. Bait.

"Indeed."

"It was nice meeting you, ma'am."

"Mm."

Barely noon, and she was already exhausted. It was the first time she'd ever made the front page of the newspaper anywhere, and hopefully, the last. The sooner they got off the damned planet, the better – but she wanted to rescue Emeline first. If it was her sister, she'd want someone to help her. The poor thing had obviously been through hell. What else would it be like to live with an authoritarian parent like Overseer Allemande?

"You done cozying up to the press corps?" Davey asked, sauntering into the hotel's main reception area.

"It's not like I enjoy this."

"Could have fooled me, you looked positively glowing."

"I *did* fool you, or have you forgotten?" Bailey hissed. "Now what did you find out?"

"As if I'm going to talk about that here, of all places."

She sighed heavily, letting all the air whoosh out of her lungs in a defiant gesture. "I hate it here."

"Yeah, and don't I know it." He handed over a thick wad of folded paper. "In here. Use heat. Then dispose of it. Discreetly."

"It's not like I'm going to go waving it around."

"You're not trained in this. I am. So stop arguing." He slid a pen into her jacket pocket. "For later. To tell me the things I asked about."

"I haven't had time for that yet."

Davey frowned. "You'd better find some time, and soon, or we won't be on good terms anymore."

"Alright, fine, I hear you," she replied, shoving the pen deeper into her pocket. She'd almost grown used to the uniform, but still desperately missed her normal clothes. If nothing else, they weren't so damned itchy.

"Today."

"Yes, okay! Today!"

"And you have another ethics committee meeting later."

"Gods, another one? What more do they want?"

He shrugged. "Protocol."

"Any word from the docks?"

"No. With any luck, we'll get the hell out of here before you-know-who shows up."

"I hope you know what you're doing."

"Listen, you do your job, and I'll handle mine, yeah?" He scribbled some notes onto a clipboard. "You have a few hours now, if you wanted to get me that information we talked about. You were supposed to be in a secondary proposal meeting, but, as you know, you've already handled that." Davey continued to scribble, avoiding eye contact. "Though not in the way I would have suggested."

Bailey pushed her long braid over her shoulder and smirked. "Too bad it wasn't your decision to make, then."

"Have you heard from Ned?"

"Yes."

"How... how is he?"

"Fine."

"Safe?"

"Yes. Why do you care?"

Davey scowled at her. "No reason."

"I'm sure you'll get your opportunity to tell him yourself."

"I just don't want you two messing things up for him. Us. The plan."

"Keep your pants on, Davey, things are going as planned. Mostly."

"It's by the far the worst plan I've ever seen in action."

"So long as it works, then you shouldn't have anything to complain about." She checked her pocket watch, making note of the time. If only she had another sandwich, like the one Amy had brought her. She couldn't waste time with the three course lunch the hotel offered. Gods, what she wouldn't give for a buffet or a basket of pastries. "You could come with me, if you want."

"Come with? Where?"

"The Armory here in the Capital. I seeded my interest, and they responded with an open invitation to tour the premises."

"Why didn't you say so? Let's go!"

* * *

The Armory was a huge, hulking building, with an imposing height that sliced into the sky with its razor-sharp spires, radio towers to send and receive official communications. It may as well have been a lion's den, and there she was, strolling right in through the front door like they wouldn't tear her limb from limb if they knew her true identity.

"Hello, I'm here for a tour," she said to the receptionist. She was pretty, in the same way that Henry was. A pang sounded in her heart, but duller now, like it was further away. "I'm General Fineglass, and this is my assistant. Don't worry, he has the requisite clearances."

"Of course, ma'am, I'll just call up for them."

Davey jabbed her in the side. "I don't have clearances," he hissed, his voice barely audible. "If I had clearances, I wouldn't need you to get in here!"

"Shh!"

"They'll be right down, ma'am. It won't be but a moment, but in the meantime, can I ask you to please sign the guest book?" The receptionist pushed a thick notebook with cream pages across the desk.

"Er—of course," Bailey replied, scanning the pages. The only familiar name that jumped out at her was Overseer Allemande. No doubt she'd come poking around, hunting for opportunities to use new technology in her sector. Ghoul.

"Are tours customary at this facility?" Davey asked innocently.

She shrugged. "Sometimes. Not every day, of course."

"No, no, of course not," he agreed, stealing a glance at the page Bailey was signing.

"General!" someone shouted from the elevator door. "We never dreamed you would take us up on our offer quite so soon!"

"I'm not in town long, I shouldn't waste the opportunity. Gods only know the next time I'll be back in the Capital."

The man stared at her quizzically. "Your official schedule says that you will be returning once a year to deal with administrative duties connected with the Outer Rim expansion project?"

"Yes, of course. I mean, who knows when I'll be back and have the time to visit," she corrected.

"If you'll just follow me, I'll take you through the labs first—oh, I'm terribly sorry, assistants aren't allowed access. You understand."

"He has clearances," she said with more confidence than she deserved, given the nervous pounding in her chest.

"Oh? How unusual." He hesitated. "I assume I can trust your word on

196

that, General?"

Bailey gave him a winning smile. "Of course, sir."

"Follow me, then! I'm sure some of our technicians will be thrilled to see a general of your caliber, not like the usual envoys and overseers we usually give tours to."

"I find it of great importance to see what's done on the ground, so to speak. Gives one a better understanding of how certain plans or policies are implemented."

"That's why you're such a fine leader, ma'am. Foresight and understanding. Two qualities I admire greatly, and that are sadly lacking in most."

"You flatter me, Mr..."

"Longfellow."

"Mr. Longfellow. It's a pleasure to tour with you today." Bailey was laying it on thick, but that kind of over the top garbage worked like a charm, here.

"Down this corridor, we have our meteorology division. It's grown tenfold in a year!"

Alarmed, Bailey jerked back. "Why? I mean, how come?"

"Important advances in weather patterning research. I have to admit, I have little knowledge of that area, myself!"

Shit. These fucks were still using the storm generators, or at least, they were planning to. No doubt the Cricket crew's stunt in Skelm had raised one hell of an alarm. "Fascinating," she finally managed to say. "Can we take a closer look?"

"I'm afraid not. Most of the teams are out for lunch this time of day, and they'd have my head if they found out I let someone in there."

Bailey poked Davey in the arm, but judging by how much tension he was holding in his shoulders, he already knew. "Shame," he said softly.

"Do you have an interest in weather?" Mr. Longfellow asked.

"Who doesn't?" Bailey answered, desperate to draw attention from Davey's face, which was frozen into stunned silence. "It affects us all!"

"Too right you are, General. Did you hear the forecast for next week? Snow! In late spring!" Mr. Longfellow shook his head in disbelief. "And I already packed away my woolens!"

"I shall be sad to miss it. I always wanted to see snow."

"Ma'am?"

Bailey cleared her throat. "In spring, that is."

"If you'll follow me up this stairwell back here, I can show you the engineering department. I assume that's more your speed."

"Mm," Bailey agreed, even though she had little to no interest in engineering as a topic. She'd picked up a few things here and there in Hjarta, but it had never been her passion like agriculture was. She sorely missed being amid rows of plants in the grow tents.

"On this floor, our engineers are working on armored suits, specifically space suits. The steam armor simply isn't sufficient anymore, not with the roving gangs of rebels and pirates that plague the skies. If you look through this window here, you can see some of the parts they are working on. This chest plate is being stress tested with torque and projectiles."

A large bullet bounced harmlessly off the piece of armor. It didn't even leave a dent.

"As you can see, they have made great strides with these improvements, and we hope that these suits will become standard issue to our MPOs within the year. Isn't that excellent, General?"

Bailey's mouth was dry with worry. "Fantastic." Rebels wouldn't have a chance against this high-tech crap.

"And down this way, we have several labs studying the effects of certain gases. Don't worry, they're hermetically sealed!" He said this in such a chipper, cheerful manner, it was like he didn't even recognize the gravity of it. He hurried them past the labs with the tiny windows so quickly, Bailey almost didn't see the restraints on the chairs. "Live trials begin next week!" Longfellow chirped.

Her stomach churned, threatening to bring up her meager breakfast. Davey dug his fingertips into the back of her arm. He'd seen them, too.

"What is the purpose of these trials?" she asked.

Mr. Longfellow tilted his head. "The same as any trials run in this building, General. It's the Armory." He turned to lead them up another set of stairs. "Though I suppose you don't have much need for some of this equipment all the way out there, do you?"

"Uh... no. Not yet, anyway."

"Let's hope it stays that way!"

"Yeah."

"This is the final floor of active labs. The next three floors are arms storage, and everything after that is just office space. Here you can see work on two of our most exciting projects. On the left, what we're calling the Hive, hundreds of miniature weaponized bugs."

"Bugs?" Davey asked.

"Yes, bugs, as in listening devices. They are solar powered, can transmit within a ten kilometer distance, and are virtually undetectable."

"What's weaponized about them?"

"They can sting, just like a wasp would, but theirs are tinged with a truth serum."

Bailey's heart dropped into her stomach. With every new advancement he showed them, she was more convinced that the Coalition would annihilate them all, in time. They had enough brute force to do it ten times over. "Truth serum?" she asked, using every ounce of control she possessed to keep her tone neutral and even.

"Yes. It wouldn't do any good to kill the informants, now would it?" He snorted a laugh and waved her away. "Most people won't even notice the initial sting, or think nothing of it. Five minutes later, they're spilling every secret they've got, and our little hive-minders are recording to transmit back to the control room."

"Wow," Davey breathed. It was a sound of horror, not admiration. "When will these be ready for deployment?"

Mr. Longfellow shrugged. "It's hard to say. Some early trials have been very encouraging, but they are still having problems with the power cells. Sometimes they can't make it back to the charging port before dying. It's not my personal area of expertise, but if I had to make an uneducated guess, I'd say we were at least three years from them being a viable tool."

"Three years?" Bailey repeated, trying not to sound relieved.

"Give or take. Now, if you want to see where my area of interest does lie, then follow me over here." Behind a large glass window, a huge cannon-like structure strapped to a rotating base on the floor. "My passion has always been heavy artillery. Guns! Explosions! Firepower! It really makes you feel human, blasting a ship out of the sky - and that's exactly what this little baby does."

"How... fascinating."

"It's the largest anti-spacecraft cannon in all the Near Systems—" He paused to laugh again and clapped a hand on Bailey's shoulder. "And the Outer Rim, too! Can't forget your team is out there now, preparing all kinds of expeditions!"

Bailey ducked out of his grasp and dusted off her uniform where he'd touched it. "How does it work?"

"It's a multi-function, this one. It has electromagnetic pulse abilities, in case we need to knock out all electronics. Disables a ship, you know, without blowing it up. It means we can board and seize prisoners or goods. Over on the left side, you can see that it has its own dedicated boiler chamber. This baby is completely mobile and can be used at any time, anywhere. It has a universal bolting mechanism, so it can be strapped to any ship, even trading vessels."

"What about that part?" Davey asked, pointing at a menacing cartridge on the side.

"That's my favorite part," Mr. Longfellow said proudly, as though he was introducing his child, and not a weapon of war. "We modified the old style projectiles they used to use in naval battles a long time ago. Inside that box there are seven missiles, each paired with a tempered steel hook. It will tear through a hull and rip it apart in seconds. It's great, isn't it?"

"Superb," Bailey said.

"I imagine once the expansion project gets underway, you'll have more filthy pirates to deal with out there. You might want to request one of these beauties as a pretty powerful deterrent. Blow up a few pirate rigs and it will send one hell of a message, don't you think, General?"

"A crystal clear message," she agreed. "And when will this one be ready?"

"Oh, it's ready now! We already have one on a gunship in areas thick with piracy. They've not had the opportunity to use it yet, unfortunately, but I live in constant hope!"

Bailey had a sudden and almost overwhelming need to contact the Cricket. What if they were the first ones targeted? "What's down that corridor there?"

"I'm afraid that's classified, General."

"I have top security clearance."

"As do I, ma'am, but it's beyond even us. Only the High Council and the small team of scientists, led by Dr. Arteo, know what's in there. If you're all through, I'll lead you back to the foyer."

Davey stepped around her, holding his hands out in desperation. "Mr. Longfellow, I hate to ask, but is there a restroom on this floor? I was very foolhardy this morning and had entirely too many cups of tea. I'd thought I could wait until we returned, but—"

"Of course, of course! It's just around the corner. We'll meet you back at reception, my good man."

Bailey threw him a warning glance. He was going to get himself killed if he wasn't careful. He might get both of them killed, actually. "Yes, don't be too long," she reminded him firmly. "We have that meeting in a little while."

"Don't worry," Davey chirped. "I'll only be a moment, General!"

Whatever they were hiding in there, it must be beyond all imagining. So terrible, not even the wide-eyed artillery fanatic knew what it was. The thought of it made her shiver. She held her tongue as she followed Mr. Longfellow back down the steps, him chattering happily away about all the different projects and how the Armory was the pride of the city. She had to get out of this terrible place. It was like poison in her veins.

"I hope you enjoyed your tour, General, we'd love to have you back some time," the receptionist said. "Maybe next time, some of the engineers will be available for lunch. I'm sure they'd love to hear about the hardships at the Outer Rim. They love a challenge!"

"I'll bet," she mumbled. Where the hell was Davey?

"You know, if you like, I could set you up with a contact here. That way, if you come across any specific needs out there, you'd have a direct line to the people who can start to work on a solution."

"Hm? Oh, sure. That would be fine." With every second that ticked by, her heart pounded faster and harder.

Mr. Longfellow shook her hand vigorously. "General, if you have time before you leave Gamma-3, I'd love to have lunch, perhaps, and discuss matters regarding funding of certain pet projects I have. I may not be a traditional contender for one of the supply contracts, but you may find my ideas around armed transport interesting."

"Armed transport."

"Yes, as a way of protecting valuable supply shipments."

"I thought transports were already armed?"

He shuffled his feet. "Yes, technically, but I would propose additional protections to shore up any gaps. You never know what those nasty pirates will get up to next, eh? And that's saying nothing of the damned rebels hijacking ships left and right?"

"I hadn't heard of that."

"No, not recently, but it does happen! Why, just last month a rebel was caught stowing away on a transport out of Skelm. The gods only know what subterfuge they were planning! They might have taken prisoners for ransom, or burst into the captain's quarters, or—"

"General!" Davey shouted from the elevator, acting as though everything was normal. "We ought to get going, we can't miss that meeting."

Bailey almost began to breathe a sigh of relief, letting air seep back into her lungs. Then, the alarm began to sound.

Chapter 22

Mae sat in the cafe, trying her best to look normal. Whatever the hell that even meant anymore. Her tea had long since gone cold, and lunch had been hours ago, but she couldn't bring herself to go home. No doubt it would just end in another argument. They'd been ready to explode the second they locked the front door after the dinner with the Allemandes. Her parents would definitely have sent her packing, if only they didn't need her so much.

"Another tea?" Aran asked, teapot in his hand. "It's fresh."

"Go on then," she answered, sliding her saucer across the vaguely sticky table.

He poured the steaming, fragrant liquid into the cup. "Getting some work done?"

"Something like that."

"It's getting late. Are you sure you don't want something more substantial than tea?"

"I'll take another slice of cake, if you've got it."

"We're all out, I'm afraid."

She sighed. "Don't worry, then. I'm sure I'll be on my way soon enough."

"May I?" He raised his eyebrows and looked at the chair across from her. "Sure."

"You know, Mae, I thought something was going on with you the first time you came in here the other day. I know it's been an eon since I saw you last but... something seemed different. On edge, maybe."

"Who isn't on edge these days?"

"Then I saw the paper yesterday, and everything started to make sense.

You could have told me, you know."

There he went, fishing for more information again. What was he getting at? "I assumed it would remain a private matter."

"I'm sure you have all kinds of reporters practically breaking down your door trying to ask you questions, but if you ever need an ear, you know where to go."

"Trust is dangerous, Aran, even for old friends."

"What about partners in crime?"

She snorted. "I hardly think some childish pranks count as crime. Not for people like us, anyway."

"Maybe not. But Amy and I, we missed you when you were gone. It's good that you're back in the Capital. Nice to see an honest face around here."

"Yeah, so honest that I'm having an affair with a high-ranking general."

"Are you, though?"

She stirred a lump of sugar into her tea, savoring the sound of the silver spoon against the fragile porcelain. "You saw the photos just like everyone else in this city."

"You and I both know the press is rarely the whole story."

"What are you saying?"

He shrugged. "I'm not saying anything. I just know that the ethics committee would be all over this, if it was true."

"And they have been. Like flies on shit."

"What did they say?"

His insistence was beginning to irritate her. She drank her tea angrily, letting it burn her throat all the way down into her stomach. "I wasn't present for that meeting. Aran, why don't you tell me what the hell it is you're fishing for? I'm no fool, I know you're angling for something specific."

"I should have known better than to try to squeeze you for information."

"Yes, you damn well should have. Now, out with it. Why have you been needling me every time I come in here?"

"Your father."

"*My father?*"

"He offered Amy and I some money if we found anything out. Not much, mind you, but... let's just say that this cafe is a little underwater, rent-wise."

"Gods' sakes, Aran, you could have just asked me for some money."

"He said you were broke, said it was why you were back here on Gamma-3 living with them."

She held out her cup for more tea, and he dutifully filled it. "It's a lie, all of it. They dragged me back here because they want to climb out of the societal grave they've dug themselves, nothing more."

"So much for that plan."

"You can say that again. I think in ten years they'd forgotten how fraught our relationship is. We achieve things in... very different ways."

"Yeah, he blackmails half the people in this city, and you wind up on the front page of the newspaper."

"No one can blackmail what's public knowledge."

"True enough, I suppose." He sat back in the rickety chair, the white-washed wood creaking under the weight. "I'm sorry I lied to you. I should have told you."

"You're damned right, you should have. Now, if you don't want me to barge into his office right now and tell him how easy it was to break you, I suggest you start being very honest with me. If I'm satisfied, then I'll make sure to mention this place in the next interview I give with the paper." She slid a piece of paper and a pen across the table. "You can start by writing down everything he told you, in explicit detail." He took the paper dutifully, folding it into his breast pocket. "And if it's not too much trouble, please set a slice of cake aside for me tomorrow. I'll be in after lunch."

"Of course. Mae, I... I really am sorry."

"He's fooled plenty of people in his time, trust me. You're not alone in that."

"No, but... I don't know, I suppose I should have known better."

Mae sipped at her tea, savoring the brutal scrape as it slid down her burnt throat. Anything to feel alive in this place. "Yes, you should have."

"I'll have to ask Amy what he said to her as well. I wasn't there for that."

"Where is she?"

"At work."

"I thought this was work."

He sighed again, casting a worried glance at the clunky register, piled high with paper receipts from chip scans. "It used to be. Once the bills started piling up, I took over everything here, and she took on work as a driver. She got lucky, and was assigned to some of the envoys and diplomats that come to the Capital for meetings and galas."

"Better than the drunks who can't hold their liquor."

"That's for sure. Still, I worry. She doesn't tell me much, but then, I suppose there isn't much to tell. I feel so guilty. She comes in early to go through the receipts. I was never any good with money." He frowned at his blurry reflection in the window. "Clearly."

"So you bake the cakes?"

"Yes."

Mae smiled encouragingly at him. "They're good cakes."

"Not good enough."

The bells on the door jingled ferociously, the teeth of the chime biting at Mae's ears. "Aran! Darling, I'm off early, I—" The woman paused, a grin spreading across her face. "Mae? Mae Machenet? Gods almighty, it's been an age, hasn't it? Aran told me you'd been in, but I didn't think I'd get the chance to say hello!"

Mae stood to embrace her. "It has been a long time, hasn't it?"

"A million years, it feels like. Maybe less for you, jetting around from place to place. I heard you were set up on Delta-4 for a time."

"Something like that."

"And look at Aran and me, two old fools growing moss in the same place we've always been. Not much has changed here, that's for sure." She set her cap on the counter and hopped over. "Is there any of that cake?"

"You're all out."

"Damn. I'm so hungry I could eat a buffet. This general has me driving all over kingdom come." She poked her head up over the register. "You'll never believe what happened today."

"Hold on, which general?"

"Steinglass or something," Aran interjected. "Amy drove her a long while back too, the last time she was in the Capital."

So she was Bailey's driver. "Fineglass?"

Amy nodded. "Yeah, that's her."

Mae blinked at her. "Do you read the paper?"

"No. Who has time to read the newspaper when you're working a solid fourteen hours a day? At dawn I'm in here, reconciling receipts. I drive all day, and then I help close up at night. I'm lucky if I get enough time to sleep for a few hours, and then it all starts up again. Why?"

Aran snickered. "Just take a look at yesterday's, Amy. It's there on the side."

"Oh, my gods!" Amy shrieked. "Mae! You're on the *front page*! With my client!" She picked up the newspaper and started to wave it around. "Mae, something's happened. Did you know? Do you know? When did you talk to her last?"

"What do you mean, something happened? What happened?"

"Up at the Armory today, she—"

"What in the hell was she doing *there*?" Gods be damned, Bailey, what were you thinking?

"A tour, or something. Her assistant set off an alarm, the whole place went into lockdown!"

"Lockdown!" Mae shouted, grateful that the cafe was empty. "Where is she? What happened?"

Amy held her hands up in apology. "I'm really sorry, I don't know! Once the alarm was triggered, I sat out in the car for at least an hour before someone came and told me to come back tomorrow."

"*Tomorrow!*"

"That's all I know, I'm really sorry, I—"

"Thank you. I have to go, I need to find out what's going on." Mae aimed for the door, panic clouding her mind. The shuttle was scheduled for tomorrow morning. If Bailey and Davey were stuck inside the Armory, they'd never make it.

"Don't be silly, I'll drive you."

"No, no, I can't involve you—"

"Mae. It will take you at least an hour to walk across the city, and you'll never get a steamcar at this hour, they're all stuck down at the docks waiting on arrivals. I don't mind, honest." Amy twirled her keys in her hand. "I bet you'd do the same for us."

"Fine. But not a word of this to my father, do you understand me?"

Amy cast a worried glance at her husband, who grimaced. "I'm sorry, Amy dear, she figured it out."

"It doesn't matter. This place was always going to be a silly dream, anyway." Shoving her hand in her pocket, she leaned against the wall. "No one else can help us keep the café. Why would they?"

Mae grabbed her hand, knowing the desperation was written all over her face. "Help me get her out of there, and I'll make all your bills current. I'll even make sure every rich asshole in this city knows this is the best place around. Please."

"I'm just a driver."

"You've always been so much more than that, Amy. Please."

Amy cracked the tiniest of mischievous smiles. "I'm at your service, ma'am."

Together, they fled the comfort of the café and ran out into the afternoon's golden light, muddled by the city's smog that hung low over the tops of the buildings. Mae slid into the passenger seat, and Amy put the long silver key into the ignition.

"Gods, does it always take this long for the engine to start?" Mae asked impatiently.

"Mae, you know full well this model is the fastest boiling steamcar on the market. See? It's already boiled." She shifted the steamcar into gear and pulled out into traffic, dodging and weaving around slow-moving transport vehicles and even more sluggish produce carts. "So how long have you and this general been... well, you know."

"That is a very strange and complicated story."

"It must be serious, if you're this worried about a lockdown protocol."

"She... struggles in confined spaces."

"I'm no fool, you know. I'm aware something else is going on. I know she's not really a general. She's not who she says she is. No scar fades like that. No general acts like that."

Mae flinched, her stomach tying itself into an uncomfortable knot. "What do you mean?"

"You know exactly what I mean."

"Please tell me that you didn't tell my father your suspicions. Please, Amy, tell me you didn't."

"I was about to, before I found you in my café."

"He's broke, Amy. He couldn't pay you for that information, even if he wanted to."

Amy ran her hands over the sleek steering wheel, chewing at her lip. "I trust you. I won't say anything, on my honor as your friend. Now, are you going to tell me what's going on?"

"It's complicated."

"Clearly, but we have at least twenty minutes to sit in the car, so there's plenty of time to spill your beans."

"Can we please just agree that this isn't the right time to talk about this?"

"Alright, fine." Amy jerked at the steering wheel. "Some things never change."

"And what is that supposed to mean?"

"Nothing."

"I have a lot going on right now, Amy, I don't have much patience for games."

"It means that this is what you do. What you've always done. You fly in, cause a lot of destruction, and leave again."

"I haven't been here in over ten years!"

Amy snorted derisively. "And look, within five minutes of seeing you, I'm driving you to an official building to help you break some impostor out of lockdown, and you won't even tell me why."

"It's important!"

"Yeah, it's always important."

"You know what, just pull over, I'll walk from here."

"Why are you like this?"

Mae stopped, her fingers curled around the handle. "Like what?"

"So guarded."

"Are you really asking me that directly after I discovered that my father was going to pay you for information about me?"

"He just wanted to know if you said anything about where you lived! He already knows where you live, so why should it matter?"

The pieces were beginning to come together in Mae's mind, and she felt the fire of a million suns began to burn in her chest. "He doesn't know. Amy, he doesn't know!"

"But he said—"

"He's a fucking liar! Gods, he lied about all of it. He lied about the whole thing!"

"What did he lie about?"

"Amy, don't be angry, but I can't tell you that, either. Not yet, anyway."

"This doesn't make any sense."

Mae's fingers dug into her thighs through the crisp taffeta of her skirts. "No. It doesn't." She turned and stared at Amy. "Where is the microphone in this car?"

"There isn't one, it's registered for diplomacy."

"Swear on it. Swear on all the gods."

"I swear on my dead mother's grave! Mae, what is going on?"

"What are your loyalties?"

"Excuse me?"

"Your loyalties, Amy, where do they lie? If you had to, where would you line up to fight? For the Coalition?"

"No."

"Then who?"

"Now that's something I can't tell *you*."

Mae's breath caught in her throat. "You're Scattered."

"Don't tell Aran."

"He doesn't know?"

"He worries."

"I can tell you that one of your empty-brained colleagues is probably who triggered that alarm today."

Amy shook her head. "Davey. He's been known to take too many risks in the field. He's always telling me 'no risk, no reward,' but I don't want to end up in a work camp." She parked the car. "Or worse."

"I'd rather we all got out of this without dealing with either of those scenarios."

"It's going to be a hell of a challenge, I won't lie to you. The Armory has enough MPOs to lay siege to the entire city, if they wanted to."

"I don't intend to go in there, guns blazing. I don't even have a gun. I don't like them."

"Then what the hell are we doing here?"

"There are more weapons than blades and projectiles. Just wait here for me, if it goes well we'll be back before you know it."

"And if it doesn't go well?"

"Then drive home and forget this ever happened. I don't want your imprisonment on my conscience."

Amy squinted at her. "To hell with that. If you don't succeed in there, I don't get to keep my cafe." She unlatched her belt and opened the door. "Just tell me what to do. How I can help."

"Can you send messages from this car?"

"Of course."

"Start telling the papers. Tell them a general has been abducted."

"Is that going to work?"

"Gods, let's hope so." Mae climbed out of the steamcar, holding her skirts in one hand, the other balled into a fist. "Wish me luck."

"Don't get killed."

"Yeah."

The pavement leading to the door was rough and uneven, so much so that the toe of her boot kept catching on pieces and threatening to send her flying. Enormous vaults worth of credits poured into the Capital Armory, and they couldn't even smooth out the sidewalk. Typical.

The door was locked behind an automated steel gate, fitted with razor wire throughout and powered by a dedicated boiler inside the courtyard. What the hell had Davey done, tried to stage his own armed insurrection? If it was anything other than that, this seemed like incredible overkill. "Hey!" she shouted through the gate, listening to her own voice echo back at her. "Let me in. I have an appointment!"

There was no answer, which didn't surprise her. "Tell Mr. Longfellow that I have information on what he was up to ten years ago in the summer, down at the docks!" She dropped her skirts and grasped the bars in between the sharp razors. "Tell him that plenty of reporters are on their way, and I'm sure they'd love to hear what I have to say!"

The gate began to hiss, lurching open one centimeter at a time. Mr. Longfellow, ten years older than the last time she'd seen him, appeared in the doorway, his hair greyer, his skin wrinklier, and angrier than she'd ever seen someone in middle management.

"I should have known it was going to be you," he spat. "Get inside. I can't guarantee I'll let you back out."

"The pleasure is all mine," she replied with a suave smile, edging through the tiny gap. "I always knew you were a man who saw reason."

"What the hell are you doing here?"

"I heard that you were holding my lover here under lock and key. A highly decorated general being kept inside like a rat? Have you lost your mind? Think what the press would say!"

"You're just like your father."

Mae smirked. "I know you mean that to be an insult, sir, please know that it was not taken as one." She sat down in a plush chair near the reception desk, arranging her skirts artfully around her. "It's untrue, in any case. He'd have someone do his dirty work for him. I do my own, in person."

"Yes, that much is clear," he grumbled. "What do you want?"

"The release of my darling, of course. She has very important meetings. You wouldn't understand, it's above your pay grade."

"Insulting me won't get this building out of lockdown any faster. It's protocol, and she knows it. She took that risk when she walked in here."

"Surely a powerful woman like General Fineglass isn't at fault for one of your technicians setting off an alarm. Why keep her here as though she is a common criminal?"

Mr. Longfellow sighed, a long, heavy exhale of breath that whistled in the back of his throat. "It wasn't a technician."

"Scientist, then. Or engineer."

"I know what you're doing, Ms. Machenet, and I won't stand for it. You can leave now, before we lock up the gates again, or you can spend the night in here while we run through our security procedures."

"I'm not leaving without her."

"Suit yourself. I won't change my mind." He pulled a large lever on the wall, and the gates outside hissed closed, pressurized by the steam. "Your threats will do no good in here. Anything said inside these walls cannot be repeated to reporters."

"Not to reporters, no."

"What is your angle, then? Announce to my coworkers that I had an affair?" He cupped his hands around his mouth. "I HAD AN AFFAIR!"

Mae raised an eyebrow. "Unorthodox, but I can respect it. Do they also know about your love child? She would be, what, nine years old now?"

"Anyone worth their salt could easily find that out. I pay for the girl's tuition, and her mother gets a monthly stipend. A secret, yes, but an affair that's been whispered around here plenty of times."

"Affair?" Mae replied with a laugh. "Who said anything about an affair?"

The color drained from his face. "What are you talking about?"

"Oh, I think you know. And unless you want to be shouting *that* into the rafters, I would suggest we cut the crap and have a civilized conversation." She didn't even know the details, not in their entirety. He'd made some deal with a shady backroom credit shark to get his position, and he was in debt to them for the rest of his life. He'd sold his soul for a middle management job, a dingy office with a mediocre paycheck. "Let's start with the basics. Who set off the alarm?"

"We don't know."

"Good. Now, I'm sure you can confirm that it wasn't General Fineglass?"

"She was with me when it happened."

"Where is she now?"

"In a holding cell."

Mae flushed with anger. "You put her into a cell? *Why?*"

"Because her damned assistant did! And she swore to me that he had the correct clearances, and he doesn't. He barely has more than a civilian, just enough to manage the general's social calendar and pick up her suit from the cleaners."

"So arrest him, then." She'd worry about getting Davey out later. The longer Bailey was in here, the more likely she'd get caught, and then they'd all wind up dead. Or worse.

"He says it wasn't intentional. That he got lost on the way to the restroom."

She breathed an undetectable sigh of relief. "And does it check out?"

"It does, he had just asked me."

"Then I have to ask you again, what in the hell are you playing at here, Mr. Longfellow? Are you trying to make sure your funding gets cut in the next budget?"

"It's protocol!"

"Don't shout at me, sir. You must understand, people will see this as you trying to influence things above your station."

"What do you propose I do, then? Ignore long-established safety protocols? Allow the reputation of the Armory as an impregnable fortress to falter, drawing every rebel and pirate in the Near Systems?"

"Hyperbole is used by fools who can't support their stance. You know as well as I do that most rebels and pirates wouldn't even make it past the docks." Mae crossed her feet at the ankles and folded her hands in her lap. "If you won't release them, can I see them, then?"

"I suppose. No funny business."

"Mr. Longfellow, what do you take me for, some kind of... of pirate, bent on destruction and the downfall of the Coalition?" In truth, that's exactly what she was.

"No, of course not, but I know you, and I know your kind, Ms. Machenet, and I won't be bamboozled."

"I just need to see her, so I can rearrange any diplomatic meetings that you've bulldozed with your clumsy attempt at notoriety." She smiled sweetly to punctuate her point.

"Fine. Follow me," he grumbled. "Keep up. Don't touch anything. Don't even look at anything, you don't have the clearance."

"I hardly think that framed portraits of previous governors is classified information."

"Why are you back in the Capital, anyway? Gods, it was bad enough with just your father slinking around in the shadows, now there are two of you."

Mae followed him down a narrow corridor, the heels of her polished boots clicking elegantly on the tile. "I think you'll find that I don't keep to the shadows, sir. I'd rather my business be in the sunlight for all to see."

"Yes, the front page of the paper this week certainly illustrated that."

"No one can use against you what is public knowledge," she chirped. "It would seem that a great many Capital residents could learn from that little adage."

"Not everyone wants their private life on public display," he muttered.

"Then don't have a private life," she answered simply. "The papers will always want to know who's leaving their boots under someone else's bed, who had a tryst with someone they shouldn't have. The longer you try to hide it, the more complicated the lies become."

"You think you know everything, but you don't." He opened the door to a room with two cells in it. One held Bailey, and Davey sat moping in the other. A camera blinked in each corner. "I'll be at reception."

"You might as well stay, it would be easier to eavesdrop," Mae said, smiling.

He scowled and pulled the door to the frame without latching it. "I don't eavesdrop."

"Dearest!" Mae shouted, playing up for their audience. "I was so worried! Are you alright?"

"I'm fine. I'd be happier out of this cell, though."

"Understandable. And Davey, my good man? Are you okay?"

He grasped the bars that separated them. "You have to get us out of here.

We have... we have that meeting."

"I know how important it is, and I'm doing my best to reschedule. My understanding, though, is that rescheduling is very difficult. The next slot likely wouldn't be until next week."

"But that's much too late!" Bailey protested. "Can't you convince them?"

"As I said, I'm doing my best, loveheart. I just can't believe they have you both locked up in here! It's an outrage! All for setting off some proximity alarm by accident." She turned her face away from the cameras to give Davey a warning glance. "They take things very seriously here."

"How long do you think they'll keep us here?" Davey asked.

"Protocol is twenty-four hours lockdown. I am trying to get you released, but some people don't know what's good for them."

Bailey touched her hand through the iron bars. "How did you find us?"

"Your driver. She was quite worried, no one would tell her anything, poor soul. So devoted to her post, she was absolutely fraught with nerves." Mae entwined her fingers with Bailey's, and even though it was a show for the cameras, the gentle, almost endearing touch made something spark deep in her heart.

"I never thought she cared that much."

"People can surprise us. Sometimes, alarmingly so."

Bailey raised an eyebrow. "Indeed. And what of the other task on the list?"

"Unfortunately, that is not a task I am up to myself, love. There are some things only a general can do." There was no way she could extricate Emeline by herself. She wasn't even sure they'd be able to manage it with all three of them on the job. The girl didn't seem like a prisoner. Not someone who wanted to leave.

"You have to try, in case we... in case we miss that meeting. You could still make the meeting, even if we didn't. Then you could drop by on your way there."

"Bai—darling, I said I'd try my hardest, but I am unfortunately not made of magic."

"What if you visited your father first? Maybe he could help us out?"

Mae shook her head wordlessly.

"Oh. But—"

"General, I think we might have to accept that we are likely going to miss that meeting," Davey interrupted. "I can only apologize profusely, given that it was my own foolishness that caused it. He said left, I went right, I've always been rather... directionally challenged."

"Mistakes happen, Davey, we've all made them. I'm sure they'll let you out of here soon."

"Gods," Bailey breathed, "if only there was some way we could beg Mr. Longfellow to see reason." She straightened her posture and released her grip on Mae's hand. "He's such an upstanding and honorable man, he's doing his best to preserve policies put into place to protect the Armory and the citizens of the city. We may not like the situation we've all landed in, but by all the gods, he's doing his best."

"*You're laying it on a little thick,*" Mae whispered.

"Oh, to be in an esteemed position to be the protector of the city's arsenal. What responsibility! I reckon even some generals don't have that level of weight on their shoulders, the burden bearing down hard." Bailey cleared her throat. "I am always in need of upstanding defenders of policy and protocol at the Outer Rim. I wish I could find someone like Longfellow to execute the complex plans we have there. Complexity that will only become more so as plans move forward."

"I understand staffing is becoming such a chore for you," Mae offered. "So many aren't ready for the challenges that the Outer Rim presents, no matter what the salary increase is."

"Don't be too hard on him, darling, he's just doing his job, just as I do mine."

"I will try, but it's so hard to see you locked up in here, having done nothing wrong. You poor, dear thing. I'll do my best to have that meeting rescheduled." She grabbed Bailey's hands through the bars again. "I will try. But I cannot work miracles." The damn shuttle was coming, and she couldn't stop it, now. It had probably already left the transport beacon. She'd have to find another way. "We may have to consider the possibility that the meeting will have to take some other form."

"Don't forget your promise," Davey reminded her. "You said you'd help me."

"And I intend to keep that promise." Mae released Bailey, and pressed her face against Davey's cell. "But you're the reason we're even in this mess, and from what I hear, it's not the first mess you've made."

"Sometimes you have to make messes to do what needs to be done."

"And sometimes, you could just *wait*." She narrowed her eyes at him threateningly, keeping her face away from the cameras. "And if you had just waited, you wouldn't have jeopardized one of the most important meetings of the general's life. So if in the future, you could just *wait*, things may proceed much more smoothly, in spite of your directional confusion."

Chapter 23

Hope sparkled in the bleak darkness the moment Mae arrived. Everything was possible and attainable in her presence. She was a force of nature, and fascinating to behold in the environment that created her. Harsh, sharp, endless climbing of a never-ending social ladder.

"Ms. Machenet, I must insist that you return with me to the reception area," Mr. Longfellow said, his tone colder and even unfriendlier than before. "There are reporters massing outside the gate."

"Reporters!" Mae said, punctuating it with a gasp. "How could they know what's going on in here?"

"I can only assume that you had something to do with that," he snarled.

"Me? I would never! I respect the sacred institution of the Coalition's armory, and endangering that sanctity is the furthest thing from my mind!" She flashed him a grin that was almost a smirk. "And if you ask any of them where their tips came from, I can guarantee that my name won't come up. After all, sir, I've been in here with you this entire time! Under surveillance! How could I possibly send wires to a dozen different reporters?"

"I'm not a fool, Maevestra. This has your father's fingerprints all over it."

"Think what you like, but he doesn't even know that I'm here."

"Regardless! Your time in here is up, because you need to go and deal with the mess outside. Call off your pack of bloodhounds, damn it!"

Mae rested her hands inside the pockets of her skirt. "They aren't my bloodhounds, sir, as I've said. But, if you like, I can be convinced to help disperse them, if I can. I must admit my relationship with the press has been rather strained as of late. Why have they said they are here?"

"Someone told them that the general was abducted from our facility. They are demanding answers. They're at the gate!" He sighed heavily, pushing his glasses up high on his nose. "You have to get rid of them, Ms. Machenet, we cannot attend to our protocols with an audience."

"I shall do my best," Mae relented, following him out of the room. The door's latch snapped closed, and they were locked in again.

"What the hell is she up to?" Davey asked.

"Trying to get us out of here, I'd imagine. And you should keep your mouth shut, there's enough surveillance in here to record our hair growing."

"It's visual only, no audio. They can't hear us. I said that before."

"And as I said before, I'm not jumping at the opportunity to put my trust in the person who landed us in lockup in the first place."

Davey rolled his eyes and tutted. "This is hardly lockup. You off-worlders have no idea."

"There are bars and a padlock. There is a door with an external deadbolt. Yes, we are locked up."

"It's procedural."

"You're damn lucky they didn't immediately haul you off to an interrogation cell."

"You're the one who assured them I had the clearances!"

"And you're the one who wanted to come here in the first place!" Bailey smacked her palm against the cold iron of the bars, the echo reverberating around the cell. "This could ruin everything, you know that, right?"

"Of course I know that!" he hissed. "But there are things larger than you and me, bigger than her, too, at play here. I wish you would understand that."

"Will you shut up?" She was tired of listening to his preachy explanations. Being a rum-runner was one thing, The Scattered was another entirely. Their methods were frequently bloody, justified by their ordained mission to overthrow the Coalition. "I'm sick of arguing with you about it."

"They could really use a woman like you, you know," he whispered. "Seeing how you've handled yourself with no preparation at all, and pulling it off is... it's astounding."

"I can assure you that this is the last gods-damned time I will ever do anything like this. I just want to get the hell out of this cell and get on with my life."

"What about the girl?"

"I've told you three times now, I'm not discussing this in here. You have no idea what they could use against us, if it came down to it. What you're doing is reckless, and I want no part of it."

"Hmm. I thought you had what it takes, but maybe not."

"That reverse-brainwave shit isn't going to work on me. Think what you want, I'm not joining your club." She made sure to keep her language as neutral as she could, in the likely scenario they were being recorded with microphones, too. "From what I've heard, it's not a club I want any part of."

"Club," Davey sneered. "How derisive."

"Remember where we are, please, for the last gods-damned time."

He was quiet for a moment, and Bailey thought she'd won the battle for silence, until he broke it with another question. "Do you think Ned will make that meeting tomorrow?"

"Gods, I hope so."

"When—if—we get out of this, and... scheduling returns to normal, it might be nice to meet for dinner. To reminisce."

"You can ask him yourself, *when* we get out of here." Bailey tugged at the loose threads on her cuff. "He's a good guy, Davey. I'm not so sure he'd want to be part of your club, either."

"He already is."

"*What?*"

Davey sighed. "I looked him up in the archives. His membership, and all associated duties, lapsed years ago, but he did run with us, for a time."

"That's ridiculous."

"It's the truth," he replied with a shrug. "I'd love to ask him about it someday."

"Yeah, you and me both, not to mention everyone else on that ship." Did

Captain Violet know that Ned had been part of The Scattered? Would she care? "I always thought I never wanted to see that vessel again, and now I find myself longing for it. Gods, how a cage can change things."

"Stop getting so sentimental, you'll get the opportunity to hate it again."

"You're very confident, for a man stuck behind two locks."

"I've always found that optimism and confidence can open many doors."

"Can you start working on these, then? Tell them you're confident that you can open them with your incredible powers of positivity."

"Shh, they're coming back."

The muffled sound of steps grew louder as they approached the door, and then the sound of the large brass key in the lock. "As I said, Mr. Longfellow, it seems like a clear solution to me. They need proof that you didn't fail in your duty to protect the general on a routine tour and inspection of the Armory. You could easily achieve that by allowing her and her assistant to go free."

"They can see her from the window, and that will put all of this to bed. The general can go tomorrow evening, when the protocols have been completed. These things take time, you know."

"While normally I would agree with you, sir, we don't live in normal, predictable times. There have been reports in other cities of lookalikes! Dupes, used to dampen the news of abductions, to keep people calm. We certainly wouldn't want the gaggle of journalists outside to think something like that was going on."

"That's poppycock. I've never heard of such a thing."

"I assure you, Mr. Longfellow, it has been done. Just last month on Delta-4 an officer was kidnapped for over a week! His manager there hid it with a doppelganger, another officer made up to look like him, or close enough, anyway - until it wasn't." Mae paused, folding her hands politely in front of her. "That manager got fired less than ten minutes after the story broke."

"Seeing as that's not what's happening here, I am in no danger of being reprimanded for following procedure."

"True, sir, but you know how the press can be. One supposition will whip them into a frenzy for weeks! Even I've been the victim of vicious gossip-mongering just this week. They've been diving into all my previous relationships, requesting interviews with colleagues I've not spoken to in ten years. Some people would really hate that kind of intense scrutiny into their private affairs."

He jangled the keys noisily in his hands, dithering. "General, how long do you anticipate being in the Capital?"

"Oh, a few more days, at least," Bailey answered.

"I suppose so long as you made yourself available to debrief, and your assistant, it wouldn't be that terrible a departure of protocol..."

"The press will herald it as a great respect for her achievements, I'm sure," Mae added. "And as you mentioned, her assistant's credentials check out. As such, we're only looking at the accidental proximity alarm. The lab wasn't even breached."

"I suppose not, but I still find it very strange that he did not have the credentials when first we checked." He turned to Davey, an eyebrow raised. "Can you explain that, Mr. Klein?"

"I'm afraid I can't, sir. I can only assume that the first data pulled was incorrect, perhaps from an outdated file, or a box ticked incorrectly. Having worked in the archives at one time in my life, I can attest that errors do occasionally happen."

The keys dangled in the air, suspended by the large bronze ring in Mr. Longfellow's hand. The promise of freedom, guarded by an up-jumped member of middle management. "I don't like being coerced into things, Machenet. Protest it all you will, but I've lived in this town my entire life, and I know when something has been orchestrated. You'd not even have got through those doors without intel you shouldn't have access to. It's clear that discretion isn't something your family values."

"It may be true that I used undue influence to get in here, but imagine if you'd been handling this without me - they'd have their articles half-written already."

"I know when I smell a rat." He thrust the key into the padlock, popping it open, allowing the door to swing free. "I'll have my eye on all three of you. Even one toe out of line, and I'll have you hauled back here for questioning, is that clear?"

"You're lucky you haven't already been demoted back down to the poor soul who scrubs the rust off the boilers, Longfellow," Bailey said. "As an esteemed general, I am not accustomed to unimportant middle-management meddlers interfering in my business."

"My deepest apologies, ma'am," he said, though his tone was flat and inauthentic. "I'm arranging an extra security detail to keep an eye on you. After all, as Ms. Machenet says, abductions are becoming far too common."

Fuck.

"How kind of you," Mae said sweetly. Her acting abilities were, quite frankly, as terrifying as they were alluring. "That's very wise, I think."

The padlock on Davey's cell snapped open too, allowing him to step out into the room, straightening his cravat. "Thank you for deigning to release us, Mr. Longfellow. You've done the Coalition a real service in allowing us to make our meeting tomorrow."

"What meeting is this, anyway?" Mr. Longfellow asked.

"It's classified! Above your pay grade, I dare say."

Walking down the hall back to the foyer was like crawling to freedom. She could feel every pair of eyes on her, boring through her uniform, willing her to slip up, waiting for the opportunity to throw her back into the cell. When she squeezed through the tiny gap in the gates, she breathed a sigh of relief.

"This is Johnson. He will be your security detail." A huge, burly man in an MPO uniform and matching cap followed them out, his hand resting on the revolver at his hip. "We'd hate for anything bad to happen to you, General."

"Yes, er... thank you," she said. "And thank you for the tour."

Without a reply, he went back into the building, and the gates creaked and popped as they closed once again.

"Nice to meet you, Johnson. I am General Fineglass."

He responded with a nod, and nothing else.

"Is Johnson your last name, or...?" Bailey asked.

Another nod.

"What's your first name?"

He gave her a cold, steely glare.

"Right, then."

"We're not all going to fit in the steamcar," Mae said, ever the pragmatic organizer. "There is room for three, but not four."

"I'll call for another," Davey said helpfully. "Perhaps you could just call from the steamcar, or—"

Johnson was herding them all towards the steamcar door, as though he was herding a flock of unruly sheep. "We'll fit," was all he said.

"Actually, I have some other matters to attend to before that meeting tomorrow, General," Mae said, ducking under his arm. "And as I am not part of this suffocating little protection detail, I will find my own way home. No doubt my parents are wondering where I am. Plus, someone has to deal with those reporters, don't you think?"

Johnson looked from the gaggle of journalists, armed with recording devices and pocket-sized notebooks, back to Bailey. He nodded.

"A man of very few words, I take it?" Mae asked. "Never you mind about the news articles, dear, now they've seen you, I'm sure that will be the end of it."

"Let's hope so. We don't have time to be dealing with such... er... that," Bailey stammered. This was a nightmare. Finally set free and saddled with the human equivalent of a surveillance camera. "What about Em—what about that, uh, personnel problem I mentioned?"

"I have to admit, I don't think that's a good idea to focus on right now."

"But it's urgent."

"I know, but I just don't see how that can work." Mae grimaced at Johnson's back. "Not under the current constraints."

Bailey pushed his arm away as he tried to get her into the steamcar. "If you don't try to make that happen, then I will. I don't care if no one else thinks it's a priority, I damn well do. I told you, my staffing challenges are my biggest challenge out there, and I will be damned by the gods if I head back out without that position filled."

Mae blinked at her. "Alright. Okay. I'll do my best. You focus on that meeting tomorrow. I'll see you there, darling. Ten in the morning, sharp. Do *not* be late. These people don't like to be kept waiting." Catching the eye of a photographer, she pulled Bailey in for a quick kiss. "See you then!" As she headed towards the group of reporters, restrained behind a barrier tape, she looked over her shoulder. "I mean it, dear. Don't be late. I can't help you if you're late."

"Okay," Bailey croaked. She got into the back seat of the steamcar, alongside her new shadow. Davey slid into the front passenger seat, glaring at Amy.

"What are you still doing here?" he asked her.

"Waiting for you, obviously. I could ask you the same question."

"Official business, of course."

"I guess we'll see about that." She shifted the car into gear. "Where to, ma'am?"

"Er, our hotel, I suppose. Davey and I have some preparations to do before our meeting in the morning."

"We could stop off for a sandwich, if you like."

Herb-crusted, fried eggplant, slathered in that garlic butter sauce, topped with stretchy, melted cheese... her stomach began to rumble just thinking about it. When was the last time she'd eaten? That pitiful breakfast? "Yes, please."

"No," Johnson said firmly. "Unauthorized locations are a heightened security risk. You can order from the hotel's room service, surely."

"They don't have sandwiches, and I want a sandwich."

"No."

"I outrank you, sir."

"As your assigned security detail, I am cleared to make unilateral decisions where locales are concerned. No. If you wish to visit this establishment in a few days, I can begin security checks right now. We'll have to verify all employees' identities, sweep the venue for bugs, secure the entrances and exits, have a detailed action plan in case of—"

"Forget it." She'd just have to sustain herself on hotel food. Always overpriced, not that she was paying, but always underwhelming. They presented it as being the best room service in the Capital, and while punctual, nearly always lukewarm and oily. She wondered where the hell their chef had gone to cooking school. She yearned for a hot meal at the Purple Pig.

* * *

Bailey slumped into an overstuffed, yellow and purple velvet chair in the room they'd reserved to discuss how the hell they were going to get out of the Capital. Her enormous room was plenty big enough, but having unmarried people in each other's rooms was apparently "unseemly," as Johnson said, despite the constant surveillance in the rooms.

"So what now?" she asked, more to herself than Davey.

"I suppose we need to prepare for this meeting tomorrow morning, don't we? How we're going to get there, what we're going to do once we are…"

Johnson followed him in and closed the door, leaning against the wood-paneled wall.

"Oh, this meeting is classified," Bailey said. "You can wait outside the door."

"I have top clearances," he replied, without moving a muscle.

"Of course you do. May I suggest that you'd be more comfortable waiting in the hall? There is a couch out there, and only two chairs in he—"

"I'm fine, thank you, ma'am. Please continue."

All the gods be damned straight into hell. As if this wasn't going to be difficult enough, now they had to talk around this giant hulking security alarm, who had no doubt been employed by Mr. Longfellow to listen in and report back. What would the real General Fineglass do?

"I would rather not discuss proprietary information within earshot of someone whose credentials I've not even seen."

"Ma'am, I served with you in Sector Five, ten years ago. When you were a sergeant."

Fuck! Blood pounded in her ears. They were done for.

"Oh, I… didn't recognize you."

"Understandable, ma'am." He inclined his head slightly. "We aren't all trained in facial recognition."

She couldn't push it any more, not without risking being found out. Of course he knew the real general - but, wait, he was trained in facial recognition? Did he already know she was a fraud? She glanced at Davey, who wore the same confused expression that she did.

"Right then, er, Davey," she began, adrenaline leaching into her veins like a poison. What use was it, if you couldn't even run? "This meeting tomorrow."

"I imagine it's the most important meeting you'll have while here in the Capital," Davey replied. "The utmost in importance."

"Mm."

"I imagine we will drive with Amy to the meeting locale?"

"Will we? I thought it might be best to... obtain other transportation. Given her schedule."

"Her schedule is free, I already confirmed it." Davey gave her an almost imperceptible wink. "We're cleared, where that's concerned."

"May I ask where this meeting is, ma'am?" Johnson asked.

"It's, er..." she trailed off, searching her mind frantically for some kind of answer. "Classified?"

"Ma'am, if this location—"

"It's at the docks," Davey interrupted. "It's been planned for weeks, and it's concerning the transportation of goods between major ports like the one here in the Capital, and the Outer Rim. The general is touring the back end of operations and discussing expectations with the management, in order to determine if her expectations are reasonable."

She nodded appreciatively. "Yes."

"I'll have to call in some additional forces," Johnson said, worried. "The docks are far too large to cordon off at this late stage. Did no one advise you of this?"

"Until about an hour ago, people trusted me to make my own decisions, and keep myself safe," she answered acerbically.

"With the growing threat of abduction, it's an inevitability that you will need more protection. Mr. Longfellow is aware of the media's perception of your state visit here and wants to ensure your safety at all costs."

Bailey rolled her eyes. "Yes, I'm sure he's very concerned about my safety, after locking me in a cell for hours." Her stomach rumbled again. "I need some sustenance. Davey?"

"Yes, that would be good."

"Johnson, could you—" Before she could finish asking him to go get food from the kitchens, he lifted a panel of wood to reveal a wire. He tapped into it with precision and slid the panel back into place.

"Someone will be here presently, ma'am."

"Uh, thank you."

Davey leaned across the table, clipboard in hand. "So, General, this meeting tomorrow - I think it best we discuss what time we should leave. Ms. Machenet implied that they do not smile upon tardiness, but also, we should be mindful of the morning rush in the tunnel."

"Why don't we leave right now, then we're sure to be on time." Bailey said it with a joking tone, but she wanted it to be true. She'd sleep in a drafty crate all night, if it meant they'd be able to get out of here safely. And what about Ned? How was he getting there?

"I suggest we leave very early in the morning," he said pointedly. "*Very* early."

"Fine. And what of our associate? Do you know how he is getting to the meeting?"

Davey sat back in his seat, sinking into the cushion like a bog. "No." He fidgeted with his pen before setting it noisily on the table. "I trust Ms. Machenet is dealing with that."

"I'm sure she is. She knows how important this meeting is."

"I just don't want our associate to get confused about the time tables, ma'am. It would be a gods-damned shame if he missed the meeting. It's the opportunity of a lifetime."

"Begging pardon, ma'am," Johnson said, opening the door. "But room service is here. They've kindly brought you the chef's special, it would seem."

Great. More oily sea bass and tepid soup. "Thank you, just set the trays on the table."

He lifted the silver domed lid off the tray, and a delicious aroma filled the room. The hotel's kitchen had certainly been holding out on them. When the steam cleared, two plates of noodles, topped with a generous pile of orange-glazed tofu and a side of roasted peppers were revealed. Bailey's mouth watered greedily, and she reached for the utensils with eagerness.

"They really pushed the boat out on this, didn't they?" Davey said, in just as much awe as she was. "I hope you're not hungry, Johnson, because I don't intend on sharing."

The guard's face held no reaction, stoney and emotionless.

"This is almost better than a sandwich," Bailey joked. She began to stir the sauce into the noodles, and discovered a tiny piece of paper with orange writing, camouflaged delicately amid the tofu.

Be ready

She glanced across to Davey, who was happily devouring his food. Had he received a note? Who had sent it? Mae? Someone else? Be ready for what? When she looked down at her plate again, the note had vanished into the sauce, dissolved into nothingness, so invisible she wasn't even sure she'd seen it at all.

"They must have hired a different chef for today," Davey said. "This isn't terrible at all."

"Mm," Bailey agreed. There were too many questions and not enough answers. She wanted off Gamma-3, and soon.

"We should also discuss the plans for after the meeting tomorrow."

"After?"

"Yes, ma'am, we still have duties to fulfill, don't we?" he asked with a laugh, trying to cover for her foolishness.

"Yes, of course. I just wonder what you have in mind for the next few days."

Davey slurped up a noodle. "I feel it's important to remember certain agreements that were made earlier during your stay here."

"Those agreements have already been completed."

"The other party might find that... debatable."

"That is too bad for the other party." If he wanted more information, he was going to have to get it himself. She was done.

"General, I'm sorry, but that's unacceptable. Agreements were made. This could damage your reputation as a fair, understanding, high-ranking official."

Bailey looked up from her plate. "To be frank, I don't care. I know that I upheld what I agreed to. Anything else would just be the other party trying to take advantage of a difficult situation."

"Fine," he grumbled. "But we're not done with this."

Chapter 24

Mae shielded her eyes against the bright setting sun. Her feet were killing her, and she just knew that her left boot had a shallow pool of blood at the heel. From here on out, it would be best if there was no record of her movements, and Amy was busy with diplomatic driving duties. Despite the reassurances of that other driver, things had changed. She'd been on the front page, and her name woven through plenty of sidelined stories about the general's visit.

The last stretch would be the most challenging, and the most difficult. If they missed the shuttle, things would spin out of control very quickly. It was a precipice, and she hated precipices.

She stopped at an old, wrought-iron bench to adjust her boot for the dozenth time, wincing at the pain. These boots were not made for walking across the Capital, a city so expansive and sprawling. She wasn't used to it, not when Bradach was a tiny fraction of the size.

Her eyelids were heavy, weighed down by a week without restful sleep. Backup plans upon backup plans constantly ran through her mind like thousands of photographs, trying to work out the best solution for any situation, any variance in her expectations. How had her father done this for decades? Secrets and lies to keep track of, always having to watch your back for the next competitor who would happily, joyfully step over your corpse to ascend the ladder.

She wouldn't be returning to her parents' home that night. They had nothing on her, their surveillance of her friends proved that. It was his riskiest bluff, and it was about to blow up in his face. It served him right for what he'd done, dragging her back here. Blackmailing your own flesh and blood wasn't out of the question, not here. Not in this infested, power-hungry place.

The Allemande's door was just ahead, and loomed large in comparison to the other, more modest houses that surrounded it. Typical that they'd hand the nicest place to an overseer who wouldn't even be living in it most of the time, instead sitting empty, darkened windows on a street where children used to play, but now creaked like the stairs of an old, untended house.

She hesitated before knocking. Should she sneak in, instead? Maybe she should have called ahead? No. This was the only way. She just hoped it wasn't about to get her killed.

Her knuckles rapped lightly against the lacquered door. There was no sound from within, no shuffling of feet, or the flick of a light. Perhaps they were out for an early dinner, or attending another function with the intent to bombard, blackmail, and harass officials into approving their contracts. Their official schedule had put the overseer in a short meeting, with Emeline on her own, for just twenty minutes. A small window. But it seemed the girl wasn't even at home.

She turned to leave, whimpering quietly at her swollen feet.

The door swung open. "Ms. Machenet? What are you doing here?"

"Ah, hello! Is your mother home, by any chance?"

"No, she's in a meeting with the Sector Ten overseer." Emeline tilted her head to the side. "Is there something I can help you with?"

Mae looked around nervously. The street wasn't a good place to discuss this, yet inside was rife with recording devices. "I wouldn't want to intrude..."

"Nonsense, come in."

"Thank you. I wouldn't usually turn up unannounced, but this is unfortunately extremely time-sensitive."

"Of course." Emeline stepped aside to let her enter and locked the door behind them. The sound of the deadbolt sliding into place made the hair on Mae's arms stand up. Something didn't feel right, but she'd promised Bailey that she would at least try to get the girl out of the Capital. Fake

General Fineglass sure as hell wouldn't have an opportunity with her shiny new armed personal protection.

"I'm sure you've heard about the lockdown at the Armory by now?" Mae asked.

"No! What happened?"

"Nothing much, to be honest, but the press is going to have a field day. I did what I could to mitigate the damage caused, but I rushed over here to discuss strategies with your mother. I'm sure she doesn't want more stories being printed about abduction attempts. In fact, I'm sure she doesn't want much attention on the Armory at all."

Emeline eyed her suspiciously. "Why do you say that?"

"I'm sure that she has her reasons, most of which involve keeping proprietary information away from rebels and pirates. It's my understanding that she's had problems with them in the past, especially in Skelm."

"Skelm."

"Yes."

"She should be home soon, if you'd like to wait in the sitting room."

"I don't mind relaying information through you. You're loyal to the Coalition, after all, aren't you?"

"Of course I am."

"Yes, of course, of course. So as I'm sure she's a very busy woman, I'm more than happy to let you pass on the information. Shall we sit?" Mae gestured at the chairs near the fire, desperate to get off her feet, even though she knew getting up would be even harder.

"Sure. Ms. Machenet—"

"You can call me Mae."

Emeline's mouth twitched downward in a split-second frown. "Mae. With all due respect, ma'am, I don't appreciate you casting aspersions at Skelm. Yes, there have been some problems in the past, but rest assured, that has all been handled now."

"Oh no, I would never! I certainly wouldn't mean any offense, and I understand your affection for the place. Wherever you grow up, come of age... it never really leaves you."

"No, it doesn't."

"Do you miss it?"

Something like surprise flashed across Emeline's face, as though it was something she hadn't even considered before. "Sometimes, yes."

"Would you..." Mae trailed off. She had to be very careful, now, as though she was stepping on shards of glass. "Would you ever go back there, if you could?"

"I suppose if a diplomatic envoy was needed, I might put my name forward. But make no mistake, Ms. Machenet, my home now is with my mother, wherever she is needed."

"Hmm."

"I know it might surprise someone like you, who was raised inside a bubble of beautiful opulence, but sometimes, the place we grew up isn't a healthy place to return to."

"I understand more than you might think."

Emeline scoffed and poured a cup of tea from a tall tea pot, emblazoned with the Coalition crest. "I'm sure you had a very challenging childhood."

The tea swirled dangerously in the cup, with a few stray leaves sticking to the sides, marring the pure white porcelain. Mae bit back the sharp reply she wanted to shoot back, that a girl so new to the Capital had no idea what she'd been through, and instead stirred a splash of milk into her tea. "It had its moments, that much is true."

"I don't understand people like you."

"What do you mean?"

"You were raised with every advantage, yet you enjoy being the center of a scandal, of upending social norms and... manners. For what? What does that achieve?"

Mae sipped at the weak tea. "Plenty."

"Not from my perspective."

"Perspectives are narrow and carry many lies and falsehoods. Emeline, what would you have done, in my position? Caught with a general, married, monogamous."

"Ms. Allemande, if you please, and I wouldn't have put myself into that

235

position to begin with. It was reckless and foolhardy, and caused your parents a mountain of embarrassment."

"Okay, Ms. Allemande, I suppose that is a fair answer."

"And another thing - what were you doing at the Armory today, anyway? I hardly think a washed-up fashion designer had any justified cause to be there." Emeline stirred her own tea and pressed the cup to her lips. "You were there with the general, weren't you?"

"Yes." No point in lying at this point, at least, not about that.

"You see? That's precisely what I don't understand."

That last word, understand, had the slightest hint of a twang that had no doubt been conditioned out of her by speech coaches. They'd probably descended on her the moment she left Skelm.

"What don't you understand?" Mae probed.

"Why you wouldn't try to stay out of the limelight. Keep a low profile, so your face stays out of the papers. Make things easier for your parents."

Mae laughed and sipped her tea. It had a strange aftertaste. "Why should I? They never made things easy for me. They still don't." The clock on the wall sliced away at the time she had left with every unforgiving pulse of the hands. She didn't have much time. She had to cut to the quick of it. "Do you ever miss your family?"

"She's only been gone a few hours."

"No, your old family. Back in Skelm."

Emeline turned her face away. "No."

"No?"

"This is highly inappropriate. Do you enjoy making people feel uncomfortable?"

"I don't mean to make you uncomfortable." She sipped at the tea and set it down on the table next to the chair. Years of living in Bradach, with hundreds of teas from all over the Near Systems, had spoiled her for taste. "I'm just a curious person. I like to analyze how people's minds work. See what makes them tick." It was obvious the girl missed her mother and sisters. Who wouldn't, after being wrenched away from them?

"Ms. Machenet, my birth mother did not provide for me. My father left us when I was very young. We lived four in one room. It was a wasteful, hard existence." She waved her arm at the velvet curtains draped against the windows, the golden tassels dragging on the rug. "Now, I am able to reach for things that were impossible before. I have food in my stomach, stockings without holes in them, access to a real education. I don't expect someone who has lived in the lap of luxury her whole life to understand that."

"I haven't always—" Mae stopped herself. Gods, she'd almost blown her cover. What was wrong with her? She cleared her throat. "What I mean to say is that no, I don't understand how challenging it must be to struggle and scrape, especially as a young girl. But similarly, I still hold a great deal of affection for people in my life, even if I can't be near them anymore." She picked up the tea and sipped it, despite the odd taste. "Even if it's too dangerous to see them."

"Dangerous?"

"Yes, you know. Prohibited."

"Who are you prohibited from seeing?"

"My friends back home." Why had she said that? She was supposed to be convincing Emeline to leave with her, not reminiscing. "Well, no, not prohibited. It's just difficult. A strenuous situation."

"Ms. Machenet, why are you here?"

Mae's thoughts began to cloud over. She shook her head to clear her mind. "To ask you to come with me."

"Where?"

"To see your family." She looked down at the teacup and blinked. Shit. "You put truth serum in my tea."

"I did."

"Why?"

Emeline tilted her head gently. "I wanted to know what you were hiding. And now I know."

"And?" Mae pressed her lips together tightly. Under the effects of the serum, she might say anything. She had to leave - but needed Emeline to answer first.

"I'm not going to go with you. Where are you even going?"

"Brada—NO!" she shouted. "No! No!" It was the only thing she could say that wasn't incriminating. She stood to leave, the pain in her feet bringing a piercing, fleeting focus. "I could take you away from here, Emeline. You don't need her. Your family is desperate to have you back."

"Tell them that they failed me. Tell them I will rise above my station, and it's thanks to Overseer Allemande." She paused, smoothing her skirts. "My mother."

Mae stumbled towards the door, her head swimming. Fucking truth serum, bastard invention. "Bailey wanted to save you, but it's clear you're past saving. They've brainwashed you!"

Emeline's brow furrowed in confusion. "Who is Bailey?"

"No!" Mae shouted again, unlocking the deadbolt and tumbling out into the street. Despite the blood in her boot, she ran. It was all falling apart.

Chapter 25

Bailey sat on her frustratingly plush bed, staring out into the darkness through the barred window. Be ready for what? Johnson was stationed outside her door, and given the amount of coffee he was drinking as she ate dinner, he wasn't going to fall asleep on the job.

The camera in the corner of her room gently cranked left and right, recording everything there was to see, which wasn't much. With all this surveillance, purportedly for her protection, she had no way of talking to Davey about getting to the shuttle in the morning, or what time they'd be sneaking out - at least, she assumed they'd be sneaking out. How, though, remained a mystery. Be ready, sure. A useless warning without any damned context. For all she knew, the message had been meant for Davey. It would make sense, given how The Scattered usually operated, with high-level espionage and crap like dissolving messages in noodles, or heat-revealed ink. Lots of tech that still hadn't achieved their goals.

Seconds ticked by like hours. Everything takes longer when you're waiting. She reached under her bed for her bag for the hundredth time. There wasn't much in there, but she'd kept the dress suit. So much effort had gone into making it, there was no way she was going to leave it here for grubby Coalition hands. What she'd do with it once she was off Gamma-3, she didn't know. Not many occasions to dress nice as a rum-runner, and even fewer to wear a Coalition general's uniform. Still, the thought of all Mae's hard work going unappreciated was heartbreaking.

A rap on the door jerked her from her daydream. "Yes?"

"Just checking on you, ma'am," came Johnson's perennially irritating baritone. Gravelly and thick and perpetually present. "There have been some reports of disturbances across the city tonight."

"Disturbances?"

"Nothing serious, don't worry. Just wanted to be sure you were still in there."

"There are bars on the windows, Johnson. I don't think it's possible for me to leave this room without your knowledge."

"It's my job to keep you safe, General."

"This level of protection certainly feels... superfluous, given the challenges I face at the Outer Rim." Maybe she could persuade him that his efforts were better off spent elsewhere. "Out there, it's life and death."

"With respect, your time here in the Capital could also be life and death, if the wrong people got their hands on you."

She'd willingly leap into the arms of any attackers, if it meant getting the hell out of there. "I can fend for myself, I assure you."

"Just the same, I will be here."

"You have to sleep sometime," she said hopefully. "I should think they aren't keeping you on duty past the recommended limits."

"I am specially trained."

"Surely you'll have a replacement in the morning?"

"No."

She sighed, but softly, so he wouldn't hear her frustration through the door. "Have you checked on my assistant? I was told that you would be ensuring his safety as well."

"You are my priority, General. He's only down the hall, and it's a dead end. No one will get past me, I can assure you of that."

"I'd like to take a walk around the hotel grounds. I can't sleep, and sometimes a bit of fresh air helps."

"I'm afraid I can't allow that, not with the reports I am hearing."

"I thought you said it wasn't anything serious?"

"It's not."

"Then why can't I get some air?"

The sound of wooden chair legs against polished marble whooshed under the door. "It's far too dangerous."

"I'm not a prisoner!" She pounded her fist against the door only once. "I can't imagine any other general of my rank being treated in this manner, it's outrageous. I only want a walk on the grounds, not to go looking for trouble. I've fought off more rebels and pirates than you can imagine."

"Of course, General, but I think we should play it safe."

A slip of paper fluttered down out of the vent that sat high on the wall. Another message? A warning? No, it was from Davey. She'd recognize his handwriting anywhere.

Contact at docks confirmed:
She's here

Her stomach leapt into her throat and then tumbled back down. They only had a few minutes, maybe an hour, if no one called ahead to the hotel. She heaved and brought up her dinner, splashing into the wastebasket beneath the desk.

"Ma'am? Everything alright?"

"I, uh... yes, Johnson, I'm fine. Just a little under the weather, perhaps dinner didn't agree with me."

"Too rich," he agreed. "Inefficient. Do you need anything? I can call the front desk if—"

"The only thing I need is some fresh air."

He shifted his stance, his boots whispering across the floor. "General, ma'am, I cannot allow it. I do apologize and please know that I do respect you and your work greatly. I've always been an admirer of yours, ever since training camp. But I can't condone you eschewing security protocols for a leisurely walk in the gardens."

Her pulse raced, pounding blood through her veins so fervent, and so insistent, that her vision began to fray at the edges. She had to get out of here, or they'd both end up dead. She had to get to Mae, had to tell her. Maybe they could all hide at the docks until morning. No, that would never work, it's the first place they'd block off once they were aware she was a fraud. Maybe the shuttle could leave sooner.

Or maybe this was all pointless, naïve hope, and their imprisonment was inevitable.

She moved across the room to stand beneath the camera. There was no way she'd get out of here with it trained on her every move, but yanking it out of the wall would alert the hotel's entire security team, not to mention Johnson, who would definitely hear it being torn from the support beam it was probably wired into. Her eyes fixed on it, she memorized its trajectory. If she could just alter the angle about fifteen degrees, she would hopefully evade detection, at least for long enough to get out.

"Ma'am?"

"Yes, Johnson, fine. I understand. I'm going to try to get some sleep. Big day tomorrow."

"Yes, ma'am."

"I'm going to have a bath first." The running water would muffle her movements. He didn't respond, and it was just as well. She didn't need any distractions. The brass handle of the tub was cold in her palm as she yanked it to the side, but soon warmed as hot water began to gush from the tap. There was no surveillance in the bathroom, but no windows or vents, either. A tiled prison.

She pushed gently at the large silver gear beneath the camera that rotated back and forth. It made an angry grinding noise, so she released it. She needed a lever, or something, and was regretting not going on that engineering course when she was Emeline's age.

Shit. Emeline. How were they going to get her off-world now?

Hastily, she eased the buckle of her belt under the gear. It lifted the camera just slightly higher, without impeding the rotation. Now, the bottom half of the window was out of reach of the camera, as was most of the floor. She strolled back into the bathroom and then crawled to the window. As far as the camera could see, she was still in the bathroom, and as far as Johnson knew, she was taking a bath. The bars were black and iron, the same as the ones that held her in the cell at the Armory. Typical.

There were no visible screws to tamper with, nor any emergency release levers. If the hotel caught on fire, would they let her burn to preserve their protocols? A distressing thought, though likely accurate. She tugged at the bars, but unsurprisingly, they didn't budge. They wouldn't go through the trouble of hiding screws just to make them easy to rip from the window. She pulled harder now, bracing her feet against the wall, biting back the soft grunt of exertion that emitted from her throat. Still, they remained in place.

Shit. What now? She didn't have a plan. She hadn't thought she would need one, at least not one like this. Panic continued to build, but her mind stayed clear. She wasn't about to make the same mistake as she had before. She was going to get out of there, and she would be damned if she left anyone behind. Not again. This was her only shot at redemption, her chance to make up for watching as her people got rounded up by Coalition thugs on Hjarta.

Leaning back, she heaved with all her might, biting her tongue to keep from shouting from the effort. The bar moved, if almost imperceptibly. It wasn't enough to become wobbly, so she pulled again, her face scrunched with concentration. It was life or death, do or die. There was no time for hesitation, no room for mistakes.

There was a crunching sound from deep within the wall, like steel grinding against iron. She coughed loudly to mask it, in case the running bathwater wasn't enough. Finally convinced that Johnson hadn't heard, she got into position again, the soles of her boots scuffing the delicate white paint on the wall. Engaging every muscle she had, she pulled, aware that once the bars were off, she'd have to make a run for it - the camera would notice the top half of the bars disappearing. Adrenaline dumped into her veins, quickening her pulse.

The bar pried loose, coming free from the wall with a deep scrape. She needed to pry one more off before she'd be able to fit through the window. It was a damn good thing that her room was on the ground floor, because she didn't relish the idea of leaping from several stories up. Scooting over, she wrapped her callused hands around the next bar and pulled, applying constant, even force, until she heard the internal supports snap. Two other bars fell to the floor with a deafening clatter.

"General?" Johnson shouted from the hall.

"I'm fine, just knocked over the table," she shouted back, her voice strained with panic. "Don't come in, I'm in the bath!"

Bailey heaved herself to her feet, preparing to kick the window out. She landed the toe of her steel-tipped boot in the center, and the cracks spider-webbed across the glass, implying her desperate freedom. Her boot connected with the glass again, this time shattering it.

"General, I'm coming in!"

There was no point in responding anymore. She thrust her legs over the windowsill, pressing her hands against the exterior brick to get herself out, the glass embedding itself in her skin. Scanning the grounds of the hotel, she searched for somewhere to run to, somewhere she could hide until morning. Where the hell was Davey? She dropped to the ground, wiping her bloody hands on the knees of her uniform, preparing to run.

"As I suspected!" Overseer Allemande said triumphantly, rounding the corner with three guards... and Davey.

"Davey! They got you too?"

"No one got me," he replied coolly.

She stared. "You're a double agent?"

He shrugged. "I go where the pay is best. You were foolish to trust me."

"I never trusted you," she spat.

"We've known for quite some time that you weren't who you said you were," Allemande interjected. "Arrest her, officers. She has to answer for her crimes against the state."

"You fucking rat!" Bailey hissed at Davey. "Does your superior know what you're up to?"

"If you mean the scum-sucking Scattered agent, then, no, and it's going to stay that way." He laughed, brushing off his shoulders with a nonchalant, pithy gesture. "It's not as though you're going to have the opportunity to pass that message on."

The damned snake! A turncoat, she should have known! He stood there with his smug smirk, watching the officers snap handcuffs around her wrists. She wanted to snap the chains that bound her and punch that smile right off his face. Several officers, their faces hidden beneath helmets, shoved her into the waiting steamtruck, clipping her cuffs to the iron chain in the bed.

Forced onto her knees, the hard metal of the steamtruck bit into her skin through the thick fabric of the uniform.

"Don't move, unless you want to get tossed around in here like a rag doll," one of them said, climbing in after her and sitting on the bench near the cab of the truck, strapping in. He knocked on the glass, signaling that the steamtruck was ready for transport.

The heavy iron cuffs rubbed against her wrists, the lock woefully impenetrable, not with her piss-poor lock pick skills. Gods, this was it. This was how it all ended for her, with her people still imprisoned or chained up in toxic waste cleanup sites. With Ned alone on the shuttle tomorrow, if they didn't already find him and lock him up, too. With Mae facing the same charges. Mae, who wasn't even supposed to be here, and shouldn't have offered her help. Bailey should have told her that people who get close, get hurt. She never should have begged for help. It was another paragraph in the book of her failures. A book that was going to end several chapters too short.

She pulled gently at the chain, testing it.

"I said, don't move," the guard said, pointing a revolver.

Bailey sat back on her haunches, defeated. Outflanked. She should have known. Should have seen, or thought even once that it had been too easy to pull this off. She was a silly, empty-headed fool, and now she was going to pay for it with her life and with Mae's, too. Poor, beautiful, talented Mae. She deserved better than a fate like this one. She deserved to go home to Bradach, sew beautiful things, meet a beautiful woman, and have a beautiful, rebellious life. Instead, she'd die in a public execution, a warning to other children of rich families not to overstep, and it was all Bailey's fault.

She wanted to melt through the truck, seep into the asphalt, and dissipate into the earth. She wasn't even good enough to be food for the worms. An utter, destructive, disappointing failure. The shame of it might kill her before the Coalition did.

A sob caught in her throat, and she pressed her palms to her forehead, the sharp edges of the cuffs gnawing into her cheeks. Tears leaked from her eyes, huge, fat globs of water that soaked the collar of her shirt and the cuffs of her shirt by the time the steamtruck came to a stop in front of the Judicature. The same place they'd sprung Ned from would be the last four walls she ever saw.

When she was young, she would dream of running her own farm someday, her hands in the earth, waking up at the crack of dawn to turn the mirrors toward the greenhouses, making coffee for a wife who'd meet her in the barn. She dreamed that one day, when she was old and grey, she would die sitting in her favorite chair, proud of how she'd lived, grateful for the loves she'd had. Instead, she'd get murdered by a government she'd not even been born into. Marshall would probably drink himself to death with guilt.

"Let's go, inmate," the guard said, unclipping her from the steamtruck and shoving her backwards. "They're waiting for you."

"Wait, don't I get an advocate, or something?"

"Not for treasonous fucks like you," he whispered malignantly. "You'll be lucky if you see the light of day again."

She never had been lucky, not with coincidences, or gambling, cards, or love. Her fate was awaiting her beyond the harsh facade of the building, all angles and iron and glass. It looked so much more threatening in the fading sunlight.

The guards pushed and dragged her along through the huge doors at the rear of the building, the hinges now caged and reinforced. Why not take her through the front, where she would be humiliated, as well? She could only hope and pray to long-dead gods that Mae would hear of her arrest before they tried to take her, too. The only thing she wanted was Mae and Ned on the first shuttle out of the docks, headed for somewhere safer than the snake pit of the Capital.

"State your name for the record," Overseer Allemande said, presiding over the small room, speaking from the slightly elevated podium.

"General Fineglass," Bailey responded.

"We know that isn't true, now, don't we? State your name."

"Bernadette Smith."

"Your *real* name, if you please."

"How do you know that's not my real name?"

"Don't try my patience. You are wasting time and costing our glorious empire credits every moment your lousy, treasonous self stands there. State. Your name."

Bailey lifted her chin in defiance. "Bernadette Smith." No way was she giving these assholes even a crumb of information that could land anyone else in one of their filthy prisons. "Is my real name."

"Fine. Why are you here, Ms. Smith?"

"To infiltrate the inner sanctum of Coalition operations in order to bring it down."

The overseer twirled a silver fountain pen through her long, spindly fingers. "Who are you working for? The Scattered?"

"Obviously not," she spat, glaring at Davey. If she ever got out of here, she'd kill him herself. A skinny waif like him would be easy pickings. "I work alone."

"You are being accused of sedition in the highest degree, of which the minimum punishment is life in a work camp. The maximum punishment is carried out by public execution, after several bouts with inspectors. With that in mind, and considering we will be kind and lenient if you confess and act accordingly, how do you plead?"

"Not guilty."

Allemande bristled. "Excuse me?"

"Not. Guilty. Firstly, you can't prove that I'm not General Fineglass, and second, the Coalition tenets—"

"You are startlingly incorrect on the first count, Ms. Smith." Allemande gestured for one of the guards. "Scan her."

The guard reached for Bailey's arm, but she wrenched it away. "How dare you treat me like this! After all, we agreed upon..." she trailed off, grasping for more of a threat. "What would the newspapers think, if they knew you had struck a deal with a filthy rat?"

"This is a closed session, Ms. Smith, as is customary in proceedings like these. I think you will find that threatening me with blackmail is a dangerous route to travel."

"Ouch!" Bailey shouted as the guard snatched at her arm again, pulling it away from her side. He scanned her, and it beeped agreeably.

"It says Officer Jones," he announced, puzzled. "But that doesn't make any sense."

"It means she's not as good at spycraft as she thinks she is," the overseer explained. "She's no different from any other traitor we see in these courts."

Chapter 26

Mae stumbled through the door of her parents' house, long after polite supper hours. Everything was so damn fuzzy, her memories all pooled into gelatinous soup. It had taken her hours to walk home. She'd lost count of the little side streets she'd wandered down, trying to find her way back to the cafe. She needed Amy's help. The last place she wanted to be was in range of her father, especially now, yet it was the only route she could recall.

"Gods above, Maevestra! Where the hell have you been? Your father has been raging all evening—" her mother stopped when Mae slumped against the banister that led upstairs. "Where are your boots?"

"I dunno," Mae slurred. They could be anywhere across the city by now. Her feet were raw, her stockings soaked in blood.

"Were you attacked? Gerard, come quickly! Maevestra was robbed!" Her mother propped her up and led her to the overstuffed chair in the sitting room. "Sit here, darling girl. I'll make you a cup of tea. We should get stories straight before we contact the authorities."

"Wasn't... mugged."

"You look like you've been wandering the streets for hours! You poor thing, I always knew that this would be too much to entrust you with, I knew something like this would happen, I—Gerard! I told you this would happen! You never listen to me, you just—"

"She's been dosed with truth serum," her father said, leaning casually against the door frame in his velvet smoking jacket.

"Maevestra, is this true?"

She wanted to shake her head, to deny it, but found herself nodding, instead. "Yes." The truth slid out of her mouth like a regurgitated slug.

"Who?" he asked simply, swirling his glass of brandy, unconcerned.

Mae bit her tongue to keep from blurting the truth. "Piss off!" she shouted instead.

"I'm only trying to help. I've seen more than one up-jumped upstart in my day, hot shots like you who thought they knew everything there was to know." He sipped at his glass. "Who?"

"I'm not telling you anything," she mumbled, her eyes locked on her bloody, torn stockings. She didn't even have a spare pair, gods be damned, not after the other pair got nicked breaking Ned out of prison. No. Mustn't think about anything incriminating, lest it slither from her lips.

"Please, dear, he's just trying to sort things. I don't think you understand the kind of situation we are in here, how dangerous—"

"I never wanted to come back here. I'd hoped I'd never see you or hear from you again. Snakes, the both of you, dragging me back here under false pretenses, blackmailing your own daughter, what kind of monsters—"

"Stay focused, please, Maevestra," her father said coolly. "What's done is done. Who dosed you with truth serum?"

"What kind of monsters put their own needs over those of their children?"

Her mother sniffled, turning her face away. "Do you have any idea what we sacrificed for you? The opportunities we turned down in order to be here for you, to provide you a stable life?"

"I never fucking asked for any of it!"

"Gladys, perhaps you should leave me and our daughter to discuss things. This is unlikely to go smoothly, and I'd hate to see you wounded by her careless and inconsiderate remarks."

"I'll make tea," her mother said icily, marching from the room with a frosty purpose.

"Maevestra, you need to tell me who did this, and what you told them. We can't be caught unawares, and if what I fear is true, then we may already have the authorities bearing down on us." He sipped again. "Or, rather, you. I hope you realize I'm not going to let *us* go down for *your* sins."

"I knew I shouldn't have come here," Mae spat, standing, wobbly, to her feet. "I just need a change of clothes, and I'll be gone."

He pushed her back down into the chair. "No, you're going to tell me who gave you that truth serum. I've had enough of your games."

"Leave me alone!" She shook her head violently, willing the serum to wear off faster. She was so tired. If only he would leave her be, she could sleep all night curled up in the chair.

"Who gave you that serum?" he asked, more gently this time. "Who was it, Maevestra? Who gave you the serum?"

Her tongue was thick and clumsy in her mouth. "I don't want to talk to you."

"Yes, you've made that much very clear, but you need to tell me who gave it to you."

"No," she tried to say, but it came out more like a muffled groan.

"Was it Winter? Marcus Winter?"

She kept her eyes trained on her feet, determined not to tell him anything.

"No, not him. Was it General Fineglass?" When she still didn't move, he crouched down next to her and set the now-empty glass on the side table. "The general's assistant, perhaps?"

Did he know? Had he known about Bailey and Davey all along? Was this all some monumental joke to him? "No."

"How about Allemande, then?"

Involuntarily, her eyes flicked up at him before she regained control and looked back down, counting every laddered hole in her stockings. There were fourteen that she could see. Ruined. No way she could mend them.

"Ah. Overseer Allemande, then. Not to be smug, dear daughter, but you should have expected that from her. She has already proved herself to be duplicitous, and it's only a matter of time before she finds another route to the outcome she desires."

"It wasn't the fucking overseer, it was her damned daughter," Mae huffed, and then clapped a hand over her mouth.

"You were outsmarted by a girl?" he said, chuckling, the laugh laced with a menacing undertone. "You, a Machenet, were bamboozled by a GIRL?" He was shouting now. "I knew you were stupid and arrogant, Maevestra, but I thought you were at least better than this!"

She needed to get this crap out of her system, and fast. Being at his mercy was worse than wandering the streets without her boots. "I want a coffee."

"I bet you do! You're a mess! Gladys! Make our daughter a coffee, and she'll need some new stockings!" He leaned in so close that she could smell the brandy on his breath. "You're a disgrace, but you're still my daughter. I'm going to get us out of this mess you've made, but you have to tell me everything."

"Why should I?"

"Because clearly, you are not up to this task."

"I told you, my sister would have been far better at this. Why you didn't ask her to bail you out, I'll never know."

"Your *sister* cut us off eighteen months ago. She said we were a liability. Can you believe that? After everything we'd done to get her into that position in the first place. Ungrateful little monster."

Mae barked a laugh in spite of her situation. "Gods, I never thought I'd see the day. Hell, maybe she and I will finally have something in common the next time I see her." She leaned forward in her chair. "You lied about everything," she whispered. "Does Mother know?"

"She knows everything. She's never been shy about getting down in the mud to maintain the lifestyle she's grown accustomed to."

"Does she know that you lied about Bradach?"

He jerked backward, searching her face. "What do you mean, lied?"

"You don't have the first clue where it is, Old Man. You really should pay your informants more."

"You think you can trust them? You don't know the half of it. I wasn't paying them, I was offering, as a kind gesture, to keep Amy's name off the desk of the investigator for subterfuge in the Capital. But hey, now that she's let it slip that I asked her for a favor, I guess I don't have to hold up my end of the bargain."

"Don't you dare."

"You don't hold all the cards, Maevestra, none of us do, but rest assured I hold more than you. You're going to tell me exactly what happened, what was said, or she'll be in a cell by Monday morning."

"You really are a bastard, aren't you?"

He smirked. "One has to be, to prosper in a place like this. You had good instincts. I could have taught you everything I know, if you hadn't left. Perhaps then you wouldn't have been outsmarted by an orphan playing house with a power-hungry inspector."

"She's not an orphan," Mae spat. "She was stolen from her family." She hadn't meant to say it, but the serum was like being far too drunk, when your head swims and words come up like vomit, unprompted and unwanted.

"And how do you know that?"

"None of your beeswax."

"I'll find out eventually, you might as well tell me."

"Piss. Off."

He sighed. "I'm only trying to help you. Without me, you're as good as dead, and you know it. Everyone under this roof knows it. Hell, half the city knows it after your little stunt that ended up with you on the front page. Be careful, I said, lie low. But no, you had to make sure that everyone knew you were back in town. Questions, questions, questions, always with the probing demands from reporters wanting to know where you'd been, why you left ten years ago."

"And did you tell them why I left? That I felt filthy after agreeing to clothe the monsters that were hunting down our friends?"

"Those people were dangerous. I couldn't let all of us get dragged down with them, you know that."

"Cowardly. *Selfish*," she hissed. "I left because I was ashamed to be part of this family."

"Have you ever considered that we are ashamed of *you*?"

Mae smiled. "I never had to consider it, trust me, it was made clear at the earliest opportunity."

"Gallivanting around with thieves. Pirates! My daughter! And why, so you could have the splendor of living without any responsibilities? And you say that I'm the selfish one?"

"Thieves are more honest than you've ever been. Scheming, undermining, it's always the same with you. Removing the knife from one back, just to plunge it into another. Aren't you tired? Wouldn't you rather take up, I don't know, gardening? Aren't you getting too old for this, Old Man?"

"I never did have a green thumb. I'm much better at this, as it turns out."

Mae snorted. "Yes, so good at it that you've ended up broke and scared, so desperate that you had to call back your wayward daughter and blackmail her into doing your work for you, because you're too old and incapable to do it yourself!"

His face began to redden with rage. "I've tried being reasonable with you, but you've left me no choice!"

"What are you going to do, throw me out? Again? Don't trouble yourself, Father, I will show myself to the door."

"Don't you dare," he spat, "even think about going out that door. If you step over that threshold, there's no coming back. I won't help you out of this." She stood and slid across the tile to the door. Even under the effects of the serum, she was faster than him. He lumbered. "I'll turn her in," he finished with a sinister hiss.

Mae hesitated, her hand poised over the door knob.

There was a sharp rap from the other side, and she jumped back. "Who's there?"

"The authorities."

"Mother, I thought you were going to wait to call—" she shouted over her shoulder.

"We're here to arrest Maevestra Machenet for crimes against the state. Open up, or we'll tear the door down!"

"Gods, there's no need for that," she said, opening the door. "I'm right here."

"You're under—"

She held her wrists out. "Yes, yes, I heard you the first time."

"You can't just come in here without the proper paperwork!" her father yelled, pushing past her onto the steps.

"It's right here, sir, with the Judge's signature. Move, or we'll arrest you, too, for aiding and abetting."

Mae's father took her hands. "Don't worry, Maevestra, we'll get you out of this."

"I doubt that."

"I love you."

She looked into his cold, unfeeling eyes and laughed. "You've never loved me. You just love the idea of me."

* * *

The ride to the Judicature was built of an uneasy silence between Mae and the guards who had arrested her. Her head, still fuzzy, was at least beginning to clear around the edges. She hadn't left of her own free will, surely that meant he wouldn't turn Amy in. He couldn't. Except she knew the rat bastard well, and he'd continue to use it as leverage. How had she started off life so unlucky as to be born to such filthy, unabashed liars? It was like they enjoyed rolling around in society's excrement. The torrid affairs, the backroom dealings, other people looked away, but not the Machenets. They reveled in it.

"We're here, inmate, time to face the music."

"I have no idea what this is about, but I want it noted for the record that I am being entirely compliant."

"We'll note everything, don't you worry," the guard answered sarcastically. "The tribunal is already in progress."

"How can they start without the star of the show?"

"Seems you have a co-star."

Bailey. Shit. Was it because she'd blurted her name out at the Allemandes, or had something else happened? Guilt gnawed at the back of her throat, the spicy acid of bile settling there. She should have known that little jerk was capable of subterfuge. Hardly a misplaced child, now fully brainwashed by the overseer. Or would it be Amy, having been turned in by her father already to win some more favor with the high-ranking officials?

"Oh, excellent, I love a good co-star." She meant to sound pithy and unconcerned, but when the words tumbled from her mouth, they were laden with a distinct air of worry.

The guard pulled her from the steamcar by the chain links that held her wrists together, the iron digging into her skin. "They're waiting for you, let's go," he said gruffly.

The Judicature's revolving doors were crisply shined, the green glass reflecting the yellow light of the street lamps so late at night. The foyer was empty, and the guards' footsteps echoed across the polished marble. Mae stumbled along, still without boots. The blisters at her heels throbbed, and she yearned for her home, where she would slide her aching feet into some soft slippers, drape a silk dressing gown around her shoulders, and curl up on the sofa with a good book. Never again, now.

She'd never wanted to come back to Gamma-3 in the first place, but she held her chin up high, proud. Even if they executed her, she'd die knowing she'd deepened the growing stain on her family's name. Good. They deserved every snide remark and whisper they'd get for the rest of their lives.

"Maevestra Machenet, you are being charged for the crime of treason against the state."

Barely through the door into the room, and already they were ready to throw her into a cell to wait to die.

"How do you plead?"

"Not guilty." Where was this co-defendant? There was no one in the room except the overseer and the guards who had dragged her in. And where were the others? "If you can give me some clue as to detailed charges, I might be able to be of more assistance."

"You aided and abetted known criminal, Bernadette Smith."

Mae burst out laughing. "I'm sorry, who? I've never heard that name in all my life." Was she here for trying to take Emeline away, or not?

"Don't play coy with me, Ms. Machenet," Overseer Allemande said in a dangerous tone. "She told us everything."

"I would love to shed light on the situation, but I am being honest, I do not know that name."

"Need I remind you that lying on the stand carries a further punishment?"

"Overseer, you all but dragged me out of bed in the middle of the night. You know my reputation and that of my family. I am more than happy to cooperate, but without a little more context, I have to admit that I am feeling rather lost."

Allemande's hand rested on the polished gavel on the bench. "If you tell us everything, then we might be able to come to an agreement."

"Everything?"

"Yes, everything."

"I had jam on toast for breakfast—"

"Don't toy with me, Ms. Machenet."

Mae rattled her iron cuffs. "If you haven't noticed, ma'am, you already have me in custody. I have nothing to gain from obfuscating the process, only more to lose, so please, enlighten me on what kind of information you are after, and I will, to the best of my ability, help you."

"Why did you come back to Gamma-3?"

Throw her parents under the bus, or wait this out, hope that her father did still have some semblance of a career left? No. He had nothing, not even her sister. "My parents summoned me."

"They *summoned* you?"

"We have had somewhat of a difficult relationship throughout my adult life. I do not enjoy the Capital."

"Why?"

Mae held up her cuffs again. "Is that really not obvious, ma'am?"

"And what did they need from you?"

"They wanted me to take over the family business."

The overseer glanced through a file. "Finance."

"Yes."

"And what did you do, once settled back in our finest city?"

"I attended several functions at the behest of my father."

"And?"

"And to tell you the truth, Overseer, they were incredibly boring."

"When did you first come into contact with Bernadette Smith?"

Who the hell were they talking about? "I'm deeply sorry, but I don't know who that is."

"Do you take me for a fool, Ms. Machenet? You were photographed together on multiple occasions, landing you on the front page of the Capital Times."

Shit. Bailey had given them a fake name. Smart, but left her on the back foot. At least she knew more of the situation. She gasped noisily. "General Fineglass? But how?"

"I find it very unlikely that you didn't know she was an impostor."

"On my honor as a Machenet, I promise you, Overseer, I had no idea. An impostor!"

"There is no need for these theatrics. She already told us how you helped her in obtaining top secret information meant to undermine operations."

Mae didn't trust people easily, but she trusted Bailey, and there was no way she would sell her out. Not even if what people said about Allemande was true. She wouldn't. "What information would that be?"

"She had access to a wide range of proprietary, classified information."

"If you are referring to the Armory incident, I think you'll find that it was her assistant who triggered the alarm, not her. She was with Mr. Longfellow the entire time."

The overseer smirked. "Her assistant was working for us."

Davey, that damned shit. She should have smelled a rat. A double agent, that wouldn't impress higher ups in The Scattered, especially not Cassius Calvetti. He'd need a personal protection detail for the rest of his life. Even then, it was no guarantee he wouldn't wind up dead in a gutter. Good. He deserved it. "Why wouldn't a general's assistant work for you?"

"I'm not in the mood for these games. I'll give you one more chance to come clean before we toss you into a cell to rot until the Judge signs off on your punishment."

"Why are you here, Overseer? Instead of the Judge, I mean."

"She was feeling under the weather."

Still? Something was up with the Judge, but she didn't have time to worry about that now. "I can say, in earnest, I did not know that the general was an impostor." She buried her face in her hands and let out a few small sobs for show. "I thought she loved me."

"Some might say that apples do not fall far from their trees, but in this case, I would beg to differ. Your father must be ashamed."

Would the overseer be ashamed of Emeline, not telling her about their meeting? What was that girl playing at? Gods, she hated the Capital. If she made it out of this alive, she was never coming back, not for anything. Though that would leave the pesky problem of her parents. "My father has much to be ashamed of, that much is true." Like making deals with shits like Overseer Allemande. Like blackmail. Like skewing stories in the papers for his personal gain. And so on.

"Put her in lockup with the other one. Not in the same cell. Who knows what they've gotten up to in recent days. Tell Davey Klein that I need him to sign his official statement before we send it to the Judge to be notarized."

"Yes, ma'am," one of the guards said, adjusting the helmet that obscured his face. The new tactical uniforms were ugly and impractical, in Mae's opinion. All flash and no substance. Hell, she could see a few fiery locks of hair peeking out from under it. A terrible fit. "I'll toss her straight in there."

He grabbed Mae by the arm and pulled her through the far door. The cells that lay beyond were the same ones they'd sprung Ned from. She hoped he would make the shuttle in the morning, even if she and Bailey wouldn't. At least someone would get the hell off this planet.

"Mae! Gods, Mae, I'm so sorry, it's all my fault. I've told them you had nothing to do with this!" Bailey shouted from one of the cells. "Please, Mae, you have to believe me!"

The guard shoved her into the cell beside Bailey's and pulled the door closed with a horribly final clank. The last four walls she'd ever see, probably. At least she could almost see Bailey through the narrow slat in the wall.

"I believe you," she said, poking her finger through the hole.

"I'm sorry," Bailey repeated, pressing her finger to Mae's in the wall.

"No, I'm sorry, I should have known."

"Fucking rat."

"If we ever get out of here, I'll slap that stupid smirk right off his face."

Bailey sighed. "Not if I do it first."

"So, *Bernadette*, who would have guessed?"

"Not me, that's for sure."

"How did they nab you?"

"The rat told me that I was in for it, so I tried to run. Ripped the bars off my window just to land straight in Allemande's clutches." Bailey paused, and the silence was heavy with what was to come. "You know what they say about her."

"Yeah. I've heard."

"Maybe she doesn't take on those duties anymore, now that she's an overseer."

"We can only hope." Mae slumped down on the bed, if it could even be called that—a hard slab, covered in a thin, threadbare sheet. "Though I don't expect the other inspectors are much better in that area."

"Did you... you know... before you got pulled in?"

"Little shit drugged me."

"No," Bailey breathed. "Mae, I... gods, I—I'm so sorry. I caused this, I—"

"They don't know," Mae answered in a tiny whisper, covering her face with her hands so whoever was watching the camera in the corner couldn't read her lips. Hell, at least Ned had a cell without twenty-four-hour monitoring. "Be careful what you say in here."

"I didn't think she was capable of that."

"As it turns out, spending all your time in this snake pit will change you."

"It didn't change you."

"Oh, it did, just in different ways, I suppose."

"Do you think we'll get out of here?"

Mae buried her face in her hands. "I have to be honest with you, Bernadette, it's not looking good for either of us. That little weasel's witness account is enough to deliver both of us life sentences." She chewed the inside of her cheek to stem the flow of tears that threatened to wash down her cheeks. "If they don't kill us first."

"I told them it was all my fault. I said you didn't know any of it," Bailey whispered. "I said they should let you go."

"That's very sweet of you, but I don't see that happening. Allemande was

260

trying to get me to flip, saying you'd told them everything."

"I wouldn't—"

"Shh. I know. Of all the serpents slithering around in this gods-forsaken city, you're the only real person left, integrity untouched. Not many people can say that, least of all me."

"So... what now?"

"No idea. Got any cards up your sleeves?"

Bailey brought her face to the slat in the wall, peering through. "Despite the exquisite construction of my clothes, I do not have any hidden plans amid the fabric."

"Shame there's not a few lock picks sewn into the pockets." Her eyes flew open. "Bai—I mean, Bernadette. Check the left inside breast pocket."

"Why, *is* there a—"

"No, a straight pin. I always forget that one, especially when I'm in a rush, which I was. Don't pull it out, don't say anything, in case they're watching. We'll have to disable the bugs before we even try, but—"

"A straight pin is never going to work," one of the guards said from the other side of the door.

Fuck.

Chapter 27

Bailey knew they hadn't been careful enough. Still, it's not as though they had much more to lose. A few extra hours staring at the yellowed walls, feeling nothing but grief and guilt, and what kind of ending was that? She peered through the narrow hole in the wall that connected their cells. Mae had her back pressed to the wall, like she was trying to get as far away as possible from the door.

"Did you hear me? I said, a straight pin won't work. Not unless you're very practiced."

Mae leaned forward. "What?"

"Here." There was a metallic scraping sound, and something long and thin slid beneath Bailey's cell door. "One each."

Neither of them said anything. Was it a trap? Try to get them to escape, to have an excuse to shoot them on sight, and remove the need for a trial? It wouldn't be the most heinous thing she'd learned about Coalition operations. She'd heard most of it firsthand from Larkin.

"It's me," the guard whispered. "Cameras and recorders are off. Try to unlock the doors, but wait for our signal to leave."

"What?" Bailey hissed. She couldn't see the guard, so didn't know who 'me' even was.

"Don't open those doors once the locks are disengaged, or you'll blow this whole thing wide open. We need a little more time."

"*What?*" she repeated.

"Shh!"

Mae pressed her face to the other side of the slat. "It's Amy!"

"Shut up! Amy hissed. "I'll circle back after we get rid of the rest of them. Stay in your cells after you get those locks picked." The percussive clicks of her boots faded down the corridor.

"Oh my gods," Bailey breathed. Relief began to flood through her, but came to a firm halt at one thought. "I don't know how to pick a lock."

"What, did Larkin never teach you? She's always making people pick locks. Says it's an invaluable skill," Mae said.

"No, I... didn't spend that much time at the Purple Pig. Not lately, anyway."

"I'll talk you through it. It's going to be hard, doing it blind. Grab your pick."

Bailey bent and picked it up off the floor, turning the smooth metal over in her hands. It was iron, and the weight lay heavily across her palm. "I've got it."

"We have to stick our arms out the cell door slat."

"I don't think I'll fit."

"Hmm, you might be right. Okay, I'll start. Are you able to lift it off, like you did with Ned?"

"No, I don't have access to the hinges in here."

"Damn, of course you don't. Hold tight, Bai, I'm on my way."

"But Amy said—"

Mae poked her finger through. "Fuck what Amy said. I'm not leaving you here."

"Thank you." She pressed the tip of her finger to Mae's, and tried to blink back the tears gathering in her eyes. When was the last time someone had done something selfless to help her? She couldn't even recall. Years of feeling like she wasn't enough, covering it with muscled bravado.

"Right! Let's get this train moving, shall we?"

It was difficult to see Mae through the tiny hole, but the brick was pleasantly cold against Bailey's flushed cheeks, so she stayed, keeping watch over her as she worked, her arm shoved through the small window in her cell door.

"Bastard thing," Mae grumbled. "This is much harder from this angle."

"You can do it," Bailey said. "I believe in you."

"I can feel the tumblers in there. There are five. I've only ever done three at a time before."

"Think how much you can gloat at the Pig. You just have to get us out of here."

Mae's skirts rustled lightly against the brick floor. "I'll have Larkin make a new cocktail and name it after me."

"She'll have to, she won't have a choice!"

"One down."

"Only four more."

"I'm going to be quiet now, I need to concentrate."

Bailey nodded, despite the fact that Mae couldn't see her. Moving to the door, she tried to peer out, but could only see the guard of the month plaque that hung on the wall opposite. It hadn't been updated in at least half a year.

"Gods blasted thing, damn it all to hell!"

"What's wrong?"

"Lock pick broke."

"Here, take mine," Bailey said, thrusting hers through the slat.

"I'll have to start all over."

"It's okay, just take your time."

"You have a lot of faith in me, Stockton."

"Why wouldn't I? You've yet to let me down, and I know you'll pull through again. I can feel it." The words weren't even a lie, or an exaggeration. Mae's presence was like warm sunlight. She was the kind of person who made other people feel capable, like they were worth something, and that was a very rare thing.

"Here I go again."

Bailey almost held her breath, so as not to create any noise that might distract Mae. The halls were silent, except for the constant, gentle gurgle from the building's boilers, bubbling away in the basement. Every so often, a guard in the next corridor would sneeze. This time of night wasn't very active, heading into the wee hours of the morning. It would still be dark outside, and yet, the inescapable press of time laid itself across her chest.

The shuttle would be leaving soon, and if they weren't on it, they'd end up back in this cell before they knew it. Or dead.

What was Amy's plan? What were they even waiting for?

"Got it!" Mae whispered triumphantly, and the door eased open with a screech. "Gods, don't they ever oil hinges around here?"

"Be *careful*, Mae."

"I'll get you unlocked before you know it."

Mae swished out of her cell and crouched in front of Bailey's. The window was too high to see anything other than the train of her skirts and the shadow she cast across the floor. The sound of the lock pick in the deadbolt was like terrifying music to Bailey's ears. Terrifying because of the dangerous hope that accompanied it. The loss of hope could kill a person faster than any execution squad.

"Almost there, Bai."

"Mae!" The guard's shadow appeared in an instant, the baton raised high. "Watch out!" But it was too late. The baton came down hard across Mae's back, landing with a sickening crack and a small whimper before she crumpled in on herself.

"What have we got here, then? A couple of rats! Where did you get these lock picks from?"

"We smuggled them in," Bailey explained quickly, desperate to get out of the cell to protect Mae. "In our pockets."

"Horseshit. We check pockets."

"They didn't check ours, we came straight from the arraignment."

The guard twirled the baton by the braided strap at the end. "Either way, you two shits aren't going anywhere other than the execution desk. Judge just signed the papers. If you're lucky, they'll give you some of that moldy oatmeal for your breakfast first."

"Please, you don't understand—"

The guard snatched at Mae's arm, dragging her back into her cell. "I told them they should have put you fucks in the high security cells. But does anyone ever listen to me? No. No, they never listen to Miller."

"Don't hurt her!" Bailey cried, utterly, desperately powerless.

The guard smirked and covered the slat in the wall with the thin sheet from the bed. There was another whump, another whimper. Rage and despair bubbled up inside Bailey, and she ran at the door, crashing into it with all her might. It didn't budge, so she did it again, and this time, one of the hinges cracked.

"Hey, what are you doing in there?" Miller shouted.

She ran at the door again, squinting at the pain in her shoulder. It was probably dislocated, but she'd worry about that later.

"I said stop!" Miller yelled.

Once more, she thrust her weight into the door, and another hinge popped. It was enough. She kicked at the edge, focusing on where the pin was, two, three times. She was blinded by anger and desperation. She didn't care if they shot her dead, so long as it earned Mae a reprieve. The pin shot across the narrow corridor, and she pressed against the door, her boots digging into the unpainted brick.

"Piss off!" a thick brogue shouted, and a body fell to the floor. What the hell was happening? "Damned MPO bastards."

"Ned?"

"Aye, it's me, I'll just—bloody hell, Stocky, you nearly took the door off its hinges."

"I had to stop that guard."

"I dunno why I'm even here, you'd have managed it with one more blast." He unlocked the door, and it swung wildly, barely hanging on to the last hinge.

"My shoulder's out, grab my arm."

"But—"

"We don't have time to argue."

"...Aye. This will hurt." He held her arm, and she swiveled, the pain flashing before her eyes, intense and hot, before it subsided with the pop back into the socket.

"I'll take her. Where's Amy?"

"Gods only know. Let's hope she's making sure we can get the hell out of here."

"How many guards did you smack to get up here?"

"Only three, including that one. Stashed the other two in a broom closet and took their uniforms. I reckon we can just... leave this one here. Lock the door."

Bailey bent and scooped up Mae as gentle and gingerly as she could. "Are you alright?"

"It hurts."

"I know it hurts. We're going to get out of here, okay?"

Mae reached up, her eyes squeezed shut, and wrapped her arms around Bailey's neck. "The Dolly Rose, Bai. The ship is waiting for us."

"We need to move," Ned whispered. "I can hear them starting their shift swap."

"Head to the back stairs, the same way we got you out, I'll—"

The lights flickered and went out.

"That will be Amy. At least, we can only hope that it's her. Without the digital locks, we can waltz out the front door."

"We'd better get to dancing, then." With Mae safely cradled in her arms, Bailey aimed for the front stairwell. It was dark, too dark, and she couldn't see each step. "Ned, I need you. You have to go first. Do you have—"

"Of course I have a cane. Marina gave me this one. It's collapsible!"

"Neat."

He unfurled a long, black cane from a cylinder the size of a pen. "Let's roll." Using the cane to find each step, he led the way, with Bailey following close behind, focusing on her boots as Ned whispered "step, step, step" with every stair.

"The door's just ahead," Bailey uttered. There was a group of guards roaming from door to door, trying to keep the building secure until the generators kicked in. Seeing as they hadn't, she could only assume that Amy had disabled those, too.

Sunlight was creeping in through the windows, the warm glow of another morning, the insistent reminder of how much time they'd wasted in the cells. If they missed that shuttle, they were doomed.

"Follow my lead," Ned said, and threw a brick through the far window.

The guards dispersed from their tightly knit squads into chaos, running to investigate the shattered glass. In the relative darkness, the sun not yet over the horizon, they crept towards the open front door, and once they reached it, began to run.

"Don't wait for me," Ned said, hobbling painfully.

"Shut up, of course I'm waiting for you," Bailey replied. "We're stealing this steamcar. Get in."

"Who's driving?"

"I'll drive. Mae showed me a shortcut that circumvents the tunnel." Bailey laid Mae delicately on the back seat. "What about Amy?"

"I don't know where she is, I—"

"Hey! Wait for me!" Davey was sprinting across the green, his cravat loose and flapping in the wind.

"You!" Bailey roared. "I ought to kill you, you snake!"

"It was put on! You're out, aren't you? Did you think Amy pulled that off without any help?"

Ned held him at arm's length. "How do we know you're not lying?"

"He's not," Amy said, emerging from the bed of a steamtruck. "I don't agree with his methods, but we didn't exactly have time to argue."

"Why take the risk to save us?" Bailey asked, suspicious.

Davey pressed his hands together, as though he was praying. "We can talk about the details later. Please let's just get in the car."

"Davey, you're with me," Amy said, wrenching open the door of the steamtruck. She tossed her keys to Bailey. "Here are the keys, so you don't have to hot-wire it."

"I'd rather stay with them, in case..." he argued.

"We don't have time for this. Get in the steamtruck or I'm leaving you here. I still have to pick up Aran."

"You can't go get him, he's a civilian! You know the rules!"

Guards began to pour out of the front doors of the Judicature. "You two can stand here and argue if you want, but I'm going," Bailey said, piling into the car and slamming the door. "We have to make that shuttle."

"Get us out of here," Ned agreed. "Floor it."

"The fucking boiler is still heating," Bailey said, the car slowly picking up speed. Much too slowly. A bullet whizzed past the window, and she ducked, crushing her body down into the yellow and purple twill upholstery of the diplomatic vehicle. "Fuck!"

"Don't panic, Stocky," Ned grunted.

"It's difficult when there are people shooting at us! We have to get rid of them!" Ned rolled down the window, yanking at the crank. "What the hell are you doing?"

"Present from Kady," he said with a smirk, and threw a small disk-shaped object out.

Bailey watched it in the rear-view mirror as it began to spin wildly and smoke before it detonated, the sound an ear-splitting screech. "What is that?" she shouted over the din.

"Portable electro-magnetic pulse!"

The gunfire stopped, and the smoke concealed them from view. The boiler kicked into gear, and Bailey stomped down on the accelerator, willing the car to go faster. "Come on, you damned thing, *move*!"

"I don't know if we'll be able to board and get the hell out of here before they figure out where we're headed, if they haven't already."

"Amy wanted it to go quietly, leave while the lights were out. She's not going to be happy about how things went down."

"It's not like we had much of a choice. There was no way I was going to fit my arm through there." In the rear-view mirror, Mae was curled in the back seat, and guilt bloomed anew in Bailey's gut. "Do you think she'll be okay?"

"Poor thing got knocked around, but I think she will be okay, with some rest. Fucking guards, Stocky. It's like they enjoy it." He kept his eyes on the road, turning left and right in his seat to check if they were being followed. "She likes you, you know."

"I can't think about that right now."

"We should change cars, in case someone clocked that we're in a diplomatic steamcar."

"Right you are. I'll pull over, there's a banged up steamcar in that lot, do you see it?"

"It looks like someone drove it off a cliff."

Bailey turned in. "That's what makes it perfect. Unassuming. Modest."

"Piece of crap, more like."

"Beggars can't be choosers, my friend." She parked the car and took one desperately needed deep breath. "I'll get Mae, you start wiring it."

"Righty-o."

Mae was looking at her when she opened the door. "You gonna save me, Bai?"

"I'm sure as hell going to try." Bailey gently lifted her out of the back seat. "I thought you were unconscious."

"In and out. Everything hurts. I feel like I'm on fire."

"We'll be on the shuttle soon, I promise."

"I trust you."

That guilt that was blooming in her stomach was threatening to become a whole forest. She was the reason why Mae was hurt, she didn't deserve that trust. "I'm going to put you in this other steamcar, okay?"

"Whatever you say, Darling." It was a callback to their role playing, but something about it felt different, and it lodged itself squarely in the middle of Bailey's heart.

"We're ready to go, Stockton, let's drive," Ned said, waving at the front seat. The driver's side door was corroded with rust, and what was visible was dented and scratched. She'd expect a steamtruck back home to look like that, not a steamcar in the middle of the Capital.

She engaged the boiler, and to her surprise, it heated to temperature almost immediately. "That was unexpected."

"Who the hell would be hiding that kind of steam power in a hunk of junk like this?"

"Ned, did we just hot-wire an Intelligence vehicle?"

"Seems like it. The sooner we get out of here, the better."

"Gods, as if we chose the most disgusting steamcar we could find, and it turns out to be Intelligence. This gods forsaken city."

"I'm as sick of it as you are."

Bailey threw the steamcar into gear and pulled back onto the road, leaning into the unexpected speed. They might just make that shuttle, but hope was a dangerous thing. "Not long now to the docks," she said, directing her comment towards Mae.

"Mm," was her only reply.

Bailey's stomach burned with bile. If they didn't get Mae medical attention soon, there was no telling what the lasting damage might be.

"We're making good time," Ned offered. "You're doing great, Stocky."

"I just hope that Amy and Davey make it there okay, too."

"I'm sure they will. Hey, where are you going? The docks are to the left."

"Mae said the back way is safer."

"Okay," Ned replied, but it was obvious that he wasn't convinced. It didn't matter. Bailey trusted Mae above all else.

The steamcar came to a stop behind the row of ships, all lined up in a row, each one in its designated bay. Transports like the one she'd arrived on to the right, cargo ships on the left, and Coalition military in the center. Those bays were walled off from the others, topped with razor wire. "Ours is a cargo ship, the Dolly Rose," Bailey said.

"Never heard of it."

"Me neither." Bailey lifted Mae from the back seat. "Let's hope they're ready to go."

They edged along the bays, looking for a ship emblazoned with that name. "I don't see it, do you?" Ned asked.

"No. It must be here, though, Mae said it would be."

A siren began to sound from one of the landing towers, and Bailey's body froze, waiting to be shot, or targeted, or tackled and dragged back to that cell.

"Shite!" Ned hissed. "How did they find us?"

Shouts emanated from the front of the docks. "Maybe it's not us?"

"Aye. Could be the others."

"Damn," Bailey whispered. "Damn, damn. What do we do now?"

"We should keep looking for that ship."

She nodded, and they kept looking, until they came upon a steel blue vessel without a name. "Maybe this is it?"

"Could be. Let's check the loading bay."

The ramp was down, maybe the first luck they'd had that day. "Hello?" Bailey called. "We're looking for the—"

A young woman with bright green hair leaped from the ship. "Gods, we thought they got you! The dock officers, they said on the local radio frequency that someone was arrested!"

"What?"

Ivy checked her pocket watch. "A few minutes ago!"

"Gods." Bailey set Mae down atop one of the smooth crates. "Where are the others, Davey and Amy?"

"We don't know."

"What are you even doing here, Ivy?"

"Helping out with Captain Tansy. I'm a valuable asset as someone who doesn't have a Coalition record." She raised a matching green eyebrow. "As I'm sure you've learned."

"You can say that again. Tell the pilot to fire up the engines. I'm going to go look for them." She turned to Ned. "Watch Mae, get her to a real bed. Get her some medicine. I'll be back."

He grabbed her arm. "You better, Stockton. I don't want to be the one to tell her we left you behind."

"I promise."

The ramp rattled under her boots as she ran back down to the docks, looking for Amy and Davey. After all they'd done to break them out, she couldn't leave them behind. There was no sign of them. Had they been arrested, too? "Davey!" she hissed. "Where the hell are you?"

There was no response. Anxiety began to creep back in, after the painfully short reprieve of finding their shuttle. Ship after ship, she couldn't find them. Rows and rows of blindingly white transport ships, all emblazoned with the Coalition crest. Had they boarded the wrong vessel?

"Amy?" she called quietly. She sighed. "Where are you?"

"Hey!" a man called, stepping out from behind a large white crate. Johnson. Fuck. "How did you get out?"

"What?"

"How many times do we have to arrest you?" he snarled, advancing on her. "Third time's the charm, that's what I always say."

"Piss off, I'm busy!"

He ran at her, arms out, and connected with her sore shoulder. She winced and threw a sloppy punch that he easily dodged.

"You're going to have to do better than that!" he shouted with a laugh. "Much better!" He ran at her again, but this time she was prepared, swerving out of the way and tripping him up with a low kick. He recovered quickly, and she was already so tired.

"Can't we just leave all this in the past?" she asked, swinging at him again, this time glancing off his frustratingly solid neck as he strafed to the left.

"Not on your life." He lunged forward and grabbed her arms, pinning them to her sides. "Let's try this again, shall we, General? You're under arrest, and may the gods help me, if you escape again, I'll shoot you myself."

Bailey strained against him. He was so strong, and he had her at a disadvantage with her shoulder. She stomped on his foot, hoping against all odds that he didn't wear steel tips. He shrieked in pain, lessening his grip the tiniest bit, enough for her to overpower him. "Fuck you!" she yelled, ducking away from his right hook. She started to run back to the Dolly Rose, but he caught her from behind, squeezing his arms around her shoulders.

Leaning back, she let him think he was getting a better grip, before she tensed and threw him over her head. He landed on the strip of grass between the bays with a dull thud. She didn't wait to see if he got up. She leaped over him and sprinted for the shuttle. They couldn't wait any longer, there wasn't time. Running behind the ships, something caught her eye. Was it Amy? Turning, she crashed into a woman, nearly knocking them both to the ground.

"Be careful!" the woman shouted in an annoyed tone. "Gods, first they arrest me on false grounds, now—"

They stared at each other.

Bailey's jaw dropped open. The woman could have been her clone, except for a faded scar that streaked across her face. "Fineglass," she managed to stutter.

"Who the hell are you?" Fineglass demanded. "What is the explanation for this?" She grabbed Bailey's wrist. "You're the one who's been gallivanting around the Capital with my face. What is it? Surgery? A top-secret cloning program?"

"I'm, uh... Bailey." It was all she could manage to say. No wonder no one had questioned her posing as General Fineglass. They looked exactly alike.

"I don't give a rat's ass what your name is, you're going straight back to that cell—"

Bailey jerked her arm away. "No!" she shouted. "I don't know why I look like you! Leave me alone!" The world around her felt unstable and threatening, like a nightmare. Nothing made sense. She had to get back to Mae. She started to run again, the Dolly Rose just ahead, the ramp drawing up into the ship.

"You'll never get off Gamma-3 alive!" Fineglass screamed. "I'll have them shoot you out of the sky!"

Chapter 28

"Go!" Bailey screamed, flinging herself into the loading bay of the Dolly Rose. "Go, go!"

"We're going!" Ivy said, scaling the ladder that led to the upper level of the loading bay. "Boiler is maxed!"

"I hope this ship has guns!"

Ivy swung around, so that she was hanging off the ladder with half her body. "No guns, you need a permit for that."

"Then it better be fast, because they're about to send the whole damn fleet after us."

"We have shields. This ship is faster—" An explosion rocked the ship, the lights flickering dangerously. "Cap!" Ivy shouted into the radio. "We're taking fire down here!"

"Boilers?"

"Full throttle, Cap! Get us out of here!"

"You don't need to tell me twice," the captain said, and the ship lurched.

"Where's Mae?" Bailey shouted over the cacophony of crates falling over, their contents spilling across the bay.

"We put her in the lounge! She's safe!"

A second blast sent Ivy flying off the ladder, landing hard on the ground. Bailey covered her head with her arms, trying to protect herself from the debris falling from the upper level. She squinted, trying to see where Ivy was, hoping she wouldn't find the kid crushed under a crate. A box of droid parts skidded across the upstairs planks and spilled out, raining tiny parts down over the bay. Springs, gears, and solar panels laid down like ice, tempting a fall.

The ship lurched again as it picked up speed, and in a moment, everything was still.

"Ivy!" Bailey yelled. "Ives, where are you?"

"I'm here," she said, brushing off her coveralls.

"Are you alright?"

"Yep. Nothing bruised except my pride. That will show me for not clipping in like I should."

Bailey allowed herself a tiny sigh of relief. "A fall like that would have killed someone else."

"It's a good thing I'm not someone else, then." The radio crackled insistently, pieces hanging off the side. "Smashed my radio. We'd better go see what Cap needs, in case it's urgent."

"What about the others, did they make it on the ship?"

"Just before you. They'll probably be on the bridge, too." Ivy stepped through the crew entrance. "We weren't sure you'd make it back."

"I wasn't sure I would, either." Her heart was still racing, her lungs burning from the effort. "I'm glad to see a familiar face, Ives."

"I practically had to beg, borrow, and steal to get this assignment. Captain Violet didn't want me to go."

A smile crept across Bailey's face. "You're the only person I know who actually seeks out danger."

"Danger is my middle name!" Ivy said with a laugh. "Actually, it's not. My middle name is Lynn. Come on, they're through here," she said, smoothing an unruly tuft of green hair back behind her ear.

Bailey ducked under the low ceiling. For a ship with advanced boilers, it sure as hell was cramped. The bridge, at least, was roomier, with a high ceiling and plenty of room for Davey to pace a hole in the dark blue carpet.

"Are you sure there's no word from Command?" he asked.

The captain sighed, facing the large window that spanned the width of the ship. "I told you, we can't take the scramblers off until we're clear of Coalition travel corridors."

"They'll be wanting to know where we are, they might already know about what happened at the docks."

"And you'll get the opportunity to make contact as soon as it's safe."

The voice was familiar. So familiar, a sob nearly caught in Bailey's throat. "Marshall?"

He turned, his face brightening. "Stockton, you wild thing! You made it!"

"What the hell are you doing here? Whose ship is this?"

"Borrowed it from a Captain Tansy. She was keen for us to run a rescue mission, let us take her out for a spin. She's fast, isn't she?"

"Marshall!" she repeated, and threw her arms around him. "You could have gotten yourself killed!"

"It was either that or wait for Bertie to kill me. You have no idea how angry she was when she found out what happened. Told me I was a fool for sending you down there in the first place." He gave her a weak smile. "I guess I am. I'm sorry. I never should have asked that of you."

"I can't believe you came for me."

"Not just for you. Some Cass lady up at Command, wherever in the hells that is, offered us a hell of a bond for getting these two out of there."

"How do you know Mae? She said she set this all up—"

He shrugged. "I don't know about any of that. It just worked out, between Command, Captain Tansy, and Bertie threatening to skin me alive if I didn't bring you back safe and sound."

"So, what now?"

"We get as much distance between us and Gamma-3 as we can, and as soon as it's safe, we double back and head to the off-grid transport beacon to drop this ship off and... well, we've got some deliveries coming up."

"How long to the beacon?"

"Oh, less than a day, I'd reckon. We're smoking through dark space right now."

"Makes you wish these boilers could be fitted standard."

"Not at those prices I don't. We'd have to pull a job like the one you just pulled every week for a year."

"I think I'll pass, thanks." Her body was still tense, a coiled spring on the verge of snapping.

He clapped her on the back. "You'd better go get what rest you can in the lounge. I'm betting you need it."

The realization that she hadn't slept in an entire day settled around her shoulders, and her eyelids were immediately heavy with exhaustion. "Yeah, I guess I'd better." She wanted to see Mae, too, to make sure she would be okay. "Any painkillers on this boat?"

"We don't have much, but whatever we do have will be in the first aid box down there."

"Seems strange to not have a medical bay. Even freighters have that."

"You've gotta cut weight when you want to move this fast," Ivy interjected. "It's not attainable for most ships, but the Dolly Rose sure can." She patted the captain's console almost lovingly. "She's a good, reliable ship. Hell, you saw how many hits we took, and we were still able to get out of there!"

"I'll be in the lounge, then, Marsh."

"Aye," he said, waving her away.

She left the bridge, hunching through the tiny corridors, the sound of Davey arguing with Marshall becoming increasingly more muffled as she went. Amy hadn't said anything on the bridge. There was no mention of anyone else - maybe the husband she'd been trying to rescue had been left behind.

Left to fend for himself, just like Emeline had been. If only they'd found her sooner, maybe...

That thought only led to thinking about her own people, how many of them had been plucked from the masses of workers to groom into Coalition management, to learn to subjugate their own families and friends in the name of progress. The endless, exhausting march forward and further into dark space. Soon, the Outer Rim would be breached, and then what? More planets and stations draped with yellow and purple? For what? More resources, more credits, more, more, always more.

She shook her head. It never made any sense to her.

The lounge was small, but at least it was quiet. Mae was curled up on the tattered couch, her bloody, swollen feet tucked up under her skirts. She was shivering as she slept, and so Bailey unbuttoned her torn, stained jacket and laid it over her, perching at the edge of the cushions.

"Bai?" she murmured. "You're here. I missed you."

"I'm here." Bailey flipped open the lid of the first aid trunk and rummaged around, fishing out a vial of slightly expired pain killer serum. Better than nothing. "Here, take this. It should help with the pain."

"Yes, ma'am," she answered, swallowing it with her eyes still closed, and in an instant they flew open. "Amy. Where's Amy? My father, he—"

"She's on the ship. She's safe."

Mae closed her eyes again. "Thank the gods. I'd never have forgiven myself." She shivered again, wrapping her arms around herself. "It's cold."

"Yeah, this ship is built for speed, not comfort. I'll just go get a blanket—"

Mae stirred and looked up at her from under her thick eyelashes. "Stay with me."

"Okay."

"Can I sleep in your lap?"

Bailey nestled back into the sofa. "Of course. How are you feeling?"

"Better now that you're here. I was worried."

"You can't get rid of me that easily."

"I don't want to be rid of you at all!"

"Shh," Bailey whispered, wrapping her arm around Mae. "Just rest, now. It won't be long before we reach the beacon, and we'll get you checked out."

"And then you'll tell me what happened?"

"Of course."

"Bailey?"

"Mm?"

Mae snuggled in closer, resting her head on Bailey's thighs. "Thanks for saving me."

"Yeah, well, thanks for saving me right back."

Chapter 29

"You don't have to carry me, you know," Mae said, her arms wrapped around Bailey's neck. "I told you, I'm feeling much better."

"Just let me do this, okay? You got smacked pretty hard."

Ned fell into step beside them, his temporary cane clicking gently against the metal flooring. "I've never seen someone take hits like that and stay conscious," he said.

"I don't want you tiring yourself out," Mae protested. "You must have been through hell, too."

Bailey looked down and gave her a smirk. "Do you really want to walk across the beacon without help?"

She grimaced. "No." Even the thought of a long walk was like torture. "I just feel so guilty, if I'd just—"

"We're not going through this again. It wasn't your fault, Mae." She sighed. "It wasn't anyone's fault. It was just a mess from start to finish."

Ned grinned. "It was a mess, but you got me the hell out of there. Without you two, I'd be a goner."

"You still haven't told me what happened," Mae pressed. She'd only been asleep a few hours, but it felt like weeks.

"I will, just as soon as we make sure you're okay."

Mae laid her palm against Bailey's cheek. "I'm okay."

"I'll believe it when someone who knows more than me about medical... stuff... confirms that."

"Stocky, you're not *squeamish*, are you?" Ned asked with a snort.

Bailey frowned. "So I don't like the sight of blood, who does?"

280

"A big strong thing like you, can't stand the idea of a little blood. Who'd have thought?"

"It's really not *that* unusual."

"If you say so." Mae held on tight, feeling safer than she had in weeks. "How far?"

"We're almost there." Bailey grinned. "If you look out the window to your left, you will see the universally infamous Cricket come into view."

"What happens if I look to the right?"

"Then you'll see an overflowing trash can and a market stall selling grey-market chips."

Ned stopped, cupping his hands around his mouth. "Oi! We're back!"

Captain Violet came sprinting down the ramp, her arms outstretched. "Ned! Nedrick, you absolute bastard, I thought we'd lost you. Kady's been absolutely beside herself, sick with worry, and Alice—"

"I'm alright, Boss."

The captain's cheeks were wet with tears. "Don't you ever do that to me again, or I'll raise you from the dead myself just to read you to rights."

"Aye, Boss."

"Bailey Stockton, you damn miracle woman! Go on inside the ship. Hyun is waiting for you both. I'll shower you with gratitude later."

"No need for that, Captain," Bailey replied humbly. "I know any of you would do the same for me. And have."

Mae didn't say anything. She didn't know Captain Violet, not really, not more than as a casual customer. She knew Alice and Larkin better, and besides, the heavy weight of exhaustion still pulled at her bones, even as she rested comfortably in Bailey's arms.

"Mae, it's nice to see you again," the captain said with a warm smile. "I know I have you to thank as well for getting my navigator back to me safe and sound."

"My pleasure." Captain Violet waved them off, and Bailey carried her up the ramp onto the ship. "You certainly seem to know your way around."

"I worked on this ship for a few months."

"I didn't realize that the Cricket did much rum-running."

"They don't. I helped their engineer with some jobs here and there, they needed some extra hands after Ivy started floating from ship to ship with Captain Tansy."

"Bailey, are you alright?"

"Mhmm," she answered, but Mae could feel her muscles tense.

"You can talk to me, you know."

"Later. Here's the med bay."

The door stood open, welcoming them inside, where Hyun was waiting to greet them, decked out in a red sequined corset and tight-fitting jodhpurs. "Bailey! So nice to see you again! The captain said you'd be coming. I'm still on for that rematch of Banríon, if you have time."

Bailey snorted a laugh. "No, thanks. I learned my lesson the first time. Should have listened to Ned."

"Set her here on this bed," Hyun instructed, grabbing a clipboard from the back of the door. "Mae, what in hells have you gotten yourself into?"

Mae gave her a weak smirk. "Trouble. Not as much trouble as that custom gown I made for you gave me, though."

"I love that dress. It's good luck, you know. I won that tournament."

"Don't you win all your tournaments?" Bailey asked.

"Yes, luckily." Hyun answered with a smirk. "Now, what have we got here? What happened?"

"A guard hit me with a baton. I'm fine, really."

"Hmm. I think I'll be the judge of that, what do you think?"

Mae nodded. "Okay."

"I'll need you to strip off this dress, so I can assess."

Before she could protest, Bailey backed out of the room. "I'll be right outside in the hallway if you need me," she said, closing the door.

"Do you need help?" Hyun asked.

"No, I can manage," Mae said, flinching with the effort of reaching behind herself to unlace her dress. It fell away to the floor, and the landscape of deep bruising was visible in the mirror on the wall. "Gods," she whispered.

"Yeah, it looks like they got you good. I'm just going to poke at you and move you around to check for breaks and fractures. Is that okay?"

Mae nodded. "Yes."

"Sounds like you lot had quite the adventure down there," Hyun said conversationally, pressing gingerly at Mae's ribs. "We were all worried sick."

"It all happened so fast, I barely even know what happened."

"Lean forward, please."

"I almost can't believe we made it out. It was a close one."

Hyun held her wrist delicately, rotating her arm. "I'll bet you're in no hurry to go back."

"I don't ever want to go back. Hell, I never even wanted to be there in the first place. The Capital is a dangerous place, and exhausting."

"I miss Gamma-3, sometimes," Hyun said sadly. "I miss the warmth of the sun, I miss snow. I miss the freedom that can only exist when you're not living in a giant fishbowl."

"I've never lived anywhere on Gamma-3 other than the Capital."

"Then I can see why you hated it," Hyun said with a laugh. "Does this hurt?"

"A little."

"And this?"

Mae shook her head. "No."

"Nothing major, just bruising. You'll be sore as hell for a few days, but that's to be expected. Just take it easy, take some warm baths with salts to keep the swelling down. The bruising should start to fade inside a week."

"Thank you." Mae slipped her dress back on, fumbling with the laces. "I told Bailey I was fine, but—"

"With bruises like that, she was right to bring you straight in here. You're very lucky, Mae, it could have been a broken rib, or internal bleeding." Hyun opened an overnight bag near the door and tossed her a pair of stockings. "Here, these are new. You look like you need some spares."

"Oh, my boots..." Mae trailed off. "It doesn't matter."

"You can *borrow* mine. You look like you're the same size. Don't run off with them, alright?" She produced a pair of silver spangled boots, fringed at the back with loops of tiny crystals.

"Don't worry, I definitely won't."

"You wouldn't be the first person to secret themselves away with my boots."

"Hyun, I give you a blood oath that I won't steal your boots. The very moment we're back in Bradach, I will gladly return them."

The medic smirked, tucking a long hair back into the braid coiled atop her head. "Here, take these. They'll help with the pain, and hopefully keep the swelling down, too. Twice a day, *with meals*. Do not take them on an empty stomach, or you will have serious regrets."

"Thanks."

"If there are any changes, if you feel more tired than usual, or—"

"I don't even know what that means anymore. I feel like I've been tired for weeks."

"—Or if you have additional swelling," Hyun continued, "come see me."

"I will."

"Captain said we'll be heading out as soon as everyone is on board and we're all stocked. You'll have that first room on the left down the second corridor." She paused, an eyebrow raised mischievously. "Unless you're planning to share with that very handsome woman out there in the hall. She seems very your type."

"Shh!"

"No judgment, of course! I certainly won't say anything. I keep my patients' secrets confidential, of course."

"Hyun!"

"Ah, okay, so you haven't made that play yet. From where I'm sitting, it looks like you're holding all the cards." She closed the open drawers and sat in her chair, nestled in the corner of the room, her feet up on the counter. "It wouldn't be the first time this ship has been the vehicle for a romance." Hyun snorted a laugh. "It's funny, because the ship *is* a vehicle."

"Yes, I got that," Mae replied. "I'll see you at dinner?"

"Of course. Ned offered to cook, and I'm not about to miss out on that."

"But he just got back!"

Hyun shrugged. "He likes cooking. Says the kitchen is where he feels most at peace. No one argues because he's the best chef among all of us. After weeks of eating the under-baked bread Alice has been making, we're all ready for a change."

"See you later, then."

Mae flinched as she climbed down off the bed, gingerly prodding her side. The med bay door was heavier than she expected, and she grunted softly with the effort of yanking it open. Bailey was waiting there, as promised, a worried expression on her face.

"Everything okay?"

"I'm fine, just like I said I was."

She breathed a sigh of relief. "Good," she said, and with a smirk, added, "nice boots."

"They're on loan."

"I assumed."

"That's the last time I go anywhere without sensible shoes."

"I'm not sure I would call crystalline fringe sensible."

Mae laughed and then groaned from the effort. "Not these, obviously."

"Shall I escort you to your room?"

"You don't have to, I—"

Bailey offered her arm. "I know I don't have to. I want to."

* * *

"Alright, people, we're on our way back to Bradach!" Captain Violet shouted from atop one of the tables, bottle of whiskey in hand. "Please, raise your glasses to the heroes of the hour, who sprung our beloved Nedrick from his cell. A cheer for Bailey Stockton and Mae Machenet!"

Alice raised her glass, nearly colliding with a small robot hovering at her shoulder. "Oops, sorry, BEEP." She grinned. "To the heroes of the hour!"

The crew cheered, downing their drinks with glee.

"And another cheer for their rescuers, Davey and Amy!"

The crew began to whoop again, but were interrupted.

"I don't want your fucking cheers. I want my husband!" Amy shouted, her eyes rimmed with red from crying. "We have to go back for him!"

The captain stepped down from the table. "We can't go back. We don't have a ship that can get through the security barricade. The Dolly Rose has been marked, now, and this ship can barely venture into Coalition space without running into trouble. I'm sorry, I really am, but—"

"If you were that sorry, you'd go back for him!"

"And how would you propose we do that? I can't risk the safety of my whole crew on a very slim margin we'd manage it. Gods, the last time I took a risk, we almost lost Ned." Captain Violet shook her head. "I'm sorry, I can't. But we've already put in a wire to Tansy—er, Captain Tansy, that is, and they'll work on getting him out of there."

"That could take years."

"It could, yes, especially as your disappearance will raise flags. They'll be watching him closely, now." She wrapped her arms around Amy and pulled her into a tight embrace. "I can only imagine what you are going through right now. I promise you, I will work with Tansy, and I will do whatever I can to help get him out of there. I am, truly, from the bottom of my heart, sorry that we didn't have time to wait."

"Oh, gods," Amy sobbed into the captain's jacket, "what am I going to do without him?"

"Hey, why don't you come and sit with me?" Alice asked, patting her back. "It's nice and quiet over there in the corner, and we can always go sit in the boiler room if this is too much for you."

"She doesn't want to sit in the boiler room, Al," the captain said.

"I'm just trying to help, Vi."

Amy sniffled, rubbing her eyes. "The boiler room sounds fine. I don't think I want to be in here right now."

"Let's get you a plate," Alice said, loading up with food from the heaping bowls on the tables. Roasted garlic potatoes, chargrilled bell peppers drizzled with oil and sea salt imported from Delta-4, a hearty slice of beetroot and mushroom wrapped in flaky pastry. "Whiskey?"

"I don't drink," Amy replied, shaking her head.

"Tea it is." Alice took the bottle gently from Captain Violet's hands, kissing her on the cheek. "This is for me. I'll bring back whatever's left." She looked at Amy, choking back another sob as she headed for the door. "We're going to need a lot of tea."

"The sooner we get back to Bradach, the better," the captain muttered. "Maybe you can install us one of those fancy engines like the Dolly Rose has, eh, Alice?"

"Did you rob a credit bank and not tell me?" Alice replied, following Amy to the door. "If you did, then I expect the parts to be in the loading bay as soon as possible."

"You wish."

Alice cast a glance back at her wife. "No, *you* wish."

"Okay," Ned said, clearing his throat loudly. "It's true that things didn't go as well as they could have... but we all have to admit that they could have gone much worse, too. I could be awaiting extradition to a work camp." He shuddered. "Without one Bailey Stockton, that's exactly where I'd be."

"I'd probably still be in a cell without you, too," Bailey called, "so let's call it even."

"A toast to calling it even, then." He swigged back his whiskey with a grimace. "Let's eat. This food won't be nearly as good cold." He sat down next to Mae, his plate heaped with steaming food. "Whiskey, Mae?"

"No thank you, I'm not one for the hard stuff," she replied. Even the smell of it was enough to turn her stomach. "I'm more of a wine drinker."

"Wine! Why didn't you say so? Stocky, you know where Boss keeps the good stuff. Why don't you get your girl a bottle?"

"She's not my girl," Mae said reflexively, immediately wishing she could swallow the words back down. "I just mean, uh—"

Bailey blinked at her. "It's fine," she said, standing up. "I'll go get you that wine."

"Hang on, wait—"

"Er, sorry," Ned said when Bailey had disappeared into the galley. "I didn't mean to make things awkward."

"I just... I don't really know where we are." Mae loaded her fork with roasted peppers. "Dinner is wonderful, Ned. You really are an excellent cook. In fact, I'm surprised that Evie and Larkin haven't snapped you up for the Purple Pig."

"Don't think they haven't tried. They're trying to lure me in by promising me a night of samplers. Larkin damn well knows that starters are my favorite." He took a swig of water from the dented metal cup next to his plate. "But I think the boss would have both their heads, and mine, on silver platters if I left to go cook fancy food. Besides, I'd miss the skies. Gods know I love a bit of excitement."

"You're not full up on excitement after that on Gamma-3?" Bailey asked, setting the open bottle on the table with a wine glass. "Your wine, Mae."

"Thanks, Bai." The nickname didn't even get a smile this time. Great. The first woman she'd been interested in for years, and she'd fucked it up. "I appreciate it. I don't really know my way around here."

"Stick around, and the boss'll have you fixing this old ship up with Georgie before you know it. Huh. They're late. Wonder where they are."

Bailey stabbed a potato so fiercely, the tines of the fork scraped unpleasantly against the plate. "It's not that big a ship, Ned. We don't have to wonder too hard."

"Sorry, Stocky, I wasn't thinking."

"I'm actually not that hungry," Bailey announced, pushing her plate away. "I'm tired. I'm going to check on Amy and Alice and then head to bed."

Mae caught her wrist. "Come on, stay. We'll have a drink, talk."

"Maybe some other time. I'll see you tomorrow."

"Shit," Ned whispered as Bailey disappeared down the corridor.

"Fill me up, Nedrick," Mae said. "Gods be damned to hell." She held out her glass, watching the ruby liquid swirl tightly. *Great job, Mae*, she thought, *you ruined it.*

Chapter 30

"Good Evening, Capital residents, I'm Delia Dodson with your nightly news. An explosion at a strip-mining operation on an asteroid caused thirty-two fatalities, among them, four managers and ten military police officers."

"Weird they're not leading with the whole fake general thing," Kady mused, her feet up on the lab table. "I mean, you'd think that they'd want to plaster your face all over the Near Systems."

"Mm," Bailey agreed in a non-committal tone. She didn't even want to be in the lab, not when Henry could walk in at any moment and just... make everything worse. But Kady had caught her walking back to her room and yanked her in for the broadcast. "Think Delia will drop any breadcrumbs tonight?"

"Who knows? It's become much more sparse since she moved up to regional reporter, she's probably under more scrutiny."

"The blast rendered the mining camp inoperable, and survivors were safely relocated to new assignments across the sector. We regret to inform our listeners that rhodium, already in short supply, will now be rationed in our district. From next week, manufacturers can collect their allowances from centralized hubs."

"Every pirate in the Near Systems is going to be aiming for those rhodium transports now," Kady said, picking at the pie crust on her plate. "So you can bet our Coalition friends are going to pack out those ships with all kinds of guns."

"Those poor people," Bailey said. Were any of them her people? Blasted into space by an unsustainable operation, barely even mentioned in the report? The thought of it turned her stomach.

"In other news, a press conference in the Capital from our very own Overseer Allemande has confirmed that Skelm, the jewel of our sector, has been granted the Outer Rim expansion contract. This will mean more jobs in Skelm for willing workers, and an influx of credits to our local economy."

Bailey sat up. No. That can't be. That wasn't supposed to happen.

"This is due to a newly formed partnership between Overseer Allemande and General Fineglass, the head of the expansion project. All glory to the Coalition."

"Great, because that jerk needs more power," Kady said, rolling her eyes. "I swear, we're never going to get rid of her."

"That contract was supposed to be canceled when the news broke that the person who signed it was an impostor."

"*You* signed it? Gods below, Bailey, why?"

"We—Mae—thought that once the news broke, it would make Allemande look like a fool. A disgrace. It was meant to undermine her, not..." she gave a frustrated growl, burying her head in her hands. "Not hand her more influence."

"So they're hiding it."

"Looks like it."

Kady took her feet off the desk, a dark look clouding her pixie-like features. "That's not good, Stockton."

"Of course it's not fucking good! It's terrible! Gods, what else am I going to be responsible for? It's a damned disaster!"

"What's a disaster?"

Bailey knew that sweet, honeyed voice. At one time, it would have made her melt into a puddle. Now it just tightened the knot in her stomach. "Nothing, Henry. I'm sure you have more important things to think about."

"No, I was just about to go get some food from the kitchen, we were..." she cleared her throat. "Busy."

"Don't let me stop you, Ms. Weaver."

"No need for all that formality, Ms. Stockton, you act like we didn't spend months working alongside each other."

And months mooning after you like a lovesick puppy, Bailey thought contemptuously. "You'd better hurry, I saw some of the others heading in for second helpings."

"Not until you tell me what's going on, it sounds serious. Maybe the captain should—"

"Honestly, Henry, you are the very last person on this ship I want to ask for help."

Henry jerked her head back, offended. "I'm just trying to—"

"What's going on?" came a drawl from behind her.

Gods, this was exactly why she wanted to get off this damned ship in the first place. Too damn crowded with too many people she didn't want to see.

"I don't know, Bailey won't tell me!"

Georgie stepped around Henry into the doorway. "Nice to see you again, Stockton."

"This is all a bit much, isn't it?" Kady said, examining her slice of pie. "Can't get a moment's peace with all this nonsense on board."

"Kady!" Henry scolded. "You don't have to always *say* things, you know."

"No one else is saying anything. Listen, your best friend Overseer Allemande landed some big contract for the Outer Rim expansion project."

"What does that have to do with Bailey?"

Bailey sighed angrily. "It's complicated, and I barely have my own thoughts clear on it!" Georgie's worried face searched her own, and it was obvious why. If she didn't say something, the guilt would digest her from the inside out. "I saw your sister, Georgie."

"You saw Emeline?" she asked hopefully, the excitement dancing at the edges of her tone. "Is she okay? What did she say?" Her face began to cloud over. "Why isn't she with you? You *left* her there? What kind of person would—"

"Whoa, Payne, lay off her, she nearly got killed trying to get Ned out. Take a breath," Kady said firmly.

"It's damned hard to be calm when we've not heard anything about her in over a month! No leads, nothing, and now here *she* is saying she spoke to my little sister, and left her there to rot."

Hot, angry tears pricked at Bailey's eyes. "I need to get out of here." She pushed past Henry and Georgie, blinking furiously to stem the tide that threatened to wash down her face. "I'll prepare a report on what happened or something, I don't know."

Georgie started to follow her down the corridor. "You can't just—"

"Let her go, George," Henry said gently.

It was the gentleness that was going to do her in. A tiny glimpse of kindness might actually kill her. Wearing your heart on your sleeve only ever meant more bruises. Gods, she almost wished she was back in that cell. At least there, she knew where she stood with all the occupants.

Bailey rounded the corner just in time for the dam to break, and tears to come flooding down her cheeks. It was all too much, too damned much. Henry never had said anything after that night when Bailey confessed her feelings. It was like it had never happened. She'd left almost immediately after to chase after Georgie and pull her out of Skelm, and almost died in the process. Bailey was just... disposable. Unwanted, and now by Mae, too. Wiping her nose on her sleeve, a tiny sob escaped her throat.

"Bai? Bailey! I was looking everywhere for you, I—" Mae caught her by the elbow. "Bailey, what's wrong?"

"Nothing. Everything!"

"I'm sorry for what I said at dinner, it's just that—"

"It doesn't matter, Mae."

Mae released her and stepped back. "Oh." She turned and squinted down the hallway, catching sight of Georgie and Henry. "Oh."

"I can't wait to get back to Bradach, I just want to get out of these clothes, and to get back to rum-running. It's just about the only thing I'm good at."

"That's obviously untrue. Ned wouldn't be drunkenly singing in the galley if not for you."

"You'd still be with your parents if it wasn't for me, building your career back up, sliding into all those fancy galas..."

"Bai, I'd rather be here with you than down there with them, that's not even a competition. I never wanted to be down there in the first place. They blackmailed me into going back."

"Blackmail?"

Mae sighed, smoothing her skirts nervously. "Yes, it's the family business. Never something I wanted any part of, and yet..."

"What did they blackmail you with?"

"My father said he knew where Bradach was, and that he would pass it to the authorities if I didn't play his sick little game."

"Gods," Bailey whispered. Her own parents were long gone, victims of a Coalition raid. They'd saved their people and paid with their lives. Not like her. She'd run and hid, and watched people be rounded up onto transports. "Now that you're gone, will he—"

"He lied to me. He never knew where it was, not really. He tried to keep me there, threatened to have Amy thrown into prison just as I was being arrested."

"It's a good thing she left, then."

"Yeah." Mae averted her eyes like she wanted to say something, but couldn't quite bring herself to say it.

"What is it?"

"Nothing. I just wouldn't be surprised if he uses everything to his own sick, twisted advantage. Anything to repaint the walls in gold leaf, no matter the body count."

"I just heard the broadcast. They announced a new partnership between Allemande and Fineglass. The real Fineglass."

"Fuck," Mae said, twisting the fabric of her skirts in her hands. "That didn't quite pan out for us, did it?"

"Mae, she looks like me. Almost exactly like me, just with a scar." Bailey drew a line across her face with her finger to illustrate. "How could she look exactly like me? How does that kind of coincidence happen?"

"What? How do you know? Did you break into the files, or—"

"I saw her. I nearly knocked her over when I was running back to the Dolly Rose after fighting off Johnson."

"Johnson? Bai, you're lucky you didn't get yourself killed. What the hell were you doing out there?"

"Looking for Amy and Davey. I didn't want them to get left behind."

Mae gave her a sad smile. "You're one of the best people I've known, Bailey Stockton."

"Given my incredible history of failures, that says a lot about the company you've kept." Bailey leaned against the wall and picked at a frayed thread. "I was there, the day everyone I knew got rounded up and taken away. I could have run in, could have saved them. Instead, I hid. I let it happen. I still don't know where they were taken." Even then, months later, the guilt and the pain sat fresh in her chest, weighing her down, sinking into every vein with its burden.

"You couldn't have stopped that. One woman against half an army? All you'd have done was get yourself killed." Mae took her hands. "And then Ned would still be stuck in that prison, or worse, and I'd be down in the Capital doing my father's dirty work." She blinked and pulled away. "Bailey, when did that happen?"

"Almost a year ago."

"Oh, my Gods. I might know where they are. Or at least, some of them. A settlement off Delta-4, Allemande mentioned it."

"That can't be. I've been searching since it happened. The entire reason I did that job in the Capital was to have the credits to hire someone to dig up information." She shook her head. "No, it can't be. That's too easy."

"There's nothing easy about a settlement armed to the teeth, bursting with MPOs."

"How do you know? The Coalition has been doing raids ever since I can remember, it might not even be the same people."

"Bai, it's a lead, at least. It's somewhere to start."

Before Bailey could respond, she found herself bracing against the sound of footsteps coming up the corridor. She wasn't going to be able to avoid them forever.

"Listen, Stockton, I'm sorry I lost my temper back there," Georgie started. "I just... it's been a lot, you know?"

"I do."

"I've not heard from my sister since she was taken that day. I spend all my time searching, wondering if she's okay."

"She is well taken care of."

"By that... that monster? How can you say that? She's just a girl, she's—"

"She dosed me with truth serum," Mae interjected, "when I went to her home to convince her to board the shuttle with us."

Georgie shook her head. "No. It can't be. Not Em, she would never."

"I'm so sorry, but I'm telling the truth."

"But—why—why would she do that? She must have been scared, or Allemande forced her to. We all know what that woman is capable of, and manipulating a girl would be a piece of cake for her."

Mae shook her head. "I don't even think Allemande knew what she was up to."

"Bullshit!"

"There's no need to—"

"You're lying!"

Henry laid a hand gently on Georgie's arm. "They wouldn't lie, George. What motivation would they possibly have to lie?"

"To cover up the fact that they never even tried to get Emeline out. To ease their guilty consciences, who knows! All I know is that my sister, who I've spent months trying to track down, was within reach, and now we're right back where we started."

"That's not strictly true, though," Bailey ventured. Georgie's outburst was understandable, but she could still stand to relax a little on the wild accusations. "We know that she's in the Capital. We also know that she's using her position to advocate for Skelm."

Georgie buried her face in her hands. "Of course. Of course Em would do that. Of course that's why she'd stay, it's the only way she can see that she can help people there." She softened. "Why didn't you say that in the first place?"

"I'm... sorry."

Mae crossed her arms in front of her chest. "We did everything we could. Bailey stayed for days longer than she should have, acting as General Fineglass, because she wanted to get your sister out of there. I can appreciate your disappointment, but please understand that she laid her life on the line for your sister, someone she'd never even met."

"Oh," Georgie said softly.

"So you can keep your little theories to yourself, Ms. Payne. You should be thanking Bailey, not interrogating her in the corridor." She smoothed invisible wrinkles from her skirts. "As for your sister, I am concerned that she has been brainwashed, or manipulated, by Overseer Allemande. She indicated that she has no intention of leaving the Capital, or her newfound position of power and influence. If you want your sister back, I'm afraid you might have to drag her out of there."

"Stockton, I'm sorry. I shouldn't have flown off the handle like that—"

"Twice," Mae interjected.

"Yes, twice. You just have no idea what it's like to lose someone, to spend months looking..."

Bailey shot a wounded look at Henry. "I guess you never told her, then, that I lost everyone close to me that day? Didn't manage to fit that in between running off to save her, and dedicating your life to finding her sister?"

"I didn't think it was mine to tell," Henry said apologetically. "She's just worried about her sister."

"I'm terrified for everyone I knew, but you don't see me accusing my gods-damned shipmates of not doing enough." She was so tired. An inescapable, crushing exhaustion that settled deep in her bones, a heartache too complicated to untangle. "Some of us have to worry about more than one person."

"I said I'm—" Georgie started.

"I'm going to bed." Bailey stalked off towards her room, closing the door quietly behind her, and wedging a chair under the handle. Tonight, she needed to be alone.

* * *

A soft knock at the door roused Bailey from her thoughts. "Yes?"

"It's me. Henry."

Bailey sighed. "Come in."

"I brought coffee. I just made it fresh in the kitchen, lots of milk, two sugars. Just how you like it."

"Thank you." The mug was warm in her hands, and the smell of sweet caffeine prickled her senses. "What are you doing here, Henry?"

"Georgie wanted to come along when she heard we were heading to the Capital. She thought—"

"No, I mean, why are you here, in my quarters?"

"I wanted to... to sort things out. Between us."

Bailey took a long sip of the coffee. "Right."

"I'm sorry that I didn't say anything to you before I left. You deserved better than that. Our friendship deserved better than that."

"I don't blame you for leaving, Henry. You love her. I understand."

"I do love her. More than anything, and I—it's not been easy, since Emeline was taken. It almost broke Georgie. I think if her sister hadn't been there with her in Skelm, she never would have made it out. She'd have given up."

"I know Georgie doesn't like me."

"She's a little jealous, it's true, but only because she knows how close we were when she and I were so far apart, with no way to write. It's a chunk of our lives we can never truly share with each other." Henry sat on the edge of the bed. "But she also admires you, Bailey. If things were different, maybe you would have been friends, first."

"It might be easier to be friends if she stopped accusing me of lying, or leaving her sister there on purpose, or—"

"She's just upset. Here, she wrote you this." Henry handed over a sealed envelope, scrawled with Bailey's name on the front. "It's an apology letter. She's better with words in writing."

"Oh."

"I hope that someday we can all grow past this, and be friends, or at least, work well together. I imagine our paths will continue to cross, and I do still care about you, Stockton. You've been a good friend to me. Better than I deserved."

"Damn right," Bailey said with a smirk.

"So what's going on between you and Mae Machenet?"

"We're not there yet, Henry."

"Alright, alright, I hear you. I won't pry—well, I might pry a little—but if I can give one word of advice, don't leave it too late. Life is short, and shorter than we realize. We may as well spend it with people we love." Henry took Bailey's empty mug and stood. "Thank you for hearing me out."

"Thank you for the coffee."

"I'll see you in the morning."

"Yep. Tell Georgie I said... thanks."

Chapter 31

It had been weeks since she'd seen Bailey. Something like a void grew daily in her chest, making it hard to breathe, a challenge to think about anything other than when she might see her again. Not that it mattered, she'd done enough to ruin what little chance they had back on the Cricket.

"Abigail, did you finish that alteration?" she asked.

"Over an hour ago. I even came back here and said, 'Mae, I finished the alteration,' and you said, 'Great, we should get a head start on that custom job,' and so I've been pattern drafting ever since. What's with you lately?"

Mae sighed heavily. "Oh, I don't know. Maybe the Capital got under my skin." She knew precisely what had gotten under her skin, and it sure as hell wasn't anyone or anything on Gamma-3.

"You seem different."

"Maybe I am." She picked at her lunch, leftover pasta and vegetables from her dinner the night before, now cold on her desk. "It's clear I'm not even needed here. You did such a wonderful job keeping the shop open while I was away."

"Uh, no. You are never allowed to take an extended leave of absence again, not without getting me some help. I was run off my feet, Mae. I've never worked so hard in my life, and I am a lazy woman by nature. I would appreciate you taking that into account the next time you jump on a shuttle."

"I just feel like... I don't know. It's complicated, I guess."

"Did you meet someone on Gamma-3?"

"No." It wasn't a lie, not technically.

"You sure about that? Because you're acting exactly like I did when I was mooning over that scrapper from Delta-4."

Mae gasped theatrically. "*Him*? Abigail, dear, you could do much better than him."

"I know. That was a million years ago now, anyway."

"So do you... have someone?"

Abigail raised an eyebrow. "Very evasive, Mae. We were talking about your love life, not mine. It's making me think that maybe my theory wasn't so far-fetched."

"Oh, please, I'm just a little out of sorts after being blackmailed by my parents and then held in a prison cell. Most people would be, I'd wager."

"Nah, I still think it's something else. Nothing fazes you, not even scary stuff like that, yet you've been gliding around the shop like a damned ghost—" Her speech was interrupted by the bells on the front door tinkling insistently. "Don't worry, I'll get it. No doubt you'd forget your own name, much less measurements."

Abigail swept out of the back room, her skirts trailing after her. Mae had gotten lucky when she hired her and knew it. Not many other shop assistants would take on all that extra work to keep the shop running smoothly, even though they were getting paid overtime.

"I, uh—is Mae here?"

Bailey.

Mae rushed towards the door, almost knocking over her lunch in the process. "I'm here!" she shouted from the back room, tripping over a felled bolt of damask. "I'm in the back! I'll be right there!" She paused by the mirror. Gods, she looked a fright. She tucked a few stray hairs back into her bun and pulled the curtain to the side. "Bailey, it's so nice to see you."

"Uh, yeah. Sorry I haven't come by, it's just... you know."

"Yes, I do."

Abigail looked from Bailey, over to Mae, and snorted. "I'm going for lunch."

"But you already went for lunch," Mae protested weakly.

"Okay, then I'm going to take myself out for the sequel. This shop is entirely too small for all three of us, I think you'd agree." She lifted her coat from the hook, slipping it on. "I'll see you tomorrow, Mae."

"See you tomorrow." She wasn't going to fight it, not when she'd been desperate to see Bailey ever since she went back to rum-running. The bells jingled as the door closed. "So, what brings you here? Need another last minute uniform?" she joked.

"Yes, actually."

Mae laughed. "Very funny."

"No, I'm serious. That lead was a good one, Mae. I know where they're keeping my people."

"What? No! You only just got here, and—and it's too dangerous for you to be seen anywhere, and—"

"They never reported that there was an impostor. No one knows to look for me. As far as any of them know, I am General Fineglass. It's their only chance of getting out of there. I have to try."

"Bailey..." she trailed off. "It's so dangerous."

"Would you do it for Abigail? Or Amy?"

"Yes, but—"

"Then you understand why I have to do this. My oldest friend, Yannick, he might be trapped in that mining camp. And I can't thank you enough for that lead, but I have to ask for your help one more time. I need a new uniform. The last one..."

"Probably looks like it's been dragged behind a steamtruck through a field of mud puddles?"

Bailey smirked. "Yeah, something like that. And I'm sorry that I couldn't save the dress uniform, not with how—"

"Please don't worry about that. It was made of curtains, hardly something to mourn."

"No, but you made it. For me. That alone makes it a shame that it got left behind."

"How long will you be gone?"

"I don't know. As long as it takes, I suppose."

"I see." Mae tried to quell the growing ache in her chest. "And when do you leave?"

"Tomorrow."

"Again with the last minute requests, eh?"

"I'm sorry, I only just got into port. I came as soon as I could."

Mae sighed. "Of course I'll do it. How could I ever say no to you?"

"If you did, I'd just go to the place across town," Bailey replied with a wry smile.

"Don't you even dare! That talentless hack would get you caught the second you disembarked. No, I'll be doing it, thank you very much, Ms. Stockton. If anyone is going to take your life into their hands, it's me."

"I do appreciate it. I'll pay the rush fee, of course, I—"

"The only payment I will take is you coming back safe. No exceptions. No refunds, either."

"Mae, I—I'm sorry, for how things went down on the Cricket. It was just a lot, and just after getting out of the Capital." Bailey ran her hands through her long auburn hair, left loose for once. "I used to carry a hell of a torch for Henry, and... I'm sure you can figure out the rest."

"That was pretty obvious." The thought of Bailey with someone else sent a sharp pang through her chest. "Still?"

"No, not anymore. We had a talk, straightened things out. Besides, it seems like my heart lies elsewhere lately."

Mae's heart leaped in her chest. "Oh?"

"I've not thought of anything other than this mission since the investigator confirmed the lead."

"Oh."

Bailey took Mae's hands. "And I have you to thank for that. I'm just sorry that I have to show up on your doorstep asking for more."

"I'd make a hundred uniforms if it meant you'd stay safe, Bai."

"No one's work even compares to yours. The replicas are perfect, almost indistinguishable."

Mae pulled her hands away. "There's a reason for that, you know. I designed them."

"Wow."

"It's my not-so-secret shame, I'm sorry to say. It's why I left the Capital in the first place. I couldn't deal with the guilt, seeing how they used those snappy uniforms to recruit thousands into their ranks. I never should have taken it on, but I did, and I have to bear that for the rest of my life."

"I think that sewing dupes for rebels might undo some of that."

Mae gave a small laugh. "Maybe."

"You know that I have to do this, right? I have to undo my own guilt. My mothers died saving their people. They gave themselves up to the Coalition raiders to protect the rest of the settlement. When I was faced with the same situation, I ran, and I hid."

"That's a hell of a legacy to live up to, Bai."

"I have to try."

"If I can be honest—"

"Of course."

She cleared her throat, turning towards the wall, where Abigail had hung a painting of Bradach at sunset. "If I can be honest," she repeated, "I care about you. Rather a lot, if truth be told, and while I'll do anything I can to help you, I hate the idea of you being in danger, and I worry that you'll follow your mothers' legacy into an early grave."

"I care about you, too," Bailey said, setting her hands on Mae's shoulders. "I promise I'll come back."

"Don't make promises you can't keep." Mae turned to face her, biting at her lip. "I don't know if my heart could take it."

"Oh," Bailey breathed. "That... complicates things."

A flush crept up Mae's neck, and she turned away. "I'm sorry. I shouldn't have said anything. I'll just get started on that uniform. Will you be needing a dress uniform this time? Better to tell me now, so that I can cut them simultaneously, and—"

"Mae."

Tears were gathering at the corners of her eyes as she scurried into the back room. She was a foolish, selfish woman, just like she'd always been. Of course Bailey didn't want her, they'd just been thrown together out of chance. "—and if you do need a dress uniform, I'm going to suggest that we use a slightly different fabric this time. After all, the last one was made out of curtains, which—"

"*Mae.*"

"Yes?" she answered, without turning to face her. She wasn't sure she could. Bailey's arm snaked around Mae's waist, bending to press her lips against Mae's neck. The warm, enticing kisses started at her shoulder, lingering at the crook of her neck, just long enough to make her tingle with anticipation.

Mae laced her fingers behind Bailey's neck, reaching up to kiss her. The moment their lips touched, it was like a new universe was being created, a brand new existence where they would be together in perpetuity, by each other's sides, laughing, touching, fighting, until they were old and grey. The excitement and relief hitched in her throat with a quiet sigh as she leaned in to deepen the kiss.

Bailey's lips were soft and sweet, like a perfectly ripe raspberry in the morning sun, dewy and plump. Mae's body came alive with the craving, wanting more of her, to drink down into her parched soul, to quench the cracked landscape of her heart. It hadn't been clear how much she'd been missing out on until that kiss, the wet hunger of it dizzying.

She was lost in a halo of red flamed hair and deep wanting, awakening something within her very core that had lain dormant for years, an electrified connection that made her feel ascended and alive, like being brought back to life from the brink of death. She pulled Bailey closer, so that their bodies were pressed tightly against each other, standing free in the center of the room, anchors for the other amid a tide of swirling need.

Her hands shaking, she reached for the toggles on Bailey's jumpsuit, flipping one open, and then another, and before she knew it, she was being swept up by strong arms, pressed against the racks of silks and satins, her legs wrapped around Bailey's waist.

"You're beautiful," Bailey murmured, her face buried in Mae's neck, slipping her hand beneath layers of taffeta skirts to rest against bare skin where the stockings ended. Her lips lingered where neck met collarbone, her breath hot against Mae's skin. Rubbing a thumb against her thigh, she hesitated, pulling back so gently, it might have been undetectable.

"It's alright," Mae whispered, her hands on Bailey's waist, pulling the toggles free of their brass clasps.

"But the shop door..."

"We're closed," Mae said, pulling the curtain across, hiding them away, alone, wrapped up in each other with no interruptions or reminders of their complicated reality. She reached inside Bailey's jumpsuit, catching the hem of the soft white undershirt and pulling it free. She gently ran her hands over Bailey's exposed breasts, her fingertips tracing around each areola. "I'd forgotten what it feels like to want someone this much," she confessed, her voice low and raspy.

"I've wanted this from the moment you kissed me in the Capital. It felt real."

"It *was* real." She twisted a lock of Bailey's hair around her finger. "I could have chosen a dozen different ways to cause a scandal. I wanted the excuse to be alone with you, even if only for a moment."

Bailey ran a hand against the laces of Mae's corset, tugging delicately at the knot in the center. "Is there somewhere we can go?"

"Upstairs," Mae answered with a nod. "Is where I live." She hoped she'd picked up her dirty laundry that morning. Shit.

Bailey held her close, carrying her up the narrow wooden stairs to her unlocked door. She kicked it open gently with the toe of her boot, setting Mae on the table, fumbling with the knots. "How do you get this thing off?"

"Like this," Mae said, guiding her hands across the firm stays to the ribbon that released the knot, loosening the corset until she could pull it off over her head.

"Mm," Bailey grunted quietly, kissing her again, laying her back against the table, her hand on Mae's thigh, inching upward, her breath ragged with excitement.

Mae felt a distantly familiar heat spread between her hips, a forbidden tightness building within that made her ravenous for Bailey's touch. Her skirts trailed off the table like a taffeta waterfall, crisp blues tumbling to the ground in a frozen painting. She groaned quietly when Bailey bent to kiss her naked breasts, a hand teasing at Mae's entrance, the anticipation almost tearing at her. When Bailey slipped inside, she cried out in the dark, biting at her lip as she stared at the whitewashed ceiling, almost navy in the unlit room.

She ground herself against Bailey's hand, savoring the deep connection that rubbed at the most sensitive part, building the tightness with every motion.

"You're so beautiful," Bailey said again, planting tiny kisses down across Mae's stomach, pausing at the neatly trimmed thatch of hair, her warm breath trailing goosebumps across Mae's skin.

"And I've never wanted any woman more," Mae replied, burying her hands in Bailey's hair, inviting her to nestle between her thighs, where she craved the sticky sweetness of her tongue the most.

When the kisses began, she cried out, stars in her eyes, her breath soft, uneven, shallow, as she gasped for air, drowning in the overwhelming sensation, the tension building to the inevitable peak. She pulled her closer, deeper, the yearning washing over her, uncontrollable.

Bailey rose up to kiss her again, and she tasted her own earthy womanliness on her tongue, and gasped again. Mae reached down to where Bailey's thighs met, and teased, pressed, until they were both panting, moaning softly into each other's mouths like they had just discovered what it meant to be alive, and maybe they had.

When the explosion of pleasure washed over Mae, she pulled Bailey close, gently biting her neck until she was crying out, too.

Bailey gently lifted her, carrying her to the bed, where they lay in each other's arms, tracing invisible patterns on exposed skin, marveling at every pore, every strand of hair, every eyelash, every faded scar and freckle, kissing each other gently. "You know this doesn't change anything, right?" Bailey whispered breathlessly. "I still have to go."

"I know."

"I'll come back to you, Mae."

"You better." She rolled onto her side, propping herself up on an elbow. "You can't do that and then leave me here, alone. I expect *plenty* more of where that came from the *second* you get back."

306

Bailey pulled her in for a tight embrace. "Knowing that you're here waiting for me is what will keep me careful."

"I'd better get a start on that uniform. Wouldn't want to miss a crucial detail."

"Just stay here one more moment. I want to burn this feeling into my memories."

* * *

The mirrors that hung over Bradach creaked as they turned inward, casting the cool, far off light into the city.

Dawn.

Mae sat in the chair in the back room of her shop, sewing patches across the breast pocket while Bailey slumbered in her bed. She'd need her sleep for what was coming next, so she'd let her rest through the night. The uniform was done, sewn from perfectly matching wool, another perfect replica. With any luck, it would keep Bailey safe as she saved her people. Pulling the iron gingerly from the fire, she pressed out the creases until it was suited for any general.

"Good morning," Bailey said with a yawn, descending the stairs, her jumpsuit still open at the front, her undershirt folded delicately on the side table. "I'm sorry, I fell asleep."

"You need a clear head. Just know that when you get back, I will absolutely be keeping *you* up all night as payment."

Bailey blushed a deep crimson. "Deal."

"Don't think you can weasel out of that, either."

"I wouldn't dare, Ms. Machenet."

"When is your shuttle?"

"We leave just before midday, but I should get down to the docks early to make sure we're all loaded in. Hell knows Marshall can't lift those crates,

and if I leave it to him, we'll all be eating tasteless trash until we're back."
She kissed Mae's hand. "I'd invite you to come with us, but—"

"I know. All extra space on that transport needs to be for your people."

"Yeah."

"Bring them back safe," Mae said, turning away to hang up the uniform, and to hide the tears gathering in her eyes. "You come back safe, too. Don't go chasing legacies, Bai. I need you here with me when this is all over."

Bailey pulled her in close for a kiss. "You can count on it." She took the uniform, smiling admiringly. "Excellent work as usual."

Mae lingered for just a moment, before dropping a small crystalline sphere into her pocket. "It's just a silly token. One of the first natural leaves grown in Bradach, encased in glass. So you remember to come home to me."

"Thank you." Bailey squeezed her tight in an embrace. "See you soon, Mae."

As Bailey left, unlocking the deadbolt and flipping the sign to 'open,' she turned back for one last wave. When the door closed, Mae crumpled into a heap, the only thing she could do to keep herself from running after her, begging her not to go.

Chapter 32

"You ready for this, Stockton?" Marshall asked, leaned against the doorway of her cramped quarters.

"No. But I don't think anyone is ever really ready for something like this."

"Still time to back out."

She dusted off the knees of her jumpsuit and hopped down from her bunk. "After months of working to get to this point? After risking my entire ass down on Gamma-3 for the credits to do this? No, Marsh, it's gotta be now."

"You got the plan all ready to go?"

"Not much of a plan, beyond breaking in, stealing some keys, and loading people onto the ship before they figure out the game."

"You promised that you'd be careful."

"And I will!"

He sighed, his hand resting against the empty holster on his hip. "I meant what I said, Stockton. You get the hell out of there at the first sign of trouble."

"Don't worry, Marsh, I've got this. Now get out so I can change into my General Fineglass costume."

He stepped out and slid the door closed, remaining on the other side. "What about the chip?"

"I'll lie that I was attacked by pirates with an EMP cannon. I still have my identification card from the Capital."

"And if someone recognizes you?"

"Marshall, for all the gods' sakes, we've been through this a thousand times already. Knock it off, you're just making me nervous."

"I just want to make sure our asses are covered."

"Our asses are very much exposed here, you know that," she said, stepping into the trousers. "The trick is to dress up as other asses and hoping no one knows the difference."

"We've got room for fifty people at a push. You really think that will be enough?"

"It has to be. A transport any bigger than this would raise too many flags. Sixty-seven were taken that day, and intel suggests some of them may have escaped before they reached this settlement. No word on the others, but we know some of them ended up in Skelm." She sighed, buttoning the jacket. "That's too hot a target for us right now with the general's new partnership with Allemande. Even if the fraud wasn't exposed publicly... *they* know that I'm around."

"I hope these folks know how lucky they are to have you," he muttered, his boots shuffling against the rusted metal in the hallway. "Gods know I'd just be thanking my lucky stars it wasn't me, and I'd never look back."

"Coming from the man who talked Captain Tansy into lending you her fastest ship to haul me out of the Capital, I'm going to call bullshit on that one."

"That's different."

"You can stop trying to convince me to turn back, it's not going to happen." Admiring herself in the small, dirty mirror on the wall, she grimaced. "Anyway, we're about to land. Too late now." She thrust open the door and gave him a cheesy grin. "What do you think?"

"Believable."

"Is that it?"

"We'd better hope so. Now go on, get to the loading bay to disembark. The less time we're parked on this asteroid, the better."

She tipped her cap in a mock salute and climbed down the ladder to the loading bay. "Ready to go, Captain," she shouted up to him.

"Don't get killed!" he shouted back.

The ship landed with a lumpy crunch, the landing gear not made for the rough surface of an asteroid. Rubbing the glass sphere in her pocket, she took a nervous, shaky breath as the loading bay door opened and the ramp descended. It was time.

The air here was smoky, polluted from the constant running of the strip mining machinery, their boilers burning coal to run faster and harder, instead of the newer waste-burning models. Profit before people, as usual with the Coalition. No wonder accidents plagued strip mining operations.

She covered her mouth to cough, her eyes watering from the acidic air.

Their ship, hidden among the other cargo vessels, was waiting for her to return with her people. Months of work, of tracking, and hoping, had all led to this moment. Now, to execute the non-plan and get the hell out of here. She approached the informational kiosk, a bored MPO sitting with his feet up on the desk, reading a newspaper.

She cleared her throat loudly to announce her presence.

"Operations tours are off-limits to civilians," he said without looking up. "Come back next week, we'll be running some of them for the press."

"I'm not a civilian," she replied.

He glanced over the top of the newspaper and choked on his sharp intake of breath. "A general! My apologies, ma'am, we just need you to sign in. Do you have your ID with you? Or I can scan your chip?"

"My ID," she said, sliding it across the desk with one hand, and signing Wilhemina Fineglass on the roster with the other. "I'm here on special orders. Is there anyone else I need to report to?"

"No, ma'am, you're the highest ranking here. It's a pleasure to have you here. My apologies for being rude, ma'am, please don't tell my commanding officer."

"I think we can keep it between us," she said politely. "I imagine the work here is painfully dull."

"You bet." He stared at her just long enough for the hair on her arms to stand up before he continued. "Sorry. A bit tired today, General. Go on through, don't hesitate to ask me if you need directions."

"I just need to know where the barracks are."

"The barracks?"

"Yes, as I said, I'm here on special orders." When he didn't respond, she smiled broadly. "It's classified."

"Ah, of course. Follow the dirt track all the way to the fork at the bottom of the hill, and turn left. Turning right will take you to the quarry."

"Noted. Thank you, Guardsman." It was getting late in the day, most of the workers should be in the barracks. The less time she was there, the better. She strode confidently down the unpaved trail, doing her best to look the part, despite the fact that, to her knowledge, no one was actually looking at her.

Cameras sat high on posts, the gears below them rotating with a quiet grinding. She pulled her cap down low over her face to hide as much of her identity as she could. With any luck, they wouldn't even put the pieces together until they were all long gone. The door to the barracks was propped open with a stack of Coalition pamphlets, and she resisted the urge to laugh. It's all they were good for.

A few people jumped up when she entered, scrambling to straighten their bunks.

"Piss off," one of them said. Marty. He had always been a grouchy curmudgeon, even when he was plowing the fields back home. "We already reached our quotas for the day! You can't squeeze blood from stones!"

"It's me," she whispered.

"By the gods," he uttered. "You came for us."

"It took a long time to find you. Now, come quickly, the transport is waiting at the top of the hill. Where is Yannick?"

"How are you going to get us out?"

She tipped her cap. "I am a general, after all."

He grabbed her hands in his leathery palms. "You are your mothers' daughter."

Tears sprang to her eyes, but she blinked them back. "Come on, you old fool, we don't have time for that right now. Tell everyone! As fast as you can!"

"Half are in the quarry," Marty said. "They've had us working round the clock for months."

So that's where Yannick was. "Damn. Get to the transport. Tell them I'm rounding up the rest. We won't be long. Go!"

They scattered, gathering up what few belongings they had, no more than what could fit in their arms. She left the barracks at almost a run, her boots kicking up dust as she headed down to the quarry. This part would be more difficult. The roar of heavy machinery rose up over the lip of the chasm, deafening and disorienting. "Yannick!" she shouted into the dark void, knowing there was no way he would hear her.

"Hey, you can't be—gods! Bailey Stockton, by my life!"

"Wendy, you have to get up the hill. I've got a transport waiting, but we don't have much time. Quick!"

"But—"

"Where's Yannick?"

"He's down in the mine!"

Bailey squeezed Wendy's shoulder reassuringly before pushing past her, descending further into the quarry. The path here was uneven, rocky, eroded by the constant blast of explosives. Every person she came across, she told them to head to the transport. An MPO foreman was up ahead, monitoring the schedule of the excavator, its huge dedicated boiler billowing clouds of coal-soaked smoke into the air.

"At ease," she said as she approached. "You're being relieved of duty. Pack your things."

"But—"

"This area is being evacuated, Foreman. Our... geological survey has suggested this asteroid is no longer fit for mining."

"This mine is practically brand new! There are years of life left—"

"The rhodium quality from this site is lacking, and has been since the inception. Are you *arguing* with your superior?"

He brushed sweat from his brow, smearing dirt across his face as he did so. "No, ma'am, of course not."

"I'll deal with the rest of the workers. You get out of here, back to the MPO barracks. Pack your things and wait for further instructions."

"Aye," he said with a salute.

Gods, it was lucky that the Coalition instilled total deference to superiors. She'd be in real trouble if she had to explain herself any further than that.

Her knowledge of rhodium or geology was woefully lacking. The path began to disintegrate, now more a mess of rock and dust, and slippery. Catching herself on the wall of rock to her right, she edged down further into the crevice. The uniforms here were grey, not by order of design, but because of all the smoke the fibers took on, staining the fabric.

"Yannick!" she shouted, the echo of her voice swallowed up by the inescapable lumbering of the machinery. "Yannick!"

She came across three more and sent them up to the transport. The longer she stayed, the greater the risk, but the transport would only be just over half full. She had to find more, and Yannick would be able to help. There was no way he'd go up the hill until they found everyone.

The control tower sat atop a tall, rickety ladder. She climbed it, rung by rung, her boots slipping every other step. The kill switch was more of a lever, painted red, outlined in yellow, and cold in her hands as she pulled it. The excavator slowed to a halt, the lights flickering on secondary power. Squinting across the cavern, she searched for any sign of movement and found none. Where was everyone else?

"Yannick!" she yelled again, climbing down. The sudden silence in the quarry was almost eerie, and left her exposed, vulnerable.

"Who the hell are you?" a worker asked. "Where is everyone?"

It was an unfamiliar face. "I'm evacuating this site, there's a transport at the top of the hill," she said evenly. "You'll be reassigned."

"Reassigned? But I only just got here last week! Where are you going to send me now, the Outer Rim?"

"I can assure you that you will not be taken to the Outer Rim."

"Hey, you're that general! The one who's been all over the public broadcasts with your husband!"

Bailey froze. "Uh, yup, that's me."

"It figures," he said with a laugh. "So what now?"

"Board the transport... don't stop to talk to anyone. We have a schedule to keep."

"What about my things?"

"Hurry."

He edged past her, climbing the rickety path to the freedom he didn't know he had yet. Hopefully someone would fill him in and keep him quiet. The last thing they needed was someone leveraging information for a better assignment.

"Wait!" she called after him. "Have you seen Yannick?"

"I don't know who that is," he answered, shrugging. "But there are others coming up from the mine now that the excavator stopped."

She ventured further down, increasingly paranoid about how long she'd been away from the ship. If they didn't get everyone out of here, the whole thing would have been for nothing, and she'd be breaking her promise to Mae that she'd get home safe, and Marshall and Bertie's imprisonment would be on her shoulders, too. How had her mothers done it? They'd always made everything look so easy, even on their last day, as they herded everyone to a secure, hidden location. No. There was no time for that now. She had to focus.

A bit farther down the eroded trail, there was a small group emerging from a crack in the cliff face, their yellow and purple helmets visible from far off. She recognized every one of them. Teachers, farmers, merchants, all people she grew up around, people she cared about. And, to her horror, children, their faces streaked with soot. Scrambling across the rocks, she couldn't help the wide grin that spread across her face.

"You're being evacuated!" she said proudly. "There's a transport at the top of the hill. Be quiet, try not to draw attention. We leave as soon as everyone is on board. Leave whatever you can, we'll be tight for space."

"Gods below," one of them said. Ms. Rowan, her teacher when she was young. "Bailey. We thought you'd died."

"Alive as ever. Now hurry! Has anyone seen Yannick?"

"He's in the cell."

"The what?"

"It's where they put the ones who don't play by the rules. It's near the freight way station at the other end of camp."

"Shit. Okay. Tell the others, get everyone you can on board. I'll get Yannick."

Ms. Rowan shook her head. "No. It's too dangerous. There are armed guards at the way station, to keep us from pocketing any rhodium."

"I'll handle it. Go!"

They shuffled past, sliding on the wet rock. She faced ahead, another ladder that led to the path for the way station. A long distance from the transport, but she wouldn't leave him here. Couldn't. Not after she'd come this far. She climbed, the rungs slimy in her hands, the sludge of grime and oil pumped out of the rocks around the clock. Just one more, and they could leave. They'd get back to Bradach, people would be fed and given shelter, she'd introduce Yannick to Mae. He'd like her.

Dragging herself over the top edge, her uniform was muddied almost beyond recognition now. She ran towards the way station, praying to all the old gods that the MPOs wouldn't be armed, or that she could sweet talk them. Once this was over, she'd never put the uniform on again. She'd have done her duty. Made her mothers proud.

The way station building was drab, a temporary building slapped together with shoddy, termite-eaten planks and broken shingles for the roof. To her surprise, the door was open, and she held her breath as she pushed it open.

"Bailey gods-damned Stockton, you fucking fool," he chimed from inside a tiny box made of iron bars. He was folded in on himself, no room to even sit up straight. "Are you trying to get yourself killed?"

"Are you? Everyone else is already on the transport. I had to make a special trip here just for you." She dug through the rickety desk drawers, looking for the key.

"I can't say I'm not happy to see you."

"Happy?" she asked, locating the key. "You should be fucking thrilled, Yannick."

"I'll be thrilled when you actually bust me out of here."

The stubby iron key clicked into the padlock and popped it open, freeing the barred door. "You are released, your highness."

"How do you plan to walk me out of here?"

"I came through the back, there was no one out there."

"Stockton, for all the gods' sakes, you look like you've been dragged

316

through a lake of mud. General's uniform or not, they're not going to let you waltz me to the transport without a few questions."

"Okay, I'll go distract them. You get to the transport. I'll be right behind you."

He stretched his arms over his head, the bones in his spine audibly crunching from the prolonged stooped position. "That's a terrible plan."

"It's the only one we've got, so take it or leave it."

"And if you get pulled in?"

She picked a large flake of mud off her sleeve. "The captain on that transport knows what to do."

"Stockton—"

"Listen, Yannick, this isn't a debate, alright? Get to the fucking transport. I will meet you there, and you can argue with me about it later."

"Be careful."

"I'm always careful. Go!"

He scrambled for the back door, and she threw open the front screen. "Officers!" she shouted. "Who is to blame for the lack of quality assurance at this site?"

They spun around, one dropped his heat gun. "General," he stuttered. "We're not scheduled a visit until next cycle."

"Are you telling me that operations are this much shoddier when you're not expecting an inspection?"

"No, we—"

"Explain yourselves!" She couldn't send them back to their barracks with the same story as she told the foreman, they'd run right into Yannick.

"We, uh... the production delays are due to the inferior quality of the laborers, and—"

"You're blaming the workers for this mess? What kind of leadership is that?"

"No, you see, they—"

She towered over him, hands on her hips. "Perhaps I should send you three to remedial training. Or, better yet, I'll go promote three of the workers, and you can take their places!"

317

"General, ma'am, please, we can explain! This mining site doesn't have the same purity as other sites, it takes much longer to extract it—"

"Are you giving me excuses?"

"It's just an explanation!"

"That's just not good enough," she spat. How long would it take Yannick to get across the gorge? "The Coalition is in dire need of rhodium, especially now that one of the mines has exploded. The future of our expansion lies at your feet, Officers, and you scoff at it with excuses and weak explanations?"

"We can do better, ma'am, if we just had some more power—"

"*More* power?"

"Yes, ma'am, our excavator runs night and day, but it's limited to how much it can carry in a load. As we said, it's much harder to extract here, it's buried deeper, and the veins aren't as pure."

"Your equipment is some of the most advanced in the Near Systems." Whether that was true or not, she had no idea, but it sounded good. "How can you look me in the face and ask for more? More, when many sites are making do with less?"

"Those sites are established, they have—"

"Your site should be established by now, and yet here I stand, covered in muck, wondering why standards in my beloved Coalition have fallen so far."

"This is a relatively new dig, we've been here less than a year, all due respect, General. With the labor shortage, it's taken much longer than usual to get set up here. It's a challenging site, and we're doing our best. I do apologize that it doesn't meet your expectations, and I can promise that we will work hard to improve conditions and efficiency here."

"I think that in this case, you need more supervision, and I will be writing to your sector's overseer to ensure that new quotas are drawn up to reflect the potential of this site. In fact, starting tomorrow, you can expect longer shifts, and—"

"Gods," one of the other officers whispered. "What the hell?"

"Is that any way to talk to your superior?"

"At ease, Officers," came a voice from behind her that turned her blood to ice. "I think you'll find that this woman isn't your superior at all. She's a fake. An impostor, and lower than the slime sitting at the bottom of that crevice."

Bailey turned slowly, despite already knowing it was going to be her own face staring back at her. "How good of you to come," she managed to squeak out. "And how unexpected."

Chapter 33

"Another?" Larkin asked, wine bottle poised over the glass.

Mae sighed. "No. I should head home."

"What if I said I had an exclusive vintage in back? Freshly imported from Delta-4."

"Tempting, but no. Drinking on an empty stomach always gives me a headache."

"What if I said that I *also* have an enormous plate of leftover paella? José made it, so you know it's good."

"I'm not hungry."

Larkin perched on the bar, the long tails of her hooded jacket sweeping over the side. "You have to eat, you know. The last thing she'd want is to come back to find you all gaunt and emaciated. Come on. Half a plate. Or Eves can fix you something?"

"I just don't know how I'm supposed to pretend everything is normal, when I'm worried sick. I can't think about anything else, Larkin. I wish I'd have been able to go with her."

"You haven't known Bailey as long as I have. She's strong. She'll be back."

"I just don't know what to do with myself until then."

"What if I said that I was going to have some, and if you happened to steal a few bites, that would be absolutely fine and not at all my sole intention?"

"Fine," Mae said with a laugh, resigned. "I appreciate you listening to me, day in, and day out."

"I'm a bartender. That's my job."

"You're very good at it."

"It's just a shame you're not a spirits drinker, I just created something brand new that people are raving about. Chocolate, good rum, and cinnamon, served in an eggshell."

Mae wrinkled her nose. "And who exactly is raving about that?"

"People." Larkin grinned and jumped down, smacking her palm lightly against the bar. "Right. I'm gonna hop in back. Watch the bar for me, will you?"

"Sure." She was left alone to nurse the dregs of her wine, the last few ruby droplets collecting at the bottom. Without the Purple Pig, she'd be at home, alone, again. Something that had never bothered her before was now a waking nightmare. It was probably nothing compared to whatever Bailey was dealing with. They'd be nearly there now, if her calculations were right. They were. She'd checked them at least two dozen times.

"I don't *care* if it's protocol, gods be damned!"

"Keep your voice down."

She hadn't noticed when she arrived, but Amy, Davey, and Hector, Mr. Hawkins' 'dead' husband, were sitting at a table positioned in the darkest corner of the tavern. Keeping her focus on her glass, she watched from the corner of her eye, and strained her ears to hear more.

"You have to let me go back for Aran," Amy begged, emotion heavy in her voice. "He'll be worried sick. Who knows what they told him! What if they told him I left him?"

"Then it would be a kindness. Anger is easier to process than grief," Hector replied. "You knew what you were signing up for. We all did."

"I never thought it would end like this."

"No one ever does."

She leaned across the table. "What if I go by myself? Without authorization?"

"Then you'd be a fool," Davey said. "You're telling us your plans right now, and we'd be obligated to report your insubordination."

"Oh, piss off, Klein. You have no idea how hard this is," Hector spat. "We all know how far you'll go to complete a mission, regardless of the planned operations. You have no place lecturing anyone else on their choices." He pushed his empty glass across the table with a hollow scrape. "That said, Amy, you can't go back for him. You absolutely cannot. It would put our entire squadron into danger, and your husband as well. They'll be watching his every movement, you know this. I'm sorry it's worked out like this, I know it's challenging. I can only offer that things do get easier, with time."

Amy shook her head. "That's not good enough."

"It's been two years since I've seen my husband. You think I'd have willingly chosen that? To know he's probably moving on without me, falling in love with someone else—"

"Stop!" she sobbed, burying her face in her hands. "I never should have joined The Scattered. I'd be at home with him right now."

Hector laid a hand on her arm. "Someone has to stand up against the Coalition's power over the Near Systems. Once they breach the Outer Rim, there's no telling how bad things will get. They'll have total control, Amy."

"You don't need to give her the sales pitch, she's already here," Davey said. "We're going to have a hell of a time drawing in new recruits if part of the pamphlet reminds them that joining up could ruin your life and leave you with a whole ocean of regrets." He ruffled his hair and cleared his throat. "We've all made mistakes. We've all done things we regret, every one of us, and I don't mean just at this table."

"What do you suggest, then?"

Davey shrugged. "What the superiors don't know can't hurt them."

"That's patently untrue, and you know it." He leaned back in his chair. "A moment ago you were threatening to turn her in, now you're proposing what, mutiny?"

"It's only mutiny if you're on a ship, and I only said that we'd be *obligated* to report it. Not everything gets reported."

"Aran can't stay in the Capital alone," Amy said between sniffles. "He's not cut out for it. That fucking Mr. Machenet is sure to show up again and try to shake poor Aran down for information he doesn't have and doesn't know how to get."

At the mention of her father's name, Mae eased off the bar stool and approached the table, much to the horror of its occupants.

322

"Mae," Amy said, "I—we didn't know you were there."

"No, that much is clear," she replied. "Amy, my father knew about you, and your involvement in The Scattered. He threatened me with turning you in just before I was arrested in the Capital."

"But—he—why the hell didn't you tell me before?"

"Because you left with us, and, if I am honest, I've been distracted, and I didn't know where to find you. It's not as if your kind leave calling cards."

"You should have told me when we were on the Cricket."

"And for that, I can only apologize. The trip was relatively short, all things considered with the speed of the Dolly Rose, and, well, my mind was... elsewhere."

Hector sat back in his chair, rubbing his temples. "How could he possibly have known?"

"My father knows a great deal more than he should. It's his business to know things, and use them as leverage. He's a liar and a con artist. I couldn't be more thrilled that he's lost his bargaining chip where I am concerned, and that he can no longer summon me back there. I thought I would be stuck in the Capital forever." She sighed. "Though this partnership with Overseer Allemande is sure to cause problems sooner or later."

"It seems like a sloppy move to assume you'd care about the welfare of someone you hadn't seen in over a decade," he said. "You might have just shrugged and let him turn her in, without ever setting foot on Gamma-3."

"You weren't the initial threat. He convinced me that he knew where Bradach was, that he'd had me followed."

Davey almost knocked his chair over, he stood so fast. "He knows where Bradach is?"

"It was a ruse. His information was inefficient to buy him any kind of influence in the Capital, and I was a fool to think he was telling the truth. If he actually knew where this place was, he never would have bothered summoning me home. He would have used it the first opportunity he got, regardless of our familial relationship." Mae pulled up a chair and sat down at the table, her hands folded neatly on the sticky wood surface. "My point is, Amy, that you can't go back there. Hector is right that Coalition Intelligence will be watching Aran like a pack of hungry wolves. Add my father into the mix, with all the people he pays to whisper him any secrets, and there's no way you'd be able to infiltrate."

"I can't just leave him there," Amy replied in a small voice, heavy with emotion. "I love him."

"Is there any way you could get word to him safely? Get him to leave the Capital under the radar, maybe head to a travel beacon, hope he isn't followed?"

Hector shook his head. "They'll follow him all the way to the Outer Rim if they think he'll lead them to The Scattered. That's why this protocol exists. It is painful, and terrible, but it keeps us safe. And it keeps our loved ones that are left behind safe, too."

"He still loves you, you know. Mr. Hawkins. Er, Alexander."

"You spoke to him? What did he say? Is he alright? Is he with someone?"

"It's clear that he misses you terribly, Hector. He's lost without you."

"It would have been easier if I hadn't even asked."

"Sometimes what's easier isn't always what's right. One of the many things that he taught me. Of course, he was talking about seam allowances, but it applies in life, too."

"I know that what's right is Aran being with me," Amy said defiantly. "I'd risk anything to get him out of there."

Hector buried his face in his hands. "There's nothing we can do. Any movement from us could trigger a terrible chain of events that would just put not just us in danger, but every single member of The Scattered. And think of the precedent it would set, if word got out!"

"How good are they with codes?" Evie asked, leaning over the second floor banister. "I'm sorry. I know I shouldn't eavesdrop, but it is my tavern, after all. Well, half my tavern. A third."

"Codes?" Amy asked. "What kind of codes?"

"Any kind of codes, numerical or alphabetical."

"I don't know, it's not something we ever discussed."

"What about a secret you two shared, something cryptic, or a favorite piece of music, or... or!" She ran to the stairs, excited. "Or a book! You know, my friends Henry and Georgie, they had a code based on a book, it's how they passed messages even though the lines were monitored. It's not a solution for, you know, daily correspondence, because it wouldn't take long for something like that to rouse suspicion, but a couple times to tell them what to do to get out of there could work."

Mae raised an eyebrow. "Evie, what—"

"Oh, I've done *loads* of research on codes now. I swear I've read a book on every kind of methodology there is! I'm no genius code breaker - that would be Henry - but coming up with a plan like this sounds like fun!"

"Fun?" Davey asked. "Gods, you need to get out more. Doesn't your girlfriend ever take you out?"

"She prefers a night in with a book, actually," Larkin called from the doorway to the backroom, an enormous plate of paella in one hand, and a dusty bottle of red wine in the other. "Are we scheming? I love a scheme, me."

"No," Hector said emphatically, "We are *not* scheming."

"Are you sure? Because the way you're all crowded around that table, barely whispering, indicates a scheme." Larkin approached the table, sauntering over and stopping to plant a kiss on Evie's cheek before setting the plate down. "Who's hungry? I always find mischievous planning makes me hungry."

"Oh, yes, please," Amy said, her eyes wide.

"Eves, you wanna grab us some bowls? I need to open this wine. I smell an all-nighter."

"We are not having an all-nighter!" Hector argued. "I want this to be a possibility more than any of us—to see my Alexander again would be the kind of joy that words cannot express—but I have to put my foot down here as the commander, and say that we cannot pursue this. It is madness, and it's likely to get us all killed."

"Wine?" Larkin asked, removing the cork with a satisfying pop that echoed around the mostly empty tavern.

Hector sighed heavily. "Fine. One glass, and that's it."

"Now we're getting somewhere!" She bent and poured a glass, a deep and complex bouquet, dark claret in the glass. "Mae?"

She couldn't resist such a fine vintage. "Yes, please."

"I'm sorry, I haven't introduced myself. I'm Larkin, and my beautiful other half getting plates is Evie. Would either of the two of you like a glass? It's on the house. I love excitement. There are some things I miss from my days as an assassin."

Davey stared wordlessly, but pushed his glass across the table.

"An experienced assassin?" Hector asked, intrigued. "Perhaps you'd be a good candidate for The Scattered, we—"

"No!" Evie shouted from the back room. "Absolutely not!"

"None for me, thank you," Amy said. "I don't drink."

"Ah! You're a prime candidate for one of my new creations then, a blend of juices and seltzer and garnish! Or, if you prefer, we also have a range of other beverages. Water. Tea. Coffee."

"The first thing?"

"Excellent!" Larkin shouted excitedly. "Eves! I'm going to try that new thing I made!"

Evie emerged from the back with a stack of bowls and forks perched precariously inside. "Should we send for Henry? After all, if we're talking codes—"

"I already did that, she's on her way," Larkin answered, bustling behind the bar, lining up several carafes of juice, a tall glass bottle, a plate of quartered limes, and a bucket of ice. "You're not allergic to anything, are you?" she called over to Amy.

"Shellfish. You don't have to bother, though, it's fine—"

"It's not *shellfish* to have a drink!" Larkin called, snorting at her own joke. "None of that here, don't worry."

"This is the weirdest tavern I've ever been in," Davey said, helping himself to a large serving of the paella, the curls of steam ascending gently to the ceiling. "But I'm not complaining."

Evie passed out the rest of the bowls. "She's just excited. Spends all night out here sometimes working on new beverages for the menu. Here, have a fork."

"Why do you even want to help us?" Hector asked. "You don't even know us."

"You're sitting with Mae, who we know to be an excellent judge of character, and you disembarked from the Cricket with some of our other closest friends, so you have to be decent people." She smirked. "Captain Violet would have thrown you out an airlock otherwise."

"She's certainly an intimidating figure," Hector agreed.

"Nah. She's a teddy bear, really. Unless you get on her bad side, like Barnaby."

"Who the hell is Barnaby?"

"No one important. Come on, everyone, eat! Larks, are you almost done over there?"

"Yes, Eves, I'm just arranging the garnish."

"Oh, I don't need garnish, I—" Amy started.

"It *needs* the garnish," Larkin argued. "There. Done!" She presented a beautiful beverage, crystalline at the top, followed by a striking magenta and at the bottom, an oceanic blue.

"Gods," Mae breathed, almost regretting not asking for one herself. "It's so... beautiful."

Larkin grinned proudly. "It's pea flower lemonade!" She set it down in front of Amy, who nodded approvingly.

"Usually when I tell a bartender I don't drink, they give me lukewarm tap water."

"Not in my establishment! Everyone deserves a beautifully crafted beverage!"

"She's very enthusiastic," Evie explained. "And it really packs in the patrons during happy hour."

Mae took a bite of the paella, the rich, spicy food bringing her back to life. "Right, we need an end goal, and we can work backwards from there."

"Get Aran and Alexander off Gamma-3, to ultimately be with us," Amy answered firmly. "But in order to do that, we need to figure out how they can get off-world without being followed or detected."

"They're going to need help," Larkin said.

"What, are you volunteering to go and escort their spouses out of the Capital?" Davey asked. "Because if not—"

"Oh, no, my Capital days are through," Larkin said, rummaging around behind the bar. "I left that city and all the poisoning behind me. I'm a settled woman now. A bartender, who'd have thought?"

Amy examined her glass suspiciously at the news, stirring it and staring at the swirling colors.

"Don't worry, I'd never poison a patron," Larkin said with a laugh. "It's bad for business."

"What about a disguise?" Evie suggested. "Not perfect, but it's somewhere to start."

"I can handle that," Mae said. "No one looks twice at MPOs. Send them some uniforms, get them on a transport. I'll start tonight."

"How can we be sure they won't be followed?" Hector asked. "As much as I am desperate to see him, and Amy to see her husband, I know that I for one wouldn't want to risk the safety of The Scattered for my own happiness."

Larkin perched on a barstool with a bowl of paella. "There's no way to be one hundred percent sure you aren't being tracked. If they want to track you, they'll damn well find a way. Trust me on that one. But if you could get hold of a scrambler or something, that would at least be insurance."

"Where the hell are we going to find scramblers that small?" Davey scoffed. "It's not like you can hide one under your coat."

"Maybe not the scramblers you've seen, but Alice and Kady, you remember them from the ship, right? I'm sure they can work on something. Last I heard, they had a few prototypes spare. Doesn't hurt to ask."

"Why would they give us the prototypes?"

Larkin stuffed a heaping forkful of food into her mouth. "What else are they going to do with them? Besides, I'm sure you'll all find some way to pay them back when they need it, right?"

"I suppose something could be arranged," Hector grumbled. "As long as they aren't going to be demanding the services of The Scattered for every minor scuffle."

"I think you'll find that the Cricket can handle itself," Evie mused. "Okay, so, we're waiting on Henry to talk codes, we've got uniforms at the ready, or almost, anyway, and maybe some scramblers. What else?"

"I'm here!" Henry shouted from the doorway, hanging her coat on the hook.

"That was fast."

"Larkin said codes. You know how I love codes."

"I thought that you'd be busy with the research facility?"

Henry shrugged. "I'm always busy. But we've got a good team down there now, they can do without me for a night. Besides, Roger is managing a new project, an atmospheric shield to protect the more vulnerable rebel settlements. We can't handle another round of those storms, we don't have the damn resources."

"So you'll help us?" Amy asked.

"I don't know what we're doing yet."

Mae stood, offering her chair. Her legs were getting stiff, anyway. "We're smuggling a couple of friends out of the Capital."

"That's going to be a hell of a job. Even in Skelm patrols and searches were ramped up. We barely got out alive."

"We have a plan to get them some uniforms and scramblers, so they can then meet us at a transport beacon. We need your help to get them word. Any ideas?"

Henry cracked her knuckles as she sat down. "I have a few. Professions?"

"Aran works at our—the bakery," Amy offered. "And Hector's husband is a teacher, a sewing instructor."

"We can certainly work with that. I was afraid you were going to tell me that they were officials. That would have presented a much larger problem. We've had a hell of a time trying to get the Judge out, and now she's gone no-contact. Do you think they're up to the challenge?"

"Alexander once crashed the Governor's party," Hector said with a wistful laugh. "I'm sure he'll have no problems with getting himself out."

"Excellent. You'll both have to come up with some kind of secret, or inside joke that they would know could only come from you. Otherwise they might think it was some kind of ruse, or a trap. Next, we'll use that as the basis for our code, so they can easily memorize it. I would say we can get... two messages through per person, before they get flagged as suspicious and trigger an investigation. That doesn't leave us a lot of wiggle room, but it should be enough."

"Thank you for helping us," Amy said earnestly. "I don't think I could live the rest of my life without Aran."

Henry nodded. "I know what it's like to miss someone so much that your bones ache. That awful emptiness when you think you might never see them again. I'm happy to help, if it means reuniting people who love each other."

She was pretty, in that alluring and mysterious, bookish way. Not Mae's type, but she could see why Bailey had fallen for Henry. Smart, capable, kind. She only hoped that she could measure up, with her own guilty past that followed her like a hungry shadow.

"I don't know you all that well," Henry continued, twisting around in her chair to face Mae, "but I know you must be worried about Bailey, whatever your relationship together is. I'm worried about her too. She's a good person, you know."

"Yes, I know." Mae said. "Better than either of us, that's certain."

Chapter 34

"Arrest her," Fineglass ordered. "Put her in the way station, I'll deal with her myself. You three, scour the site. We have it on good authority she's engaging in trafficking workers."

Iron cuffs clamped hard around her wrists, and all she could think about was how she'd broken her promise to Mae. She wouldn't be making it home, after all. Marshall would lift off the second Yannick was on board. He knew the rules. They all did.

"I knew you'd show up here," the real general said, shoving her towards the way station shack. "I've been keeping an eye on this backwater just for you. Do you have any idea what I've had to do to clean up the mess you made in the Capital? Journalists paid off or blackmailed, covering up the escape to preserve my sterling reputation. You deserve even worse than what's about to happen to you."

"And what is going to happen to me?" Bailey asked, tripping over the uneven threshold of the way station, back where she'd just liberated Yannick from.

"Let's not spoil the surprise! I should say, we have quite a bit of catching up to do." She clipped a padlock around the cuffs, locking Bailey to the long pipe in the corner that fed heat from the main boiler below. At least it wasn't the cage. "Let me have a real look at you." Fineglass hovered around her like a gnat, inspecting her face, her jawline, even her hair. "The resemblance really is uncanny. How did you do it? Surgery?"

"I told you back on Gamma-3, no surgery. I just look like this."

"That's impossible. Coincidences like that don't happen. Who recruited you for this? The Scattered?"

"No one recruited me."

"We've done research into you, Bailey Stockton." She said the name like it was crushed glass in her mouth. "It wasn't easy, given the lack of records. No photo, either, though I can see now why that is. Born to rebel parents, raised off-world." She dropped Bailey's journal on the desk. "You left this behind. Quite the unique story. It's not hard to see how you would fall into a life of villainy."

"I'd hardly call it villainy."

"Your perception has been warped by a lack of rules. You've spent your life doing as you please, with no regard for the greater good or the necessity of expansion. Here you are, trying to reclaim people that were never yours in the first place. You may have known them from childhood, but every one of them, except the children of course, had lives in the Coalition. They abandoned their contracts, their responsibilities, to play at being farming folks on that piece of shit spit of land you called home."

"It's gone now, anyway," Bailey said bitterly. "Your glorious Coalition saw to that."

"That was recorded as a meteorological anomaly."

"It was a storm generator, and you know it."

"A what?"

Bailey stared at her. What was this, some kind of act to get her to give up information? "A storm generator. To generate high-powered storms. Usually to target rebels, though sometimes Coalition citizens in cases of insubordination."

"Don't be ridiculous." Fineglass paced the narrow length of the shed. "What of your parentage?"

"My mothers both died when I was young." Including information on the circumstances of their deaths was only going to further convince the general that she'd been involved in some kind of grand conspiracy. "What about *your* parentage?"

"I was raised by law-abiding parents in the farming district on Gamma-3. Though that's really none of your business."

332

"Aren't you at least a little curious why we look alike?"

"You may not be admitting it, but I know beyond a shadow of a doubt that you... affected this face, somehow."

"On my honor as a filthy vagrant, I did not."

Fineglass narrowed her eyes. "Lies."

"Do you really think you're that important, that someone would willingly undergo medical treatments to look like you? You're a general, not a member of the High Council, for fuck's sake."

"I am very well regarded, and I have a sterling reputation, or at least, I did, before you came along and mucked it all up with your rampant nonsense. Amateur tactics, predictable moves, it was almost too easy to track you down, to anticipate your plan."

"Surely my inadequacy should prove to you that it's not some huge heist that's been planned for years."

"Hmm. You do have a point, though even the most delicately placed members of The Scattered have been rooted out. Perhaps it's just that the Coalition is demonstrably better than any hackneyed rebellion." She continued to pace, her hands clasped behind her back. "Even that deep placement in Skelm was found out before he went missing."

Bailey swallowed hard. Was she about to go missing, too? A gentle Coalition euphemism for having your corpse dumped into a lake, or tossed out into the dark. How many bodies were out there, floating around? Would she add her own to the horde of bones drifting through space?

"Let's make a deal," Fineglass continued, the scar over her eye shining in the dim light. "You tell me why you have my face, and maybe I'll convince the Judge to grant you life in a work camp, instead of a public execution."

"You wouldn't want my face in a public execution, even I know that would raise far too many questions that you don't want to be answering. All it would take is one person in the Capital to question it, and all your hard work of covering up my many indiscretions would go down the drain."

"I'll bet you think you're some genius little negotiator, don't you?"

"No."

"Trained for years, I'll bet, on my mannerisms, on how to conduct business in the Capital, on the best methods to cover up the extraction of a prisoner. Oh, yes, I know all about that. Francoise. A fake name, no doubt, but I am interested in why he was valuable enough to concoct such a dangerous plan."

Bailey pulled at her cuffs, the metal rubbing angrily at her skin. "Listen, lady, I'm telling you the gods' honest truths. I wasn't trained by some secret, dark cabal. I did not have medical intervention to look like you. There was no plan. I am a rum-runner, born off-world, and the whole thing was a huge accident. I spent the entire week terrified I'd be found out, which I was. I never wanted to impersonate you in the first place. Some jerk dragged me off the docks. The chip I had in was imprinted with someone else's data. I was supposed to deliver a shipment of very expensive whiskey and go home the same day."

"Hmm," the general said again, now paused from her relentless pacing. "A rum-runner."

"Yes, as I said."

"Who were you running rum to?"

Shit. She couldn't give up Marina, not after all she'd done to help Ned. "I dunno. Some speakeasy. I never saw it, they collected it from the depot."

"Bullshit."

"Do you really think I'd risk my life over some pissant little tavern in a city I hope I never see again?"

"You strike me as the annoyingly virtuous type. I suspect you would risk your life many times over, if it meant going out the way your mothers did."

Bailey grunted softly at the pain in her wrists. "My mothers... were foolish. And brave. They were many things, to many people."

"Do you ever feel angry about how they abandoned you? Chose some trashy little settlement over a life of safety with their daughter?"

"Grief is complicated. I don't envy the decision they had to make, and nor do I wish to repeat it."

"What of their families, then?"

"I don't know."

The general flipped through the file angrily and snapped it shut. "Their genetic records are sealed."

"Yes, I am aware."

"Why would they be sealed?"

"General Fineglass, I was fourteen years old when my mothers died. It's my understanding that they had their own records sealed, so that no one from Coalition controlled space could lay claim on me. I'm sure you're aware that often, when an orphan is placed with distant family, they typically end up farmed out for dangerous work contracts. They did not want as such for me. They did everything that they could to hide me, in case... well, in case what happened, happened."

"This is preposterous."

The general's sidearm glinted in the narrow gap between her crisply ironed shirt and the uniform jacket buttoned over the top. If she could just get free of the damned cuffs, maybe she could overpower her, but the cuffs were ironclad, the links forged for strength. Even she couldn't break them, not without a sledgehammer or a heat gun.

"Do you agree that this is preposterous?" General Fineglass prompted.

"Yes?"

"If what you say is true, which I doubt, then there is no reasonable explanation for our likeness. You understand it is difficult for me to believe you, under the circumstances."

Bailey shifted her weight. "I do." The general was curious, or she'd have already thrown her onto a prison transport. "I don't know what the explanation is." She leaned against the pipe, warm from the hot water, but a welcome balm for her sore muscles. "Perhaps we are related in some way."

"No."

"There aren't many other viable explanations, General."

"Impossible. My family comes from years of good Coalition stock. Both my father and my mother were generals for our glorious empire, they—" she stopped short.

"They what?"

General Fineglass turned away, shaking her head. "They spent their lives working towards a better future, up until the very last. They made sure I

335

had every opportunity that I had my heart set on."

"They're gone, then. Your parents."

"Yes."

"I'm sorry," Bailey said, and meant it. "Losing your parents is difficult, no matter the age."

"They were very old. In fact, they were already approaching advanced years when I was born. A surprise, long awaited, they always said."

She was being sentimental, and despite the fact that she was chained inside a shack, Bailey softened towards her, though maybe it was because it was eerily like looking into a mirror. "I am sorry that you didn't get more time with them."

"I need your cooperation, Bailey Stockton. I understand your position, and you understand mine even more thoroughly, having lived in my life for a week, though clumsily."

"It doesn't feel like I have much of a choice in refusing," Bailey replied, gesturing to her cuffs.

"Yes, well, I'm not taking them off. No doubt you'd try to overpower me, reach for my sidearm."

Damn.

"I wouldn't think of it," Bailey said innocently.

"I need your cooperations with a genetic test."

"So you *do* think we're related."

The general scowled. "No, but it needs to be officially ruled out. The Judge is preparing to seek additional charges against you for premeditated impersonation of an officer. If we do not share genetics, which I suspect is the case, then it is all but proven that you undertook significant medical intervention in order to steal my face."

"Okay."

"It is a rapid test. The results will be available in just a few moments after I collect the samples."

"You came prepared."

"I was not willing to let this information get out through a leak. I've dealt with enough press lately, thanks to you, and I am not eager to place myself back in the spotlight. The Judge will accept my word as to the results, as a personal favor to me. She owes me one."

"What did you do, get her kid a placement in the military, or something?"

General Finegless looked up from the file. "I took a bullet for her several years back, on an assignment. Before I went to the Outer Rim. Why did you think she specifically requested my name when she wasn't able to perform her duties? Not just because I am a general, but because she trusts me implicitly. Saving someone's life will do that." She glanced back down at the file. "Not that you would know that."

So much for fucking sentiment. Bailey bristled at the jab, searching for the right words to cut with. "Yeah, well—uh—"

"Open your mouth. I need a swab. The sooner this is over, and I have confirmation, the better."

"Fine."

She swabbed her own mouth first, placing it into a sealed test tube, and then stepped forward, shoving a dry medical swap into Bailey's mouth.

"Gods," Bailey coughed. "You don't have to try to remove my tonsils."

"It's best to have an accurate sample. Don't be a baby." The second tube sealed with a click. "Not long now." She placed the tubes into a small brass chamber and clamped the lid down. "This test aims to match certain genetic markers."

"I know how it works."

"Well, then, I suppose I don't have to explain to you that it will take a few moments."

A far-off explosion sounded, shaking the rickety walls of the shed. Her heart raced in anticipation, fearing that it was Yannick coming back for her. It better not be, he'd get himself killed. It's not as if they'd brought weapons with them, it was supposed to be a stealth retrieval, not a standoff.

"What in all the gods' names was that?" General Fineglass barked, already at the window, peering out.

"It's a mining quarry. I imagine explosions are customary here." Not explosions like that, but she didn't want to draw any attention if it was Yannick. Or Marshall. Either of them were equally likely to jeopardize an entire mission to play the hero. She'd never forgive them if they did.

"General!" one of the officers shouted, gasping as he nearly fell through the door. "General Fineglass, a transport—"

"What in blazes are you talking about?"

"I—"

"Spit it out!"

"General, a transport escaped. Almost all of our workers are missing."

Fineglass turned slowly, rage crawling up her face, red and poisonous. "*You*," she spat. "You did this!"

"Uh, ma'am, I'm also obliged to tell you that they dropped an explosive on our communications array. We can't get word in or out."

Bailey snorted a laugh. That would have been Marshall. Smart. They'd have hours now to cover their tracks, and she knew now that they'd gotten out safely. Relief flooded through her veins, despite her own precarious situation.

"Get out!" the general roared, sending the officer scrambling backwards. "Fix the damned array!" She clenched her fists, her meaty knuckles pulsing white as she turned her glare back to Bailey. "How did you do it, then? Hide a whole transport, load people up, and what, you acted as a distraction to give them time to get away?"

"Something like that."

"You disgust me."

"The feeling is mutual."

"Me? What have I done, other than faithfully serve my people?"

"I could ask you the same question."

The bronze chamber on the wobbly table lit a green light with a chirpy chime, and it was like all the air had been sucked out of the room.

"No," Fineglass whispered. "It can't be." She snatched the tiny print out from the chamber, scanning it angrily. "No! The test must have been faulty, or the chamber—" She reached into her pockets and pulled out two more swabs. "We test again."

"I thought these were one hundred percent accurate?"

"We. Test. *Again*."

338

"Alright, fine, shit, it's not like I have a choice." Bailey opened her mouth for the second swab and flinched from the force. "Ouch!"

"You're lucky I'm not taking the sample from your corpse. Shut up." The fresh samples went into the chamber, this time the lid being slammed down and latched with barely concealed rage. "Piece of garbage. You'd think they would test these things before signing them out, especially for such important applications like this."

With the transport gone, Bailey was all but trapped on this crappy asteroid, and with the comms out, there wouldn't be any way to patch into the array to get word out... not that she would want anyone risking their hides on a foolish mission to save her, anyway. What would Mae think, when the transport showed up in Bradach without her? Would she feel angry? Betrayed? What options were there, other than to accept whatever fate the general bestowed on her?

"Allemande is going to lose it," Fineglass said, her eyes fixed on the chamber. "I barely kept her from coming here herself."

"Not the new best friend you'd hoped for?"

"She's extremely capable, and assisted in keeping the more lurid details out of the press. She is useful, and her daughter has a mountain of potential." The chamber whirred quietly as it worked. "But if it's true, if this... is true, she will want to intervene. She will see my position as compromised." Fineglass sighed angrily. "I am on the precipice with the Outer Rim expansion. I cannot be compromised. I have worked my entire life for this, for the crowning opportunity."

"Mm," Bailey replied. What was she supposed to say? What the hell was even going on? The general's rage and sentiment oscillated wildly, unpredictable, like a dangerous storm.

The chamber chirped again, lighting up the green bulb at the top.

"Gods be fucking damned!" Fineglass screamed, hurling it at the wall, where the segments separated, falling to the floor in a pile of shining components. A spring, a cog, a solar panel, shining crisply in the dim light. "This can't be. It can't!"

"I'm sorry," Bailey offered, quietly afraid she was about to be murdered.

"I wouldn't want to be related to me, either."

"My whole life has been a lie. They *lied* to me. My own parents fabricated my entire existence, they—what was I, some pathetic orphan they found in a basket on the streets? I come from... who knows where the hell I come from! Rebels, probably!" She tossed the paper into the air, and it fluttered gently to the ground.

Half-siblings

"Gods below," Bailey breathed.

"Yeah, you're telling me."

"You're my... sister."

"It would seem so."

"So then my parents lied to me, too."

Why had they hidden her? How could one of her mothers have just walked away from one child, and not the other? Too many questions, and not enough answers.

Chapter 35

Mae hung the iron back in its place next to the fire and wiped her brow, admiring the uniforms. Not bad for a night's work, and they would catch the early shuttle out of Bradach, to reach them in just a few days. If everything went as planned, and the Dolly Rose met them at the transport beacon as planned, Aran and Mr. Hawkins would be reunited with their loves within the week. It was strange to call him Alexander, even if she was grown now.

"Morning, Sunshine," Abigail chirped, unlocking the front door and flipping the sign to open. "Gods, were you up *all night*? What in gods' hells, Mae?"

"Volunteered to help some friends."

"Of course you did. I don't suppose you got a head start on those alterations?"

"Didn't have time."

Abigail tutted and tossed a muffin, wrapped in brown paper, across the room. "And to think, I even brought you breakfast."

"Thank you."

"It's almost as if I somehow knew that you were up to something. Coffee?"

"In the carafe back here, it's fresh." Mae bit into the muffin, a little stale, but edible, the blueberries rehydrated from a pack, probably. "Where did this muffin come from?"

"I made them."

"They're good!"

"Oh, shut up Mae, I know they're terrible. Even my dog wouldn't have it." Abigail shot her a look, and then laughed. "I had to offload them somewhere.

Gods, what I wouldn't give for a cute little bakery here in Bradach. Shame the Pig doesn't open til lunch."

"I think you'd have a hard time getting those two up at dawn to bake, especially when they're open so late."

"I know, I know." She poured herself a mug of coffee, adding a cube of sugar and a splash of milk. "Need a refill?"

"No, thank you. I have to get down to the docks with these before the early shuttle departs, and I still have to wrap them up. I'll probably drink the rest of the pot when I return though, I don't think I'll get through the day without immense levels of caffeine."

"I don't mind taking them."

Mae shook her head. "It's alright, I'll go." She trusted Abigail almost implicitly, but this plan was so fragile, she wanted to see them make it on the shuttle herself. Anything else and she'd be fretting for days that something had gone wrong, and it would be her fault when they ended up trapped in the Capital, or worse.

"If you insist." Abigail leaned against the back room wall, biting into her own muffin. "I guess they aren't the worst muffins I've ever had. Hey, if you're going out anyway, maybe you could stop and get some more sweets for the bowl on the front desk? We're almost out."

"Only because you keep eating them."

"Don't get good sweets, then, and I won't eat them."

"Seems to defeat the purpose, Ab. Okay, I will pick up some sweets, those citrusy ones we had last time."

"I seem to remember that *you* are the one who ate those."

"I'll get a double portion, then."

Abigail lifted the uniforms from their hangers. "Finish your muffin. I'll wrap these. Paper or fabric?"

"Both. We want it to look... normal. If they get pulled and searched, they'll never make it to the Capital." Mae chewed at her lip. "Actually, why don't you use boxes, paper, and fabric? Will keep the wrinkles out if laid flat. We don't want them having to re-press the uniforms, it's much better if they arrive ready."

"Ever the perfectionist."

"This time it's life and death." Even saying it out loud made her shoulders tense. It was all well and good to dream up a dangerous plan. It was another entirely to execute it. The last thing she needed was more blood on her hands. "Better double wrap them before boxing."

"Aye, I got it," Abigail said, cutting a length of wrapping paper. "These people you're rescuing, will they come here to Bradach?"

"I'm not sure."

"Some people aren't happy with the refugee influx. Say the city's too crowded."

"Not you though, right Ab? You don't think that, do you?"

"No, I don't. How could I, when my family showed up here with nothing five years ago? Hell, there was no refugee camp then, no help. Without you giving me a job, we'd have ended up back on Delta-4, running from the authorities."

"Please, I would have been a fool not to hire you. I never would have been able to expand without you. Not to mention you covering for me, without notice. You're one of the most talented tailors I know." Mae sighed heavily. "I feel that things with the Coalition are going to get worse before they get better. Things feel... dangerous."

Abigail taped the boxes shut carefully, smoothing over the seams to ensure the contents wouldn't come loose. "Yeah. When I realized there was no way to contact you, I was panicked."

"Hell, I was panicked, too."

"Better make that a triple portion of sweets, Mae."

"Why don't I just buy out the entire stall?"

"I wouldn't complain."

Mae laughed and tossed the muffin paper into the waste bin. "I'd better get these down to the docks. Thanks for wrapping."

"You might be the better seamstress, but we both know I'm much better at wrapping."

"True." Mae took the large boxes into her arms and opened the door. "I'll be back in a few. Make another pot of coffee, will you? I feel like I'm about to pass out."

As the door latched shut, Mae raised her face to the morning light, reflected down from the enormous mirrors above the city. After being on Gamma-3, the rays didn't feel nearly as bright. Not like in the Capital, where the sunrise could burn your eyes. The Capital, which could burn every inch of you down for the good of the empire.

Bradach's cobblestone streets were wet with dew from the terraformers, the chilly temperatures at night not enough to freeze, instead leaving a delicate sheen across the stones that glinted in the mirror's reflections. Abigail was right. The city *had* grown, and even more so over the past year. Bradach was a refuge, a haven for so many. How could they resent others trying to do the same for their families? It didn't make any sense to her, but then, the Coalition attitude of superiority never had either.

The roads were livening up as shops opened their doors, the day traders showing up to line the pavement along the grass with carts packed with food and other supplies fresh from the cargo ships at the docks. One held an array of shining crystals and tall beeswax candles amid piles of dried flowers, another lined with tiny jars of herbs and medicinal ointments, probably stolen from a Coalition merchant vessel. Dried synthetic meats, aged cheeses, there was plenty to purchase, if you had credits or something to barter. A tempting bazaar, and she hadn't even made it to the stall that always had new silks.

Mae's boots clicked noisily against the cobblestones, and she was grateful that she had her old, reliable pair back. Hyun's spangled footwear, while beautiful, wasn't really practical, and she'd spent the entire time on the Cricket terrified that she'd accidentally ruin them. The refugee camp near the docks bustled with people, many of them spending their days working at the research facility nearby, doing whatever they could to help the cause.

The cargo ship was being loaded with huge wooden crates, most of it illegal alcohol to be smuggled into Coalition-controlled areas like Delta-4, where the stringent import laws weren't quite as strict as on Gamma-3. It was Bradach's main export, aside from the small amounts of artisan goods that had been sold to traveling merchants, who would visit the more remote settlements with goods for trade. The Coalition certainly wasn't going to make sure people had anything more than the bare minimum, and sometimes, not even that.

"This needs to go to the Capital, express," she said, setting the boxes down on top of the crate next to the dock manager's table. "I'd like them on the first ship out."

"That's going to cost you," she grumbled. "Express is a hefty fee, these days, with all the damned barricades everywhere."

"I know." She held out her arm, and the chip gun chirped as it read her details. "The names are on the respective packages."

"Nothing illegal?"

"No." It wasn't a lie, not really. There was nothing illegal about officer uniforms. They'd only be illegal once Aran and Mr. Hawkins put them on. "No contraband."

The dock manager raised an eyebrow. "You sure about that?"

"Yes."

"Because we've reached our contraband quota for this vessel already."

"It's not contraband."

"Very well, we'll load it up. Ship's leaving in an hour."

"Thank you."

There was a soft rumble as a ship behind her touched down. Not unusual, it was a busy port for a city this small, but what did make her turn was the screaming cheer that went up as it touched the ground. Gods. Marshall's ship. She ran to the ramp as it unfurled, her heart racing, willing Bailey to step off the transport. One by one, people disembarked, some reuniting with waiting family with hugs and plentiful tears, some looking a bit lost as they took in their new temporary home. One man knelt down and kissed the dock, openly weeping.

Georgie's mother, Sandrine, and her beau, José, were on hand, waiting with packs filled with necessities and fresh clothes. Mae's eyes were trained on the ship, her heart pounding harder every time a new face appeared that wasn't Bailey's. When Marshall and a man about her age disembarked, she ran over, her throat tight with emotion.

"Captain Marshall," she said, "don't tell me she's not with you. Please, you can't tell me that. You can't. She promised me, Marshall. She promised."

"Mae, I'm so sorry," he began.

A sob escaped from her throat. "No. No, this is some terrible joke, you've got her on that ship, Marshall, don't you dare lie to me."

"I'm sorry, things went sideways. We had to leave her behind. This ship, it's got no weapons. We were like sitting ducks with nearly sixty people on board. It would have been suicide to stay."

"No!" she shouted, and collapsed onto the dock. "No, it can't be. I only just found her, Marshall. They can't take her away from me, they can't."

"We don't know what happened after we left, maybe—"

"She promised," Mae whispered. "She promised me that she would come back."

"If I know Stockton, and I damn well do, she'll find a way out of that mess." The other man gently pulled her up and held her arm. "I'm Yannick, we—"

"I know who you are. She told me about you."

"I didn't want to leave without her. She insisted. Said it wasn't worth risking everyone's lives just for her."

Mae buried her face in her hands, her skin sticky with tears. "That sounds like my Bailey." A sob escaped her throat again. "I don't know what to do now."

"We wait," Marshall said with a grim face. "Not much else we can do. That place is going to be locked down tighter than a banker's wallet now, and we won't hear anything until they get that communications array working. We disabled it on our way out to be sure we'd make a clean exit."

"How long do we wait?"

"As long as it takes."

* * *

How could it be that the very moment she'd found real love, a real affection

346

for someone who felt it too, that she'd have it ripped away from her? It was like some terrible cosmic joke, to tease and tempt her with happiness, just to end up laying on the floor of her apartment in a heap, exhausted from hours of crying.

"Bailey, oh, Love, what have you gone and done?" she asked the painfully empty room. "You promised me that you would come back." She pounded her fist on the floor. "You promised!"

Her cheek pressed against the cool, smooth wood floor, another tear fell from her eye. "I wish I'd never gone to Gamma-3. I wish I'd never told her where her people were." Even as she said it, she knew that it wasn't true. She never would have been able to live with the guilt of keeping something like that from Bailey. Yet, the love of her life and the most beautiful person she'd ever known was stuck on some fucking asteroid strip-mining operation. The gods only knew what had happened to her.

The thought of Bailey's lifeless body wrenched another sob from her lungs. It couldn't be. How could she go on living if it were true?

Confident footsteps paraded up the back stairs, and Mae flinched away from the door. She didn't want to see anyone. She wanted to sleep until she woke up from the nightmare of Bailey's absence.

"Mae."

"Go away, Abigail," she mumbled into the floor. "I just need to be left alone."

"I sort of think that's exactly what you *don't* need, actually."

"I can't think about anything else."

Abigail sighed and set two glass containers on the table. "I brought dinner. You should eat."

"I'm not hungry."

"That Yannick guy came to the shop, looking for you. He wanted to talk."

"I don't have anything to say."

"He thinks she's still alive, Mae."

"Impossible."

"He just wants to talk."

Mae sat up and wiped her face with the back of her sleeve. "She promised me that she'd come back, Ab."

"I know. And maybe she still will. Listen, Mae, the rest of the mission group, they need you. That plan *needs* you. It wouldn't exist without you and your skills. You can't abandon them now. What would happen to Aran and Mr. Hawkins?"

"They just needed me for uniforms."

"I was just at the Pig getting food, and they're worried about you. They're also worried because now there's about a dozen refugees begging them to help get their loved ones out of Coalition-controlled areas. They can't do that without you, Mae."

"What areas?"

"All over. Gamma-3, Delta-4, some mid-sized settlements, Skelm. They're going to need you. Yannick, or whatever his name is, said that Captain Tansy is up there and looking for you, too."

"Tansy?" Mae sniffed. "She's not due back for weeks."

"She came back to see you, you melon. She heard about the plan. Wants to help." Abigail gestured at her with a fork. "You can either eat dinner with me here at your table, or you can eat up at the Pig, but you're eating either way. I'm not going to let you waste away with grief before we even know anything for sure. Gods, Mae, you all managed to get out of the Capital when there were warrants out for you. You broke out of prison."

"Jail."

"It had bars, didn't it? My point is, she's not a helpless woman. But if you don't get your skinny ass back up to the Pig, you'll never know what plans you might be able to make to get her out of there."

Mae sniffled. "What did you get for dinner?"

"Fried noodles with peppers."

"My favorite."

"I know it's your favorite. Why else would I have convinced Evie to make it?" Abigail nudged the container towards her. "Not that it took much convincing. All I had to do was tell her it was for you. They're worried, Mae."

"I'll eat here. It will give me some time to get my nerves together."

"Do you want me to stay, or would you prefer some privacy to wash those tears off your face?"

"Stay."

Abigail sat down at the table and tucked into the noodles, slurping noisily. "You know I do this because I care, right?"

"I know."

"Because I could easily have gone home early and be deep in a bath right now."

"Thank you, Ab."

"You don't have to thank me. Just... help more of those people. I can't imagine what that's like. I feel very lucky that my family is still together, still whole." She shoved in another bite of noodles. "I volunteer to help with the uniforms. Can't have you staying up all night, every night, we'd never get anything done for our paying customers, and we'll need those credits to pay for all the fabric we'll need."

"Hmm." Abigail was right. It would cost a small fortune if they were going to keep this up. "I'll talk to Captain Violet. Maybe they can be on the lookout for us."

"It would be poetic, in a way, wouldn't it? Making Coalition uniforms from textiles stolen from them, all to undermine their laws."

Mae smirked, the first spark of hope she'd felt in hours. "I wonder how many we can get out before they figure it out."

"If everyone keeps a low profile... hopefully a few hundred. You realize this is going to put one hell of a target on your back, right? They'll know that it's you."

"I've had a target on my back in some form for over a decade. I'm sure this one will feel the same."

"They're going to try harder to get to you."

"Yes." Mae poked at her noodles, unearthing a perfectly charred crimson pepper. "I don't care. What else am I going to do until we know what happened to Bailey?"

"Hurry up and eat, they're holding another meeting in thirty minutes."

"It takes fifteen just to walk up there!"

Abigail shoved in another bite. "Better eat up, then."

Chapter 36

"You can't keep me here forever, you know," Bailey grumbled, swallowing another mouthful of bland porridge. "And what the hell is this crap? Do you hate flavor, or something?"

"I'm keeping you here until I know what to do with you."

"I don't know why you're so afraid of Allemande, anyway. You outrank her."

Fineglass set her mug down angrily, rattling the pens corralled into a cup on the desk. "I'm not afraid of her, you ingrate. It's a blossoming partnership, and I don't want it all mucked up just because you decided to show up and make my life hell."

"To be fair, if you hadn't showed up at that mining camp, you wouldn't know that I'm your long-lost sister. So really, this is all your fault."

"Are you always this irritating?"

"Usually." Bailey rattled her cuffs noisily. She couldn't escape the shackles, and Fineglass was too smart to make any wrong moves. You didn't get to be a general by being reckless.

"Stop making so much noise, I'm trying to work."

"This room would be silent as the grave if you'd just let me go. I'll find my own way home."

The general looked up and scowled. "I wouldn't be talking about graves flippantly, if I was you. I could have had you killed."

"And yet, you haven't."

"I want to unravel more of this mystery, and I can't do that if you're dead." She signed another paper and slid it into a file. "But if you test my patience,

I might change my mind."

"Listen, Wilhemina—"

"Regardless of whatever genetic connection we may have, you will still address me as 'General,' I think I have earned that much."

"Alright then, *General*, I think we can agree that this is unsustainable. I propose a radically honest conversation. I will answer anything you ask truthfully, and you do the same."

Fineglass sighed heavily. "No. I very strongly doubt that you would behave honorably, given the situation at hand. What would that do for me, anyway? If what you already said was true, you don't have any more answers than I do. If I let you go, you will continue to gallivant around the Near Systems, impersonating me, wreaking havoc and destroying my reputation. Do you know how difficult you have made things for me? Having to parade around with my odious little toad of a legal husband, pretending to be happily married? Having to appear on public broadcasts to talk about the importance of family as part of the Coalition's expansion plans? It's an embarrassment, and there is no way I will allow you to continue."

"So, what happened with him? Your husband. Before I... impersonated you, that is."

"None of your business."

"Did he... sneak around behind your back?"

"No."

"Was he... too distant and cold? Not enough hugs?"

"*No.*"

"Did he try to undermine your career?"

"Why don't you just shut up, you little weasel?"

Bailey sat back on her haunches. "Ah, so that's it then. Well, understandable that you'd hate him so much. You've worked hard to be head of the colonization committee, no doubt that you'd resent any attempt to keep you away from shooting the Coalition past the Outer Rim."

"It's not called the 'colonization committee,' I am the lead general for the expansion project." Fineglass looked up, glowering. "Do you really think that your beloved band of little miscreants would be able to achieve what the Coalition has?"

"Maybe life should be about more than achievement."

"Okay, so how much strength and ingenuity did you witness in that dirty little backwater you grew up in? Ever since I discovered that I am... somewhat genetically related to you, I have been thanking the gods that I was born here on Gamma-3, and not there. Think of the potential wasted."

"Potential for what?"

"For the advancement of the human race, Bailey."

"That's a lot of weight for one pair of shoulders, Wilhemina."

"I said—"

"Fine, General, whatever."

"Now, shut that hole in your face, and let me work."

The sidearm sat on the desk, glittering with temptation. If she could just get a few more inches of reach, maybe... but would she be able to kill someone? Even more so, what kind of horrifying guilt would she carry if she killed her only living relative, no matter how much of a monster she was? Bailey gritted her teeth, pulling the cuffs taut. Gods be damned, fucking iron. Even she couldn't snap the links, and Fineglass knew it.

Bailey had been smuggled back onto Gamma-3 in a private transport, a bag over her head to conceal her inconvenient likeness to the general. It had been days holed up in this strange remote office, far from the Capital. No mountains as far as the eye could see, no landmarks through the window other than the airfield in the distance, where occasionally dirigibles would ascend and land in a bizarre dance.

"Why do you work here?" Bailey asked.

"To get some peace and quiet, not that you're helping."

"Do you find the Capital too distracting?"

"I detest the Capital. It is necessary for the function of the Coalition, of course, but I work best in total solitude." The general signed another paper and set it aside. "But I also thought it would be too dangerous to bring you back there. Too many eyes in the Capital, looking for a way to climb the ladder of success with blackmail, with information, instead of hard work. It disgusts me."

"The sun is so bright here. On Gamma-3. No mirrors, no terraformers."

"I'm glad you see why we have to work hard to preserve it. We don't know if there is another planet even remotely like this one out there, yet your squalid little friends want to halt industry and progress, no doubt to let our society backslide hundreds of years."

"That's a very odd way of saying that people want to live in safe homes and be able to feed their children."

"Oh, please. They could have that if they wanted it." Fineglass paused over a page, her pen poised in the air. "After all, you managed to carve a life from your meager circumstances."

"I'm a rum-runner."

"Still with that excuse, eh?"

"I told you, it's the truth."

"Where will all those people you secreted away go? Tell me that much, if you so crave radical honesty."

"I will tell you anything about *myself*. I will not endanger people, or make it easier for you to go and scoop them back up, delivering them back into indentured servitude."

"They had better lives on that asteroid than they ever will in work camps. That's what you have condemned them to, Stockton."

"Just kill me or let me go. I'm tired of this. I have offered you information on what you say you want to know, yet it's become clear that what you really want is to round up all my people and shove them into toxic working camps, you want to make sure that your reputation as a heartless shit stays intact."

"Do you have any idea what I've had to do to cover up that little stunt at the mining camp?" She pushed the papers off her desk, leaving them to flutter down to the floor. "What do you think all this is? It's deciding whether to declare them all dead, the sad consequences of another badly maintained mining operation, or to admit that I was there when it happened, and let them slip through my fingers, questions about who would have helped them, and that all leads to *you*."

Bailey sat up straight. Signed death certificates would be de facto freedom for her people. They'd cease to exist. They'd be free to take on different identities, live freely out of the clutches of the Coalition. Maybe start a new settlement, or work to repair Hjarta. It was possibility. Hope. "So why don't you sign them?"

"Don't play coy with me. You're smarter than that."

"Is there anything I can do—other than tell you where they all are, because I couldn't if I tried—to convince you to sign them?"

The general tapped her black fountain pen against the side of the desk, tiny splatters of deep navy ink splashed across the parquet floor. "Are you trying to negotiate with me?"

"I'd rather not be chained up in your office for the rest of my days, dear sister."

"*Don't* call me that."

"Let me go and you'll never hear it from me again."

"You're a terrible negotiator."

Bailey smirked. "Probably because I am a rum-runner. I carry crates. I deliver them. Repeat, repeat, repeat. It is not the life of excitement you've become accustomed to, Wilhemina."

"So, you want to have an honest talk," Fineglass said. "Perhaps we should."

"Are you ever normal, or do you always act this way?"

"You want me to sign these death certificates, yes? Grant your people a life of freedom, wherever they've ended up, shirking their responsibilities as Coalition workers?"

"Something like that."

"Then perhaps we can make a deal. I have to come out of this the victor, you see, but I don't have the time nor the inclination to spend weeks, or even months, wearing you down. Nor do I have access to truth serum, unfortunately. That is available only to inspectors and Intelligence operatives." She bent, sweeping up the papers that had fallen to the floor. "Give me the information I ask for, all of it, and I will sign these, all of them."

"What kind of information?"

"If I'm to sign these, then their location is no longer of any significance to me other than curiosity. No, I need something to give Allemande, so that we can show the High Council that together, we can move mountains. It's the only way that our plans for the Outer Rim expansion can proceed unimpeded by bureaucratic nonsense." She straightened the papers and dipped her pen into the inkwell. "We know that the pirate contingent has a base somewhere."

"No—"

"Don't argue. I already know that it exists, just not where. I know that you won't tell me where it is, you're far too irritatingly noble for that, but I will ask this: is the main export illegal alcohol?"

Bailey swallowed hard. "Yes."

"And does the bulk of that end up here on Gamma-3 via hidden shipments?"

"Maybe not here, but Coalition-controlled space, yes."

"Are there Coalition officers making money from these deals?"

This question surprised her. "Er—yes, occasionally. More so in the smaller settlements than in big cities. There, it tends to be higher-ups, like generals, for example, who overlook the trade for a cut of the credits."

"This deal you went to the Capital for, the one that very unfortunately thrust us together. Was it a large deal?"

"Yes."

Fineglass raised an eyebrow. "Good. How large?"

"I don't know the specifics, but enough for two of my crew to retire comfortably. Not a lavish life, but they don't want for basics."

"And what did you do with your share?"

"Uh..." Bailey trailed off. Should she admit that she paid for an investigator? What if Fineglass wanted a name?

"What did you do with your share, Stockton?"

Bailey cleared her throat. "I paid for an investigator to find where my people were. We had a lead, and—"

"Where did the lead come from?"

"Mr. Machenet," she replied without hesitation. "He told me explicitly where people who had been rounded up were being dumped. The investigator determined which site."

"Mr. Machenet," the general repeated, surprised. "You'd think a slimy, sniveling snake like him would know better than to casually mention classified information, even if he did think that you were me."

"It's my understanding that he's become desperate."

"Indeed. What else did he tell you?"

"I didn't have that much contact with him, in honesty."

"You were found in a broom closet with his daughter, Bailey."

"And I'm sure you realize that would hardly endear me to the man."

"Where was the shipment going?"

"I told you, a speakeasy in—"

"The name, I need the name."

Shit. She couldn't sell out the speakeasy, could she? Endanger Marina and her employees? Possibly send them to work camps... or worse? "I don't know the name," she finally said.

Fineglass dropped the pen back on the desk, dripping fat droplets of ink onto its surface. "I can't help you, if you don't help me."

"Argh!" Bailey growled, rattling her cuffs. "Why do you have to be like this?"

"The name."

"What good is that? You know as well as I do that even if you shut it down, another will crop up in its place. You can never squash the black market in its entirety, what's even the point?"

"I will crush every speakeasy in the Capital, especially if it means taking down officers and officials who are allowing it to take place. The name, Bailey."

"The Dark Owl."

"And the location?"

"Find it yourself."

Fineglass picked up one of the papers, her hands poised to tear it in half. "The location."

"The mercantile quarter, in the back of an old apothecary." Her stomach roiled angrily, threatening to bring up her bland, disgusting breakfast. "There's a purple mushroom on the sign."

"Good." She dipped the pen into ink again. "One more question, *dear sister*. Who runs that establishment?"

Tears pricked at Bailey's eyes, hot and angry, totally powerless. "Marina. I don't know her last name."

"Excellent." The general put pen to paper and began to sign the pages, one after the other, blowing gently on each one to dry the ink before sliding them into a blue folder. "See how much can be accomplished, when we work together? Perhaps you might have been an asset for the Coalition, after all. If you agreed to facial reconstruction—"

"Never," Bailey spat. "I'll never be like you."

"You already are. You chose your own people, a selfish declaration, over the life and livelihood of a tavern owner. We are not so different, it seems."

"Ten minutes ago you were ashamed to share my genetics, now you're proudly crowing about how we're one and the same."

"Apples don't fall far from their trees, so they say. Our mother was duplicitous. It seems we are, as well."

"You didn't know her. She gave her life for her people, to protect them against monsters like you."

"And she left me on Gamma-3 to rot. People are complex."

Bailey clenched her jaw, with nowhere else for the anger to go. "I'm not going to join the damn Coalition."

"Suit yourself." She tucked the folder under her arm and unlocked the deadbolt. "I'll go file these."

"What about me?"

"Your freedom was not part of our agreement."

Chapter 37

Mae was standing in the square of the transport beacon, watching the arrivals board nervously as it ticked from one bay to the next. Ships landed and departed, but there was still no sign of the Dolly Rose. "They should be here by now," she said.

"Give it time," Davey replied. "The last message received said they were heading to the docks together."

"What if they didn't board?"

"Relax, you're going to make the others nervous." Amy and Hector were both standing beneath the board, staring up at it as though their rapt attention would summon the ship faster. "This is going to work, just you wait and see." He placed a hand on her shoulder. "It's a good plan, Mae."

"I just hope nothing goes wrong." Even then, her thoughts were on Bailey. It had been almost a week since the transport arrived back in Bradach, and there was still no sign of her. The light of hope grew dimmer with every passing day, with no word from the mining camp or General Fineglass. "I feel so... responsible."

"You have to detach yourself from feelings of guilt. They aren't productive, and they hamper missions."

"Gods, you Scattered sound just like the Coalition, sometimes. Productivity, efficiency, it's two sides of the same coin."

Davey scowled. "It's rather different, thank you."

"How come we haven't heard from Captain Tansy?"

"Risk assessment. This should be quiet enough, but if someone back in the Capital is looking for them, they'll be scanning all frequencies."

"Seems like a lot of effort for a baker and a teacher."

"They've already made three ship changes to be sure, but you never know. Better safe than sorry."

The board's tiles clacked into place, announcing the Cricket's arrival in bay three. "Looks like their ride is here."

"It's not unusual for Captain Violet to be early." He fumbled with his pocket watch, checking the time. "She has an excellent navigator."

Mae glanced at him sideways. "You should just ask him to dinner," she said.

"Who?"

"Ned, obviously. You've been mooning over him since the day you met."

"The Scattered doesn't encourage relationships."

"Sounds like Coalition claptrap to me."

"Fine," he said, "I will."

"Good."

The Cricket pressurized in the bay, the ramp extending out, with Alice bounding out first, Captain Violet in tow. "Are they here yet?" she shouted over the din of the beacon.

"No," Mae shouted back. "Hopefully soon."

"This is a hell of a plan," Captain Violet said admiringly. "If this goes off without a hitch, Mae, I think you're going to have a lot of work on your hands."

"I meant to talk to you about that, actually. We're going to need a damn lot of fabric."

The captain smirked mischievously. "You mean like the four crates we're taking back to Bradach with us?"

"Four *crates*? But how—"

"Your assistant sent a wire, said it was urgent."

"I wasn't going to mention it until we knew for sure it was going to work." Alice grinned widely. "Let's just say we have total faith in this plan."

"That makes one of us," Mae replied.

"Hold your cynicism, Machenet, because look what ship just pulled in." The board flipped its tiles, showing the Dolly Rose in a recently vacated bay.

"Oh, my gods," she whispered. Still, nothing was for certain until they walked off that vessel.

Amy and Hector were already running for the bay, skidding across the slick tiles. She beat him to the bay's glass pressure door, her hands pressed against it in anticipation. "Aran!" she was screaming, even though everyone knew those doors were hermetically sealed until cleared by the beacon's bay operator.

Steam rolled off the Dolly Rose in waves, the ramp descending slowly. The glass door's pressure latch released, and when Aran and Mr. Hawkins appeared in the doorway, everyone started screaming. Tears flooded Mae's eyes, relieved the plan had worked, envious that they were reunited when she didn't even yet know if Bailey was still alive.

"Aran, gods, I thought I'd never see you again," Amy said through sobs, her arms locked tight around him. "I'm so sorry I never told you, I—"

"Shh, it's alright," he soothed. "I'm here now."

Hector rushed for Mr. Hawkins, who stood stiffly at the base of the ramp. "Alexander, my love, I—"

"I thought you were dead, Hector. You let me think you were dead. For *years*."

"I'm sorry, I—"

"You silly fucking radish. I'd have followed you anywhere. I'd have joined any rebel cause, no matter how dangerous, if it meant being with you. When you disappeared, I'd been feeding information to underground cells for months already."

"Why didn't you tell me?"

"You were never home towards the end! Hells below, Hector, I could kill you for leaving me alone." He threw his arms around his husband, tears leaking from his eyes. "If you ever do that again, I will bury you myself."

"We didn't have a viable plan, not until Mae's idea."

Mr. Hawkins released Hector and wrapped her in a tight embrace. "I knew it would be you. My best and most talented student. No one sews like you do."

"I had to do something to erase that black mark against my name," she said. "This was the only thing I could think of."

"It's brilliant. A brilliant, smart plan. It won't work forever, no, they'll figure it out eventually, but for now, well... this is going to do a lot of good." He took Hector's hand. "A damn lot of good."

"We already have over a dozen people we're trying to work out plans for."

"I hope you realize I'm going to be invading your shop to help sew these uniforms, Mae."

She laughed, the first bit of joy she'd felt since Bailey left. "I wouldn't dream of keeping you away, sir."

"Mae! Gods, woman, if I'd have known you designed the gods-damned uniforms, I would have asked for your help months ago." Captain Tansy swaggered off the ship, her cybernetic leg proudly on display. She was crisply dressed, as always, though Mae didn't recognize the embroidery work on the waistcoat. She knew from one glance at the tricorn hat, though, that it had been made by that talented milliner on Delta-4. She'd know their work anywhere.

"Captain Tansy, a pleasure, as always."

"This plan is genius. We're already working out flight patterns for all the people who requested it. Genius, I tell you. I'm angry I didn't think of it myself."

"Nice hat."

"Thank you. My new paramour made it."

Mae cocked an eyebrow. "Been spending time on Delta-4, have you?"

"I should have known you'd know their work from one hundred meters away. You've got a keen eye and a big, beautiful brain."

"Their work is impressive and speaks for itself."

"I'll tell them you said so. I think this idea is fantastic, Machenet."

"No doubt the Coalition will be so embarrassed, they'll lock everything down. Maybe even change the uniforms."

"I bet you'd be able to duplicate anything they came up with."

Mae smiled. "You can bet on that, Captain."

"We'll cross that asteroid belt when we come to it, shall we? Now, where's that strapping woman who organized that mining site operation? I want to shake her hand."

"Captain, she..." Mae's throat became tight with emotion, strangling her words. "She didn't come back with the rest. I thought you knew."

"Gods. No one told me. Any word?"

Mae shook her head. "No. Nothing."

"I'm so sorry, I never would have—"

"It's alright, Captain. We still have faith that she's out there somewhere." Even as she said the words, her heart deeply ached through her very core.

"Maybe we could run a ship by the mining site?"

"I don't know what good it would do. If she was there, she'd be in trouble, and we can't get to her."

"It's likely they shipped her off somewhere. I'll ask around, press some of my contacts for information. If she's in a prison, we'll find her, and that's half the battle." Captain Tansy tipped her hat. "You have my word on that. I'm not going to give up on someone who pulled off a hell of an operation like that. She's a hell of a fighter."

"She saved her people. I just hope that we can save her."

Chapter 38

Bailey leaned her head against the pole she was chained to and sighed. Over a week now, and she was still stuck in that horrible office in the middle of nowhere. Fineglass never made a mistake, at least, not one that would allow her to get the advantage. Short of tearing the pole out of the wall with her bare hands, she was stuck - and unlike the jail cell, she was constantly monitored here. The general slept on the other side of the wall, and spent her days at her desk, reading, signing, mumbling.

"You could at least get me something to read!" she shouted through the wall. "If I don't die of malnutrition, I'll die of boredom!"

Still, she'd stayed in worse accommodation. At least she was regularly fed, taken to the water closet, and given a pillow to sleep on, despite remaining shackled at all times. Maybe this wasn't the first time the general had kept a prisoner in this remote office.

"Here, you can read this," Fineglass said, opening the door. "It's for you."

"For me?"

A yellowed slip of paper fluttered to the ground. A wire from the Capital.

ILLEGAL VENUE OPERATOR MARINA SYKES APPREHENDED. TRIAL TO BEGIN THREE WEEKS FROM TODAY. GOOD WORK. NEXT WE TAKE ON THE SUPPLIERS.

-ALLEMANDE

"You shit," Bailey spat.

"Did you think I asked you for that information as a joke?"

"You're made of ruination and spite."

Fineglass smirked. "Maybe so, but now we can complete our deal."

"What deal?"

"You don't think I'm going to keep you chained here forever, do you? You're terrible for my concentration."

"I suppose I'm free to go now, so you can shoot me in the back as I run for it? Is that how this works?"

"Try as I may, I am finding the prospect of killing you... rather difficult to swallow, despite your insolence and terrible choice in lifestyles. A rum-runner, I mean *really*. A woman like you, with your potential—"

"I told you before, I am not joining the ranks of your soulless, corporate enterprise."

"Very well, then. No one can say I didn't try. In any case, even if I did kill you, it leaves me with the unpleasant job of disposing of your corpse, a difficult feat with so many eyes on me. All it would take is one false move, one person to ask too many questions, and I'd have more to answer for. There are only so many airfield attendants I can pay off to keep them quiet, and I don't want a word of this getting back to Overseer Allemande, especially not so close to the start of the expansion project."

"She needs you more than you need her."

"Are you trying to convince me to kill you?"

"No, just stating facts. She's a conwoman, Wilhemina."

"Clearly. Yet, I need her cooperation, so I must tread carefully. I want to be clear, now. I don't ever want to see your face again."

Bailey snorted. "Don't look in the mirror, then."

"And I don't want to hear your voice. If you ever decide to masquerade as me again, you can be sure that I will gladly pour piles of credits upon the meanest, most monstrous assassin to take you out, as well as that little strumpet you were parading around with. I know enough to find you both, Bailey. Are we understood?"

"Why now?"

"I certainly couldn't let you go directly after giving me that information, now could I? You'd have run straight to the first pirate you could find and warn them. No, I had to be sure everything was secured, first, and now, it has been."

"So, what, you're going to unlock these cuffs and let me free? Where I will definitely get picked up by an MPO within ten minutes and imprisoned shortly after?"

"Don't be daft, Bailey. Someone seeing you would undermine the story I have so carefully built, about an unfortunate mining accident."

"What about the officers that were there on the asteroid? Did you have them knocked off?"

Fineglass shot her a look. "Of course not. They were thrilled to be merely reassigned, and not brought up on charges for gross misconduct in action. They have been shipped off to the Outer Rim, where they will work for me, under close watch."

"How do you expect me to get off this rock, then?"

"With a personal shuttle, obviously."

"I'm not a pilot. I've never flown."

"Lucky for you, you'll be taking the same small vessel of mine that we arrived on. The auto-pilot will take you to the nearest transport beacon, and I assume you can find your way home from there. Don't think you can steal my ship, either, I'll be tracking you the entire way."

"What about when the bay controller asks me for verification?"

"You pretended to me for a full week in front of the entire Capital, I'm sure you can manage that. Let that be the last time my name ever leaves your mouth. Leave it there, someone will collect it after you've left. Try to keep a low profile, will you? I have no qualms about cleaning up messes, as I hope I've made clear."

"Crystal."

Fineglass bent, holding the key to the cuffs. "Don't punch me, or I'll shoot you in the knee, and you can stay here while you recuperate."

"I'm not going to punch you." She did really want to punch her, but she wouldn't win against a revolver. She needed to get back to Mae. The tiny iron key clicked in the lock, and Bailey rubbed her wrists when the cuffs released, rising to her feet. "Thank you, I guess. For not murdering me."

"I'll admit, it was tempting. You're lucky you look like me."

"Until we meet again, Wilhemina."

"We'd better not meet again, Bailey."

"Better not look over your shoulder, then. You never know when I'll come back for a reunion. The gods know everyone wants quality time with their evil twin."

"I thank the gods we didn't grow up together."

Bailey snorted. "That's a shame, I always wanted a sister." She opened the door, and without turning around, continued, "just never one like you."

* * *

Bailey's hand hesitated over the handle of the shop door. What if Mae, having had time to think, didn't want her anymore? What if she'd come all the way back to Bradach just to find a door slammed in her face? With a deep breath, she pushed open the door.

Mae was standing with her back to the door, noting something down in the logbook. "I'll be right with you," she said.

Reaching out for her, Bailey pulled her arms back, unsure. She stepped behind her. "I told you I'd come back," she whispered.

"Bailey!" Mae squealed, spinning around, throwing her arms around her neck and pulling her into a deep kiss. "Bai, oh gods, I've been worried sick, I—" She kissed again, lightly, her lips soft and warm. "I was terrified when you didn't come back on the transport, I—" Another kiss, more fervent now. "I've been so lost without you, I thought I lost you, I—" Their mouths melted into each other, a hundred kisses at once, fierce and hungry.

"I love you, Mae," Bailey blurted out, and then pulled away. "I'm sorry, I—"

Mae kissed her again, reaching behind to lock the door, then pulling her towards the stairs. "I love you, I love you, I love you," she repeated between kisses. "I'll love you for an eternity, Bailey Stockton." This last admission was whispered, her voice tight with emotion as she led Bailey up the stairs. "An eternity, and then some." Her hands were pulling down Bailey's suspenders, letting them droop at her waist, her nimble fingers releasing every button, sliding inside her shirt and caressing her waist.

Before she knew it they were on the bed, and Mae was stripping off her skirts, her corset, her stockings, until her naked body was on top of Bailey, crying, and laughing all at once as she stripped her, too, clothes falling into untidy piles at the side of the bed, their hands all over each other, greedily caressing.

When Mae's head trailed lower, kissing across Bailey's hips, lingering where thighs met, she sighed and let the deep yearning wash over her. "Yes," she uttered, letting all of the fear and bad memories be stripped away. She felt at home with Mae, more than with any other woman, and as she trailed her fingertips through soft hair, the ache that had pulsed beneath her skin for weeks drew to the surface. The gentle pressure of Mae's tongue sent rivulets of excitement coursing through her. Bailey moaned through her breathlessness, giving way to the inevitable joining of their bodies.

And there they stayed, grasping, and giving, until both were dewy with sweat, gulping for breath as they came up for air, held tight in each other's arms.

Epilogue

A dozen new refugees piled into the Purple Pig, each of them holding tight to their loved ones, cheeks wet with tears of relief. One by one, they returned their borrowed Coalition uniforms, having been given fresh clothes down at the refugee camp.

"Eat up, everyone!" Evie shouted, whipping a deep purple cloth off of trays upon trays of food, covered with sterling silver lids.

Larkin set down several large pitchers of the beautiful pea flower lemonade, the magical colors swirling under the lamplight. "Try the new concoction! Trialled to great acclaim!"

"Welcome! Everyone gets a drink on me!" Captain Tansy yelled from the doorway, laughing. "It's still half my tavern, after all!"

A little girl, her hair in tight braids, tugged at Mae's skirt. "Miss?"

"What's wrong?"

"I made this for you. To say thank you for helping my mommy come back." It was a handmade card, crudely drawn in a child's hand, a picture of her newly reunited family.

"Thank you! I'm not the only one who helped, you know."

"I know! I have a card for everyone." She skipped off, rushing back to her mother, wrapping herself around her skirts.

"You did a good thing, love," Bailey said. "You're one of the best people I've ever known. And you're all mine." She gave Mae's hand a gentle squeeze, rubbing her thumb across soft skin.

Mae wrapped her arms around Bailey's waist. "Same to you, darling." She pecked her on the cheek and handed her a lemonade. "Don't look now, but I think Davey's about to make his move."

He was standing at Ned's table, shifting his weight nervously from foot to foot, before taking Ned's hand and leading him to the improvised dance floor.

"Oh, gods, there's no music," Bailey said. "He's a total amateur."

"You'd better help him out, then."

"I think you're right. Hand me my fiddle." She took her instrument and stood on the table, clearing her throat loudly for attention. "Anyone who would like to join in, we're going to start with one of my personal favorites, 'Where Rebel Hearts Reside.' Common Key." She gave the fiddle a quick tune, and set the bow against the strings, drawing forth a sweet yearning melody. She wasn't more than eight bars into the song before Tansy pulled a small guitar from behind the bar, traded for booze by a pirate who'd probably stolen it off an officer, and strummed chords beneath. Henry hummed along in harmony, and one of the new refugees pulled an old viola off the wall, left there by one of the traveling musicians, joining with an arpeggiated counter melody.

Couples danced, people sang, and as the song came to a close, Bailey called out, "Let's bring this barn down!"

Alice whooped in appreciation while Violet laughed, and Georgie pulled out a harmonica to join in.

They stomped, and danced, and spun, and for once, something a little like hope hung in the air.

End of book four

Keep reading for a sneak peek into the next novel in the series, **A Recipe for Regret.**

Sign up for my newsletter and get information about convention appearances, book launch parties, new releases, and more! Get bonus content for the Cricket Chronicles series like deleted scenes and extended cuts. You can unsubscribe at any time with no obligation.

http://eepurl.com/gOQBaP

You can follow me on Twitter at @IMRyannFletcher, on Facebook @RyannFletcherWrites, Instagram @RyannFletcherWrites, or email at RyannFletcherBooks@Gmail.com. It's always great to hear from you!

A Recipe for Revenge preview

The Overseer's voice rang out into the corridor. "Ms. Dodson!"

Delia cringed. That woman's voice was like gears grinding in a poorly-maintained ship. At least back on Gamma-3, gods, even in Skelm, she could escape it for a while. Here at the Outer Rim, there was no getting away from her. "Yes?" she answered in her usual bright, obedient tone. "What can I do for you, Overseer?"

"I need you to draft an announcement for tomorrow morning's broad-cast."

"I thought you already signed off—"

"The situation has changed."

"I'll be right in," Delia said, swallowing back an aggrieved sigh. What she wouldn't give for a moment's peace. She slid off the rickety stool and made sure that her shirt was tucked in. The overseer's lectures on presentation were unbearable.

"Bring a pad of paper with you."

"Of course!" Rolling her eyes to the bare, unfinished ceiling, she mouthed a swear and tucked a pen behind her ear. She knocked on the adjacent doorway and poked her head in. "Are you ready for me?"

"I've been waiting what feels like several days, yes, I am ready."

"Alright, what did you want to add to the broadcast?"

"Sit. We need to rework the entire thing."

Clawing her eyes out was preferable to another session with Allemande, but still, she sat down in the high-backed chair opposite her. "Okay."

"First of all, we need to scrap the story about nutritional needs here at the station. As it happens, one of the laborers has been writing home, telling them all about the appalling food here. We have now instituted censoring on wires home, but the damage has been done." The overseer glared at the paper in her hand. "Now, we've had to hire a cook for at least the higher ups here on site. We can still use this piece, once we can prove that any communications suggesting otherwise are nothing more than exaggerations."

"Mhmm. Understood."

"Ms. Dodson, if I may ask, what is your opinion of the nutritional offerings here?"

"Er—perfectly adequate, ma'am."

"If only every worker here was like you, we wouldn't have to trouble ourselves with this trivial nonsense!"

"Yes, ma'am. Thank you." It was easier to agree with her. The food, if you could even call it that, on the station was nothing short of disgusting, and Delia had been living almost entirely off the stash of illicit imported chocolate in her cramped quarters. "And what of the progress report regarding construction here? Are we going to scrap that from the broadcast as well?"

"Move that to the evening. We will have additional information to add concerning the ventilation systems here, as well as proposed improvements to crew quarters. While I find it entirely preposterous, it is proving a challenge to recruit skilled laborers to work out here. Other stations get by just fine using indentured workers, but this place has sensitive information, we just can't risk it."

"Mm," Delia agreed. Maybe if the Coalition agreed to pay laborers more than a pittance, they'd find an easier time of obtaining craftspeople. "What did you want to replace the rest of the morning broadcast with, then?"

"Have you spoken to Mr. Cross?"

"No, I haven't seen Thomas all day." She'd spent half the afternoon looking for him, too. How the hell was she supposed to deliver the evening broadcast without an operator?

"I'm afraid I have some grave news, Ms. Dodson."

"What happened? Is he alright?"

"We made the unfortunate discovery that Mr. Cross had been passing information to The Scattered."

Every muscle in Delia's body tensed. Thomas? A spy? "Gods," she managed to squeak. "How did you find that out?"

"An anonymous member of the work crew tipped off General Fineglass last week. She said that she had seen him scavenging through the shredded document discards, trying to piece together papers. We laid a cunning trap, and he eagerly stepped directly into it."

"I can't believe it," she breathed, and it was the first true thing she'd said to Allemande in days. "To think, I'd worked alongside him for years, and never knew."

"Yes, I'd have thought a dedicated reporter like yourself would have noticed that something was awry with him, or at least suspect." The overseer arched an eyebrow. "You didn't, did you?"

"No, of course not."

"Then I am very disappointed in you. I expect my hires to be observant, keenly so. To think that a traitor loomed under your nose for years, undetected!"

"They are getting more sophisticated lately."

Allemande frowned. "Yes, I suppose that is true, after all. In any case, General Fineglass has already seen to his punishment. I appreciate that you are now in need of a new operator—"

"Punishment?"

"Yes, of course, Ms. Dodson. Thomas Cross was a traitor."

Was. The word hung in the air, heavy and inescapable. "I just thought, a trial—"

"We don't have time for trials out here, you know better than that."

"Of course." She blinked furiously, desperate to keep the tears from pooling in her eyes. Dangerous to show any affection for a traitor, and even more fraught to show weakness this far from Gamma-3.

"Do not cry for him," Allemande scolded. "He was an enemy. A treasonous snake. He wanted nothing more than to see us all suffocate. The paperwork he was stealing from the incineration pile was concerning the ventilators on this station, and we can only assume that he was passing that information to The Scattered to give them an edge over us."

"Did he already pass the information on?"

"Don't be ridiculous. The information was planted. General Fineglass is no fool, and no stranger to the activities of miscreants."

Delia nodded. "It is good that he didn't put the station in danger." She'd find whoever ratted him out, and push them out of the airlock herself. Thomas was a good man, a friend. She hadn't even known that they shared an alliance beyond broadcasting, though she should have guessed when he didn't intervene when she reworded scripts back in Skelm. Some reporter she was, missing the obvious.

"Quite right. As it stands, we have to get out in front of this mess before word gets out. I've already informed the workers that communications off the station will be limited going forward due to cost analysis and staffing shortages, but someone will notice that he is missing."

"Missing."

"We can't have people knowing that The Scattered were so close to infiltrating us, Ms. Dodson. It will only encourage them."

"Yes."

"I propose a statement about the hazards of mind-altering substances. Poor Mr. Cross, having smuggled illegal spirits onto the station, became rather inebriated, and decided to go for an unsupervised space jump. Tragically, he did so without a protective suit."

"Understood."

"Offer your personal condolences. After all, you knew him best of anyone on the station." Overseer Allemande glared at her over the smooth, polished desk. "Do you swear that you didn't know about his proclivities?"

"Of course, ma'am."

"Hmm. Very well then, I suppose. You will be assigned a new operator, some volunteer from the new crew arrivals. She has assured the general that she has experience with broadcasting, but I am sure you will need to guide her along in the beginning."

"Yes, ma'am."

"If she is not suitable, we will have to send for someone, but it would be at least a month before we could get someone out here, you understand."

"I'm sure the new operator will be just fine." Her heart squeezed in her chest. Thomas, gone, just like that. Her own demise felt even more inevitable than usual. She couldn't keep this up forever, certainly not with a new operator who would be quick to snitch to Allemande. "Did you want any other changes for tomorrow morning? Or evening?"

"No, that will be all. Work up a draft and bring it back in twenty minutes for approval."

"I'll be as quick as I can."

"And Ms. Dodson, if you see my daughter, please tell her that I need to speak with her urgently."

"If I see Emeline, I will send her here."

"You are dismissed."

Delia nodded, pushing herself up out of her chair, her limbs heavy, her chest tight with anxiety and sadness. Without Thomas, she really was alone out here, all by herself in the crushing, endless darkness of space.

About the Author

With this fourth book in the series, I'm reflecting a lot on all the people who helped The Cricket Chronicles get this far. My wife, of course, who drives so much enthusiasm for these characters and the setting they were created in, is by far my biggest cheerleader. I can't thank her enough for her tireless musings on where the story is going, or for her deep and unending support for the story to even get this far.

And my writing group, who have made me laugh until I cry, even on days I wasn't sure I could go on putting words on the page.

My beta readers, a growing but vehemently opinionated team whose thoughts matter so much to me. Thank you, too, for your effort.

And finally, I want to thank YOU, reader, for getting this far in the series. I hope you will join us in book five, *A Recipe for Regret*.

Ryann Fletcher is a writer who lives with her wife and too many craft supplies. She writes sapphic science fiction and fantasy, and likes to cook.

You can connect with me on:

- https://ryannfletcher.com
- https://twitter.com/IMRyannFletcher
- https://facebook.com/RyannFletcherWrites
- https://instagram.com/RyannFletcherWrites

Subscribe to my newsletter:

- http://eepurl.com/gOQBaP

Also by Ryann Fletcher

A Recipe for Regret

When Rosie took the job as the Outer Rim's only cook, she never thought she'd run into her old flame - her old flame who was now, apparently, married. With strange, cryptic notes being delivered to her quarters in the middle of the night and nothing more than canned beans, she has her work cut out for her to keep her head down and her profile low.

Delia spent her entire career working towards this point, so why now does everything seem so off-balance? Her husband is busy making deals with General Fineglass, she's reporting on how the station is about to become the Gateway Beyond the Rim, but when her friend and co-worker mysteriously turns up dead, it's up to her to find out why.

In book 5 of The Cricket Chronicles, we're traveling to the Outer Rim - where everything is far more dangerous.